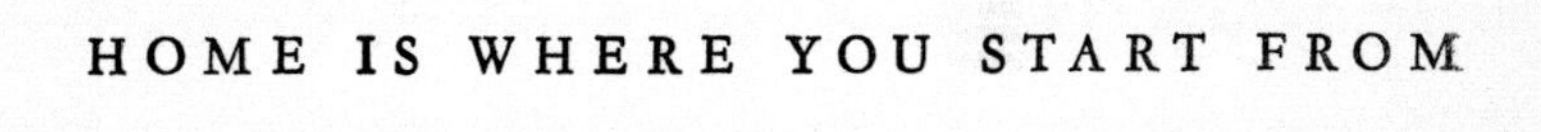

HOME IS WHERE YOU START FROM

Home is where you start from

A NOVEL BY

Gene Horowitz

NEW YORK  W · W · NORTON & COMPANY · INC ·

Published simultaneously in Canada by George J. McLeod Limited, Toronto.
First Edition
Library of Congress Catalog Card No. 65-24923
Printed in the United States of America for the publishers
by the Vail-Ballou Press, Inc.
1 2 3 4 5 6 7 8 9 0

FOR MY MOTHER AND FATHER

Home is where one starts from . . .
We must be still and still moving
Into another intensity . . .
. . . In my end is my beginning.

—T. S. Eliot, "East Coker," *Four Quartets*
(Harcourt, Brace & World, Inc.)

HOME IS WHERE YOU START FROM

Home is where you start from.
Pushed, pulled, lured forward,
Dragging after all that is not understood,
You leave.

Going where?

To life, they say.
Life. So big!
And you and they are small,
Smaller than one single ticking of the kitchen clock.

Midway there is a new home growing,
Perpetuated, made by deciduous transits
From a past that darkens to a bright, remembered flame,
Lighting present, future into
Nothing!

You remember those that helped you.
You remember that there is no help
And help your own to help themselves.

Moving, waiting, living through
The deaths and years that lead you to a knowledge
Which has no use.
The past is unredeemable. There are no coupons.
You have done this, done that,
Hoped, found,
Too late or early,
That this was wise, or that was wrong.
You bite your lip,
Arrange the furniture once more,
Wash a floor that is not dirty,
Twist your wedding band,

And wait;

And that which was turned inward always—
        A fire in the bloodstream screaming,
        Growing with you inward, older—
Seeks larger, still larger confinements
Beyond the organ,
Flows, stops, within the largest, wildest smallness of each cell.

Suddenly, there is no time for waiting.
Growing inside, the fire, your death,
Races down the stream that feeds you.

You told no one what you found.
They, at the end, said nothing.
They kissed you, moving away from them,
Took the few things you had:
        The gold band,
        The false teeth,
        Living.

That was an end to waiting,
An end, which you did, as with your other doing,
Silently angry,
But straining to smile,
For them.

PART I

CHAPTER *One*

TONIGHT, COMING TO THIS PLACE, alone, and last year married here, angered Ellie more than the dress she wore and didn't like, more than being Toby's matron of honor, even more than the argument with Morrie before she left their apartment; the fact that she would be alone, and alone in this place was enough to eat up the remaining pieces of her determination to have a good time tonight, no matter what.

The stone steps first and at the top of the stairs the intricately carved wooden door with polished brass rings hanging from lions' mouths, the brass shining, fading in the alternating light and dark rhythm of the overhead sign that read, "Kutsher's Catering," the steps, the door, the sign all remembered from that other time, but seen again, differently now, because she was alone, her irritation, as she stepped higher, spreading a false warmth throughout her body. She leaned into the waves of wind, let the whipping spray beat against her face. It was March. It would snow before the night was over. Ellie sensed that in the wind and pulled at the edges of her sleeves, made fists inside the cuffs of her coat, darted glances at the other guests who moved with her. Lured by the warmth they knew would be inside, they went to the wedding. Puffing, groaning sounds of age and eagerness surrounded her, and then the door was opened. She was pushed forward on a surge of their desire to be inside.

Now she could straighten up, settle her shoulders inside the cold satin lining of her coat. The forward movement was stopped, arrested by the sudden lights, the blast of heat. People stamped around her. But as they collected in a knot others erupted through the door behind them, pushed into the corridor, moved them forward once more. Ellie was caught in the center of this new urge to be inside. The knot dissolved and became people, and then special people to whom she was related, or a friend and honored tonight because she was in the wedding family and because, last year, they had been to her wedding here. She was kissed and embraced. Coats and shawls were removed, and she was asked by eyes, mouths still too cold to ask, and hands thrusting hats at her, 'Where do these go?'

She led them to the checkroom. Silence disappeared with the coats. They waited to be looked at. They kissed again.

"You're cold, Ellie. That way?" an aunt questioned.

Ellie straightened the skirt of her sleeveless blue crepe dress, nodding 'no' vigorously, then pulling at the crushed petals of the corsage pinned to her waist.

"So why you're shivering then?" The aunt reached beneath a rhinestone clasp at her shoulder to retrieve a fallen brassière strap. "*Nu?*" Ellie turned to smile at her uncle. "All right. No answer. So let's march instead."

The loud swish of taffeta, the whine of silk accompanied them down the corridor. And other words, greetings from other aunts, uncles, and cousins sounded in the foyer, swelled the beginning noises of the wedding. An arm, an itchy blue-serge arm, her uncle's, was draped over Ellie's shoulder. She endured it, added it to her own private, prickling annoyance as they walked cautiously, on display, to the reception room and Toby.

The question that she did not want to answer, did not want anyone to ask yet, knowing, of course, that everyone before long would ask, she posed to herself, and then did not answer because at that moment they passed by an entranceway and all heads turned automatically toward the screeching sound of a tuning violin. In the dimly lit room she could see four men. The band was almost ready.

"Where's Morrie?" The question was shouted. Her cousin, at the end of an advancing line of relatives, had asked it. No longer need Ellie experiment with possible answers which, a moment before, had been forming in her mind. No fights! That was all she had time to tell herself. They were waiting. "He has to work tonight."

"Tonight? Saturday?" Her uncle removed his arm from her shoulder.

"Yes." She started moving again. They followed quickly.

"He works every night?" Her aunt's words grew into a rising, taunting question.

"No. Not every, most." Ellie gazed down at the maroon carpeting. It wouldn't hurt if she suddenly pushed her aunt on it.

"That's terrible." Her aunt ground her dentures. "When can you go anywhere?"

"We can't very much." Ellie tried to lock her lips for control. "That's when they deliver milk. At night. You get up in the morning, and there it is outside your door."

They had reached the entrance to the reception room, and in front of the far wall was the raised mahogany seat, like a throne. Toby was erect, looking down across the awe-filled distance, sometimes smiling, sometimes talking to the guests that stood below. But one hand pulled at the long lace train. Ellie saw that. The others wouldn't, but she knew how heavy the gown was and how Mr. Kutsher, himself, arranged the train so that it forced you to sit up straight. She remembered his words. "The bride should look like a queen. Don't you worry. Sit and I'll fix."

A respectful murmur of appreciation hung in the air above the heads of the milling people. Smiling, they looked and turned and bumped into one another, retreating then into the safety of distant observation to wait for the moment when the murmur would dare to become laughter and noise.

Ellie stood at the base of the raised seat. "You look beautiful, Toby. Perfect."

"I'm frightened to death. I thought you'd never get here." Toby glanced away from her sister, toward the entrance. Consternation pinched her powdered forehead into young, firm wrinkles. "Did you see Leon? He's around somewhere. . . . Come up here already. You're supposed to stand here."

Ellie obeyed, stepping carefully over the twisted lace, turning, the redness of her accumulated irritation frozen now on her blushing face, defenseless, surveying the crowd with her sister who maintained a nervous, whispered complaint. "Of course everything will go wrong. . . . Our family! Not one of them is here yet. Can you imagine that! Not one. Except you and it took you long enough to get here. Couldn't they for once leave. . . ." Toby interrupted herself, decided to smile down at her friends to wave.

"Don't worry. They'll be here on time." Ellie leaned toward Toby. "I assure you nothing will go wrong."

But Toby's gracefully long, oval face seemed to gather its features into a familiar circle of disbelief so that the tiny bump on the center of her straight nose—a family bump which on Ellie's nose was more obvious, as if from the oldest daughter to the youngest the effects of evolution were clearly apparent—became whitely prominent. "*You* assure me?"

"It's *Shabbath* still. They're walking." Ellie nodded to passing relatives.

"You look so pale, Toby," a cousin shouted. "Don't be nervous."

Toby's smile widened with malice. "Thanks for your advice. When was the last time you were married?" The cousin recoiled into folds of shaking obesity and turned sadly away. Ellie did not look at Toby, but she could see the blur and fidget of whiteness on the periphery of her outward gaze. Then she heard more words streaming past. "Now they're really coming. There's Uncle Mischa and Aunt Lena. Look at the dress she's wearing. The same one she wore to your wedding, remember? . . . with the gold thread in it? What gall. At least Rachel and Alvin—they're right behind them, see?—the younger ones look like *menches* . . . I wonder where Leon is . . . Damn him. Wait till . . ."

"Smile Toby. Smile." Ellie issued the command out of her clenched, grinning mouth. "They're all watching you. Now's no time . . ."

"God," Toby groaned, "I'm afraid."

"No need to be. None whatsoever. Before you know it, it'll be over."

They waved; they wriggled their fingers at the advancing relatives. Some of the close ones, the *seder* relatives, blew kisses; others, the *brith*, wedding, and funeral ones whispered behind raised hands. And the friends remained poised on the fringes of the crowd. The group before them diminished, was constantly replenished by new arrivals. The murmur gradually rose in volume. The band could be heard playing in the dining room where, by now, the tables would have been pushed to the walls to create the dance floor. Mr. Kutsher's staff was at work.

"Where's Morrie?" Toby suddenly asked. "I didn't notice till this minute he wasn't here."

"He has to work tonight."

"So? He doesn't go in until late. Why couldn't he come for awhile?"

"He just couldn't." Toby's logic was the same that Ellie had used earlier that evening. "Not even for a little while? As a favor to me?"

"Favor?" Morrie had shouted. "*I* need a favor. Some sleep. Can't you go without me? You backward or something?"

"Please?" she begged, hating the need to do so.

"I said no. I'm not changing my mind, so you might as well give up." Then Morrie had placed the newspaper in front of his face blocking out her view.

"Thank you for your consideration. And also thank you for not letting me get a new dress, and for being such a good husband. . . ."

"And thank you for the peace and quiet I'm going to have when you get the hell out of here." The newspaper was lowered, the dark eyes glared, daring her to say another word.

Toby repeated her question. "What do you mean couldn't?"

"I'll be back. I'm going to the Ladies' room." Ellie stepped back over the train of lace.

"You don't have to come back. I'm fine now. Go hide somewhere."

Exasperation made Ellie stop. But why answer her? There's no satisfaction. She hurried away.

In the dining room she found an uninhabited corner behind a wooden column. Slowly the clenched fists opened. Slowly she peered out, dared to display her false composure. The hors d'oeuvres were being snatched up from the long, low table temporarily set up near the bandstand. Thin strips of smoked salmon, finely chopped liver and onions, both pasted onto small squares of rye bread, disappeared down the throats of the inspecting guests. Tightly corseted, gowned women roamed the shiny dance floor, children pulling at and being pulled away from their skirts. Their husbands, following unwillingly, it seemed to Ellie, but talking louder now, opening up to others they hadn't seen for a long time, eyed the bar. And gradually, as if by prearranged signal, they moved toward it, circled it indifferently, then back-slapping their acquiescence, approached. The liquor would do what words could not. Its flow would carry them to laughter. The clean shaven look would disappear. The screaming and the sweat would commence. The next phase of the wedding, the reason for having it at all, would eat its way out of a protective cocoon. Children, as if on roller skates, would slide across the dance floor . . . Mothers would holler. Fathers would turn from that and have another drink.

Through that beginning the band played. Ellie accepted their fixed-smile boredom. Their shiny, aging tuxedos had appeared at how many weddings? Four men playing happy music together, waiting for all this to be over so that they could go home to bed. And no one ever danced immediately. The guests had to be urged on by hellos and food and whisky. They played a waltz. Ellie danced to it in her mind, imagining a long gown, instead of the blue one she wore, brushing the floor, her body tall, ample, twisting, slowly turning, on display, alone. But the violin screeched off key. The children laughed shrilly. Ellie opened her eyes.

The spreading stream of noise swirled around her. She felt warmer, yes, but conspicuous. It was the dress that did it, the bareness of her arms and shoulders. Not at all what she wanted. She retreated to the edge of a partition, nervously tried to arrange the corsage of sweet peas at her waist. Everytime she swung her arms it brushed against the skin, annoying her, making her think of what really annoyed her so that the flowers became a hated object that got in the way. A small thing, small in size and purpose, the way she was. And the dress. The wrong color blue. Much too light for her dark brown hair. Such a horrible combination. Just to be matron of honor. Some honor. Toby should have had a friend, not a sister. But, of course, she realized, I'm responsible for that too. By making Mollie my maid of honor, I started a new tradition. Just like that!

Aunt Dora, leaning on her cane, stood next to the bandstand. She motioned for Ellie's attention, pointed toward the entranceway. Harry had arrived. He walked briskly across the dance floor, weaving lithely in and out of the reaching hands of running children, nodding ceremoniously to relatives, conscious of the eyes that scrutinized him, the whispered words that announced his alien situation. A cynical grin told everyone that he was more than equal to the stares. Tall, without the slightest trace of self-conscious slouch, he showed everyone, instantly, that he had no time to waste with people who wanted only to tell him how they disapproved of what he had done. He stopped to kiss his Aunt Dora then continued picking his path toward Ellie.

They kissed the ritual public kiss of brother and sister: the offered cheek, the patting hand on the back. Harry straightened up, folded his arms across his chest. "Here we go again."

"You've seen Toby already?"

"No."

"Is Martha in there?"

"No."

"Didn't she come?" Ellie flattened her corsage, her brother's ever-bearing calm further troubling her.

"No, she didn't come and I didn't make her."

"But Harry, Mama's going . . ."

"Mama will be very happy she didn't come. You know she will."

"That isn't true. She'll be . . ."

"Glad."

Ellie shrugged. "Have it your way."

"What's the difference? If Mama's unhappy about it, then Mollie and Clara will be glad. It balances out. And Toby," he unfolded his arms to swing them at his side toward Ellie, "that ringleader, she won't even know Martha's not here. This way we won't have any fights."

"Nobody would fight. You're being unfair."

"Good girl. The oldest child has learned her lesson from Papa. Keep peace." He draped an arm on Ellie's shoulder, playfully rubbing it across her skin. "If you don't mind my asking, where's Morrie?"

Ellie lifted his arm from her shoulder. "He's not here either. He had to work."

"Well! So now we're even-Steven. Okay?"

"Maybe we should mingle, Harry, instead of talking this way."

"I'd rather stay right here. It's protected from . . ." His waving arm completed the statement.

"At least you should see Toby before the ceremony."

"I'll see her soon enough. She can wait for my congratulations."

"Why still hold a grudge, Harry? You're married now. You got what you wanted. The past is the past."

"You don't really believe that, do you El? My gentile wife doesn't believe that. Her Jewish 'in-laws' don't believe it. Just you?"

"No arguments, please." Ellie touched his cheek. "I was just suggesting."

"You're better off suggesting it to your sisters. They're the ones who drive us nuts." His voice was raised in sudden anger. People standing nearby turned immediately, as if all along they had been listening. Harry glared back defiantly.

"Harry, please. Ssh."

"All right." He turned to face her. "I won't yell, but just give me credit for some sense. I'm young, not stupid. I married the person I wanted to. Papa didn't have to tell me who."

"And what is that remark supposed to mean?" Although she knew, because, instantly, he reached out to embrace her, to pat her back, that his words were not meant to hurt, nevertheless, she had to react; she was human too; she had to defend herself just as he was doing. And all along she had been trying to show him, whenever Martha was present, that she was on their side, that she understood doing what you had to do even if others hated you for it. After all, running off, at nineteen, wasn't the easiest thing in the world for her or the others to accept. And so this is what she was going to get in return for the effort. Okay. That's what happens. Everyone for himself. "You can't answer all of a sudden? You want revenge on me because I listened to Papa?" She covered her eyes, embarrassed that she could start to cry so easily, and walked quickly away. He called to her, but she refused to stop.

Alone on the dance floor, unconsciously her steps moved in time to the fox-trot rhythm. She stifled a wild urge to go back to Harry, to make him dance with her. And even if Morrie were here, they wouldn't dance. Not him! She would never dance, never. Not now. Not in the future. A sad inner stillness, a stillness through which drifted, stretching endlessly, the color of gray, stopped her movement. Looking out at the dancing people, hearing the rising noise, the music, she saw inside a glimpse of something beyond this moment for which she had no word. Gray, she called it. But the encircling children were tugging, pulling her away from the sight. She bent to them, forced her mind back through time to remember how they must feel, free, with space to run in, to scream into and not be heard above the larger noise, remembering suddenly that even that she had stopped herself from doing.

"Doesn't Toby look beautiful?" Her Aunt Minnie was shouting to her. "Just like your mother."

"She does. Very beautiful," Ellie answered, gazing through imagined distance.

"I think I'll like her husband. What does he do?"

"I don't know. Mama knows. Excuse me, Aunt Minnie, I'm going to eat."

"Sure, darling, go. But where's Morrie? I don't see him anywhere."

"At work," she screamed, moving once more toward the edge of the dance floor.

Waiters were already replenishing platters. The guests, caring little for the beauty of the floral arrangements, had long since destroyed the original design. A *gefilte* fish ball was sticking in the mush of a chopped herring bowl; horseradish red was splashed atop the white tablecloths; used toothpicks, removed from knishes, littered the table and surrounding floor. Surely she could not, if even the simple beauty of this table could not—Ellie pushed at the repulsive remnants of it—avoid moving past stillness into change. She pierced a slice of gray, pickled herring. It dangled dangerously at the end of the toothpick, and, as she lifted it carefully toward her mouth, a push from behind made it slither to the floor.

"Oh, I'm so sorry," her Cousin Rose shrieked.

Ellie blushed, grabbed a napkin to dispose of the now ugly herring.

She moved down the length of table, in front of, around the munching people, managing a slab of pink lox, some green olives, and, best of all, a wedge of strong white radish. Grape punch washed it down. The maneuvering left her breathless.

The band began "The Blue Danube" and now all danced: mothers and young sons, fathers and daughters, old couples shuffling sadly to the strains of their private nostalgia. The cigarette and cigar smoke rose upward toward the scintillating dimness of the revolving chandelier. The men below, near the bar, laughed hoarsely. The wedding was on. Time was pushing it to its inevitable finale: a crushing crescendo of sobs. All around her dancers whirled; excitement reddened each face so that they looked like new people, joyously taking part in a great event. Even Harry was dancing, laughing as he tried to direct a puffing Aunt Rose to keep time with the swaying rhythm.

Then she saw them all in the entranceway: Mama, Papa, Mollie and Clara: the Perlins. Harry immediately started toward them. Ellie watched them move into the room and, by their presence, quiet the noise. Only the music continued, now muted. Harry kissed each of them. They smiled 'hellos,' nodding to all that gazed. They showed, bending graciously together, a modest strength. Mrs. Perlin took Harry's offered arm. Mr. Perlin, erect, his graying beard trimmed fastidiously to form a silver triangle beneath his full red lips, held his arms protectively around his unmarried daughters, urged them imperiously forward. Right out of the Bible, Ellie thought, loving, holding on to what was proudly his. And she, married, was now outside those arms, unable to depend on them for help.

Once more the music became louder. The crowd stirred, resumed the dance.

"Ellie, you look wonderful." Mr. Perlin kissed her forehead, and, as he always did, rubbed his beard across her nose. She smiled obediently. His gaze scanned the people waiting to say hello. "Morrie?" His lips soundlessly formed the name. She nodded 'no' and stepped forward to kiss her mother. "Mama, the dress is beautiful."

"It's just my old *shmata*."

"Old maybe, but not a *shmata*." Mollie brushed the front of her long, black crepe dress. "That's the prettiest wine velvet Papa ever worked on." She looked directly at Ellie. "And you? That's not a very covered up dress."

"It's blue." Mrs. Perlin responded for Ellie. "Very appropriate."

"Did you see Toby?" shouted Clara above the swell of music, grabbing for Ellie's arm with the same nervous animation that made even her ironing of a dress a celebration. "She's marvelous."

"Come," Mr. Perlin interrupted. "We shouldn't stand here right in the middle." He beckoned them into motion. Two lines advanced in the direction of Leon's parents. Harry, taciturn and aloof, Ellie, gazing determinedly ahead, each holding onto their mother; Mollie and Clara behind them still held within the circle of their father's arms. Heads turned to watch. Relatives edged closer. But then the band began the Wedding March, and the doors of the chapel were pushed open by Mr. Kutsher.

First sniffles, then choking sobs could be heard. Even Ellie, standing with the rest of the two families on the raised platform, found it necessary to dart her crumpled handkerchief up to her eyes. Toby and Leon seemed shapeless tremors, not real people, through her tears.

The cantor's tenor voice soared thinly, purely trilled, then glided even higher above the trivial noises of the present moment, reaching into the darkness and then the brightness of ancient, perpetuated melodies. His audience would feel that awesome chill of recognition, a vague but startling force that prodded memory, that recalled their magnificent tradition of misery, misery which, through the centuries and here in the third decade of the Twentieth, had never really diminished. Some wore the fact of its effect proudly; others tried always to hide the truth; but all trembled when confronted by it. The cantor made the tears flow easily. They expected that, desired it.

Toby swayed before the rabbi. And Leon, who soon would hold her securely, now touched her tentatively, to support her.

Numbly, Ellie played her part, wondered, seeing Leon's hand move, why at one moment it was necessary to use caution, to fear the power that issued from an unseeable source; and at the next moment to be brutish, to demand. The rabbi was in contact with the Law, with the mystery of the Why, with the unquestioned explanations handed down from above. He stood beneath the sacred canopy, his beard long and scraggly, smelling sour from age like a fetid wrinkled rag, one hand waving slightly before the couple in benediction, in warning, beating out an accompaniment to the cantor's music, his voice, raspy with phlegm, intoning the Hebrew words that would finally say to Leon, kiss her, take her and make her heavy with child, the way the Talmud prescribes; but be kind, fear, respect, understand that there is One who sees all that you do, One who smiles benignly at compassion and frowns at cruelty.

None of this is true. Ellie roused herself to doubt again what she wanted to believe. No one sees me here or at home with Morrie, in bed, covered by his long body. Does God say I must do that? Does God care about love? A suppressed sob swelled her throat with pain.

Toby's veil was lifted. She drank the consecrated wine. The silver goblet was passed to Leon. He drank. Toby's veil was lowered once more, and the rabbi proceeded. All those on the platform arched forward expectantly, together in their hushed waiting.

Behind Ellie the guests seated in the chapel were now still, their breath sucked in, anxious for the moment that was rapidly approaching. The rabbi's voice wobbled toward its carefully prepared climax of happiness and despair. "Take and make of your life together all that you are able; God wills it so; only He will help you attain contentment; only He will punish you for transgression." Leon's lifted foot stamped down on the sacred wine glass, shattering it to bits inside the white covering. The people exhaled. Their chairs creaked with a new expectation.

The couple kissed. The rabbi smiled. The ceremony was consummated. The gates of the past were locked again, the presence of mysterious, hovering figures departed, and the names of Toby and Leon Levinson, together now, were sealed within.

Everyone moved, stirred by a collective reflex to be closer. Amid smiles and new waves of tears Leon, confident now, kissed Toby once more. Hands and mouths fell upon her as she was shunted from one to another carelessly down the steps of the platform, onto the carpeted aisle of the chapel, out into the spaciousness of the dining room where the tables had been set up for the meal. The guests erupted into a chorus of *Mazeltovs*. The band started up loudly.

Toby twirled, radiant; the pallor had disappeared. She was married. There was only one further ordeal, as Ellie viewed it, to be met with and overcome. She wondered, as she was pushed past tables, if Toby would meet lust as successfully as she had met God. Seeing her stumble, Harry put his hand on Ellie's shoulder to steady her, and in that instant, the touch of skin to skin, she remembered Morrie and her awkward incompetence on their first night together.

CHAPTER *Two*

THE SNOW, which had begun to fall when she left Kutsher's, was now, as she opened the door to their apartment, well on its way to becoming one of those legendary March blizzards that everyone recalls, years later, as the worst they ever experienced. Ellie's fatigue stemmed more from the burden of having to explain Morrie's absence than from the wedding itself; that had finished appropriately with lingering goodbyes and the guests disappearing into the swirl of snow, not to be seen until the next occasion provided a reason for being together.

She did not switch on the light in the living room but walked instead, debating with her desire for sleep, to the window to watch the snow fall past the street lamp. The flakes were large, energetic, rushing noiselessly to join the unmarked whiteness covering the sidewalks, to coat the fire escapes of the darkened houses across the street. Behind her was the banging sound of radiators hissing the early morning heat through the apartment house. The solitude was comforting. She estimated that Morrie would not be home for at least another hour, perhaps two, since the snow would make the horse and wagon hard to manage. She was glad to have all that time to herself. Time enough in the morning to talk about the wedding, make the inevitable comparisons to their own, argue some more about why he didn't go. Yes, in the morning it would be easier to talk. She could prepare her anger, control it better than she usually did.

She sighed, leaned her head against the cold glass of the window. The snow, beautifully sad and quick, falling for what? To melt? To turn black overnight in the city. Remembering other snows, she cried, feeling lonely, small, but captured, enjoying, for awhile, memories of the winter at the old house in New Jersey where snow stayed white as long as you cared to play with it, of a sled, of a *Chanukah* gift. There were no more gifts for each new candle at *Chanukah*. She pushed away from the window, not wanting to cry, instinct moving her to the bedroom. It doesn't change anything to cry.

Once in bed, feeling the coldness of clean sheets against her skin, she relaxed. The tension of the evening waved out of her arms and legs. She stretched diagonally across the double bed, shuddered, searching for warmth, raised her legs so that she could hold her feet in her hands. Twisting toward the window, she could still see the falling snow framed in the diamond of glass left between the folds of the white organdy curtains. Sleep was what she wanted now. Just plain sleep. Before Morrie came home. Poor Morrie. Out in the snow, probably pulling the wagon because the horse wouldn't move. Milkmen always had to work, regardless of the weather. That kind of work made some people better. Or worse . . . either one . . . or both. For him it's both. She extended her legs cautiously down across the sheet. What *is* wrong with him? And what's wrong with me too? He knows about everything in the world. More than I do. If only I could admit that and let him win all the arguments, he'd be better in a second. But he'll never be like Papa or Harry. Handsome like them. Yes. But not loving. That he knows nothing about. She stretched her head toward the snow, toward the past, toward sleep. Away from the question that settled, sifted deeply to the bottom of her mind, always disturbing whatever comfortable drowsiness she felt. Why did he marry me? He wanted Mollie. She's prettier. Why did he do it? She plunged her head beneath the blanket. He'll be cold and wet when he comes in. Probably make a lot of noise too. Well, he's got a right. After all. He can sleep late tomorrow and I'll make a big breakfast. I'll really try with the coffee. If I drank it, I'd know when it's good. The things we find to argue about. But it takes so long to learn everything. Much more than a year. He'll be kinder. We won't yell. He must care something for me. He married me. And that's that. He didn't have to. So he has to care. Once more she looked toward the snow. All right now, no more thinking. Enough. Just sleep. The snow. The cold. And warm. Sleep.

THE DOOR SLAMMED. It must be the door. Ellie sat up, pulling the blanket toward her throat, frightened.

"I'm sorry, El. It slipped." Morrie's voice, a loud whisper, satisfied her fear. She fell back against the pillow. The room was filled with gray. The clock on the nightstand said 6:30. He was much later than she thought he would be. Holding her breath, she tried to fall back into sleep. But she heard him moving toward her. Then saw him silhouetted in the doorway of the bedroom, stopping, his leather lumberjacket crackling as he strained forward to see if she were awake. She couldn't lie still.

The bed squeaked as he sat down, his peaked cap still on, drops of water dribbling to the edge of the celluloid brim. A yellow pencil was sticking out of its holder above his ear. He bent over to kiss her, searching clumsily for her mouth in the dimness, leaning heavily.

"Oh Morrie, you're soaking wet."

"I know," he said wearily. "Am I glad to be home. It's still snowing hard." He moved his cold hand up and down her exposed arm.

"Morrie, please get up from the quilt before it gets all wet."

"It'll dry. Don't worry about it." He tried to lean toward her once more, but her hand pushed him back.

"I know it'll dry, but why get it wet in the first place?"

"For Christ's sake forget about the quilt." He sat up, remaining on the bed. "Is that all you can think about? I'm the one who's wet and I don't mind it."

Ellie turned away from his angry glare, to the snow.

"No answer for that?"

She closed her eyes.

He slapped his knee loudly. "I come home. The first thing I do is come in to kiss you, and all you care about is getting the goddamned quilt wet. Look at me, Ellie."

She didn't move.

"I said look at me, Ellie." He leaned over, twisting her body, pulling her face toward his. "Didn't you hear me?"

She freed her head, kept her eyes closed.

"Now," leaning across her, "you can really feel how wet I am.

What are you going to do about it?"

As he waited, his fingers squeezing the flesh of her arms, her drowsy anger, her panic were mixed with helpless pity for him, for herself. What could she do now that it had started? "Why don't you change into your pajamas and come to bed?"

"No. I want you to get out of bed. I want something to eat." His fingers pressed harder as if to hold on to her were all that he could accomplish.

"There's a pot of coffee on the stove." Her voice was soft, conciliatory. "Have some and come to bed."

"No. I said I wanted you to get out of bed. I want more than coffee."

"Please, Morrie. Be sensible. It's so early."

"Damn it." His exploding rage made his body tremble. "I don't give a shit how early it is." Drops of water rolled onto Ellie's face.

"Please, Morrie, let go of my arms. You're hurting me." She tried to pull back, but he pressed down, pinning her beneath him. "Morrie, Morrie, please. Come to bed. Sleep for a while. It's Sunday morning."

He let go of her arms, kissed her face, scraping his stubbled chin across her skin.

"Don't you care if you're hurting me?" she screamed, the sound muffled by his jacket.

"I don't give a shit. You do what I want you to do."

"All right, I will, only let me get up."

Gradually, as if he were afraid that she would slither away, he sat up.

"What foolishness," she dared as she wiped herself with the sheet.

"Well, if you weren't so stupid, none of this would happen."

"I'm stupid?" She moaned with pain as she rubbed her arms. "If you would just use your brains to understand a little bit . . ."

"Understand? Damn it, you're the one who can't do that. With all that snow I rush through my route to get home to bed with you, and right away you're bitching like a goddamn kid. And when I ask you to do something for me, Madame High-Horse decides she can't."

"Okay. Have it your way." It was useless to talk, to reason. "Only don't yell, Morrie. The neighbors are still trying to sleep."

"Who gives a shit for the neighbors." He waved his arm menacingly, raising his voice once again.

"Ssh. No need to yell now."

"Don't ssh me," he screamed louder. "Do you hear! Just don't ssh me ever," and as his words exploded in the gray light his raised hand slapped down heavily onto Ellie's face.

A noiseless moment of snow falling past the dim light of the window. Neither of them moved, both looking at the other, shocked, surprised. And then Ellie's hand touched her cheek, touched the place where it hurt, as if just now the reflex had caught up with the thought. Bewildered, she slowly edged away from him until she reached the other side of the bed.

He lowered his hand to rub the silky quilt, gazed dumbly toward the rustling sound of her leaving the bed and then the room. He stood up, flung his cap onto the bed, and walked to the window. Looking out, he arched his hand across his forehead, felt the strong beat of anger in his temples, anger directed at himself now, sorry for the slap and for his never knowing how to make simple words, simple acts do what he wanted them to do. His whole idea was so easy. A quiet morning with the snow outside and the two of them in bed together, warm and comfortable. Now it'll be cold words to apologize and the snow wasted. I should have gone to the wedding. That's why it happened. That's what she wanted.

From the kitchen he heard the sounds of a pot being banged on the gas stove, then water running in the sink. What the hell was she doing this for now? He had expected her to run to the bathroom and lock herself in. She always did that when he yelled at her. Only this time—nodding his head as the fact worked its way deeper into his understanding—there's a difference. This time I hit her.

He was unwilling to walk to the kitchen, to stop her, yet he knew that if he waited too long, it would be worse. And so, finally changing into his pajamas and robe, he went meekly toward the bright electric glare in the other room.

Ellie was in front of the stove stirring a pan of cereal, clanging the spoon against the metal side. With each sound her body shivered.

"Would you like me to get your bathrobe, El?"

The sound of his subdued voice stopped her hand, started it up again with increased speed so that the liquid sloshed over the rim of the pan. She said nothing.

"Ellie, would you turn around for a minute so I can tell you something?"

"No. The cereal will stick."

"Please, Ellie. I can't talk to your back."

"You want to tell me you're sorry. That I know." Her voice was low, even. "You've told me that already, for all the other yelling." She did not interrupt the stirring. "For a whole year you've been yelling and apologizing. I know those words. What good are they. You don't change," she hesitated, "and neither do I." She twisted the gas jet shut and turned it, "Why didn't you ever yell before we were married? And if that's all you need me for, why did you ever marry me?"

Morrie sat down at the kitchen table, nervously rubbed his hand back and forth across the clean white cloth. "I don't want to yell, Ellie. I swear I don't. I just can't seem to help it."

"I know, Morrie." Her bitterness made her wince. "Just like I don't want to make you angry. All the same it happens and I hate it."

"Come on, Ellie. Things like that are bound to happen."

"Hitting me, too?"

"No! Of course not. I didn't mean . . ."

"I know. I said I knew. But this is just going to be a new thing to apologize for."

Ellie poured the cereal into a bowl and set it before him. "Eat!" She remained standing next to him, pointing at the bowl. "You asked for food. Now eat!" Her voice thickened with unaccustomed strength. Rarely was he so docile, so guilty, and although the moment was painful, she was determined to draw it out, to endure her body's coldness for the sake of his discomfort. The moments that would shortly confront them, she wanted to stop from occurring.

Then it came, his voice childish now, cajoling. "Ellie, you talk as if you don't care anything about how I feel." He completely ignored the cereal that steamed before him.

"What do you expect me to say? That I love you to yell at me and hit me? Well, I don't. And what's more, I don't think I want any more of it." She sat down on the chair opposite to him. An expression of distant speculation glazed her eyes. She brushed a strand of hair from her forehead, distracted, as if she were thinking of something beautiful and possible. Morrie hunched over the table, his head tilted upward so that he could watch her. She began speaking again, her tone even softer than it had been earlier. "What I want to say, Morrie, is that I don't see how it can ever be any good for us. Other married people don't act this way. We fight so much because we can't help it. There doesn't seem to be anything else we can do. We never should have gotten married." Morrie lowered his gaze. "I'm sorry to have to put it that way, but it's the truth. You should have married Mollie. She wanted you to. You've said that often enough."

"Oh Ellie, you know I was only kidding when I said that. I thought you understood."

"Well, that's how little you understand me."

"You said you did."

"What else could I say? Could I complain? You'd only have screamed more. Could I kiss you and say don't tease me? You would've been embarrassed."

"So what? You should have. Don't you care anything for me?"

"I thought I did. I even thought I loved you—and that's the first time anyone ever used that word in this house. Love. It must have been something entirely different I felt. You would have a name for it. Anyway, my father convinced me to get married. You know that's the truth."

"He didn't have to convince me." He tried to reach for her hand. Instantly she withdrew it from the tabletop.

"My father told me you'd be good, you'd amount to something."

"Wait a minute." He was immediately less contrite. "You haven't even given me a chance. It's such a short time."

"True, but it's long enough to know I'm unhappy. Nobody ever treated me the way you do. I never expected you to act like an animal. You never did before we were married. And now . . ." Her courage was suddenly gone. She looked toward the stove.

Once more his hand moved across the table toward her, stopped, afraid to touch, defeated by the truth of what she said. "What can I do, Ellie? You seem so determined."

"Determined?"

"Yes, like you've made up your mind to leave me."

"I don't want to say anything as definite as that. But, who

knows, maybe it would be for the best. We don't have any children." She stood up, hesitating, then walked to the sink, leaning against it, staring down at him.

Nothing was left of Morrie's anger now, except inside the taut fingers, the hard circle of hand that aimlessly stirred the cooling bowl of cereal, he felt it waiting along with a sense of undiminished pride that told him he was better than she said, better than he acted. He stared blankly toward the window at the beginnings of another Sunday.

CHAPTER *Three*

ELLIE LEFT THE APARTMENT in the early afternoon when she was sure Morrie was asleep. It was still snowing outside and the cold, soft air urged her away from thoughts of the morning discussion which had ended in a tense silence of nothing really decided. Animated by the hush of falling snow, she could shiver her need to decide into a vacant smiling at the playing, yelling children, or at the people, huddled together, walking against the weather.

The wind whisked through the wrap-around folds of her coat, lifted her umbrella in loud puffs, stung her tense face into vivid redness. It was relief she felt, natural, exhilarating.

The trolley car took her within a block of her parents' apartment house, further downtown. There the snow was black and slushy. The street was crowded with pushcarts whose wares were covered by wet tarpaulins. Sunday was a work day on the Lower East Side. Women pushed close to the carts, briskly lifting up the edges of the coverings, peering underneath, quickly making a selection. Snow laced their blinking eyes. They pointed and paid while the peddler scurried around the cart, indifferent to the snow. Ellie stopped long enough to buy some hot chestnuts from a bundled, bearded old man who, after expertly tossing the hot nuts into a bag, returned his hands close to the warmth of his small stove, lowered his head inside a bulky shawl.

When she entered the apartment, her father was bending before the stove, stoking the coals with a metal poker, a remnant of their old house fireplace. Smiling, he turned, straightened up with effort, kissed Ellie's upturned face. "Morrie couldn't come today either?"

"He's sleeping. He had a very bad night. Where's Mollie and Clara?"

"They went to the movies."

"And Mama?" Ellie gestured toward the bedroom.

Mr. Perlin nodded. "Yes. She's resting. The wedding was too much for her." He moved from the stove and saw the bag of chestnuts on the table. "Always thoughtful, my daughter." He kissed her again.

Ellie warmed her hands over the stove. "You think she's sleeping?"

"Probably not. She was only tired. Must be the blood pressure. The doctor always tells her to stay in bed when she feels the spinning inside." He sat down at the table, gazed lifelessly toward the bedroom door. His dark eyes were ringed with wrinkles. Ellie stepped behind his chair and let a hand rest on his shoulder. The blue woolen muffler, the one she had knitted for him years ago, was pulled tightly around his neck, the ends tucked neatly inside the front of his fraying but tidy jacket. Under her hand she felt a yielding, soft weariness. Last night at the wedding he had smiled proudly, and today his flesh sagged submissively as she massaged his shoulders. "That's good," he moaned for more. Old, older his face said, however crisply he smiled, and the white flecks in his beard, prominent against the blue muffler, proved it to her. Another daughter married; another hour passing on the clock by which a father measured time.

"I'll go in to see Mama." Her hand stopped moving. "Eat those chestnuts before they get cold." She leaned her cheek against his. "Why don't you rest in the other room for a while?"

"As long as you're here, I'd better go downstairs to the shop and catch up with the sewing."

"Can't it wait, Pa? You look too tired."

"It's relaxing in the shop. No one will come in there today."

"Okay. But dress warm. It's still snowing." She hesitated, measuring her need alongside his, then went on. "And Papa, I have to talk to you before I leave." It was the wrong time to bother him, but for what she had to say there would never be a right time. And he was the only one she could say it to.

"It's important, darling?"

"It'll wait, Pa. Go down to the shop first." She helped him with his coat, kissed him, watched him leave before she quietly opened the door to the bedroom.

It was brighter in there. Her mother, propped up in the big double bed, gazed out at the snow. Waxen immobility tightened the skin stretched across her high cheek bones so that its pallor seemed to glow with a newer whiteness. The long gray hair, now unbraided, lay splayed upon the shoulders of her lace bed jacket. She didn't hear Ellie enter.

"Hello Mama." Ellie sat down at the edge of the bed.

"Ellie darling." Mrs. Perlin, speaking softly, did not disturb her gaze, her mood. "You came out in such a weather." She took hold of Ellie's hand, caressed it, squeezed it as if she did not want to let go.

"You looked so pretty lying there I hated to bother you."

"Your mother is no longer so pretty, and for what I was thinking it's all right to bother me." She looked directly at Ellie for the first time. "Believe it or not Ripley, I was trying to add up all the snow I've had in my lifetime. A lot. A terrible lot. Still, I like it."

"And why shouldn't you? It's beautiful." Ellie felt obliged to agree with vigor. The rueful whiteness of her mother's fatigue demanded that, as if announcing the fact that last night's event had diminished much more than her strength.

"I know it is, but I thought how in Budapest it was more beautiful." She raised one hand then let it fall limply on the blanket. "Papa went downstairs?" Ellie nodded. "He had so much sewing to do, but he wouldn't leave me alone. Your sisters with the movies."

Ellie moved to a chair near the bed. "Do you want me to get something for you? Some tea, maybe?"

"No darling. Just sit here and talk to me."

"Sure Mama."

"It must be so cold outside. Look at how those clothes on the line are frozen stiff. I don't understand why those women don't take them inside."

"They probably had them outside during the night. Remember it only started to snow when we left Kutsher's. And it was worse when Morrie came home this morning."

"Oy," her mother put her hand on her cheek, slapping it gently, "how did I forget to ask you before this about Morrie?"

"He's all right." She looked away from her mother.

"You don't sound so sure." Leaning slightly forward, Mrs. Perlin waited for a reply as if she had asked a question for which she must have an answer.

Just because, today, for a few hours, her mother seemed softer, more willing, perhaps, to admit that there were degrees of 'being all right,' was not reason enough for Ellie to talk, suddenly. That approach, in the past, had never been successful. And now, if Mrs. Perlin, reverting to the familiar cold aloofness reserved for moments of crisis, said 'I told you so,' how could that help either of them. The illusion of understanding would once more be tested and fail. No, Ellie knew that she would have to talk to her father. "Really, Mama, he's fine."

"But?"

"But nothing." Ellie smiled weakly, a quickly fading smile that revealed her insistent lie.

"All right. I wouldn't ask you no more." She shifted her gaze back to the window and the snow. "How I hope Toby and Leon will be happy. I always hope that everyone should be as happy as your father and me. Sure bad things happened . . . with Harry . . . no more house . . ." she paused, obviously thinking thoughts she would not tell Ellie, ". . . how you children loved the snow when we had the house. And you, you stayed out until you were frozen stiff like those clothes."

"I still love the snow, only it's not the same fun anymore."

A silence followed, a silence of private memory in which Ellie saw herself with Harry, Mollie and Clara, very little Toby, on the hill behind their house, belly-whopping, and mama watching from the kitchen window. And when papa came back from the shop in New York, just before it got very dark, it was so good to run to him, while the others continued to play, and enter the warmth of the house together, separate from everyone else, even mama. Snow was always this for her. But today, when she had left her own apartment and allowed memory to mix with the new snow, her image of the past had been vague, almost beyond recall, as if darkness had descended in her mind and there was no light to turn on. The thought of Morrie, her husband, had dimmed the familiar recollections which, now, like magic, her mother had retrieved. "No more crazy presents for *Chanukah*," said Ellie, smiling wistfully, barely disturbing the quiet of the room.

"Sure not. Now I give dishes and silverware so you can become a regular *balabusta*."

"Don't joke, Ma. You know I can't even cook eggs right. You never let us do anything in the kitchen."

"Then, that was for me to do. You'll learn the same way I did. Don't worry."

"I'll never learn. Morrie's always complaining. About my coffee, about everything. Nothing's as good as his mother's."

"Of course it's not. A wife never makes good coffee for her husband. That's a fact of life like Mama's is always the best." Mrs. Perlin nodded knowingly, proud of her wisdom. "Why not ask your mother-in-law for help? She'll be glad to teach."

"I suppose that would be the thing to do," Ellie agreed, immediately dismissing the possibility. Her gaze wandered from the window. She was attracted by the framed wedding picture on the dressing table. Morrie looked like a funny cartoon figure dressed in a tuxedo that was too small for his long arms. And the tiny girl next to him just couldn't be herself. Impossible. The face smiled, looked young. And now she felt so much older, so tired, not knowing how to decide the end of something which the picture proved had really happened. And if she loved Morrie then, that was then. Now what did she feel? Nothing? If every day, every minute you have to figure out, what's the good. Just to be married?

Ellie? . . . Ellie, where's your mind?"

"I'm sorry Mama. I was just thinking of something."

"I know you were, but what?"

"Nothing important."

"All right, but what is that nothing important?"

"Please, Ma, don't make a *megillah* out of it. I was only thinking what I should make Morrie for supper tonight."

"If that's all, you can take some lamb stew from me. In the icebox. It's from a few days so it'll be good."

"Thanks, Ma. He likes that."

"Better he should like me more than my lamb stew."

"He does. Don't be silly."

"You dasn't lie to me. I know different. I remember. When he spoke to papa about marrying you, I said no right away. The three of us were sitting right there," and she pointed for emphasis, toward the door. The pale hue of her skin reddened with animation. "And I said no and right away he hated me. I don't blame him. I only say that you're too good for him. Mollie was too. It's a difference if he's really a decent man. But how could he be when all he knows is for himself. All the time himself. That I could tell. I knew better. On this I knew better than your father."

"Don't get so excited, Ma. Please. It's not necessary." Ellie stood up.

"I'm not excited. It's all right. You're married now. So let it be that way. All I want is for you to be happy. If you are, I'm satisfied. I want to die knowing that if not my son, at least my daughters are all right."

"I can't stand it when you talk that way." Ellie walked to the door, but the familiarity of her mother's words stopped her from leaving as if they represented a litany of life that she was forced to share. To deny what her mother would say now was to deny the source of herself.

"When we had the house and money, you all had what you needed and more. Harry was in school. My only son in school to become something here, in this country. All of you . . ." Mrs. Perlin stopped suddenly, her eyes filling with tears. She dabbed at them with the edge of her bed jacket, shook her head, as if that way she could make the tears stop. "If I had what to give you now, you can be sure you would never have to be without. And papa too. All he has left is the tailor shop. All he can do is make dresses for you . . ."

"Ma. It's enough. You gave. He gave. That's finished."

"No. It's not enough." Mrs. Perlin waved her hand at Ellie. "At night, when your father goes to bed, he lies here and tells how he wanted to give you a house for your wedding, with fine furniture, like we had in the old country. For me, I didn't care about that. I wanted you should go to college, and Harry, and the rest of you, to be a lady, not to get married quick, in a hurry. . . . Who knows what your Morrie will ever become? If he'll ever forget himself enough to give you something. One thing I know, he's not kind, Ellie. That I knew right away."

Ellie looked down at her mother's grinding mouth, at the pointing hand. The words had been the same, yet today they meant something different. Accusing Morrie for everything that had gone wrong in the Perlin family was unfair. "You're always talking about being kind and giving. Always saying that Morrie's the bad one. Maybe I'm the bad one. Maybe if I were kinder, he could be. Did you ever think of that Ma?" For the first time Ellie wanted to defend Morrie as if by doing that she was helping herself to move away from the center of her unhappiness. "It's not Morrie's fault. Not all of it."

The two women looked at each other, calmly aware that they had, this afternoon, ruffled the familiar texture of their conversation, broken a tenuous strand of understanding. It was the wedding that had done it. Ellie was sure that it had ended something old in herself. She had no word yet for what would come next. "I'm going to make coffee for papa. Do you want some?"

The older lady turned her gaze once more back to the window. "No darling. You go," she whispered. "Cut cake for it."

"I will." Ellie left the room, closing the door with exaggerated care.

By the time her father returned to the apartment, Ellie was sitting at the kitchen table trying to drink a cup of coffee. There was a pan of untouched apple cake in the center of the table.

"You're drinking coffee? Since when?"

"Since now, Pa, but I'm not very successful. I really made it for you. Want some?"

"An excellent idea. It's getting colder out." He warmed his hands over the stove. "Mama's sleeping?"

"I think so." Ellie poured her father's coffee into a shallow bowl, cut some cake. For some time they sat silently together, Ellie's thoughts removed from this dim, building-enclosed kitchen, settling definitely on what she would do.

Finally, troubled by her nervous movement with the coffee cup, Mr. Perlin said gently, "You wanted to talk to me?"

"Papa, I . . ." She hesitated, certainty vanishing as her father's solicitous smile appeared.

"Take your time and tell me. What is it?"

Then, in a determined rush of words, as if this was the only way she would be able to speak, she went on, "Papa, I'm sorry I married Morrie."

Mr. Perlin's smile which, at all moments of Ellie's life had represented a faith older than suffering dissolved as she stumbled into further explanation. First astonishment, then disbelief, and then, as Ellie stopped talking, tears filled Mr. Perlin's eyes. Only the remnant of the habitual smile creased the corners of his mouth.

"Don't cry, Papa. Please don't cry," Ellie pleaded. "And don't say anything yet. Just let me talk." She stood up and walked to the front of the stove. The warmth was there, and those eyes, the sad, tired eyes of her father, could not see her. "When I came here before, I thought I was going to tell you I would leave Morrie. Sure we've argued before. He yelled right away like he always does. But this time when he ended up slapping me . . ."

"Slapped you?" His hand reached up to his cheek in incredible wonder. He turned to look at her.

"Don't say anything yet or I won't be able to finish."

"All right. I won't. But how could he slap you?"

"That's what I thought. How could he slap me. You never did. Mama didn't. At that minute I hated him so I couldn't wait to come here and tell you. I wondered how it was that I married him, why you thought he was so good. I always believed you papa; you were never wrong, so I thought you knew Morrie too, and I married him. But I don't love him anymore. This whole year, every day I knew more and more that I didn't care about him. And I came here to tell you."

Mr. Perlin remained silent, his body swaying to the melody of some secret prayer.

Ellie moved closer, placed her hands on his shoulders. "Then, when you went out, I spoke to mama. Not about this, but about Morrie generally. She started in. You know, about how she doesn't like him, how he isn't good enough for me and'll never give me anything. But today it was like I was hearing it for the first time. Mama means things, to give things. I don't blame her. I know why she feels that way, but Morrie does try hard. Regardless of what happened this morning, he does. And didn't he have the right to expect more from me too? What did I do for him? It's not only his fault. Like they say, there's always two sides."

"Sure two sides. I say that too, but who cares to look." Mr. Perlin pulled at his beard.

"So now I feel guilty," she continued, calmer now that she had struggled with the worst of it. "I'm not going to leave him. I don't know exactly what to do. I have to make up my mind, alone. I just know I won't leave him."

Her father stood up, tears collecting, glistening in the soft neatness of his beard, held Ellie in his arms, pressed her head onto his chest. "You're right. What you say is sensible, but to know you're unhappy . . . it's terrible, terrible . . . and to know that I did it to you . . ."

"Don't say that, Papa." Gently she pushed back to look up at him.

"How could it not be my fault? How could you not blame me?"

"What's the point of blaming anybody?"

"You're right. There's no point. But listen to me. For the last time listen and understand. The whole trouble is I never knew to tell you what to expect. I didn't know from arguments. Maybe you don't realize, but your mother and I had a peaceful marriage. Sure there was trouble, we lost our money, all that you know, but mostly it has been all right. And when you were born, that was all we needed—the first child. But when you got married last year, and last night Toby, and Harry's, well," he paused, brushed at his eyes with his muffler, "soon, perhaps, we'll be alone again, the way we were a long time ago. It seems such a long time ago to remember. But to be old means to remember. If things were good when we were young, then being old is not so terrible. I ask myself why I didn't speak like this before. I don't know why. Except who can be so cruel to tell children, your own children, that they best make good memories so that when they get old it will be easier? You can only hope and pray that it will be all right for them. Some things you can do nothing about. You'll see that's true." Once more he paused, raised Ellie's chin. His deep voice quivered the way it did in synagogue, "Try. Try more. Don't get a . . . a divorce from Morrie. For your mother's sake and for mine. You'll help Morrie to change. I know that."

He held her hands and neither of them spoke. Ellie saw in her father's eyes a desperate, helpless pleading. Inside herself, the gray stillness that she had seen last night at the wedding, on the dance floor, alone, returned. Now she felt compelled to give it a name. It was more than loneliness. It was, somehow, life. Not her father's, perhaps, but her own.

CHAPTER *Four*

Morrie was sitting in his overstuffed easy chair reading the *Sunday Daily News* when Ellie returned home. The parts of the paper he had already read littered the floor near his hassock. He sat up as the door slammed and lowered the newspaper. "Still snowing, El?" His tone was cautious, expectant.

"Yes," she murmured.

He got up and walked to her. "Need some help?"

She extended a package wrapped in brown paper. "Take that to the kitchen please." She held her hand beneath the point of the umbrella so that the water wouldn't drip on the floor. Meekly, Morrie followed her from the kitchen to the bathroom where she opened the umbrella and placed it in the bathtub. "I'm glad I don't have to work tonight."

Ellie hung her wet coat on one of the shower curtain rings and brushed past him on her way to the kitchen.

"What's in the package, honey?" He stood behind her, near the table, fingering the package then trying to brush an imaginary crumb from the cloth. There was nothing for him to do except wait for Ellie to set the tone. If she were willing to talk, he had a chance. If not, well, he would have to wait.

"Just leave it alone," she snapped. "It's lamb stew. My mother sent it for you."

"Good. I love your mother's lamb stew." He sat down. Even her anger was a hopeful sign. "How are they feeling?"

Ellie lit a burner and emptied the contents of the package into another saucepan, setting the pan down noisily on the burner. "My mother's not well. From the wedding. She was in bed."

"It must have been quite an affair," said Morrie, feigning, she realized, great interest. "Was it as good as ours?"

"Better."

"How better?"

"Maybe not better . . ." If she didn't soften her voice, they would soon be having another argument, ". . . but the ceremony was more effective."

"Oh," he replied, nodding as if he immediately understood Ellie's distinction. "How's this guy Leon?"

"Fine, as far as I can tell. He's a shoe salesman." Ellie was setting the table now and motioned for Morrie to lift his arms as she put down his napkin, plate, and silverware with ceremony. "I've decided to invite everyone to dinner when Toby comes back from her honeymoon. You'll meet him then since you couldn't meet him last night." He nodded and touched her hand intentionally, trying to stop her movements, but she shrugged it off.

"Where'd they go on their honeymoon?" He would have to be casual, for once let her lead him.

Ellie, preparing this meal with great deliberation, let his question go unanswered for the time being. She cut thick slices of rye bread and placed them on a plate. She bent before the stove, adjusting the flame beneath the saucepan so the stew wouldn't burn, carefully measured the amounts of water and coffee she placed in the percolator. Only then was she ready to answer his question. "You don't remember well, do you? I told you they were going to your father's hotel. I even called your mother the other day."

"Oh yeah. Now I remember."

"They only have a few days. Toby has to be back at work on Thursday."

"That's a shame, but they'll have a good time there. The food—not that they'll care about the food—well, anyway my mother will take care of them." Morrie watched Ellie as she moved briskly around the kitchen. She felt his staring helplessness, and it made her resolve stronger.

The snow started up harder again. She could hear it ticking the windowpane. "My silly sisters had to go to the movies in this weather. I hope they're home already."

"How would you like to go to the movies tonight, El?"

"Don't be foolish. One minute you're glad you don't have to go to work, and the next minute you want to go out to the movies." She shook her head incredulously as if she were speaking to a child.

"It was just an idea. Forget it. I thought it might be relaxing." He sounded hurt. "You used to like to walk in the snow."

"Thanks for your thoughtfulness but I feel very relaxed now."

"You do? I wish I could say the same." The sense of gratification released by his remark felt odd. To feel pleasure from someone else's discomfort was not Ellie's habit. But it told her he was feeling, that he could feel. All this time, as they talked, she was making up her mind to say nothing directly to Morrie about the morning or her decision. She would simply go about her routine activities with firmness, with a set mouth, a pout, perhaps, until he apologized. Or, if he didn't apologize, it was all right. By continuing to perform as if nothing had happened, she would make him understand that she planned nothing drastic. The hard part would be behaving with determination, with discipline, never to relax, yet to seem relaxed. Spontaneity would be lost, but she would gain control, quietly.

"Ellie? I think the stew's bubbling."

She turned from the window, recovering the sense of where she was, where she would always be. Even emptying the stew into a bowl, carrying it and a plate of rye bread to the table became a momentous act of will. "Start eating while it's hot." Before sitting down opposite Morrie, she lowered the flame under the coffeepot.

They ate in silence except for the noise Morrie made when he dipped rye bread into the sauce and then rushed the dripping bread to his mouth, blowing it loudly while it oozed juice back into his plate. In the past that kind of eating annoyed her. Now she said nothing. And when he looked at her, sure that she would react, the challenge of the stare only intensified her desire not to complain. Her expression must remain indifferent, like the faces of people you meet but don't know well. The plan would work. Even now his surprise pleased her. His mouth opened slightly, and his nostrils quivered involuntarily like an animal that catches a far off, indistinct scent. Confused by his failure to rouse her, he continued to eat.

"This is great, El. Must be a few days old."

"I'm glad you like it." She got up to turn the gas off under the coffee. "I'll have to remember to tell my mother."

"Give me some coffee now. And put some cream in it." It was the familiar Morrie who spoke then, the thin edge of anger sounding hard and hollow, his head trembling slightly.

But Ellie was not frightened now. "You can have coffee, but you're not getting cream. Not after meat. As long as I'm around, the kitchen stays kosher."

He strained, thinking of the morning, pulled the crust from another piece of rye bread. "All right."

She filled two cups of coffee—she would try it again—and handed one to him.

"You're drinking it?" She nodded 'yes' as if it were the most trivial of events. "When did you decide that?"

"This afternoon."

"You like it?"

"No." She sipped. "I don't know how you can drink it."

"Next thing you'll have to learn is how to smoke." Morrie laughed.

"That I'll never do. I can assure you of that."

"Ellie?" He reached for her hand, held it loosely. "Ellie, I . . ."

"I've got to clear the dishes." She stood up quickly, leaving his hand stretched across the table, useless.

"But El, I . . ." Her back was toward him and he stopped talking. She spilled old coffee grounds into a paper bag, cleaned, very carefully, the parts of the percolator as she had read somewhere it was important to do. Morrie watched, waiting for his moment, hoping that he could tell her what he had been thinking all afternoon. She dawdled; she made noise; in spite of her resolve, she wanted to provoke him, to hurt him some more. She could be as cruel as he, but she had a right to be.

"For Christ's sake, Ellie, come and finish your coffee. I have to talk to you."

She did not tell him not to holler; she did not react at all; but she did sit down and stare at him.

"Now look, El. I'm going to apologize once more. But I'm not going to kiss your ass forever. I'm a man. I work hard for you and for myself. I make a decent living. We're married and we're going to stay that way."

Ellie nodded when he paused.

"You haven't had it so bad," Morrie continued, his voice raised self-righteously. "You get what you want, whatever I'm able to give you now. I'm not an educated man like your father, his royal highness, but I'm all right. And even though you're so high and mighty, when we get to bed you like it too."

She winced, instinct still in control; he saw it. To play her part correctly that was not allowed. But she couldn't gain immunity immediately or completely. It would take a long time; and then, she realized, there would always be some hurt to sustain, some slur that would stir her. Human beings endure; they don't live very much.

He said nothing further. There was no need to. His power had been reinstated by her quiet acceptance. That was, after all, what he wanted most of all. He placed both hands on the table and leaned down hard on the palms, fingers stretching, tense, waiting for a rebuttal.

"Okay Morrie? You're finished?" She waited. "If you are, go to the living room and finish with your newspaper. I'll do the dishes. After all, I'm your wife. That's why you hired me."

And in this next moment of hesitation, his jaw dropping as if readying itself to deny, with some joke, what she had said, his hand raised from the table, perhaps to wave and point 'no,' Ellie felt that if he would say a word, even grudgingly, it would be enough for now and for the future. But the moment was without its promise. She could only imagine the word spoken. He got up and left the room just as she had suggested.

"ARE YOU SLEEPING YET, EL?" Morrie whispered, extending his hand so that it rested lightly on her breast. Her breathing was regular, slow, as if the air were being sucked in by some well-run machine. "Ellie?" She stirred, finally, and his hand, with anxious but tender deliberation, glided to unseen spots along her arm. She was awake now, but unmoving. She felt the nervous fingers urging her sleeping senses into awareness. She wanted to sleep. It seemed, after this difficult day, the only sensible desire. And even her sleep he had broken into. It wasn't nearly morning. The darkness in the room told her that.

"Ellie? You awake? Please wake up."

"What is it?" she mumbled without turning toward him.

"You're going to stay, aren't you?" The serious, childish tone now, underneath it the quiet plea, 'I want, I want.'

"Yes. I guess so." The postponed answer easier in the darkness.

"I'm glad." He rested his hand on her exposed arm. She felt it warm and protective, almost comforting. So much of what hurt her was so easily soothed by a gesture. She had never received much more, only gestures of devotion, from her father, her brother. These would have to be enough. There never would be more than that.

He moved her slowly towards himself, pulling so slowly there was no sound of it in the room. And she went, her senses alert, waiting to be caressed. Anger, control ebbed out of her body. Huddled inside his strong arms, she felt no fear. There *was* more than just the yelling.

He stroked her hair, nudged her head onto his chest. There was no resistance to offer up, no reason for it. It yielded, had to yield in his, in hers, in everyone's nighttime of need. Firmness was for daylight, for controlling what others had made each of them become, the start of that making reaching back, too far back for anyone to have changed a thing.

"Ellie! Ellie!" He moaned his lamentation of growing desire—she could call it affection—rocking himself, gradually faster, against her. "I'll try. I promise I'll try. Help me. You can help me."

She thought of nothing but his presence, his crying, moaning need. This moment held itself apart from the knowledge of what he was or what she was. Brief, yes, but limitlessly powerful, sustaining. We are most nearly ourselves now, she thought, at this instant. She pushed harder against his chest, and his arms squeezed tightly around her.

"There's no one else, Ellie. Never will be. I promise that."

His rocking became a man again; the familiar rhythm became a force, demanding her. She felt it too. Strong but gentle, kind, atoning. Only she could know that about him.

"You'll be glad," said Morrie, pushing deep inside her.

CHAPTER *Five*

SOMETHING IMPORTANT had softened Mollie. Each member of the Perlin family, separately or talking together when Mollie wasn't present, could tell that. When she left for work in the morning, she managed to keep peace with Clara and Toby. She didn't borrow their dresses, nor did she suggest it. As for Ellie, although Mr. Perlin made certain his oldest daughter would have the respect due her, now Mollie didn't have to strain to be dutiful, nor did her father have to remind her. Some mornings she could even find time to hug Ellie when she entered the kitchen, although late for breakfast. Mrs. Perlin realized what had happened. She had not been told about a young man, but she knew there had to be one.

However, it was at least three months from the time that Mrs. Perlin first spoke to her husband, warning him about the change in their daughter, three months during which time Mollie was trying to 'make sure' about Morrie before she finally decided that it would be best to bring him home and have him meet the family. She wanted to marry him, had wanted to from the moment she met him at the milk plant, but she knew she faced a major obstacle: Mr. Perlin. The prospects of an early marriage for Ellie were not promising, and Mollie had, often enough to respect the iron of his intention, heard her father say, "The oldest daughter will marry first. That's final." Even Ellie tried to argue him away from his decision, but Mr. Perlin remained adamant. "Maybe this is a new world," and his finger would point to the sky as he paused, "nevertheless, I'm from the old world and an old man. My laws, my people's laws are just. On this there can be no disagreement. Sha!" And he would bang the table for silence the way he banged his prayer desk in the synagogue when there was talking around him. If Mr. Perlin liked Morrie, really got to know him, he might change his mind. That was Mollie's hope.

"Mama, I'm going to bring a friend of mine home for dinner tomorrow night," Mollie announced at the breakfast table one morning. Only the girls were present; Mr. Perlin had left for the shop.

"It's about time." Mrs. Perlin's sarcasm was never subtle. "Is he Jewish?"

"How do you know it's a he? I only said a friend."

"If it was a she, would you be so nervous? Would you be such a different girl? Would you spend so much time curling your hair?"

"All right, Ma. You're so smart. It's a he."

"Where did you meet him? What does he do?" Clara exploded into questions, unable to conceal the fact any longer that they had all felt as their mother felt. Ellie kissed Mollie, Clara's outburst releasing her from the need to wait for her mother's expected questions. Toby remained bored and quietly ate her cereal. The youngest child of any family of many children is always quiet until he can do the most damage with a few words.

"I'm not answering any questions until you meet him tomorrow night. So don't grunt, Clara."

"For me you'll answer questions." Mrs. Perlin stood next to Mollie's chair. "First, how long have you known him?" Mollie remained silent, sipped her coffee. "How long? I'm asking, and you'll answer, Miss America."

"All right, Ma. All right." Mollie pushed her cup away. "A number of months."

"Is he Jewish?"

"Of course he's Jewish. His name's Morris Howard. Okay? Can I go to work now?"

"No. Sit. Have more coffee." Mrs. Perlin moved the cup back toward Mollie. "It's good he's Jewish. You, I knew I could trust. Your brother, that's a different story. Where did you meet him?"

"Is he handsome, Mol?" Clara had to interrupt, her curiosity was making her pull her stringy blond hair into little nervous circles.

"Either go to work, Clara, or keep quiet." Mrs. Perlin pointed her finger ominously. "Where did you meet him?" she continued.

"At the plant. He's a driver."

"A driver? What do you mean a driver?"

"He delivers milk. He's what you would call a milkman." Mollie wanted it to sound more acceptable, but the fact was too plain to embellish. Her father would like it even less than her mother did.

"He can't be doing very well," Toby suggested, looking at Mollie for the first time.

"Thank you," Mollie shouted. "I knew I could count on your help."

"Why do you need my help? You planning to marry him?"

"Why don't you shut up, Toby?" Clara pushed her sister's chair.

"Stop it. Both of you." Mrs. Perlin's voice, even when raised, sounded calmly controlling.

"Yes. Let's just stop it," echoed Ellie.

"And now the big sister has to have her word," Toby said sharply.

"Enough children!" Mrs. Perlin's fierce demand ended the outburst. "You dasn't speak that way, Toby. If your father was here. . . ." She pointed her finger. "Mollie, go to work. You'll bring him home and we'll all see."

"That's what I wanted in the beginning." Mollie stood up, elaborately scanning the faces of her sisters and mother. "What a bunch."

"Enough I said." Mrs. Perlin began to clear the table. "Ellie, hurry or you'll be late too. The doctor will call for his assistant; where is she. And Clara, before you leave, I want you to get coffee at the store. I'll give you money. Papa will be up for breakfast and I don't have anymore."

"Oh, Ma. I'll be late too. Send Toby. She's got more time." Clara tried to help her mother with the dishes.

"Don't help me. Go. Toby's got to iron her dress. The iron's heating on the stove already." Toby got up and went to the bedroom she shared with all her sisters. "Go, Clara. While you're waiting, it's getting later." Clara took the extended money, reached for her coat hanging on the clothes pole near the door, and left, mumbling her annoyance, slamming the door.

On her way out Ellie kissed her mother and then stood next to Mollie. "I hope it works out. If papa doesn't want to change his mind, I'll do my best to help you."

"Thanks," mumbled Mollie, embarrassed by all that her sister was trying to convey.

"Ellie," Mrs. Perlin held her arm, "remember one thing. Papa decides what's right and what isn't. Both of you know that. So you shouldn't have any business between the two of you."

"Yes, Ma. I know. But sometimes papa gets . . . well, he gets so stubborn about things."

"What things may I ask?"

"You know. You don't have to make me say it." Ellie tried to leave the apartment once more. Mrs. Perlin would not let go of her arm.

"My darling daughter," and there was no longer any sarcasm in her voice, "in the old country your sister would not meet a boy without we should know about it." She put her hand to Ellie's cheek. "Don't worry. Go. You too, Mollie. Papa will see for himself."

After Ellie had left, Mollie followed her mother to the sink. "Ma, I do want to . . ."

"No more now, please." Mrs. Perlin did not turn around. She started the water running. "I must do the dishes."

YES, THE YOUNG MAN was nervous, but, clearly, he showed that he would not be overcome by nervousness. Ellie, seated opposite to him at the table, recognized that by the cold defiant sound of his voice as he responded to Mr. Perlin's questions. When he reached for a dish, when he looked at Mollie, when he stared down Toby, he did it with a total lack of self-consciousness. His ruddy but gaunt handsomeness, guarded by the straight slope—Ellie could think of it only as being un-Jewish—of his nose, seemed fiercely alert to the impression he made. Mollie, sitting next to Morrie, smiled proudly as she followed the exchange of answer for question.

"And where does your family live now, Morris?" Mr. Perlin sat at the head of the table, his black skull cap gleaming in the light from the lamp which, on Friday nights, was always placed next to him. That would be, along with the flickering candles now in the center of the table but later put on top of the ice-box, the only light permitted in the apartment until sundown on Saturday.

"They live up near Ellenville, in the Catskills. They have a small hotel. Not much." Morrie handed his soup plate to Mollie who passed it on to Mrs. Perlin, seated at the foot of the table. When, finally, Toby was silently nudged by Ellie into taking the rest of the soup plates, Mrs. Perlin got up to serve the next course.

"So who do you live with then?"

"With cousins in Bayonne, New Jersey, where we used to live. It's just across the river."

"We lived near there too for a while. You must have a lot of traveling every day to work."

"I suppose. But I don't mind. The plant's here in New York, but I like to travel. I expect to travel all over this country someday, maybe even around the world."

Mr. Perlin stroked his beard, cleared his throat, embarrassed by the energy of Morrie's words. Even Toby lifted her head to look at this young man who could so foolishly predict what he would do. To Ellie, who had never been west of New Jersey, the prospect was only exciting, possible, not boasting. "That's wonderful. I hope it comes true."

"Oh, he'll do it," said Mollie, "if anyone can."

"I'll do it, all right." He spoke directly to Ellie, ignoring Mollie's support. "I get vacation time, and after a few years of saving, I'll be able to. No doubt in my mind."

"You must have a very good job," said Mr. Perlin. His wife handed him a platter heaped with steaming stuffed cabbage, and she, looking briefly at Morrie, seemed to be saying, 'Eat, don't talk so big.'

Morrie would eat, but he was not responsive to her disbelief. "It's not the job so much. I'll have better ones soon. It's the union. We're getting stronger all the time. As soon as we can make some strong demands, we'll be on our way."

"I suppose that's very important these days," Mr. Perlin was apologizing for his wife. "I don't know what I should about these unions."

Since everyone had helped himself to the stuffed cabbage, Mrs. Perlin once more sat down.

"Not very many people do, so you don't have to feel bad. They will though." Morrie paused to wipe the cabbage juice from his mouth. "Very good stuff, Mrs. Perlin." She nodded her thanks. "The whole thing is if you get in good with the leaders, the organizers, you stand a good chance of really moving up. That's what I'm doing." He hesitated, looked around the table to make sure that each of them was listening, then said, exaggerating the natural bass richness of his voice, "I'm not going to be a milk deliverer forever, believe me. I've got a damn good chance of getting into personnel work. That's what I really want. I can judge people. They like me."

Mr. Perlin, finished with the cabbage, pushed the plate to the side, out of his way, toward Clara. "It's good, this personnel?"

"The best. So's this cabbage. Just like my mother's." He lifted his plate and Mollie eagerly gave him another helping.

"For a thin fellow you certainly can eat," Clara dared, blushed immediately, quickly looked to see if her parents were annoyed by her interruption.

But Morrie answered good-naturedly, "I just seem to burn it up." He set to work on the new offering of food.

"What part of Europe is your mother from?" asked Mrs. Perlin. It was her first question.

"From Minsk, Russia. I was born there too. I was three when they brought me over."

"We're from Budapest . . . *Galitzianers*." Mrs. Perlin waited for a negative response, but there was none, not even a joke about how snobbish *Galitzianers* were supposed to be. "I'm surprised the cabbage tastes like your mother's. *Litvaks* usually cook sour." Her tone was deprecating, serious. "I don't like that style."

"Well, it's all what you get used to, I guess." Morrie registered her bitterness, but he did not reflect any crack in his composure. "Myself, I'm liberal. I like good food. That's what counts."

Mrs. Perlin did not pursue the topic, but the polite smile on her face was, to Ellie, an indication that she was not satisfied with the answer nor with the young man. It must be his boldness; nothing seemed to soften it. Surely he knew why he had been brought to the house. He couldn't be so indifferent to that. And the way he ate, attacking the food, ferociously, as if that were the way to enjoy it. That would really bother her mother, Ellie decided, as she began stacking the cabbage dishes. No refinement. But why should he have? He seemed strong enough to make that unimportant. Mollie, who in the past had complained about the dirty fingernails of other 'friends,' didn't mind his brusqueness. Now she was in love, and the indulgence of faults was part of love. Ellie, suddenly anxious to get away from the table, was motioned to stillness by her mother's tacit demand.

"Are there any other children in your family?" asked Mr. Perlin.

"There were three others." Morrie stopped eating, and when he spoke again it was to Mrs. Perlin. "Last year my younger brother was drowned in the bay near Bayonne. And before that, when my sister developed T.B., my family decided to buy that little hotel in the country so that she could get fresh air. But she died anyway, right after they moved." He resumed eating sure that they would be affected by the facts; he himself was too occupied by the moment and the mood to be stirred. "That leaves one other sister and me."

"Your poor mother," mumbled Mrs. Perlin, raising her hand to her cheek, rocking her head back and forth.

"Yes, it sure was hard for her. My brother was so good. He was going to college at night. She wanted that, even wanted me to go, but I don't have time for college."

"Your mother is right." Mrs. Perlin spoke emphatically. "In these days it's important."

"I agree with you completely." Once more Morrie would snatch the advantage from this woman who was trying to beat him down. "That's why I didn't move away with them." His smile was complacent, unrelenting. "I had so much to do here, in the city. There was nothing in Ellenville. And you've got to be where the opportunities are. Right?" Mollie offered more food, but this time, suddenly becoming aware of the fact that the others had long since finished, he declined.

The table remained cluttered with dishes. No one attempted to clear them away. If Mrs. Perlin didn't move, the girls knew that they shouldn't. The difficult phase of Morrie's test was about to begin. A silence of staring, expectant faces settled on the small kitchen-dining room. There was no place else to go for serious talk. Mollie coughed, fidgeted, played with the knife that was on her plate. Mr. Perlin folded his hands across his stomach. Toby leaned her head on the palm of her hand, gazed blankly at the victim, tried to blink back sleep. Only Morrie smiled, and only Ellie watched him. Clara slumped in her chair, knowing, as they all knew, that there was no escape. There were just the two bedrooms and the kitchen. Actually, the girls' bedroom was supposed to be a living room, but necessity had forced another function. Before Harry ran off, the situation had been more desperate. He had had to sleep on a folding cot in the kitchen. Ellie suddenly cleared her throat; all heads snapped up. Morrie began laughing then stopped when no one else joined him. The setting had become too solemn for laughter, and he recognized his responsibility for it. The faces peered at him; his natural ebullience froze into a display mask. Unseen, his hand moved to pat Mollie's which rested on her lap at the edge of the white tablecloth. She dug her nails into the palm of his hand, signalling her own helplessness.

When the kettle began to hiss, Mrs. Perlin stood up and announced, "We'll have tea and cake as soon as I clear the table." Clara tried, half raising herself, to show how much she wanted to help. The mother, imperiously, waved her down. "Everyone will please to remain seated." She was enjoying the tension. She moved around the table in silence, accepting dishes as if they were good wishes.

"Does anyone mind if I smoke a cigarette?" Morrie turned to Mr. Perlin.

"Please do." He stopped stroking his beard.

"It's *Shabbath*." Mrs. Perlin's words sounded a rebuke.

"If he wants to smoke, he'll smoke." Mr. Perlin disregarded his wife's sputtering anger, watched Morrie light his cigarette, then drop the used match on a dirty plate. Mollie frantically retrieved it before her mother could say a word. She gave him a saucer to use as an ashtray.

When the tea and cake were served, Mr. Perlin began anew. "You have been seeing a lot of our Mollie?"

"I guess you might say that." Morrie smiled at Mollie's blushing face.

"And I suppose, Mollie, that you didn't see fit to tell me about this before now?" The sternness of Mr. Perlin's words surprised her. She hadn't expected that to be part of the discussion; that should have been left for a time when Morrie wasn't present. "What did you want me to tell you, Papa?" She asked weakly.

"You dasn't answer that way, Mollie. You know better. I must tell you, Morris, that I am a man very much from the old school." Morrie, annoyed for the first time that evening, stared back challengingly. "Morris, Mollie is not my oldest daughter." Everyone, as though moved by a single reflex, shifted nervously on their chairs. Clara gasped. Ellie lowered her head. "Please papa," was all she could force out.

"No pleases, Ellie." Mr. Perlin's beard shook as he ground his teeth in anger. "This is a family. Morris must know that. I am a father and there are rules and laws, laws that I did not make, that my father gave to me. Not by words, mind you, but by actions. I wear this *yarmulka*," he moved his hand slowly to the top of his black skull cap, "why? Because my father wore it and his father before him and because I believe it is right I should wear it." Excited now, he paused, waited, sought everyone's attention. "I didn't say to Morrie that he must wear one at our table. That's his business. And smoking is his business. But when it comes to what is going to happen to my children, then it is my business." Mrs. Perlin, sitting rigidly straight at the other end of the table, nodded proudly.

Morrie's composure throughout Mr. Perlin's speech seemed to gather further stores of confidence. He smiled broadly, placed both his arms on the table, ready for anything that might come.

Mollie gloomily regarded her father. Her mouth twisted into speech. "The rules didn't work for Harry, Papa. Why didn't they work then?"

As if he had been hit, Mr. Perlin pushed back, away from the table, away from the words.

"That's a lousy thing to dare to say." It was Toby who spoke, ready to argue.

"Shut up," Mollie screamed. "Stay out of it."

"Sha! Both of you," demanded Mr. Perlin. "Maybe you know already, Morris, but my son married a gentile girl. He ran off and married her." His breath was labored, prayer-like, as if by speaking this way, openly, of a sin, he was making atonement. "I couldn't stop him because I didn't know."

"Don't you think that's a little different situation? After all, Mollie and I are only seeing each other, and I am Jewish, and I am sitting at your table. I'm not the kind who runs away from anything."

"I don't mean to insult you. I'm only saying beforehand." He sighed, resigned to embarrassment, understanding that was part of his faith. "I want you both should know that my first daughter will marry first. That's all I want."

"You must be kidding." Morrie laughed, but the others and Mr. Perlin solemnly expressed reproach. He stopped.

"I am not, what you call it, kidding."

"But Mr. Perlin, this is America. Not the old country. People do differently here."

"That I know all right. I also know the words when in Rome to do what the Romans do. So see what happened to them." He moved his head back and forth. "No. Some things are good and some things are bad. You have to know one from the other. I'm glad to be in America. Very glad. I'm already a citizen here, but I'm also a Jew. I'm not to forget that too." He leaned forward, and his gaze, which took in Morrie's challenging, animated face, was, at the same time, seeing the image of a memory deep within himself, as if this moment existed only in the reflecting mirror of the past. "My son, Harry, he too said what you say. He too wants to be American first and Jewish when he has time. So let it be for him and for you. But for me the past is too important. I must try to keep inside me what makes it important. Even now, in the Holy Land, my people go through too much suffering to forget them."

A silence ensued in which only Mollie's soft crying could be heard. Then Morrie slammed his hand on the table, and Ellie, who had sat immobile throughout her father's speech, jumped. Eyes turned toward her, expectantly. She cleared her throat. She wanted to speak, but the words she picked out of her mind seemed futile. Her sigh encouraged Mr. Perlin to continue. "And so, Morris, I have to think of my Ellen. It was that way in my father's house and in my grandfather's house. It will not change in mine. That much I can protect from changing. What already has happened I can't control." He hid his eyes momentarily. "You shouldn't think I don't like you. You have ambition. You'll be successful. But if you had ideas to marry Mollie right away, you'll have to forget them." With these words Mollie jumped away from the table, sobbing, ran to the bedroom, slammed the door. Clara got up to follow her. "You don't understand, Papa. I thought you understood about love, or didn't they have that in the old country?"

"Go!" shouted Mrs. Perlin. "Go to her!"

"Mr. Perlin," said Morrie without emotion. "I didn't say for sure that I was going to marry Mollie. Everyone took that for granted.

We're only seeing each other."

"And what else do you see someone for if not to marry them?" Mrs. Perlin's angry question did not unsettle Morrie's resolve.

"Look Mrs. Perlin, I came here because I was asked to dinner. I'm willing to be honest, not to do things behind your back. That's what you want. And all I want is to go on seeing Mollie. What happens, happens. Maybe in the meantime Ellie will find herself a husband. Who knows." He smiled sympathetically at Ellie, and she, instinctively defensive, responded, like an echo, but much less hopefully, "Who knows. Maybe I will."

"All right. It's enough," said Mr. Perlin simply, shrugging his shoulders. "Toby, go bring your sisters back to the table."

In the months that followed that dinner, Morrie did come to the apartment often, sometimes even when he knew that Mollie would not be there. It did not seem to make any difference to him. He spent most of his time engaged in conversation with Mr. Perlin who, in spite of his wife's warnings, listened attentively to this excitable young man express his opinions. And Morrie had opinions on all matters. "I only went to school until the 8th grade. But I read. All the time. Newspapers, books, the *Saturday Evening Post*. I'll teach myself whatever I need to know." Mr. Perlin would nod affirmatively to all that Morrie claimed except when they touched on family matters. Then the tired eyes of the old man would squint his mind into blankness, and he would interrupt, muttering through his beard, "No fights. Not tonight. No family. No religion. Other things, yes."

"All right," Morrie pointed his finger, "but if you take that attitude you'll only get what you deserve. We've had one war. People don't want another one and . . ."

"You fought in Europe? Morris?"

"No. I got in at the very end, but I know what it was like. People are just not going to take crap forever. You saw what went on in Russia . . ."

With Mrs. Perlin's feelings there was no change. At night, in bed, she could express herself freely, and her husband would have to listen. "And you're so sure because he has ambition he has a heart? That I don't see. Mollie worries about the time they're losing, but not him. He doesn't care even. I can tell."

"He's got other things on his mind, Minnie. A young man alone has a hard time."

"So? Does he have to be alone? He could be with his mother and father. But have it your way if you want. I only want our Mollie to be happy."

"And don't I?" Mr. Perlin would say fiercely, but with a calm that respected the darkness. "Don't I?" He was angrier with his own stubborn temperament than with his wife's querulousness. "Some things must be as they are. It's God's will. I do only what He tells me is right."

"Who says otherwise. Of course it's right."

"It's more than Mollie," he went on speaking as if he had not heard his wife. "It's my life. My believing. And for Ellie and the others." He hesitated, arguing with himself, "What if she doesn't find a husband? What then?"

"What then? What nothing, Avram." She held his hand. "She'll get married. She's got a good job in the doctor's office. Every day she meets more people. Maybe even the doctor himself." For Mrs. Perlin that was security. That would be a chance for Ellie to regain what the family had had once, to be a lady with pride, to be a Jew in a world which cared little for you when you had very little to give to it.

The two of them would lull themselves into a sleep of fear, a fear that they would lose whatever was left of their future peace. Harry they had lost. Mollie they were determined to save. And Ellie . . . "Sleep, Avram. Sleep and don't worry. God will take care."

But God, the God she had inherited from her father's belief, without reservation or question, did not immediately solve Ellie's dilemma. She had to think of herself as a curiosity, a ridiculous obstacle, not quite five feet tall, yet able to prevent events from taking place. Such power only embarrassed her. As she grew up, her father had taught her how to act in his place, how to force compliance from her brother and sisters. But she had never deceived herself. Her authority was on loan. She seldom sought more. Now her father had placed her, alone, on a stage whose boundaries were unfamiliar. Some nights, lying in the darkness of the bedroom, surrounded by her sleeping sisters, she would toss and turn her mind into a spiral of confused thoughts about marriage, about having to leave home, thoughts that threatened to twist past the exploding inside light of her closed eyelids. She was in the way and Mollie would hate her for it.

But, apparently, Mollie did not hate her. On Saturday afternoons, when they went out for long walks uptown, along Fifth Avenue, where the air seemed freer and the fabled richness of the people they passed on the street made all thoughts possible, Ellie would talk about what was happening inside herself. And for a few hours the two of them would laugh together, exchanging dreams about the future, of travel and clothes and love. They forgot about their suffocating apartment and their jobs. They stood before the solid, ornate private homes, meekly looking up, as if just to stop was trespassing, yet daring to tell the stone what they hoped for.

"Just wait, Ellie. Wait 'til you feel it. When you're sure you're in love, a house like that won't mean anything."

"I wouldn't mind feeling that way already, whatever it is you feel."

"I can't describe it, really. Only what it does to me. Like even if it's dark outside, you still see the sun." Mollie hugged Ellie and then held her at arm's length. "It's like you're so rich."

"And the other person probably feels the same way?"

"You just have to hope so, otherwise . . ." Mollie, instead of completing the thought, hugged Ellie again, this time holding on to her.

"Otherwise," Ellie continued, as if to herself, "you're not very rich at all, and it *is* dark."

"I guess so." Mollie pushed Ellie into motion. "Let's walk."

"I'll never get married, Mollie. I just know it."

"Don't be silly. Of course you will and we'll wait. Morrie doesn't mind."

Continuing their walk, they would before long enter the busy streets of downtown, and finally, the Saturday quiet of the Lower East Side. The pushcarts were missing; the unashamed banners of bedclothes did not dangle from fire escapes. The talking ceased. They were home.

Sometimes Morrie joined them on these walks. He was always willing to include Ellie, wherever they went. Often he invited her to go to the movies with them. At first she accepted these invitations only after Morrie convinced her she would not 'be in the way.'

And when the three of them walked, the girls on either side of him, listening avidly to his 'plans,' it was impossible to determine which of these girls would be his wife.

"When I get into personnel, then I'll really be a gentleman. Can you imagine me, a gentleman?"

"You're almost a gentleman now," Mollie teased. "At least you know how to please ladies. That's being a gentleman."

"That's the easiest part of it. It's the men, the businessmen you have to work hard to impress. They're tough to figure. Women, you know, are crafty, but they're not so smart that you can't figure out their next move. Right Ellie?"

She assumed that his speaking to her this way, including her, was part of a generous nature, and instead of guilt, she felt elation. He, too, understood that she wanted, more than anything else, to help them be together. "It sounds very complicated, but being a woman I never thought of it quite that way." She tried to sound sophisticated, but curious. "Don't you have to treat all people as if they are a combination of good and bad. People are people, they say."

"That's what they say." Morrie laughed loudly. "You're the most gullible baby in the world. Don't you know that some people are always going to be a lot more than others are? That's a law of democracy, to be born equal but never to die that way."

"That's an interesting thought. Where did you get it from?" Ellie's desire was only to have him go on talking.

"From my own head. I read and I think and I end up with ideas. That's important to do." Suddenly, he stopped walking. "For example, take Mollie here." He nudged her arm. "She never reads anything, as far as I can tell, so she never has anything to think about except whether Clara's wearing one of her dresses. Isn't that right, Mollie?"

Mollie laughed, but when she looked up at his face, saw his lips pursed, she realized that he wanted a serious answer. And then, just as suddenly as his mood had changed, Mollie became annoyed with Ellie's presence, that she too waited for an answer. She could admit her failures to Morrie and make him forget them. That was permissible. She loved him. But Ellie was a different matter.

"You never do any thinking, do you Mollie?" He was cruelly persistent. "What goes on inside your head? Not once have you told me."

"What's gotten into you all of a sudden? What're you making such a big issue of this for?"

Ellie let go of Morrie's arm and moved a few steps away. She was alarmed by the shift of his darting gaiety, his ebullience into this iron glare.

Mollie refused to answer his question. She took his hand from her arm and walked on, alone. Morrie grabbed for Ellie, forcing her forward, as if he had a right to do so. They caught up with Mollie and walked the rest of the way home in silence.

Later, when she reviewed all of the events leading up to her own engagement, she realized that the unanswered question had ended whatever harmony existed in the crowded apartment. Undeniably, Morrie paid more attention to Ellie. Clara and Toby both said so. Mrs. Perlin tried to quiet them, "for Mollie's sake," but Mollie insisted on talking about it, insisted on finding fault with him. "He's so smart," she would say, "it's a shame he can't become president. He doesn't know what *he's* doing either." Ellie, in spite of the fact that she knew it would have to anger Mollie, in spite of the fact that whatever she said now would imply the truth of her sisters' claim, felt obliged to defend Morrie, to honor his patience while waiting for a wedding. It seemed only fair. He had been generous to her, but surely not for the reasons her sisters offered.

"What do you know about him? He's on his best behavior when he's with someone else. But when he's alone with me now he's horrible. I'm not blaming you, Ellie. I'm just telling the truth. I still love him, but I don't understand him anymore."

Morrie was at the house almost every evening now, and Mr. Perlin more warmly welcomed his presence. His wife had hidden the disturbance from him, and the chance to talk with another man had become a great source of joy, especially when Morrie talked of the future. "I like this about becoming modernized, but, unfortunately, I won't be around long enough to know whether the new lasts as long as the old. All I know is . . ."

"All you know is that the old was good enough for all the old people you ever knew, so why shouldn't it be good enough for me." There was no malice in Morrie's voice, only enjoyment, the enjoyment of forming words into ideas. "How do you know that our famous ancestors aren't responsible for the fact that the Jews still have no place to call their own?"

"Who knows the answer to that? No one. Only we see that wherever Jews live, they endure. That's not enough?"

"No! It's not enough." Morrie rocked his chair back and forth. "People have a right to more than just getting by. Look at all of you here, crowded into these rooms . . ." he waited, nodded toward Mrs. Perlin bent over the sink, finishing the dishes, and at Ellie who sat next to her father. No one else was at home. "How can your daughters ever find a husband if they don't have anywhere to go with their boyfriends, a place to sit alone and talk. We all need more room." He let his chair come to rest again.

"You do all right here." Ellie grinned.

"Sure, but if we were alone, I'd have a lot more to say."

Mrs. Perlin instantly turned from the sink, looked toward her husband. Ellie, startled by the remark, remained grinning, until the meaning of it gradually dissolved her eagerness into an expression of nervous discovery.

"What is this you're saying?" Mr. Perlin cautiously broke the silence.

Now that Morrie had spoken those words, he was unsure of exactly how he should proceed. "All I'm trying to say is . . . Well, I only wanted to say what everyone else knows and that is that. . . . For Christ's sake, is it wrong for me to like Ellie?"

"Wrong?" echoed Mr. Perlin.

"Yes, wrong? She's all right, isn't she?" He ignored her presence.

Mr. Perlin watched Ellie pleating and unpleating the tablecloth. "She's excellent, only I am naturally surprised . . ."

"I'm glad Mollie isn't here right now," Morrie lowered his voice, "because, honestly, I never said for sure that I was going to marry her, did I?"

"Morris," it was Mrs. Perlin who interrupted, "everyone in this house expected it, Mollie herself most of all."

"It's always been her idea, Mrs. Perlin. I never said for sure."

"Well, why else did you keep coming here for if you had no intentions?" Mr. Perlin reached for his beard, a reflex of defense against whatever Morrie answered.

"Finally, because of Ellie."

Ellie gazed at her parents, bewildered, her eyes like hands reaching out for help.

Mrs. Perlin moved from the sink, wiped her hands carefully on her apron and sat down. "*Nu?*" She prompted her husband. "So what now?"

Mr. Perlin held up his hand, letting her know that she was not to interfere. "Morris, you're willing to tell Mollie you will not marry her?"

"I'm not interested in what he's willing." Mrs. Perlin would not be stopped by gestures. She leaned close to Morrie. "This house is not a stable for you to choose from. My daughters are good girls. You're going to hurt one and then maybe hurt another one?" Her rising inflection ended in a sputtering, coughing disbelief. "What kind of person are you?"

"Take it easy, Mrs. Perlin." Her anger was something familiar to Morrie, the dare which, compulsively, he enjoyed accepting. "I'm not going to hurt anyone intentionally. Just remember that Mollie asked me to come here. How did I know this would happen?" He faced Mr. Perlin. "You asked us to wait. Your laws, remember? Well, I'm glad you did." For the first time, he confronted her. "Maybe the best thing is to ask Ellie how she feels."

"I . . . I . . ." she stammered, but Mr. Perlin did not let her even attempt speech.

"Go now, Morris, before Mollie comes home. Please."

Morrie got up slowly, relieved but unsatisfied by the uncertain outcome. He wanted swift finality, needed definition, expected to control. As he reached for the knob of the door, it was opened by Mollie, carrying packages and smiling.

"Are you leaving already?" In a glance she took in the tense stillness of the room. She watched Morrie's hesitation at the door. "What's the matter?" She put her packages on the table, pushed back her falling hair.

"I've got to go," Morrie raised his voice defiantly. "But you'll see me again. I promise." He looked sympathetically toward Ellie and left the apartment.

"What's the matter?" Mollie's voice deepened with the dry, hollow tones of panic.

No one spoke.

"Doesn't anyone hear me? What's the matter?" She leaned over the table, demanding an answer.

"Nothing." But Mrs. Perlin conveyed the sense of 'everything.'

"What did Morrie say?" She was yelling now. "Would someone

please, please answer me."

"How could he," muttered Ellie, still trapped in a trance of bewilderment.

"How could he what?"

"He's nothing. *Dreck.*" Mrs. Perlin moaned, rocked her disbelief.

"Please. Stop this." Mr. Perlin lowered his beard against his chest. "He only said what he felt. What's to blame him for? Better we should be thankful he did say it."

"Tell me already, Papa. What?" Mollie moved to the front of the stove alongside her father.

"Sit down, darling."

"I don't want to sit down. Just tell me."

He spoke quietly then, sure that no matter how he said it there would be no helping her. "He is not going to marry you."

Her mouth fell open. One hand leaned on the hot coal stove behind her. For an instant it was as if she felt nothing, then quickly she jerked her fingers to her mouth. She waved them in the air. "What do you mean he's not going to . . . When did he say that?"

"Just now, before he left." His lowered head made the words indistinct, muted.

"I don't believe you," she screamed. "I don't. He wouldn't say that. He wants to marry me. I know it." She stopped, suddenly quiet, a questioning, doubting expression on her face. And then, in what seemed like a dialogue with herself, her voice growing once more in volume, she spoke, "No! I don't know it . . . He never said he would . . . I only thought so . . . I said it . . . I don't understand." She put her hands to her face, pulled at the skin. "I love him."

Mrs. Perlin went to her, rubbed and patted her back. "Don't cry, darling. He's not worth it. I knew it. All along I was sure. And Ellie, hear me, you're not to see him. Make certain of that."

Ellie did not respond, but Mollie did, her sobs ceasing. "What are you saying, Mama? What has Ellie got to do with it?"

"Thank you," said Mr. Perlin bitterly. "You've helped me."

"What is this?" Mollie pushed her mother's arms down, backed away. "Ellie, what are they talking about? Tell me?"

And although Ellie expected the question, or one like it, she could find no answer. What did she have to do with it? She liked

Morrie; that was all; nothing more, she thought, and wondered if it were not the continuation of some joke that Morrie had begun when he first became known to the family. And now the punch line had been delivered. Or did all this happen just because she had never thought of it or encouraged it? Perhaps that *was* it. Events would occur in spite of stillness, sometimes because of it. And life, like a morbidly smiling presence, manipulated our actions even when we refused to act. Walking away or toward the center of someone else's life was no protection against involvement or hurt. It was impossible to know that sometimes just walking away represented the proper meshing, the secret mechanics of mutual need. Nothing she did now could prevent the movement forward, the step that placed her outside this room, outside these lives. "Mollie," she began, hesitated, not knowing how to explain, "I swear I don't understand."

"You can try. It's very simple."

"Leave her alone," pleaded Mr. Perlin. "It's not her fault."

"No! Talk now, Ellie." Mrs. Perlin wanted an end to this presence in her house. "Get it over with now and it'll be easier for always."

"But I can't say everything just like that." With trembling fingers Ellie drew on the air a touch, a dot of time. She stood up, wanting to approach Mollie. But she remained behind her chair, gripping the back of it. "I was just as surprised as everyone else. He's your boyfriend. I only thought if I was nice to him he wouldn't mind having to wait so long. That part is my fault," as if realizing it suddenly, "and yours, Papa. More yours." Ellie gazed at her father who, by a nod of his head, acknowledged guilt. "But Mollie, I can't say . . . I can't say even right now that I hate him for what happened."

"What you really mean is you love him." Mollie's tears made her words sound spongy and sad like noise under water. "And he really loves you." Mollie walked to the bedroom door. "Don't ever speak to me again, Ellie. Never. You spoiled my only chance." The door opened and closed softly. Ellie's mind and then her own tears did not want her gone. "Mollie, please. I . . ."

"*Kinder, kinder,*" muttered Mrs. Perlin, her head shaking to a rhythm of familiar despair.

ALTHOUGH MRS. PERLIN ATTEMPTED to block Morrie's return to the apartment Mr. Perlin decided, a decision which reluctantly but automatically subdued his wife, that the shift in affection was, after all, not the most inhuman of crimes. Secretly, he could understand why Morrie would choose Ellie. Inside her was an unobtrusive stillness that must have been as attractive to Morrie's energy and ambition as Mollie's unconcealed desire had been at first. Ellie, small and attentive, seemed so vulnerable that a man would want to protect her from harm. Mr. Perlin, instead of discouraging the relationship, looked forward to the prospect of a good marriage. He even thought of it as his particular function to hasten the event.

Ellie, as she went to work and came home and lived among the people whom she loved long past the time she knew why she did, out of habit, wanted Mollie to need her once more as a sister needs. Inside herself she had not completely accepted the fact that a man wanted her. Mollie, because for all of Ellie's life it had been that way, longer than the fact of Morrie's asking, was more important to her. But Mollie, conscious of her final words to Ellie, would not speak. Toby and Clara could not joke her into it; Mr. Perlin could not force her, nor could the longing sighs of her mother do it. When Morrie was present in the apartment, accompanied by sounds of grunted hate, Mollie would disappear into the bedroom.

Morrie, not laughing at these retreats but youthfully rational, as practical about emotions, it seemed to Mr. Perlin, as he was about his future, would say, "I'm sorry for her, but I know what I want. I can't let her stop me."

It was cruel of him to speak that way, Ellie admitted to herself. But, after all, he was allowed to be present, and she, by her acceptance of that presence, approved of what was going to happen because of it. Yes, Mollie's loss and withdrawal saddened Ellie, but, at the same time, she felt the joy, unhoped for and so denied in the thinking she understood, of being wanted. Guilt was there, but so was Morrie. She was being moved toward him, offered to him by her father who made it all seem quite reasonable.

Morrie and Ellie were engaged to be married. Ellie was irrevocably spilled out of the container of familiar affection onto a broad, limitless expanse of time where now Morrie, self-assured and smiling, was expected to care for her.

A few weeks before the wedding Harry, alone and unexpected, arrived for dinner. There was more than the usual amount of tension in the apartment that night. Ellie, surrounded by an indifference that threatened to dissolve her thimbleful of courage and pleasure, had attended to, without the offer of help from her sisters, the printing of invitations, mailing them, fitting her gown—her mother had grudgingly acquiesced to give hers—hiring a hall with money her father had secured in a manner he would not discuss, all the details which tend to cage the most intimate participants of a wedding into a vise of questioning: Why do it at all? Ellie said it to herself over and over again. Nobody cared; nobody but her father encouraged her.

They all sat around the kitchen table after dinner, talking very little, watching Ellie check the names of guests whose R.S.V.P.'s had been received. Morrie would not be there this evening. He was with his own family in New Jersey. They had come down from the hotel in order to meet Ellie.

Mollie, coldly aloof, aimlessly rubbed her hand across the patch of tablecloth before her. Mr. Perlin and Clara were still drinking their tea. They lingered over it, Mr. Perlin sipping loudly as if he wanted to allay conversation.

Occasionally, Toby spoke to Harry, asking him questions about night school or if he had seen any of the new musicals uptown. His answers were brief, disinterested.

"You mean you haven't been to any? Not at all? Doesn't Martha mind that?" Toby shrieked with delight.

As if brushing all that she had been saying aside, Harry's voice was suddenly raised in irritation. "Why don't you help her, Toby?"

"She can do it herself. She does everything herself."

"That's because you're all so thoughtful."

Ellie looked up at Harry, and with her eyes said, 'No, it isn't necessary for you to do this.'

"Why don't you help her, Harry," Clara suggested, giggling.

"If she wants me to, I will."

"No one has to help her," said Mr. Perlin. He handed his empty tea glass to his wife. "She'll do it nicely herself. The sisters have no time. You can see how busy they are."

"I'm glad to see the group hasn't changed any." Harry grinned wryly. "Always a million laughs in this house."

"The big time kidder," said Mollie sharply, rousing herself for an attack. "You don't have to live with us. Aren't you lucky. By the way, how is your darling wife?"

"Yes, how is your darling wife?" Clara mimicked.

Harry remained unperturbed by sarcasm. It was the natural element of his growing up. "She's wonderful. Should I tell her how concerned you both are about her health?"

"Don't be so smart." Mollie didn't want to continue the game.

"You don't like intelligence?" Harry leaned closer to her, tauntingly.

"Oh why don't you just shut up!" Clara turned her tea glass upside down, banging it loudly in the saucer.

"I won't shut up, as you suggest, but I'll be glad to change the subject. How about the new prospect for happiness in the Perlin family. This wedding?" Once more Ellie urged him to be quiet. Mrs. Perlin folded her arms across her chest, waiting. "I can tell you're all so happy to see your oldest sister on the doorstep of a new life and that you're more accepting of her choice than of mine."

"Everyone likes Martha, Harry. You dasn't talk that way." But Mrs. Perlin's words carried little conviction.

"Thank you, Mama, but it doesn't bother me one way or the other. I judge by actions, not words, so I can tell you all think Morris Howard's perfect for Ellie. Right? Don't you? You especially, Mollie?"

Mollie would not answer. As she started up, Harry's words forced her down again. "How about it, Mollie? Don't you approve? If he was good enough for you, isn't he good enough for Ellie?"

"Please, Harry . . . stop," Mr. Perlin begged. "Let her alone."

"No, Papa. I know what I'm doing. I need to do it." The sarcasm was absent from his voice now. "I never saw people so unwilling to face facts. Why do you think I got out of here so fast? What's wrong with all of you? You just sit in this cramped kitchen, night after night, making it seem even smaller by being nasty to one another. I know I'm not much better, but it's the only way I can ever get an idea across." He paused, and realizing that everyone, including Mollie, was attentive, he continued. "I don't want to hurt you, Mollie, and I don't want to embarrass Ellie, but for once let's look at the truth as it exists. Can't we talk together without yelling? Is it too late to change us a little bit? Outside this apartment everybody's talking about progress, but in here . . ." Abruptly he lapsed into silence, as if he were waiting for someone to prove that his hope was not a futile one. The silence was filled with the sound of Mrs. Perlin's tears. Once more Mollie regarded the tablecloth, the expression of weariness replacing the pinched bitterness her face had worn for so many weeks. But the pattern of reticence which it had taken accumulated lifetimes to construct could not be destroyed in a moment. The great wall that separated Harry's desire for confession from their reflexive sense of personal privacy had seldom, if ever, been scaled. It wouldn't crumble now without a battle. "Damn it, the guy chose Ellie, and she, I suppose, although she hardly shows it, is glad."

"How could she be as glad as she's entitled," Mr. Perlin erupted into words. "Like you said, no one cares. Only you. Thank God at least for that." He surveyed the ceiling, mumbling a Hebrew prayer.

"That's unfair, Papa." Clara was subdued, ready to reason with the facts. "After all, Morrie was Mollie's intended. You know that's the truth."

"Whose truth was that? Mollie's?" Harry was quick but no longer curt.

"He's right," Mollie said softly as if no greater volume could be managed.

"And why blame Ellie for what happened?" Harry felt more confident now that Mollie had understood. "Did she try to steal him away?" His insistence forced them to nod in agreement. "You know she wouldn't do that kind of thing. And frankly, it's not even Morrie's fault. I met him. I talked to him about everything. When you get married, you want it to be right, don't you?"

"Harry is right." Mollie looked at them, recovering a sense of herself, not listening to her brother's words any longer but to the thoughts they had forced her to think. "It's my fault. I'm stupid, dumb . . . But also I'm human. Don't forget that. What would I be if I accepted everything that happened. I have a right to some pride." Mollie's hands covered her eyes, pressed hard into them as if each finger was saying no, no, don't cry. Ellie stood alongside her chair, wanting to reach toward Mollie, but afraid of being pushed away.

"It's all so simple. Everything's simple," said Harry, bitterly compassionate. "Life's so simple and so beyond us all because somehow, who knows why, we don't really care about what happens to each other . . . I know Clara. Don't say it. You neither Toby. I include myself. It's my weakness too, although once in a while I try."

"We're to blame?" Mrs. Perlin questioned, her gaze blank,

inward.

"No, Mama. Not you or Papa. Not anyone." When he saw Ellie's hand resting on Mollie's shoulder, when he saw Mollie's hand reach up to touch it, he stood up, satisfied that this much had been accomplished. He kissed his mother, squeezed his father's shoulder and left the apartment.

In that moment of giving up, not so much to her brother's logic as to her stronger urge—stronger because it was buried, hidden so often—to share excitement and affection, an urge which had been the largest part of her love for Morrie, Mollie also relinquished the right to act in whatever way her nature prescribed. It was her function, and she was bitterly aware of it, that she would have to help maintain the atmosphere of precarious calm which, after Harry's words, had descended on the family. Her younger sisters, she knew, waited for an outbreak of new anger. None came. Ellie, moodily, never expansively, caught up in the final details of the wedding preparations, labored successfully to win back part of her sister's support. Mollie did not refuse the role of Maid of Honor, offered pessimistically, nor did she refuse to speak to Morrie. She accepted what was inevitable, but this moment of giving up was something she had never known before, and she would have to wait for the wedding itself to understand how it would settle into the painful churning that wouldn't let her sleep at night.

Ellie's excitement spilled into words. Mollie listened to them. Toby and Clara, watching as if from a periphery of hushed surprise, felt the pull of Mollie's effort and they too gave a grudging assistance. Mr. Perlin was pleased, soothed by what Harry had accomplished, and Mrs. Perlin, now stoically and irrevocably opposed to the marriage, was nevertheless heartened by Mollie's attitude and began to seem interested in Ellie's chances for contentment. Mollie, if self-sacrifice was required, was determined to sacrifice until the pleasure of the pain was unbearable.

When Morrie came to the apartment, she experienced the most perfect moments of her perverse enjoyment. She chatted with him about their mutual acquaintances at the milk plant. She asked about honeymoon plans. She even went so far with the dissimulation that one evening, briefly alone with him, she spoke of their times together, of, at least, her enjoyment of them and so she wouldn't harbor any hard feelings. As long as he made her sister happy, that was all that mattered now. His surprise and embarrassment nourished her satisfaction. That, she thought, would be her revenge. She would always be present to make Morrie remember. And Ellie, who was soft, would find it difficult to stand up against that memory.

Only at the moment that she stood next to Ellie, under the canopy, while the rabbi blessed the couple, did she cry tears of rage. And only when it was over, when the glass was broken, when Ellie was being kissed and fondled by the guests and she watched them moving off to the dining hall did she understand that her rage would probably stretch on unbroken for as long as she lived, silently crippling her desire for anything else.

The band played. Couples marched out onto the dance floor. Mollie took her seat at the 'family' table. Morrie, tall but surprisingly graceful moved before her holding Ellie against his chest with threatening possessiveness.

Throughout the meal Mollie was aware of only one intrusion into her private brooding and that was the silent scrutiny of her by Morrie's mother. Only Mrs. Howard observed what Mollie could not altogether hide. At one point, when everyone else was either dancing or talking between courses, Mrs. Howard reached over and held Mollie's hand. "Don't be sorry," she whispered. "He's my son, but I tell you you're better off without him. Believe me. I only worry about your sister."

For Mollie, the evening became an endless waiting. The guests reluctantly took their leave of the brightness and noise. Finally, when most of them had gone and Mollie stood in the drafty entrance hall, Ellie came to her. They embraced and Ellie's wistful, grateful thank you stirred the fixed smile from her face. She said nothing. Harry, standing nearby, helping Martha with her coat, called out, "Mollie, *Myetz ashem bei dir*."

Looking at him, anger flared instantly then died. Yes, the same for me. Never, she thought. Never.

Ellie and Morrie left Kutsher's shortly after to begin their honeymoon in Atlantic City. Morrie waved; he didn't stop to speak to her. The last guests left, and then she, with her mother, father, and sisters walked down the steps away from the battered hall. At home would be another empty bed.

CHAPTER *Six*

Ellie did carry out her plans to have the entire family, including the 'newlyweds,' to their apartment for a Friday night dinner. This first, full scale attempt, too long postponed, at becoming a capable housewife had grown out of that moment of choice—sitting in their living room the night before the event, playing with rather than reading the newspaper while Morrie dozed across the room, she traced it back to that moment—when, standing before her father, she accepted the need to 'stay' with Morrie. But, you just can't say, all right, I'm staying. She had wanted to do that. The last week had shown her how impossible that plan was. She kept looking around the apartment for things to do, and cleaning the same floor, dusting the same woodwork wasn't enough. There had to be something about which she could say, "Look! I've done this. I'm better at this than anyone else." And if he yelled at her again—which he would do, certainly—if he slapped her again, she could, at least, complain with a sense of justifiable anger.

Quietly, she folded her unread section of the newspaper. She watched Morrie's head bob between reading and sleeping. His eyelids blinked open, wide, startled, then closed. With great effort he forced them open, pulled the paper closer to his eyes. His lips formed the shape of the words until, once more, the urge to sleep overwhelmed him. Ellie concentrated on his struggle, enjoyed his defenselessness, the ferocious will fighting with diminishing strength.

But ashamed, as if she were eavesdropping, she called out, "Morrie, why don't you go to bed?"

His head jerked up, instantly awake. "What? What's wrong?"

"Nothing." She laughed. "I only thought you'd be more comfortable in bed."

"You coming too?"

"In a while. I've got things to do."

"What kind of things?" Getting up, he stretched his arms until the bones cracked.

"For tomorrow night." She followed his movement toward her.

"Tomorrow night? What's tomorrow night?" He sat on the hassock in front of her chair.

"Oh Morrie, I told you." She had, but not since the night of their last argument had she mentioned it.

"Never. You never said a word."

"You just don't remember. That's all."

"All right." He shrugged his shoulders. "Have it your way. Tell me again now. What about tomorrow night?"

"I'm having everybody for dinner." His surprise, his smile—was it pride?—satisfied her.

"Can you do all that cooking?" He reached for and held her hand. "You know how to make fish and everything?"

"I wrote to your mother. Your sister sent all the recipes. All I have to do is follow them. I bought all the different fish and . . ."

"You wrote to my mother?"

"Yes. What's so shocking about . . ."

"That's what I call a good wife." He patted her hand, exaggerating his pleasure. "My mother can teach you a lot."

"And I guess you think I have a lot to learn?" Even though it's true, let him deny it.

"In lots of things, yes, you do. But so do I."

She nodded, unfolded the newspaper, pretended to read it.

"Who's coming?"

Her eyes scanned the paper. Only when he repeated the question insistently did she respond, but she did not lower the paper. "Toby and Leon, of course. It's in their honor. And my mother and father . . . not that they'll eat anything . . ." Because he remained listening, her own excitement was fired. ". . . maybe papa will . . . And Harry and Martha . . . I hope she comes. Harry said he would make her come . . . Clara and Mollie."

"That's a lot of people for this apartment."

"If my mother can get them all in, we surely can. We'll eat in this room." She dropped the paper, expecting his irritation.

"That means I have to move the kitchen table in here and set up the bridge table and . . . Why the hell didn't you tell me about this before? What if I were working tomorrow night? What then?"

"We went through this once already. And you mentioned the other night that you'd be home."

"That's not the point." He waved his finger at her. "I want to know what's going on in my house always. Is that all right with you?"

"Oh Morrie." She stood up.

"Don't 'oh Morrie' me. You've got to learn to tell me these things a few times at least."

"Yes. I do." She walked quickly out of the room. An argument would ruin everything. In the bedroom she switched on the night table lamp and stretched out across the bed. All he is is a child. One minute he smiles and the next minute he's crazy. What a life. She'd have to be careful of every word she said. Day after day. She pushed her face into the chenille spread until, pressing hard, the little bumps felt like sharp rocks that pierced to the center of her resolution to be good, through the optimism that said she could take one moment at a time and make it all bearable. Leaning up on an elbow, a reflection of herself appeared in the dressing table mirror. Brown hair splashed onto the frowning face. In the dim light the shadows seemed to make the crooked nose straight. She smiled from the mirror, laughed out loud and fell back against the springy bed. It doesn't matter any more how I look, she thought. I've got a husband. She closed her eyes, hoping that when she opened them again, the thought would be less depressing. Her fingers pressed against her eyes, but the bright explosions inside formed ugly shapes. Even that delight was gone. But it, this feeling now, would not pass, and she had decided that. Tomorrow night she would prepare her first *Shabbath* dinner and it would be good. Even if he doesn't understand its purpose, it makes no difference.

The door opened.

"What are you doing?" He put on the overhead light.

"Nothing. Just resting." She didn't move.

"Why don't you get into bed?" There was the sound of a smile in his voice.

"I will." She put her hand up to cut the glare of the light.

He sat down next to her. "I don't know what you have to be tired about. I'm the one who has to go to work later, running around with the milk bottles . . ."

His voice droned on above her. It said things which she understood, but they were unimportant. Underneath the words was the important sound, a low hum of warmth that insisted he was decent, concerned. She looked at him leaning over her, smiling. "Yes. I think I'll go to bed now. I'm tired from not doing anything all day."

She started to sit up, but he pushed her back, gently, leaned closer, kissed her surprised eyes.

"You look very good," he whispered, awkwardly kissing her neck now.

"Thank you," she sighed and relaxed with a passion that included the feel of his kisses and not the words that made no sense.

WHAT THEIR REACTION WOULD BE to the *gefilte fish* was only one of the anxieties she lived with all that day. Another was that there would not be enough room in the living room. Early that morning, just after Morrie returned from work, she had gotten him to move his easy chair and hassock into the bedroom and then, by appealing to his sense of strength and not to his easily provoked annoyance, she had convinced him to transfer the kitchen table to the other room. She tried to judge distances. "It'll have to do." When the bridge table was pushed against the larger one, it did add space, but at a lower level, and she told herself to remember that that would be one of the danger spots.

"Everything's going to spill," said Morrie, observing his work.

"We'll be careful. That's all we can do." She walked around the tables, frowned at how little space there was. "I won't worry about it now."

Morrie moved the standing tiered lamp close to the head of the table, certain that he would sit there.

"Okay. Now have your breakfast and go to sleep." Ellie was not going to tell him now that her father was to have that seat. "I've got lots of work to do."

He obeyed every request this morning and when he left for the bedroom, Ellie thrilled to what lay before her. The movements, the actions were imitations of scenes from the past that flashed vividly through her mind as she worked. It was her mother's hand that patted the ground carp, fluke, and white fish into oblong shapes, like small potatoes. It was as if her mother-in-law stood behind her, examining the way she wrapped the dark-colored fish skin around the familiar shapes. The huge pan of spiced water bubbled steam into her face. Ellie's hand hesitated above it and then the first piece slipped deftly down, under the water. Another piece and another until all of them were comfortably squeezed together. She looked down, admiring what she had started, and a pleasure as serene as any she had ever experienced made her smile. Unwillingly she covered the pan, leaving a little air space, for its long period of cooking. Next, she started grating the carrots and potatoes so that the *tzimmis* and pudding would be ready for the afternoon. As long as she followed directions, all would go well.

The large chickens had been salted by the butcher and she proceeded to pluck, with the edge of a sharp knife, the remnants of feathers, so small that only an experienced housewife would know that they were there. Ellie saw them, as if through other eyes, and scraped and pulled until the fat-yellow of the skin was unblemished. With a hand at first timid then happily compelled, she gouged the insides of the fowl for little scraps of clotted blood then placed both chickens into the huge turkey pan she had borrowed from her mother. She set the pan down on the drain section of the sink, alongside the carrots and potatoes. Standing back, observing the still-life of her preparations, she could not fight back a flush of self-satisfaction. There was no need to. No one watched. She was relaxed. All went smoothly. Each detail seemed correct. Every movement springing naturally from an instinct, a reservoir of dexterity unused before this morning, yet mysteriously there, ready. All that casual watching was responsible. All those Fridays of standing behind her mother who had worked at the sink had, like magic, provided her now with a skill beyond understanding. Being happy this way, absorbed with doing, was a new freedom, an escape from the nervousness that had always seemed the dues you had to pay for being alive.

By the time the late afternoon sunshine spotted the kitchen floor, the fish was done, the chickens were roasting, the puddings were resting on top of the stove, beautifully browned and crisp to the touch, and the sponge cakes, for the tea, were just beginning to rise.

She went back into the living room for the first time since the morning to examine the tables once again. The arrangement appeared more plausible. Anyway, the meal would be good, and if they were uncomfortable with the seating . . . well, they would just have to be uncomfortable. No use worrying about it when she couldn't help it.

Morrie came out of the bedroom, stretching and rubbing the sleep from his eyes. "My God the house smells good. What the hell you making, a banquet?"

"It does smell good." She smiled. "Morrie? Do you honestly think we'll have enough room?"

"Don't worry. It's enough." He moved on to the bathroom.

She began setting the tables. Previously unused wedding presents were taken from the hall closet. The filigree silver from her 'in-laws,' the dishes from Aunt Dora, and the white damask cloths from . . . who? She couldn't remember. Just a year and she had forgotten. Oh well, it would come to her later. You have to forget about trying to remember and then suddenly, when you least expect it, you remember. Linen napkins tonight. Yes.

"Ellie," Morrie called from the bathroom, the sound of dripping water accompanying his words, "you got a little something for me to eat?"

"Yes. Don't worry. I've got something. Just don't dirty the floor in there. It's already been cleaned."

"And don't you start sounding like a nag so soon," he shouted back. "I'm being careful."

Later, after every detail had been checked off her list and Morrie had his sample *nosh* of the chicken, Ellie gratefully lowered herself into a hot bath. Lounging, wiggling her legs contentedly, she felt that she was on the edge of a special victory, that she had performed an act of will that would win. The bath became a reward for hard work. The weight of her mood had moved from dead center and here was an unexpected source of contentment. She leaned back against the rim of the tub and sloshed water on her floating breasts. "A *machia*. A *machia*." She laughed. An old woman sitting in her bath and splashing her joy.

Finally there was only the ring of soap to wipe from the tub, then the floor, for the third time that day, to be cleaned. By the time she finished drying herself, a twinge of anticipation churned in her stomach and perspiration rose to her skin, caking the bath powder as she rubbed it on. As long as there are no fights. No fights and the fish has to be perfect.

SINCE AT THE VERY LAST MOMENT Ellie had convinced Morrie to move the sofa and coffee table into their bedroom, when the family arrived, all at once, there was nothing to have them do but squeeze into place at the table.

"Papa, you're at the head of the table." Ellie led her father to the seat while Morrie struggled with the hanging up of coats. Mr. Perlin, surprised and timid, tried to refuse. "Come on, Pa, up there, next to the lamp, and Mama at the other end." They moved to their seats. Ellie kissed Toby and Leon. "You both look wonderful." Mollie and Clara were next. Harry leaned down for a kiss and Ellie clutched Martha's hand, whispering, "I'm so glad you came." Martha's defensive smile thawed into one of genuine relief.

They stood behind the seats that Ellie had assigned, gazing down at the gleaming silver, the sparkling glasses, the whiteness that lay before them.

"Well, come on people, move," shouted Morrie, reentering the room.

"I think maybe Morrie should sit here." Mr. Perlin pointed to the arm chair.

"No. He doesn't mind. Do you Morrie?" Ellie dared him to object.

He didn't. Ellie's glow of pleasure warmed him to obedience; his father-in-law's embarrassed, wanting-to-please expression deserved this little tribute. "I don't mind at all so let's get settled. I'm hungry."

Harry held the chair out for his mother. She sat down silently, her silence a warning, almost a conviction that all could not possibly go well. Ellie, seeing the thought clearly, flashing it to her mind, was equally determined to have nothing dull the sharpness of these few hours.

Ellie and Morrie watched the others seat themselves, heard the scraping sounds of chairs coming to rest in that instant of stillness that precedes all meals, that hushed waiting that wants to be disturbed. Mr. Perlin's solitary skull cap shone in the bright lamp light. Heads turned to one another. They were in place. There was room. Ellie smiled with a warmth that divorced the event, however briefly, from any unpleasantness that had come before or would come after. Morrie squeezed her hand then sat down between his mother-in-law and Mollie. "Bring on the food. I'm hungry."

"I'll get the fish." Leaving the room, she heard Toby say, "She made fish too?" and Mr. Perlin's answer, "Your sister's a *balabusta*. You didn't know?" And remembering the last conversation with her father, Ellie was grateful that at least he understood the importance of this dinner.

In the kitchen she could hear the tense beginning of conversation. Harry laughed, and then Clara and Morrie, in unison, shouted, "Ellie, a glass of wine first."

A good idea. Insurance. "I'll bring it right in," she called.

First the fish: a platter on each section of the table. Then she ran back to the kitchen for the wine and set the bottle down before her father.

"God, that fish looks good," said Clara. "When did you learn how to make fish?"

"I learned today . . . I hope it's not bad." She knew it wasn't bad, but if she acted as if she were unsure, the praise would be greater.

"You make a toast, Papa," said Toby after the wine glasses had been filled ceremoniously by Morrie and passed around.

Mollie leaned forward to whisper something to Ellie which made her jump up screaming, "Wait, Papa, wait 'til I bring in the horseradish." They all laughed, even Mrs. Perlin, the laughter sustained, bursting anew as Ellie raced back into the room. "Now, Papa." She raised her glass.

"All right, children, and Mama." He lifted his glass, inclining it toward his wife, but Mrs. Perlin's hands remained folded on her lap. He did not call attention to the fact that she wouldn't toast. "Here's to God and the happiness of my wife and children. A long smile and a long life. *Boruch attaw adonai* . . ." The glasses remained poised until the prayer was concluded. "Amen," he whispered, and then, his glass raised even higher for the extra "*L'Chayim.*"

"*L'Chayim,*" they answered and drank.

"Now let's pass that fish around." Morrie slapped his palms together.

Hands reached out. The platters moved quickly around the table, bypassing Mrs. Perlin who held her hand over her plate.

"You won't eat, Minnie?" Mr. Perlin frowned.

"You didn't have your wine either," said Clara.

"I'm not hungry." Mrs. Perlin looked straight ahead, toward her husband.

"You can eat here, Mama." Ellie's voice conveyed defeat on this issue, but she was expected to try. "My house is kosher."

"I'm sure it is, but I'm not hungry."

"Come on, Ma. Be a sport." Harry tried his special approach. "It's not fair to Ellie. If this were my house, that would be a different story." He looked at Martha. Her eyes told him that it was all right for him to continue. "We understand that. But here there's no reason to . . ."

"Leave her alone!" Mollie interrupted.

Mr. Perlin's hand tugged at Harry's sleeve, begging for silence.

Leon, a newcomer to this kind of exchange, attacked his fish with embarrassed energy. Toby never disturbed her familiar boredom. Her eyes remained downcast, indifferent; she picked at the fish.

"Well, anyway, El, the fish *is* delicious." Clara reached for another piece.

"That we agree on. My wife's all right." Morrie decided it was his duty to change the subject. "Well, Leon, how'd you like the hotel? Good honeymoon place this time of year, I'll bet."

"Swell." Leon blushed. "Your mother's a good cook too."

"You hear that, El? He's comparing you to my mother already." Ellie nodded self-consciously. "Was anyone else there? Any guests?"

Toby spoke up. "Just your parents, your sister and of course Max." Her voice lingered coldly on the name.

"You know, it's funny how things work out." Morrie paused in his eating. "My sister married to your brother, Leon. You married to Ellie's sister. It's crazy. Like royalty. Of course my sister's no queen and Toby's no . . ."

"Have more fish," Ellie interrupted frantically. "Martha? Some more . . . I mean if you really like it."

"I love it, but I want to leave room for the rest of the meal.

Thank you." Martha moved her fish plate to the side. She was grateful for Ellie's attempt to include her in the group, but she had learned, very early in her marriage, to remain as inconspicuous as possible. Harry spoke for both of them when the conversation became dangerous. That was their plan. Ellie knew it and honored it.

"How's school going, Harry?" Morrie speared his third piece of fish.

"It's a grind but coming along. Two more years and law school. The roughest part is that Martha has to keep working."

"You don't mind, do you, Martha?" Toby never tried to be subtle.

"No. Not at all." Martha's composure remained unruffled.

The conversation turned into the general area of working wives, thanks to Leon's comment that if a wife wanted to share in her husband's future she had to be willing to help out in the present. Although Toby's irritation was apparent, she said nothing. Leon was pleased.

"My wife will never work," Morrie barked. "No sir. I'll make whatever money's in my family."

"It's not a question of money," Harry continued. "More and more women want to make that kind of investment. Don't you feel that way, Martha?"

"What can she say?" Mr. Perlin smiled benignly. "There's no answer to that question. A woman does what her husband wants her to do. For myself, I wouldn't want my wife should work anyplace but in the house."

"But Papa," said Leon, meekly now, for he was not used to addressing his father-in-law by that title, "if you can let her work in the kitchen, what's the difference if she works anywhere else?"

"A big difference because if she's somewhere else, then the house suffers."

"Does your house suffer, Harry?" Clara twitted good-naturedly.

"What do you think, darling sister?"

Ellie jumped up. "Everyone please let me have your fish plates and the silverware." Clara offered to help. "No one is to get up. I'll do it myself."

The talk subsided once more to the level of neighborly exchange. Only Mrs. Perlin and Mollie remained rigidly out of touch.

"By the way," Toby called to Morrie, "your mother asked when the two of you are going up there."

"For Passover, I hope. What about it El?" She had returned with a steaming tureen of chicken soup and absorbed in the duty of serving it nodded yes without having heard the request.

"What about our *seder?*" Mrs. Perlin roused herself.

"We were there last year for both of them, Ma," Morrie answered.

"So?"

"So my mother would like a chance."

"She doesn't have a real *seder.*" Mrs. Perlin's frankness started Morrie's head trembling, but Harry interrupted before his brother-in-law could speak.

"It's only fair to alternate." Once more Harry wanted to reason.

"Let's not talk about it now," Mr. Perlin demanded. "We're eating a good meal, so let's eat." Sipping and blowing obedience followed. Mrs. Perlin, having rejected the soup as well, retreated further behind the brooding screen of obduracy.

"How's your job doing, Leon?" Harry asked as if to protect his mother from the next attempt to make her eat.

"Not bad, but I was thinking and hoping that," he hesitated, glanced quickly at Morrie, then continued, ". . . that maybe I could get a job with Morrie's company. My salesman's job keeps me on the road too much and . . . What do you think, Morrie?"

"I can ask around." Morrie slurped his soup.

"Remember Leon," Ellie was dissatisfied with Morrie's lack of enthusiasm, "that being a driver keeps you working most of the night."

"True, but I was thinking about the future."

"The future . . . the future," Toby mumbled.

"Well, honey, you've got to think about it. When we have kids I'd like to be around them once in a while."

"I've heard all that. But being a milk . . ." Remembering suddenly, Toby stopped. But Morrie had looked up and was ready for her.

"You people give me a swift pain in the ass. You think you were all in the '400' or something. There's nothing wrong with being a milkman so don't screw your nose up as if you were smelling crap."

"It's right." Mr. Perlin scanned the anxious faces. "What matter your job as long as you shall be honest. In the old country I was rich.

So even being that, specially that, you must be honest. Now I can call myself an honest tailor." He laughed, but no one joined him.

"You are Papa, but so what?" Mollie's remark was aimed at Morrie, not her father.

"What do you mean, so what?" Harry was eager to stir his sister, but she refused the challenge, returned to the eating of her soup.

"It's all solved anyway. Right Leon? Your wife's going to direct you away from low class jobs." Morrie wanted to return to Toby, to force her to anger. That he could handle.

"Come on, Morrie. Toby's my wife, but she's not going to tell me everything. I got a mind of my own."

"You got a lot to learn about your wife."

"Do you mind dropping it please," Toby snapped. "Leon's not like you. He's got a heart."

Morrie shook off Ellie's restraining hand. "No! I'm not going to stop. It's my house and I'm not dropping the subject just because it gets too hard to take. Papa, you should have taught your daughters better manners if they're going to be in society."

"Look who's talking about manners," Clara burst out, but Mrs. Perlin's shouted "Quiet" silenced her.

"Morris, my daughters are both good and bad, like most people. I tried to teach them the right thing."

"Yeah, to do the right thing, but that's a hell of a lot different from thinking the right thing."

"You so sure you think right," said Mollie with tightlipped force.

"I try at least."

"Well, so do we."

"Is that right. Should I ask Martha about that?"

Martha looked toward Harry. Ellie saw the frightened glance, but Morrie was beyond the point where a 'ssh' would stop him.

"You're right about that," Harry answered. "But that's not my father's fault. It goes back past him. Far back."

"I don't blame anybody for anything." Martha smiled proudly. "I'm happy."

The simple admission, spoken calmly, stunned the others to defensive silence as if, yielding here, they could conserve energy for another opportunity. Ellie sighed, collected the soup plates, filled the moment with the reality of clattering dishes.

"Can I help you?" Mrs. Perlin wanted urgently to leave the room.

"No, Mama. Just sit there. I'll manage."

Ellie stood before the stove in the kitchen, straining her ears for the sound of talk. None came. She gazed at the waiting platters, but the triumph of handsome, deeply browned chicken, the correct tart taste of the orange carrot *tzimmis*, the crisp crustiness of the potato *kugel* faded into grayness. Nevertheless, she forced herself to smile as she returned to the other room laden with the products of her own ingenuity.

They ate and slowly the good food did revive the appearance of warmth.

"Delicious *tzimmis*," said Harry. "And this is the first time you ever made this stuff?"

"Even the chicken's good." Mollie's compliment was grudging but sincere. Ellie smiled meekly, but inside the unfamiliar praise returned the sense of victory. If only her mother would eat something. "Not even a wing, Mama?"

"Let's not go through that business again." Morrie's greasy fingers waved through the air. "Your mother's a religious fanatic. She sets back the Jewish cause a thousand years."

"I didn't ask for your comments." Ellie knew her sharpness was dangerous. Morrie stared at her.

"He's right," said Mrs. Perlin, surprising everyone to attention. "But what I can't do, I can't do."

"Papa's eating." Morrie pushed his advantage. "He's as religious as you."

"He does as he sees fit. That's the way it is. I'm sorry."

"Eat and don't worry." Mr. Perlin motioned to Morrie contritely.

"No one's worried," Morrie was insistent now, "but it's about time someone did. We go on this way and we're all going to be lost. In the old country they know the world's changing. Look at Russia. And if we don't smarten up that revolution's going to be the beginning of trouble everywhere. That's all I mean, El. I'm not looking for a fight."

"I don't know what you mean right now. Just eat and we'll talk later."

"For Christ's sake, what an answer."

There it was again, his quickly flaring anger; and her sighing consternation, matching it, visible to all. She said nothing; he relented. Ellie forced second helpings on the men; the girls picked at small pieces until the platters were almost empty and the chicken grease began to form a thick milky film.

Mr. Perlin patted his stomach, pushed his chair back from the table. "Not another thing more. Everything was excellent. Morris, you're lucky to have such a wife."

"I'm glad everyone's agreed on at least one thing."

"Thanks for your confidence. I'll get the tea and cake in a few minutes. *Now* you can talk, Morrie, if you have anything left to say."

Once more Mrs. Perlin offered to help, but Ellie firmly refused. "You didn't eat, so you don't help." Her sisters remained motionless, unspeaking.

"You girls are pretty strong stock. Why don't you help Ellie?" Morrie suggested.

Ellie called from the kitchen that she did not, absolutely did not want any help.

"Leon, you play pinochle?" asked Morrie.

"Yes, but not good."

"You want to have a game later, Harry?"

"I guess so." Harry waited for Martha's nod.

"Not cards tonight, on *Shabbath*." Mr. Perlin addressed his words to Harry.

But Morrie responded. "We're not going to play for money. Just a friendly family game to break Leon in. You're supposed to relax on *Shabbath* and pinochle's relaxing."

"Not cards." Mr. Perlin became stern for the first time that evening.

"Pa," Morrie's voice was taunting, coy, "when they were making the rules, they didn't play pinochle so how do you know it's forbidden?"

"Nothing is forbidden if you don't see it that way." Mrs. Perlin did not look at him as she spoke.

"I don't see what harm it could do. We're all in the family." Morrie was pleased with his sarcasm.

"You wouldn't see," retorted Mollie. "You don't know right

from wrong anyway."

"And you do?"

"In some things, yes." Mollie chose this moment not to retreat.

"Well, for Christ's sake then, why don't you go out to the kitchen and help your sister instead of butting in here?"

"Why don't you shut up, for once," Clara yelled.

"Don't get excited, Clara." Toby was calm. "Leon's not going to play anyway. We have to go home early."

"What for?" Leon blurted out, then, too late, realized what he had done.

"If you don't know, I'll have to tell you later."

"Damn it," Harry shifted in his seat to face as many of them as he could, "what a circus this is. Why the hell do we ever sit down together? I'm going to swear that this is the last time." The arc of his moving head included his mother and father. "You know Martha, with the exception of Ellie, you're the only one with any sense."

"Thank you, Mr. Big Shot." Toby's face was filled with hate.

"Big shot hell." Harry's voice was raised higher than he wished. "For a little girl you've got the most nerve of all—and don't interrupt, Leon, I've known her longer than you."

Mr. Perlin stood up, trying to silence them.

"Not this time, Papa," Harry shouted. "I'm not stopping. Here's Ellie making a great dinner for her newly married sister, her darling, sweet, appreciative sister, and what happens?"

"Give it to them!" Morrie screamed. "Harder!"

"You're not much better either. You bait everyone. You always do. Believe me, this is the last time I'm acting as peacemaker for this family."

"Where's the war, peacemaker?" Clara shouted.

"Of course you're too dumb to know there is one."

Clara burst into tears, but she did not leave the table.

Ellie stood in the doorway to the kitchen, her face reflecting a bitterness, a disappointment so keen that, for the moment, she could find no words to express it. She walked to Clara and put her hand comfortingly on her shoulder. "Harry, right now you're not helping me one bit, and believe me, you're not going to change a thing. We might as well understand that. I don't like to talk this way but since it's started we might as well continue." She paused, looked around the room at the sullen faces. "No use denying what's the truth. We're not the nicest people around. Myself included. Sure we know better. That we learned all right. I don't blame Mama and Papa. Not them. It's us. Each of us . . . each of us thinking to get *our* rights, *our* way. Why must it be that way? I . . . I . . ." she struggled to find words for thoughts that were just forming in her mind. Like blocks of light the phrases fell too quickly into the darkness of her anger to be retrieved. Her hands made desperate arcs and darts of emotion above Clara's bent head. "Picking . . . picking at each other. Always the same thing instead of being glad to be together. What's the point of being alive if you can't know how everyone's trying to control themselves . . . to make sense . . ." Her mind would yield no words. It was filled with darkness and she was afraid to mention love. ". . . Oh, what's the difference . . ." She turned away. "I'm going to serve tea and cake and after that if you want to play pinochle, you're welcome to . . . Clara, stop crying. There's nothing to cry about." She left the room, conscious only of their eyes, feeling shame for daring to speak. There was no sense in hurting her mother and father anymore. They could do nothing more than feel regret for the wasted effort of their lives. And the others, she thought, will have to find their own ways to die their lives away. She knew that she was on the verge of discovering her way. Nothing, not tears, not screams were going to prevent her from seeing this meal through to its conclusion.

She filled the kettle with water, banged it down on the stove, and lit the burner, concentrating, concentrating only on this. The tea pot was ready. The red and gold tin of 'Swee-Toch-Nee' was alongside it. And the sponge cake was waiting to be cut. Noises from the other room intruded. She shrugged them out of her mind. Only the burning gas mattered, and the need for boiling water.

PART *II*

CHAPTER *Seven*

THE SOUNDS OF CHILDREN returning from school, the shouts, the unleashed laughter mixed with the snap of wind against window. Ellie straightened her shoulders, checked the rearrangement of furniture in the living room. Now that she had moved it, the plan no longer seemed a good one. The mohair sofa! That's what always caused the trouble. It's just too big. This way it sticks too far into the dining room entrance. She had a moment of wanting everything as it had been: Morrie's chair back near the window where, sensibly, it could get the outside light over his shoulder; his hassock in front of *his* chair—it *was* ridiculous with the wing chair; and, of course, the sofa should be along the only unbroken wall. Only it's not going to be. Too bad if they don't like it. It'll stay right where it is.

The kitchen door slammed. Ellie readied herself for the first comment.

"Not again, Ma!" Evelyn marched to the center of the room. She whirled around, the long, dark curls swinging, tumbling, still; the chubby, dimpled cheeks splashed with the rosy energy of the wind.

"All right. So you don't like it." Ellie walked toward the kitchen. There criticism was impossible. "Just wait before you make up your mind. . . . Change your clothes. And have some milk. . . . I made new cookies." Evelyn was already in the bedroom she shared with her younger brothers.

"Is Irving with you?" Ellie collected her cleaning rags, folding each one neatly. The oily one she kept separate, placed it in a container under the sink. "Evelyn?" There was no response except for the loud thump of the closet door being banged shut. "Don't you hear me? Where's Irving?"

"Don't have to scream, Ma." Evelyn was at the icebox searching for the milk. "I don't know where he is. I waited after school and he didn't come. Maybe he went to fly kites near the bay. I didn't see any of his friends either."

"How many times have I told you to make sure he comes home first before going anywhere?" Ellie moved her daughter to the small, porcelain top table near the kitchen window. "I don't want crumbs on the floor. Eat here."

Evelyn nibbled her cookies. "There's no sense in waiting for him all afternoon when he's not coming, Ma."

"You're so busy with your friends?" Ellie snapped.

"I'm sorry, Ma, but I didn't know what else to do except come home. I thought maybe he was home already."

"All right. It's enough." Ellie opened the oven door, checked the progress of the roasting chicken. "Don't drip that glass on the floor and no more of those cookies."

"I love pinwheels." Evelyn smiled. "You make those the best."

"Thank you. Now go down to the boulevard so you can cross David when he gets there. Don't go anywhere else. Do you hear me? Nowhere else!"

Evelyn nodded obediently. Her legs swung freely beneath the table; she munched the remnant of her last cookie. Two crescents remained of the pinwheel; she saved the chocolate strip for last. Her gaze scrutinized the square outside the kitchen window. Friday afternoon. The whole weekend. "Ma, why do you put papers on the floor after you wash it? You can't see that it's clean that way?"

"Never mind asking. Just go meet your brother." Ellie ushered her away from the table. "I've got too much to do. And after you meet David, find Irving and tell him I want him home. Kites or no kites."

Evelyn slowly buttoned her new leatherette jacket, the kind all the girls had, the kind her mother had so long refused to buy just because all the girls had one. "Ma, we're having a meeting of the club tonight. You remember I told you we were? Well, we're going to have the meeting here because the other girls' mothers don't want it and I said you wouldn't mind. Do you think Daddy'll mind?"

"Your father's playing pinochle here tonight, but maybe they'll let you use the basement. Go upstairs and ask Fanny if she will let . . ." Evelyn was tramping heavily up the stairs before Ellie could finish her statement. "Don't forget the other things I asked you to do," she shouted, walking to the side door which Evelyn had left open. "Evelyn?" Ellie screamed so that the footsteps stopped immediately. "Also go to the bakery and pick up the *challah*. I almost forgot with all your clubs. It's paid for already."

"Yes, Ma."

Ellie closed the door, walked to the sink and swirled water on the crumbs of food, washed Evelyn's glass. She could hear the voices of Fanny and Evelyn discussing the basement. Fanny would say yes; Ben would object later, but Fanny could out-yell her husband. Thank God at least one of Morrie's cousins was decent. When they had to move from New York to Bayonne because Morrie's promotion meant that he would be in New Jersey, Ellie had resisted stubbornly. To be someplace new, away from her mother, with one child then, had threatened to dissolve her carefully constructed resolve, a resolve which, during the years, no amount of arguing had disturbed. But Morrie insisted. He was getting too old for that kind of traveling everyday. Sure I used to do it, but so what. Now is now. They fought each day for weeks: he behind the newspaper when he ate; she at the stove or the sink. Only when Fanny's two-family house became available did Ellie yield. First, she wanted Morrie to buy the house. That, too, he refused. "Never. Let Fanny and Ben have the headaches." They rented the lower floor. Mrs. Perlin convinced her to give in. "The children could use the space darling. Like you had."

Ellie checked the chicken once more, and then the March wind, rattling the loose window panes in the living room, called her back to the front of the house. Perhaps now the furniture would have a settled, natural look.

No, she admitted, it will have to be temporary. Morrie will hate it. She almost decided to move it back the way it had been, but fatigue stopped her. She sat down on the sofa, rubbed her hand across the prickly maroon mohair. How could there ever be enough time to do so much on a Friday afternoon? Yet, each week, the cleaning, the cooking, the baking was done with time to spare. Sixteen years of Fridays teach you how to juggle hours like a vaudeville performer. So many performances. Sixteen years. Almost. And how many times had she arranged the furniture? Even the children knew it was a joke. Probably, even the furniture knew it. She smiled, poked at the cushion. The telephone rang; the smile disappeared. She was quickly in motion once more.

Morrie'll be late for dinner again. By the third ring, the receiver was in her hand. "Hello. Clara? . . . Everything all right?"

"Of course it is. What kind of catastrophe were you expecting? I just wanted to make sure that you'll be at Mama's tomorrow with the kids."

"If nothing changes by then, I plan to."

"Nothing will change except maybe we'll buy our house."

"In one day?" Ellie screamed into the receiver.

"One day? It's months we've looked at it. Anyway, we're deciding tonight. We'll give you the news tomorrow. Also, Simon will drive you all home after Mama's."

"Good. You can have something to eat here when we get back."

"Okay, El, if it's not too much trouble."

"Trouble? It's no trouble at all. How's the children?"

"Fine. El? I've got to get dinner started so I can't talk."

"Started? So late?"

"I'm not you, remember."

"All right. Send my love."

"Mine too. Bye."

"Bye." Ellie's thoughts turned immediately to food for tomorrow night. Not Clara's house. She forced herself not to think about that. Everyone else will own something, and what'll I have? She sat down at the porcelain table, brushed crumbs from Evelyn's cookies into a cupped palm, transferred them to her apron pocket. Another landmark. Clara and Simon buying a house. This one was more important for all of them because this landmark her father would never see. But that Ellie surely didn't want to think about. And Mollie left alone with her mother was another fact to try and forget now. She picked up the metal chopper, gripped the wooden handle, reached to the stove for the wooden bowl. The best thing is to chop the liver. The metal, glinting in the sunlight, sliced through the chunks. Automatically, with practiced precision, she threw shreds of fried onions into the bowl. The chopping hand never stopped. Her eyes remained fixed on the outside. The window could stand a cleaning. Not today. It's enough for today. The meal was almost ready. The house was clean. It was 'kept,' ready for her children, her husband. Soon she would feed them and if they liked what they ate, they would, perhaps, tell her and she would be satisfied. Maybe there were other ways of showing love, but this was hers. There was no question of change now. The children are all right. If only Morrie would yell less . . . The liver was done. She looked down at its dryness and added a few globs of chicken fat, folded it deeply into the mound.

"Mama? I'm home." Irving had entered quietly, holding the door so his mother wouldn't be angry about that too.

"I see you're home. Why weren't you here with Evelyn?"

"They were going to fly kites . . ."

"Who's they?" The chopper was poised midair.

Irving's eyes, the cautious but confident eyes of an eight year old who knows he is loved, widened with mock fear. His mother never hit him. His father, yes. Never his mother. "You know who, Ma. My friends." He crossed his legs, anxious to get back outside.

"I know only that you are always to come home," she set the chopper down noisily, "after school. No 'ifs,' 'ands,' or 'theys.' "

Irving smiled, unsure that he should. His hand searched through his blond hair, scratching, spilling it onto his forehead. He moved to stand alongside his mother's chair, testing, challenging her seriousness.

Looking down at him, she relented, swept his hair from his eyes, and offered him a piece of liver on her fingertip. He took it gleefully on his extended tongue then turned toward the door. "I'll be in soon, Ma. Georgie's outside with his dog." And he was gone before Ellie had a chance to forgive him.

The sunlight looked colder now, but still it felt warm on her arms. She lingered by the window, watching the children as they paraded in and out of the candy store across the street. She saw Irving pushing his face in front of George's patient police dog. Then Evelyn, holding on to David's hand, approached Irving. Ellie knew that she was scolding him. She could see her daughter's mouth purse and pout self-righteously, the way fourteen year old girls get angry. Irving skipped wildly, tauntingly away from her, secure. He snatched at the brown bag that David held, darted away, looked inside, and threw it back to Evelyn who just managed to grab it before it fell to the ground. Her head bobbed with fury. David tugged at her hand, pointed to their house. They crossed the street and disappeared from Ellie's view. Irving, legs spread apart proudly laughed with his friends.

She got up, busied herself at the sink, awaiting the next arrival. She would have liked a high stool on coasters so that she could swing herself from sink to stove to table to ice-box. What energy she could store up then! What energy! For what? For washing and ironing more clothes? Moving more furiture? More screaming power for Morrie? It was better to stand up. The door opened.

David ran to his mother and waited to be kissed. Ellie leaned over, let herself be hugged, and then gently moved him away. "Was it a good afternoon in school, Davey? . . . Evelyn, put the *challah* down already please. You don't have to wait to be told, do you? . . . Did you Dave? . . . Stay away from that cake, Davey. It's too hot."

David froze. "Ma?" the sound whistled through the gap created by lost teeth. "Why can't you eat hot cake if you can eat hot soup?"

Ellie sighed, exasperated. "It's different."

"How, Ma?" He stood before her looking up, so small and demanding.

But Ellie had no time to talk now. "It's just different Davey." She turned back to the sink. "How was school?" she asked again.

"Okay." David hoisted himself onto one of the chairs at the porcelain table. Evelyn disappeared into her bedroom. "Teacher says I don't listen to her 'cause I don't build things. I don't like to build buildings, Ma. I don't and she put me in the wardrobe closet for ten minutes."

"The wardrobe?" Ellie whirled around. "You must have been very bad if she did that." Annoyed with the teacher's punishment, but unwilling to let David see that, she turned away, reached for a ladle and stirred the big pot of chicken soup.

"I wasn't, Ma. I wasn't. I promise. She only kept saying you're naughty, you're naughty. Just because I didn't want to do what the other kids did. And then she put me in the wardrobe closet. She stinks."

Impulsively, Ellie walked over to David. She brushed the soft brown hair back from his forehead, watched it slide back into place. "Don't worry about it. Maybe I'll go speak to her."

"Don't, Ma. Please don't. She'll get angry with you too."

"I said don't worry. So don't. Go outside and play in the yard. And don't go looking for Irving . . . Take a cookie with you."

David tugged at his mother's hand. Ellie, instead of kissing him, touched his cheek and motioned for him to go. "Kisses and kisses. That's all you want."

"I'm gonna go see Fanny, Ma."

"No, Davey. Outside. Fanny's busy."

Obediently, David left the kitchen. Ellie waited near the window until he appeared in the yard. He stood motionless near the entranceway to the alley, so sad, unsure of what to do next. The sun seemed to be setting on him as he slid slowly into a sitting position against the house. He munched on the cookie and looked, blinking, into the deepening, cloudless blue of the afternoon sky. No friends came to call for him. No noise attracted his attention. He squatted and looked, waiting for nothing but the call to come inside. So lonely, my poor son. Ellie tapped on the window. David waved with his cookie. It's this Bayonne, with all the churches, that does it to him. No ghetto of squalor here to bind people to each other. No pushcarts! She left the window. And what is there instead? Kites? Sure, and then comes 'kike' and 'sheeny.' That's what the Jew is when he leaves Delancey Street. Okay—Ellie looked into the oven, nodded, satisfied, turned off the gas—but they're not going to beat my children. No sir! Jews they'll stay. Clean and strong, well-dressed. And if Morrie never takes them to the synagogue, then I will. And to Hebrew School and *bar-mitzvah*. The last laugh I'll get when they see how their father, the great Jew, accomplished so much when everyone else suffered in the Depression—always working; always providing; always reading about Dale Carnegie and Lincoln and the *Saturday Evening Post*. They'll know that was important. What they learn when he yells at me, calls me stupid bitch, even that's good. They'll learn to stand up instead of sliding down against a wall. "Evelyn," she called out, "come and set the table. Your father will be home soon."

Carefully, she placed the various pots and pans on the stove. They'll stay warm enough. The fish, the liver. Everything ready. "Evelyn?"

"I'll be right there."

"Now!" Ellie put a clean white cloth on the dining room table, set the two candle holders on it. "Evelyn, I'm not going to call you again."

"I'm here, Ma. I'm here." Evelyn stood in the entranceway to the kitchen, her long curls twisting neatly into spirals that rested on her shoulders.

"All this time you've been curling your hair?"

"Yes. Do you really like them still, Ma?"

"Of course I do. They're beautiful. Maybe with your talent you should become a beautician." Ellie placed candles in the holders. "Now set the table."

Evelyn didn't move. "Fanny said I could have the meeting downstairs."

"I thought she would."

"Ma?"

Ellie stopped moving around. She recognized the 'I want' sound. "What?"

"Ma, could I buy . . ."

"Buying again? You just got your fancy jacket. What now?"

"Wait, Ma. Please. What I want isn't going to cost a lot of money."

"Let me hear. What could you want. Not clothes?"

Evelyn hesitated, then finally blurted it out, "Lipstick." She sucked in her breath, waited, followed her mother into the kitchen, moaned as she exhaled.

Ellie turned to the *gefilte fish*, started to drain the juice, and said, quietly, "No."

"But Ma, all the girls . . ."

"No. I said no, and I mean no. You're only fourteen. It's too young for that sort of thing."

"What sort of thing is it?" asked Evelyn, too quickly belligerent.

Ellie sighed, realized that it would take a long time to talk her out of it. And there was so much to do right now. Of course that's why she started it. It's lipstick time already. The make-up, the decorations, the signals that Ellie wanted to ignore. It's too soon for the life outside the kitchen of her world to claim her daughter. Growing was one thing. That you couldn't stop. Of course not. When Evelyn had complained about her stomach and the blood, Ellie had shown her what to do, but she would not explain why it happened. Then she had said, "All the girls had it." Now, she couldn't repeat the magic phrase. Evelyn just had to be strong enough to know that she didn't need to paint her face while around her 'all the girls' did so. To live right—Ellie wanted Evelyn to know it without being told—means sometimes being alone, without lipstick if necessary.

"Why don't you say something, Ma? You're just standing there not listening to me."

"I'm listening, but all I can say is no. The question is will you hear me." Ellie roused herself. "Go set the table now. We'll talk about it later, when your father's home."

"He won't care. He never cares about what *I* want."

"I don't like that kind of talk. Especially now when there's so much to do. Please? The table?"

Evelyn shrugged her shoulders. For the moment, she would obey. The silverware tray was taken from its buffet compartment, and the dishes, removed from their racks in the dining room cabinet by angry fingers, rattled loudly.

So, another Friday night will end in an argument, thought Ellie.

Unfortunately for all the family, Morrie was brooding when he returned from the office. Office problems seldom stayed in the office. All activity spilled into his home, made it, in fact, a continuation of the day. He, in his imaginings was what he thought he should be: the center of the household. His family only needed to arrange themselves around his hard work in order to survive. Wasn't he responsible for all they had. Okay! Then they had nothing to complain about. They watched his silent eating and, as if by dumb habit, did the same. Only Ellie, passing the platters, urging her children to take more, spoke.

When they reached the soup course and Morrie began to slurp, the children, made less frightened by the familiar sound, dared more.

"Georgie got a new bike," said Irving tentatively, pulling at his blond hair for reassurance.

"Is it a three wheeler?" questioned David, who sat alone on one side of the table.

"Na-a-a!" Irving was manfully disgusted. "Three wheelers are for kids like you."

"Don't tease," said Ellie sternly.

"No bicycles for you." Morrie peered over his soup spoon. "You'll only get into trouble with them. Your mother's got enough to do now."

"When are the men coming over?" Ellie, sensing some kind of special trouble, felt that she must get him to talk, even if he only issued orders.

"Eight o'clock. Same as always."

"Evelyn's having her club meeting downstairs tonight. Fanny gave her permission."

"For Christ's sake! Why'd you let her, Ellie? They'll be making all kinds of noise."

"We won't," Evelyn spoke up quickly. "I promise, Dad." She was afraid that now, at the last minute, as he had done in the past, he would cancel her plans with a sudden, firm 'No.'

"Can I come to the meeting?" Irving beamed playfully.

"Can I?" echoed David.

"Both of you will have your baths and get to bed with no fooling around," commented Ellie as she returned from the kitchen carrying the chicken.

"And no noise here or downstairs," added Morrie. "Understand?"

The boys nodded; Evelyn sighed her relief.

"Clara called this afternoon. She wants to come over tomorrow with Simon and the children."

"Is she?" Annoyance stopped Morrie's fork inches from his mouth.

"Of course. But first I'm taking the children to my mother's and then we'll all come back together." The children looked up, smiled, gladdened by the prospect of the trip. They were now prepared to follow the exchange between their parents.

"And what am I supposed to do while all this is going on?"

"Aren't you working tomorrow?"

"Only 'til two o'clock." Morrie ladled a fresh supply of potato *kugel* onto his plate.

"Well maybe you'll come to Mama's from work. Simon's going to drive us home." Ordinarily, he would reject such a plan. Tonight, Ellie was unsure. He keeps on eating so he can't be very worried.

"I can't."

"Why not?"

"I've got too much to think about."

"What's wrong, Morrie? Something at work?" By this time in their married life, Ellie could distinguish the rippling, watery edge, that ever shifting boundary that separated habitual, tired preoccupation from those matters that made him grunt because he was profoundly worried. Tonight, when he arrived home and greeted no one, not even his favorite David, Ellie knew that grunting would follow.

"What's bothering me is important." Morrie stopped eating, looked around the table. "It concerns all of you."

"Maybe you should tell me later." Ellie's instinct reacted to the serious tone of his voice. Family discussions of important matters she distrusted. If Morrie had lost his job, which was her darkest thought, the children should not know it, at least not until she could decide how they should know it. That was the only kind of overprotection she allowed for them.

Morrie reached for his fork once more, hesitated, and Ellie repeated, "Later we'll talk." She gazed at him, hoping he would yield, turned away, letting him think that he was making up his own mind. "David some more chicken if you're not going to eat the other things."

The children, of one mind, knowing the usual result of such an appeal, waited expectantly for Morrie's raised voice and angry words. But just then his fork resumed its natural rhythm. "All right. Later," he muttered.

Ellie sighed loudly. This little victory offered little relief. Ordinarily, she would have deemed it a milestone. But tonight, his giving in so easily, made her feel anything but comfortable.

Ellie had both boys in the bathtub, scrubbing whatever arm or leg was carelessly offered up to her. She could hear, from the kitchen, the voices raised to bid and then the even louder post-game discussion of the four men playing pinochle. And down below, in the basement, the twelve girls were remarkably quiet. Occasionally Evelyn's voice could be heard warning her friends to be 'good.' When you demand, thought Ellie, most of the time you win. Evelyn makes an excellent president. All she had to do was copy her father.

"All right. Stand up, Davey. You're finished."

"Two more minutes, Ma? Please? Let Irving go first. I want to watch the water go out."

"Come on sonny boy. Stand up. You were second last week."

David splashed his foot in the water, but he obeyed. Ellie draped the huge white towel, its edges trailing dangerously close to the water, around the reluctant body of her son, then lifted him to the toilet seat where, immediately, she began rubbing vigorously, as if she were trying to start the circulation of an almost drowned victim.

"Fan me dry, Ma. Come on."

Ellie folded the towel neatly and waved it wildly in front of him. David giggled, laughed, hugged her neck with pleasure. That done, she reached into the medicine chest and removed, what even she had to call her instruments of hygienic torture: the fine tooth comb and the cuticle scissors. That was why she, personally, gave them their bath on Friday night. David's lingering smile disappeared.

There was a bang at the door and then Morrie's voice shouting, "How about some tea and cake, El? We're ready for it."

"Soon. Right away." She dug ferociously into the matted, wet head before her. The fine teeth dragged along the scalp, parting the hair, twisting the escaping strands.

"Ma! That hurts me!" David tried to push her hand down, but, as he knew he must, lost the battle.

"It's better if it hurts. At least I know you're clean. You're not going to be sent home from school for bugs in your hair." She proceeded; the howls continued. But Bayonne would never contribute contagion. "Irving! Put down that back scratcher and pull the plug."

"A few more minutes."

"Now!"

"Okay." Irving growled and lunged for the rubber plug.

David's hair was slicked back, but clumps of it refused the downward pressure of the comb. "Your hair dries too quickly. I can never keep it in place." She stood back, surveyed her work. "It's as good as I can get it. Now sit down and let me cut your nails." Again the child obeyed, trapped, and Ellie, down on her knees in front of the commode, snipped cautiously, but completely, as David wriggled his toes. Ellie powdered, she patted, and even kissed him before she rushed him into his pajamas and bathrobe. "Go say goodnight to Daddy and the men, and then go directly to your bedroom. No side trips. No questions to Daddy. Understand?"

David nodded and stealthily crept through the small opening of the door. He knew by now that no cold air was allowed inside the bathroom.

Hurriedly, Ellie turned, as she slammed the door shut, ready for a repeat performance. "All right, Irving!" A fresh towel was poised.

"MORE TEA, MR. KLUGMAN?" asked Ellie. The bearded, paunchy, sour-smelling man had just turned his glass upside down on the saucer.

"No thanks, Ellie . . . 300." His bid escaped on the explosion of a belch. He said nothing further. Actually, they never really stopped for refreshments. Ellie had to work around them. She collected cups and saucers and piled them into the sink. Morrie motioned to her with his head. She removed the plate of cookies and apple cake.

"310," said Benny, Fanny's husband.

It was Mr. Epstein's turn. He chewed the corner of his mouth, lifted his gaze toward the ceiling of the kitchen where they preferred playing, then, convinced that God would want it that way, quietly passed.

"350." Morrie studied his cards intently.

"Pass," the others said in unison, closing the fans of their cards, each placing the pack on the porcelain table top.

"Here's a flush in spades." Morrie spread the cards for them to inspect. "Plus a hundred aces." He looked quickly at the 'to loan,' smiled smugly. There was another piece of trump in it. "You want to play it out gentlemen?"

"Of course we'll play it," said Benny, always willing to hope that fate would award him a renege or a misplay.

"All right," Morrie grabbed for his cards, "we'll play it." Silence, except for the slap of cards on the table, followed. Ellie was especially careful not to make noise at the sink. She troubled the sudsy water with her fingers, leaned against the cold edge. She raised one foot. I must get that corn removed, she thought, staring dreamily into the water. And then, as though with great effort, she stood erect, rousing herself from the luxury of aimlessness. But I am tired. Tired. Tired. The last one sounded as a noiseless scream inside her head. I wish they'd all go home. Right now. But then she remembered that sleep, tonight, was a long way off. Morrie wanted to talk, and what he had to say she would want to hear. The last hand was completed, and as Morrie explained the strategy used in playing it, she couldn't detect the faintest trace of weariness or desperation.

It can't be his job then.

"So it wasn't so great then," Benny was saying. "If I had cards like that, I'd do good too." Ellie noticed that the pile of dollar bills had dwindled from in front of him and were now in Morrie's possession. It was as if some great power had come down from above and rearranged the earth. "Deal, Klugman," Benny ordered.

"Ben," Morrie taunted confidently, "you gotta know how to play the game. Take chances. I got the extra piece of trump in the 'to loan,' remember."

"All right, so you got. Deal, already, Klugman."

Now Ellie listened to the sounds of the swishing cards and the thump of the hands that reached out to get them. All the sounds she knew. She could listen with eyes blindfolded and tell exactly what was happening in the house. She sifted the other noises as she worked. Her mind left the kitchen. Upstairs, Fanny was talking, screaming to her mother, who was hard of hearing. From another part of the house—yes, the bedroom—Irving was still talking to David.—That I'll stop, Mister, in a few minutes.—The shuffling of feet was the only recognizable basement sound. She checked the clock on the kitchen wall. 10:30. The fact was registered in her mind and the response was automatic: 15 minutes more for the meeting. A dizzying, whirling sensation began to disturb the flow of thoughts. And then her body seemed to be spinning. She leaned heavily against the sink, over it. Suddenly, she wanted to scream again, this time so that everyone would hear it. She was frightened. She swayed with the dizziness. Her eyes fastened their gaze on the face of the clock; the second hand seemed to be moving faster than it should. Circling, passing under the twelve. And nothing else was happening. She was standing at the sink, spinning too, with it, a dish in her hand. The thousands upon thousands of dishes she had washed, the thousands upon thousands of dishes yet to wash stared down at her, smiling, mocking. Tears sprang into her now closed eyes. And there was no longer any one to talk to. No father, no friends that mattered to her. Every pain, every regret was encased in an eternally sealed phial of duty which she herself had sealed. Morrie, you stink, stink . . . She felt her body sag. She gripped the slippery sink ledge. She didn't call out. I don't need any help. Who's to help me? I did this all to myself. And it'll pass.

"Ellie? What's the matter?" the urgency of Morrie's call,

touched, stopped the throbbing pulse in her head. But she was unable to answer.

"You all right?" A chair scraped and he was beside her, his hand on her back.

She forced herself up, tried to move away from his hand. "Go back to the game," she whispered, embarrassed. "My corn hurts. That's all." He hesitated, turned, shrugged, moved back to his seat. "Who's dealing?"

THE NUMBERS of the electric clock glowed in the darkness of the bedroom. 1:30 and they were still wide awake. ". . . and that's what's bothering you? What a man you are. All night you let me think a great disaster was taking place and instead it's good news."

"You told me not to talk."

"And for once, the wrong time, you listened."

"I always listen."

"Of course."

"Look, El. It isn't as simple as you make out. We're going to have to move again. To Brooklyn, I guess."

"So? We'll move. You've gotten a promotion. Doesn't that make it worthwhile? And a raise too, I hope?"

"Yes. I'll get a raise, but . . ."

"But nothing." Annoyed, Ellie twisted from beneath his hand. "I never saw anything like it. A promotion. The first Jew I'll bet in your company to become a plant manager and you're worried. Can you tell me why?"

"I'm not worried. I'm glad." He moved closer to her. "It's the moving I don't like. You'll have plenty of work and I don't like disrupting everything."

"Disrupting? It'll be a pleasure to move from this town."

"Do you realize we've been living in this house ever since Evelyn was born?" Morrie reached for and held her hand beneath the quilt. He felt the veins throbbing, standing up in relief like little ridges on one of those mountain maps. Her fingers seemed longer as if they had been stretched by reaching for things so many years. "Fourteen years," he said nostalgically.

"You think it's a long time?" she questioned drowsily, warmed by this proof that beneath the yelling there was feeling.

"No. It's been quick. Too quick. I almost forget I'm getting older."

"I don't forget." She placed her hands outside the quilt.

Morrie turned on his side, facing her profile, pushing up against her. "What happened at the sink tonight, El?"

"Nothing."

"It must have been something. I thought you were going to faint."

"I told you. My corn hurt."

"That's all? You're sure?" He rubbed one hand back and forth across her stomach.

"That's all," she murmured, lulled by his rubbing, moving toward sleep, but hearing the children tossing in the other room, the beds squeaking, the electric clock humming its message of no stillness anywhere. Even sleep is movement beyond this moment; and sleeping, we settle ourselves deeper into the earth.

David whimpered; Morrie lifted himself on an elbow, listening. He heard someone shuffle barefooted across the floor, and then, moments later, the great rush of water down the toilet bowl. The sound of feet returning was lost in the greater noise. The whimpering had stopped. He fell back against the pillow. "You asleep, El?"

"I was almost. Now I'm just thinking. We should buy a house *this time* when we move."

He didn't answer.

"Now you're sleeping so quickly?"

"No! Of course I'm not." He turned away from her. "We got enough to take care of already without adding to it."

"I'm not talking about bicycles now. We could afford a down payment." He offered no denial. "There must be places in Brooklyn you could get a good house cheaply. It's not so built up there yet."

"We're not going to, Ellie, so get the idea out of your head. We'll rent. I don't want any problems."

"You won't have the problems. I will. You'll just pay. For the children you should do it."

"You got fancy ideas about a house." It was the daylight Morrie talking now. "You got them from your mother. What if I lost my job in a year? What then with the payments. It could happen, you know, with my company."

"Don't be silly. They gave you another promotion. They must like you." Her mind was made up. This time for sure. If she got nothing else out of her life, she would own a house first and then she would concentrate on Morrie's share of his mother's hotel. Nothing else. Just how to convince him!

"What if we ever want to take a trip somewhere? What if I buy a car? We can't afford everything." He gazed at his suit hanging on the outside of the closet, ready for the morning rush to the office.

"We'll be able to do all those things, someday." Why was he so different? Why didn't he want to own one thing? That she would never understand. "But first things first. If we don't get a house now, when the children are young, later, who needs it."

"Look," his voice was suddenly louder, the signal that his control was going, "we're not going to, and that's final. Finished. I got to sleep. It's late." He turned back toward her, but she could not respond. He pulled her roughly. "Come here."

She went because there was no choice but that. She had learned that much. The children slept. The house was quiet, and it was dark, mercifully dark. His fingers pulled at her hair. Disgusted by their demand, she tried to move back, pushing at him.

"We'll think about the house some more, El," he whispered, kissing her neck. Still resisting, knowing that she could not much longer, she let herself rest inside his arms.

"We are going to, Morrie. I won't let you forget."

"Whatever you say." His arms were locked behind her back.

THE TRAIN WAS OFF AGAIN, this time racing under the Hudson River for its last stop, New York City.

Ellie managed the buses with firm control. And there were the tall buildings to keep the boys quiet. On the Lower East Side this Saturday morning was a quiet one. The pushcarts were missing. The shops were closed. The emptiness of the streets forced a whispering respect for the Sabbath. The only noises were distant ones, coming from that other world, a world that seemed closer, that worked on Saturday.

"Right on time." Clara let them into the apartment. "Mama's still in her bedroom." The sisters kissed. David and Irving pushed past them toward their grandmother.

"Where are Rose and Charlie?" asked Ellie about Clara's children, hoping that she had not left them somewhere else. She pushed Evelyn to the open door of her mother's room, from which there now came delighted clucking noises as Mrs. Perlin first squeezed Irving and then kissed David's upturned face.

"I told them to take a walk until you got here."

"Ellie? *Nu?* Come here already with Evelyn." Mrs. Perlin's once splendidly, fastidiously arrayed hair was twirled haphazardly into a falling bun at the back of her head. Wisps of it always escaped her indifferent fingers when she combed it. Her face glowed gray, the skin oddly tight, the eyes deeply sunken and feverish. "Tonight," she spoke to the children, "when the sun sets, I'll make *blintzes* for you. I prepared it already. You'll like that Irving?"

They stood around the bed, except Irving, who rested his head on his grandmother's chest. He nodded. "Only don't fill the pages with cheese."

It had become a ritual of deception, a chief joy, for Mrs. Perlin to start making *blintzes* and leave the cooling outer covering on a plate at the edge of the stove. Her grandchildren would take them, while she turned away, as quickly as they came from the skillet, hold them suspended on a finger, and then stuff them into their mouths. "How can I stuff the pages," she would say, "if you keep eating them? I'll have to waste the cheese now." No one had ever seen evidence of the cheese filling.

"Later I'll make them and you'll have my coffee with *matzo*. Yes? You'll like that?"

"Go find Rose and Charlie, boys." Ellie moved them away from her mother. "They'll be outside. Play nicely. No going away." Instantly acting upon the suggestion, the boys were already out of the apartment.

Mrs. Perlin pulled Evelyn to a position alongside the bed. "Every time you're bigger. And the curls. So beautiful. You dasn't let her cut them, Ellie."

"She'll have to soon, Ma," said Clara. "It's too much trouble. I had the same problem." Instinctively Clara patted her hair. It was no longer blond or long. Streaks of brown covered its brightness. In other ways, Clara had remained the same. She was pleasantly stuffed, not fat, but ample, in the way that, as a child, had always made her pinchable.

"Have you seen the doctor recently, Ma?" That too was a deception. Ellie hoped her mother would relent. But since Mr. Perlin's death, no doctor was allowed into the apartment.

"Who needs a doctor. When my children and grandchildren come, I feel fine."

"And Mollie? How's she?"

"How should she be? The same. Tonight she's going to Toby and Leon." Mrs. Perlin turned toward the window and smoothed, with a regular, weak motion, the unused portion of the bed. "We'll go to the cemetery before *Pesach?*"

"Sure Mama." Ellie watched her mother's hand moving across the bedspread. Outside, the clothesline hung free on this Saturday morning, and in the background, away from the shadowed courtyard the backs of buildings reflected the brilliant March sunlight. On the dressing table opposite the bed stood the gallery: Ellie and Morrie; Toby and Leon; Clara and Simon; a double frame of Harry, taken when he was *bar-mitzvahed*, in *tallith* and skull cap, and Mr. Perlin, smiling, just before he died. Atop the night table were the grandchildren: five pictures. This was Mrs. Perlin's world: the pictures, the memories. How often, thought Ellie, did she shuffle through the record of events, relive what only had life because she, only she, now, knew that all her memories had happened? How often did Mollie stand before her mother, alone, a reminder that there was one thing she had not accomplished, would probably never accomplish. Ellie listened to the talk of her mother, her daughter, her sister, continued to gaze around the room, out of the window, knew that being inside this room, with the pictures, the bed, the familiar smell from the kitchen, there seemed little use for a future which ended, always in another photograph. And in the other bedroom, where Mollie now slept alone, the empty beds were enough to retrieve, all too vividly, the family as it had been. The inhabitants had left, but nothing, no physical part of it, had been changed. Ellie tried never to enter that room.

". . . no, Grandma, but all the other girls wear it. That's what I told her. Don't you think I'm old enough?" Evelyn looked fearfully at her mother.

"She's the boss, darling." Mrs. Perlin twirled Evelyn's curls. "You don't want her to, Ellie?"

"No. It's not necessary."

"Don't be so old-fashioned," said Clara, reverting to her role of interfering sister. "Even Rosie wants some already."

"You dasn't let her." Mrs. Perlin's sternness flickered briefly, dissolved.

Clara laughed. "I'm just kidding, Ma."

"I hope so," said Ellie. "Evelyn, go get your brothers and cousins. We'll have lunch."

"But Ma? Can't I please get some lipstick?"

"We're not going to discuss it now. Just do what I asked you to do."

"You never want to discuss anything," mumbled Evelyn as she left the room. "Never," she shouted, leaving the apartment.

FINALLY, they all did manage to fit into Simon's La Salle. Morrie, who decided to surprise everyone by going to his mother-in-law's, had David on his lap, in front, next to Clara and Simon; Ellie was in the back with the four children.

They drove up Canal Street toward the Holland Tunnel. Only when they reached the entrance to the tunnel did the traffic slow down, crawl forward, stop. Car horns honked impatiently. Simon remained calm, squeezing closer to the toll booth, while Morrie's head bobbed back and forth, directing the strategy of getting into the proper lane. "What they need is another set of tubes. Dumb fools. They never realize what the future's going to be like." He extended toll money to Simon. "Go ahead. Take it."

"I got it, Morrie." He nudged Clara to get some change. She fumbled with her purse while Morrie forced the coins onto her lap.

"Come on. Take it. What's the difference. It's your turn already." Morrie pointed impatiently forward.

"Why do you have to pay money to go underneath the water?" David asked his father.

"Because they have to keep fixing the leaks in the tunnel."

"Leaks?" David's freckled face registered horror. Morrie laughed. In the back, Irving joined him.

They moved into the opening of the tunnel.

"Does the house have a good basement, Clara?" All afternoon Ellie had been trying to talk about the house, but each time she did, Morrie had changed the subject. Now, with everyone squeezed into the car, she might get her way.

"Tremendous one, El. The kids could have it for playing with lots of room left over."

"Mama says," Rose said proudly, "that I can even have my own room, and Charlie too."

"That's right, Honey," Simon smiled happily. "It really is a buy, Morrie."

"Where's it located exactly?" Morrie's angry tone told Ellie that he was ready to defeat her scheme.

"Not far from where we are now in Jersey City. But now I'll have to get a bus to work."

"It's not a long ride though." Clara placed her arm behind Simon's neck.

"It's got a backyard," Simon continued. Charlie and Rose leaned forward, put their hands on their parents' shoulders.

"It's none of my business," Morrie broke the mood of optimism, "but where in hell does a shoe salesman get that kind of money?"

"It ain't going to be easy, I can assure you. My father's giving me some. I got some saved. I'd rather have it hard in my own house than an apartment. Why should I make my landlord richer?"

"There'll be plenty of headaches taking care of it." Morrie shook his head disapprovingly.

"I guess so, but my family's going to enjoy it." Simon turned his head slightly, smiled at Clara.

"Couldn't you convince Morrie of that?" Ellie spoke quietly. She heard Morrie's grumbling, "Here we go again." "He's afraid we'll starve or he'll lose his job or the world'll collapse tomorrow."

Ellie's challenge remained unanswered. They drove on in silence, reached Hudson Boulevard, turned left toward Journal Square. The newly planted bare trees that lined the center island of the boulevard swayed under the pressure of a gusty, shifting March wind. In the spaciousness of the square, newspapers sailed into the glowing darkness above the street lights. A long line of people waited outside the Loew's Jersey City. Red and green neon flashed dazzlingly. Waiting busses started, moved with them out of the square, on to the extension of the Boulevard toward Bayonne. Soon the lights were gone. The car passed long stretches of empty lots and small parks. In the distance, off to the right, Newark Bay, a dark clot, was visible. The children were quiet. The low whir of the car's motor sounded distant, muted by the wind.

They crossed the city line into Bayonne. Here, the older trees lining either side of the broad avenue blocked the view of the bay. "I'm afraid we're going to be moving out of all this soon." Morrie sighed the words mournfully.

"Morrie! Not now. Please!" Ellie leaned forward.

"What's the difference. Might as well let everyone know. It's definite." Now his voice boomed proudly. "I'll be taking over in the beginning of July. We'll have to move sometime in June."

"What's happening?" Simon seemed to slow the car.

"They're transferring me to the Brooklyn branch. Better job. The first Jew in my company to get such a job."

"You mean we're going to move to Brooklyn?" Evelyn sounded agonized.

"That's right."

"Where's Brooklyn?" David turned his head to look into his father's face. "Where, Daddy?"

Morrie tousled his son's soft brown hair, squeezed him against his chest. "Very far. Across two rivers."

"Farther than Bubby's hotel in the country?" David referred to his other grandmother as if that was the only way he could measure distance.

"No. Not that far, though it might just as well be."

Ellie remained silent, listening to the questions, Clara's congratulations, bitterly aware that once again Morrie had outmaneuvered her. Irving, who had been sleeping with his head on her lap, woke up as her hand brushed across his hair. "We home, Ma?"

"No. Very soon. Sit up . . . Charlie, move over a little bit . . . Rose, wake Charlie up . . . Evelyn, stop pouting. Brooklyn's not the end of the world."

"It is for me."

"What's she talking about, Ma?" Irving asked.

"We're going to move."

"Will I still have to go to Hebrew School when we move?" Even Evelyn found herself joining the others in laughter.

"You'll go until you're *bar-mitzvahed* even if we live in China." She pinched his cheeks lovingly.

"Seems like now would be the perfect time to buy a house too," said Simon. Clara nodded in agreement.

"What are you, my wife's henchmen? That's all she's bellyachin' about since I told her."

"She's right." Clara looked at him defiantly. "You can afford it for sure now. You'll get a raise."

"And how do you know? You know what I have in the bank?"

"You worked right through the depression. How many people can say that? And your job's steady now."

"Steady my foot. They could fire me tomorrow." Morrie pushed David to a sitting position.

"You think my husband's sane?"

"You just shut up, Ellie. I know what's going on and you don't. You'll never know with your great East Side education."

"Of course. That's the only thing your brilliant mind knows how to say." Ellie's rage exploded. "But one thing my dumb mind knows is that you're afraid of everything. That's what you are. A house, owning anything's too much for you." Morrie raised his voice louder in warning, but Ellie could not stop now. "Why can't you give something to your children before it's too late?"

David looked past Morrie's shoulder toward his mother, frightened. Irving sat up, leaned to the side, ready to guard himself if his father turned around. Evelyn held onto her mother's arm as if she wanted to pull her out of danger.

But once again Morrie let her win. "I don't want to say another word about it. I've got too many other things to worry about."

They drove on, tensely silent. Ellie's determination on this issue was fixed, settled. Regardless of the consequences, she was going to fight him. Let him holler all he wants. I've lost for the last time.

The car stopped. They were home.

"You'll have coffee and cake," Ellie commanded, even as Clara nodded 'no.' "You'll stay for a while."

Morrie walked rapidly up the steps to the front door, pulling David with him.

Ellie grabbed for Clara's arm. "Don't go yet."

And for her sister's sake, Clara relented. "Simon, we'll stay for a while."

Ellie sat up in bed as quietly as possible, not that she was afraid of waking Morrie. He was snoring, lying on his back. She listened to the night noises comforted by the knowledge that the cold water in the kitchen always dripped no matter how many times she tried to fix the washer or that the bathroom commode would gurgle forever unless it was replaced. The wind rattled that loose pane in the front room. Ellie pulled the quilt up to her neck. Relax.

For a few hours relax. There never seemed to be a time during the day when that was possible. Don't people ever have a time when absolutely nothing bothers them? When, for a minute, they say everything's fine? She watched the glowing second hand of the electric clock revolving. Her eyes grew heavy, as if she were being hypnotized. Suddenly Morrie turned on his side; the snoring stopped. She held her breath, hoping that he wouldn't awaken.

Slowly, the breathing resumed its regularity, the snore returned, muffled now by the pillow. She gazed toward the window, wishing that the darkness would remain forever. This precious privacy to use for herself, to think with, of what she had, of what she wanted. Would a house really help? And if Morrie worked to get his mother's hotel . . . nothing! It was all the same. In the end, nothing. What she wanted to feel, openly, she buried, sifting it down with the flour in her cakes, dousing it in pails of water for the floors. She lowered herself beneath the quilt, closed her eyes, waited for sleep. The house I'll get. Just that.

On his back again, Morrie was snoring loudly. He gets promoted and he sleeps. Ellie tried to push him on his side. He wouldn't budge. His predictions come true. He told my father and it's true. The big success . . .

Ellie felt her head spinning, the way it had at the sink, the night before. Get sick. That's one way out of it. Be sick—and tired. She twisted her gold wedding band until it cut into the skin. She cried, not wanting to. 1937. And she was thirty-seven years old. As old as the century with nothing to feel good about. Nothing, except the children.

CHAPTER *Eight*

THEY MADE MANY TRIPS to Brooklyn looking for a place to live and each time they returned home angry, sullen, neither able to convince the other of his point of view. Morrie kept finding out about solid two-family houses in good Jewish areas that could be rented at a sensible rate. He had a friend at the plant who put his money in property, "You know Louis Kriegel, El? Well, anyway he knows about all this and he says it's crazy to buy a private house now. Building is lousy and the houses are too expensive. You have to be out of your mind, he says."

"None of those things stopped him from buying. Why is that?"

"Ellie, once and for all, we can't buy. Not now."

"Why? Why can't we? You never convince me and until I am I'm not raising a finger to help you."

They were coming off the Manhattan Bridge, moving onto Flatbush Avenue Extension. The shiny black company car which Morrie used for these scouting trips passed the Fabian Fox theatre, the colorful shops, the tall buildings, the downtown of Brooklyn which seemed too much like the center of any big city to be credited with distinction. Yet, Ellie, watching intently, saw light and not the drab, milk-gray of Jersey. Then there was Grand Army Plaza and the imitation Arc de Triomphe guarding the entrance to Prospect Park.

"There's a great zoo in there. The kids'll love it." Morrie tried to capture Ellie's hand but she swiftly moved it behind his head on the back of the seat, like a weapon held poised, ready for the remainder of the trip. They sped past churches, synagogues, new shopping areas, from one tree-lined street to another. Finally, Morrie stopped the car in front of a row of semidetached, new, two-family houses on Lenox Road. "This is it, El."

She followed him up the stone steps to the front door of the house second from the corner. Each of the other houses on that side of the street was the same: a porch fronting the downstairs windows, stone flower boxes filled with cemetery evergreens, brownish red brick façades. Between each set of houses was an alleyway.

A dark, crinkly-haired, big breasted woman met them at the door. "Howards? From Jersey?" Morrie nodded. "Kriegel said you'd come today. My name's Silver. Leah Silver. Come in," she motioned them past her without waiting for a response, "and I'll show you."

In the vestibule there were two, small-paned, glass doors, one of which, at the right, with the faces of two children peering through a gauzy curtain, led to Mrs. Silver's floor. The other, different only in the fact that it had no curtain yet, led up a flight of stairs. Mrs. Silver lunged ahead, grunting as she ascended, her words, like a shrill whistle, directing them to follow, "We bought this house last year. Just went up. It's sturdy. Very good. A good neighborhood. Nice people. This side of the street's all Jewish. The shopping's easy, Mrs. Howard. This part of Brooklyn's just beginning to grow. Used to be swamp, East Flatbush, like Canarsie, but now . . ." Ellie's determination to reject the house, regardless of its merit, now had a focus.

But the house was—she couldn't deny it—a good one. The living room, in the front, was very large, with two windows providing an excellent view of the street. The Silvers had obviously just planted a tree in front of the house which just reached the second floor level. The dining room was almost as big as the front room and had three windows looking out onto the sister house across the alleyway. Off the dining room was a small bedroom with one window. Good for Evelyn. Ellie registered the fact even as her silent opposition grew with each word from Mrs. Silver.

"Kitchen's beautiful. All new equipment. Two windows. And another feature's this dinette. You can get a whole family around a big table. We always eat that way downstairs. The four of us. How many children you got, Mrs. Howard?"

Since Ellie did not answer, Morrie did. But Mrs. Silver was only momentarily surprised. Ellie turned away to inspect the fixtures in the kitchen. "This door's a small bathroom. Nothing fancy, just useful. Sink. Commode. At the other end of this corridor's the big bathroom with a stalled shower. A needle shower. Plenty of closets in the corridor." She opened each of the doors. "Lots of space. And the second bedroom. Two windows again on the alley. I keep twin beds in this one for the kids." They followed, examining the cedar-lined closets, measuring off space as if, by now, they were experts. At the end of the corridor, adjoining the bathroom, was the master bedroom. It was the back corner of the house and so had two exposures. It was huge. Again Ellie had to admit that it was larger and airier than any house they had seen before. No question about it. Surely hard to find a better one.

". . . and what's the rent?" Morrie interrupted Mrs. Silver's description, and for the first time since they had entered the house, she hesitated. She re-walked the length of the corridor, into the dinette, up to the new stove in the kitchen, brushed away an imaginary speck of dirt. This could save me, Ellie prayed. It'll be too high. Too high, please.

"Sixty-five dollars," Mrs. Silver said finally, adding quickly, "and that's plenty cheap for all you're getting here." She let the water run down the sink, pointed proudly to the drainage. She opened the refrigerator door, "Look inside that," closed it before they could look. "Too much room . . . and we have oil heat," indicating the radiator in front of the two kitchen windows. "The best. Nice and warm in winter, cool in summer. You can adjust them."

"Sixty-five's a lot of money." Morrie felt obliged to try and lower the amount. "We'll have to think about it."

"Better not think too long. Lots of people been here looking. I only held them off because you're a good friend of Kriegel. He helped us get this place. Good man."

"Well, I'll call your husband tomorrow morning and let him know."

"My husband won't be home. He's away. I take care of that kind of thing anyway. It's my house." Mrs. Silver led them down the stairs, ushered them out, nodded goodbye.

When they were pulling away from the curb, Ellie spoke, "I can tell that the answer's going to be yes."

"Well, it is a good place. You can't deny that."

"I don't deny it, but I still want a house. If Louis can help them get one why can't he . . ."

"Give in already. Give in on this one little thing." His impatience threatened to become attack. "We're going to settle this once and for all. This place is too good to miss."

As they drove, Ellie measured the futility of her dream against the injustice of Morrie's request, and she realized, as she had always realized, that being adamant would accomplish nothing. He would decide to do whatever he wanted to do. He would have his way, make her feel guilty for holding out. That was his justice. The pattern had become as hard as a rock. Her fingers were too frail to crush it. "All right." Her disgust was like nausea. "Rent it. Do what you want."

"Good girl!" He patted her knee. "I knew you'd come around to seeing it my way."

"I was only acting like a child," she tried irony, but Morrie had no time for that.

"We'll move at the end of May. That gives you a month to get ready. Plenty of time."

"Too much."

"Of course," Morrie was oblivious to any other emotion but his own satisfaction, "the kids'll have a tough time, changing schools so late in the year."

"Only Evelyn." Ellie resumed her mother role again. Anger, irony were pointless. The decision was made. "Maybe she'll stay with Fanny 'til the end of the year. She'd probably like that."

"Perhaps." Morrie's brightness now was expansive, easy. "I do have one surprise for you, El. A good one."

"A surprise? From you? That's a surprise in itself."

He refused to be dismayed. "We're going on a trip."

"To your mother's." She laughed. "The trip we take every summer. Some surprise."

"No, damn it. A real trip. My mother's staying with the kids and we're going to Canada."

He expected her to be pleased, but she was not. "We don't have money to buy a house but we do have it for a trip? Is that the way it goes?"

He pushed down on the accelerator and then had to apply the brakes quickly for a red light. "Go ahead. Spoil it. The whole thing, the way you always do."

"How can we move, take a trip, and go to your mother's for the summer? Answer that?" She didn't care how much she angered him. She wanted a small moment of revenge.

"If you want to, you do it, stupid."

"Thanks for the information. And you're so sure your mother will stay? You asked her already?"

"Yes, I asked her already. She said yes already."

"And of course you said nothing to me. Why should you! I'm only your wife."

"It was a surprise. Remember?"

"You surprised me all right."

They turned off Utica Avenue onto Eastern Parkway, heading back toward the bridge. The sun shone through the budding trees, checkered the asphalt with spots of brightness. Ellie wished it would rain, suddenly and forever. "Not once. Never will I get my way." She hadn't meant to say those words out loud.

"I thought you'd like the trip." Morrie's disappointment had, by now, softened his anger.

"I might have . . . And how are we going to go? Walk?"

"This car. The company's lending it."

"And you might as well let me know when you scheduled it for?"

"Right after we move."

"That'll be my present for working to get us moved. You're very thoughtful. A good husband who never remembers an anniversary but never forgets every other occasion."

"Very thoughtful. That's me. For example, you want to stop off and see your mother? We'll be going right near there?"

How wise he was. Each time he hurt you, he offered a gift. When he decided against buying his own car, and she argued about that, the next thing he does is tell her to buy a new dress, a coat, anything she wanted. Five minutes after he called her dirty names, he was crying. Sure, she admitted she was a child, but he was worse. At least she had some control. "Yes. I would like that very much. You can also take me out to lunch as long as you have the day off."

He hesitated, but finally nodded yes. She wasn't kidding now and he didn't want to fight anymore today.

Harry arrived early, before Morrie went to work. He was going to help with the moving since Morrie said he couldn't take another day off from work. "I've got to wind things up. I'll leave early, though, in time to help you set up."

"Of course," Ellie told him, "that's just your way to do it."

Ellie and Fanny supervised the removal of the more fragile items into the moving van. The boys, freed from school illegally, stayed close to to the house without being told to. Evelyn sulked. For her, the move represented an upheaval, the effects of which, she swore repeatedly, she would never be able to stand. She had been on the telephone continuously during the days prior to this all important one speaking with the girls from her club or the members of the Girl Scout troop she led. At least, since she would be staying with Fanny for the rest of the school year, she would be able to go on the final overnight hike sponsored by her troop. But, that would be the end of her leadership. She would never join a troop in Brooklyn, never start at the bottom again. Life would never be the same she told her uncle, sitting with him on the porch, watching the two movers trudging in and out of the house loaded with crates of dishes, pots and pans, linen, towels, the accumulation of fifteen years of married life. Soon the heavier furniture was on its way.

Morrie left for work, silently stealing away with only a nod for Harry and a quick kiss for Evelyn. It was to be his final day at the Jersey plant. He expected some kind of going away celebration.

Fanny, one hand curled under her breasts and the other cupping her cheek, watched, tears filling her eyes as the furniture which had filled the bottom part of her house for so long was carried out. Ellie pleaded with the men to "take care," "watch out for the door frames."

"Don't worry about my frames, darling. As long as you're happy where you're going. It's too far away, Brooklyn. I'll never get to see you." David came to stand near Fanny. Instinctively she smoothed down his hair. You should be a good boy, Davele. You'll come to see me all the time?"

"I will. I promise." He put his hands around her legs and hugged.

"Irving, get away from the truck. Next thing you know you'll be hurt," Ellie shouted as the mohair sofa came through the front door. "We'll really have to get a new living room set, Fanny. This one's taken an awful beating. . . . Evelyn, maybe you could help a little, please?"

Evelyn squirmed but did not leave her porch chair.

"Go ahead, Ev," Harry suggested. "You'll be sorry later if you don't do something."

"Never mind, Harry, Miss Independent will get hers later, all right." Ellie walked rapidly inside the house.

"Uncle Harry," Irving screamed from below, "can I ride in the truck instead of the car?"

"I don't think your mother will agree to that."

"If you asked her . . ."

"But I'm not going to. You ask for yourself. She's your mother."

"Uncle Harry?" David left the weeping Fanny and leaned against his uncle's chair. "Does it take very long to get to Brooklyn?"

"Not too long. Maybe an hour and a half."

"Will we go across a lot of bridges?"

"Some."

David stood in front of his sister. "I'm going to miss you. Mama says you have your own room there, and I'm going to sleep in it until you come for good. Is that all right?"

Evelyn's indifference dissolved instantly. Tears splashed onto the rosy fullness of her cheeks. She pulled her brother onto her lap. "Stay with me for awhile, Davie."

The beds were being removed from the house now, and an almost stifled wail issued from Fanny's trembling mouth. Ellie embraced her as much to comfort herself as Fanny. "It's not across the country you know. We'll be back and you have Evelyn to take care of."

"Where will I find tenants like you." She swayed back and forth. "Never. Never. I know it. It's impossible."

Ellie moved to the head of the wooden steps. "All right boys. Go to the bathroom. We'll be leaving in a little while. Harry, would you come check the house with me?"

A few cartons remained in the living room. All of the shades had been pulled down, and the rugs rolled and tied, waited to be removed. "Doesn't look like much now, does it El?"

"No. It doesn't. But, then again, it never was." She walked through the rooms, touching the walls or rubbing the floors to see if she had left them clean enough. "I worked so hard. I don't want Fanny to complain about anything."

"I seriously doubt that she would." He watched her go to the sink and stand before it, her hands resting on the faded metal spigots. She closed her eyes.

"You all right, Ellie?"

She didn't answer. Harry placed his hand on her shoulder, repeating the question softly.

"I'm all right. Just a little dizzy and a little sad."

"Let's go then." He tried to move her, but she resisted.

"In a minute. You go get the boys settled. Then send Evelyn in, please." She waited until he had left before she went into her empty bedroom. Only the deep impressions the bed's legs had made on the linoleum floor served as a reminder of the room's life. From far off she heard her sons' laughter, then Harry's shouted commands. And then the lifting, groaning sounds of the workmen as they shuffled across the bare floors. She shrugged her shoulders as if to tell the room that she was ending one thing only to begin another, for the years of giving in, of commitment to something far removed from love, were not finished, not yet. She sagged against the window sill, stared down at the ugly rose pattern of the linoleum. In the new place I'll definitely have a real rug. That's a promise, whether he wants one or not.

"Ma?" Evelyn stood in the doorway. Her call was soft, as if she understood that she should honor her mother's mood. Nor did Ellie respond immediately. "You wanted me, Ma? Uncle Harry said . . ."

"Yes." Ellie stared up at Evelyn dumbly, then walked to her. "Evelyn, I . . . I want you to know I understand how you feel. Believe me, I do. But there's nothing we could do about it. Your father had . . ."

Evelyn's lips trembled. She lowered her head.

"We just had to move. And it'll be less than a month. Before you know it we'll be going up to Bubby's and you'll be coming to Brooklyn every weekend."

"I can't come next weekend. I've got the hike."

"That's right. So we'll speak to you on the telephone. And you're not a baby, remember. You'll have your friends and your cousins. You like Edith and Sol. They'll take you to the movies . . ."

Evelyn walked the few paces that separated her from her mother. Ellie held her. Neither said a word. They stood together, crying quietly, Evelyn already taller than her mother. Then Harry's voice echoed through the empty house.

HARRY'S 1935 NASH pulled away from behind the moving van. Fanny and Evelyn waved from the porch, but Ellie kept her eyes forward. The boys, seated in the back, screamed with delight.

"Evelyn's waving, Ma," David shouted. "Wave to her, Ma. Go ahead and wave before we're far away."

"Just be quiet, David."

"But Ma . . ."

"We'll see her soon. Relax now."

Harry turned the lumbering car onto Hudson Boulevard. "The van will get there after us, but not too long after, I hope."

"I really appreciate your help. Your boss wasn't too angry, was he?"

"He didn't mind. He owed it to me. I wrote a great brief on the last case."

"I'm sure." Ellie turned to look at her sons. They were busy peering out the windows. "Of course I couldn't depend on my husband for any help. That's too much to expect."

"Well, El, remember it's the last day there for him, and there are things to do. You know how it is. And you'll be going away on that trip."

"You sound as if Morrie had taught you what to say." They both laughed easily and then lapsed into an observant silence as the car chugged comfortably up the boulevard. Bayonne was nothing Ellie minded leaving. Regardless of what Brooklyn had to offer, at least she would be closer to her own kind. All these years of living close to church bells had stiffened her resistance to those people. But now, with the promise of a synagogue close at hand and shops that sold the foods she wanted, she felt free to loathe the separation that she and the children had lived through. They could have friends now that didn't call them names. She could stop telling them, be proud that you're different.

The tunnel was not crowded and Canal Street offered no obstacle. Ellie felt disappointed. She did want an obstacle, something, not drastic, that would prevent their arrival. It would be pleasant to spend her life en route. Everything would be suspended, waiting, like in a dream.

They drove onto the Manhattan Bridge. "I told Mama I'd stop off on my way back. She's anxious to know how it turns out."

Ellie nodded approvingly.

The boys kneeled on the back seat, searching the retreating skyline. David clutched his brother's arm. "Could the car fall into the river, Uncle Harry?"

"Not if I'm a careful driver. I promise to stay away from the edges."

"We're in Brooklyn," David screamed as they left the bridge. "My first time in Brooklyn."

The morning grew hotter as they drove deeper into the borough. The excitement of the boys made them shift their window-watching posture constantly. There was so much to see. The stores and apartment houses were bigger than all of Bayonne put together. And then, suddenly there were stretches of empty lots with signs of new building about to begin. There were church spires and synagogues, trees and movie houses, stores and gas stations all tumbled together, squeezed between empty fields. The novelty of this newness was irresistible, and when they stopped in front of their new house, it too seemed to Ellie part of a beginning, a possibility.

"This is it, kids." Harry got out. "You're home." But they remained seated, reluctant to start what was too frightening to be called an adventure.

On the porch no one waved a greeting. Mrs. Silver, busily washing her windows hadn't seen them yet.

Ellie opened the door for the boys. "Come on now. You can't stay in the car forever."

"Mrs. Howard. So early." A wet rag in one hand, Mrs. Silver descended the porch steps. "So this is your family."

"My brother, Harry Perlin. My sons, Irving and David." The boys pulled Ellie's dress, embarrassed.

Harry extended his hand. "It's a good-looking house you have. Sturdy brick."

Mrs. Silver stuffed the wet rag into the front of her housedress, wiped her hand on it. "Pleased ta meet you." She let her gaze study Harry unashamedly. "You're right about the brick. The brick is what sold me. My husband wanted wood and shingles, and I said the three little pigs I'm not going to be. Just one of them, the smart one." She urged them up the steps. "I'll get your keys and you can go up and get settled down. When is your stuff coming? Soon?"

Ellie looked down the row of porches before she entered the house, saw other women in housedresses, standing, inspecting her family.

They trudged upstairs to another kind of emptiness. Mrs. Silver raced ahead checking each room for any signs of dirt. "I swept up but you know how it collects, the dust. The refrigerator's on so you can put things in right away. Around the corner, on Clarkson Avenue's the stores." With that, she opened the side entrance door in the dinette and started down the stairs. "I'll leave you to get acquainted." Ellie closed the door. The boys were exploring the other rooms with Harry. "It's quite a house," he called from the living room.

"It is," she shouted. Opening the refrigerator, a little light went on inside. Ellie felt thrilled by that alone. No more ice to buy. Unfortunately, there was nothing else inside. Mrs. Silver hadn't prepared a surprise banquet. But, the apartment did look clean. Everything neatly painted, and the parquet floors sparkling with fresh shellac. The radiators in each room glistened with aluminum paint. The sun streamed through the shadeless windows. A mounting feeling of joy, of pleasant expectation flushed Ellie's face as she moved from room to room, opening windows, letting in the fresh air, letting out the paint smell.

In the large bathroom the needle sprays in the stall shower captured her completely. She called for the boys, demonstrated the way it worked. "You turn these handles and water comes from the sides. And you turn these, and water comes from the top."

"What an invention and what a house, Ma," Irving screamed. "Are we going to get the front bedroom?"

"I told you already. That's going to be Evelyn's so don't try to get me to change my mind."

"Gee whiz! She always gets everything. Why can't we?" He stamped his foot definantly.

"Your room's right next to ours." Ellie motioned them down the corridor. "It's plenty big. We'll put twin beds up. That'll be something. You'll each have your own bed." Irving was satisfied and pushed on to a new discovery in the dining room. David walked to the front window and cautiously pressed his nose against the glass, watching. "There's lots of cars out there, Ma."

"Yes. You'll have to be careful the way you play. There's no more back yard remember. What time is it, Harry?"

"Almost twelve."

"What's happened to the truck, I wonder. It should be here by now." Ellie stood behind David at the window.

"It's not, Ma. I've been looking."

"How can we eat?" She pressed her palm against her cheek. "I don't have dishes. I never thought this would happen."

"You could borrow them, El." Harry pointed his thumb to the floor.

"No borrowing. Not the first thing borrowing."

"Well, let's go to some restaurant. I'll treat you all. Like a celebration."

"No sir. You can't afford that. We'll wait. The truck has to be here soon." Ellie wouldn't borrow from anyone, but she would have accepted help if Mrs. Silver had offered it. She made a mental note: her landlord was not going to be one of her great friends. And she couldn't let Harry take the children to eat. No. The first meal you must have in a new house when you move, regardless of what happens. That was a law she had inherited from Mrs. Perlin. "Let's all wait on the porch. It's too hot up here."

Mrs. Silver had finished washing her windows. Ellie noticed that they were badly streaked. She sat down on the stone division that separated this porch from the attached house. Harry lounged against the wooden entrance door, and the boys went off to explore the alleyway. "Don't go too far away," Ellie warned.

Across the street were private, one-family houses. They were not new. Their front gardens showed rich growth and purple, speckled irises lined the paths leading to their front doors. Although each house was different, each one had purple irises. "Those aren't Jewish homes." Ellie was emphatic.

"Now how can you tell that?" Harry tried to conceal his instant irritation by coughing loudly.

"I've lived among *goyim* long enough to be able to tell their houses."

"So have I. Remember? And frankly, I don't know what makes them so different. As far as I can tell they're doing as much living and dying as we are."

Ellie stared dumbly at her brother's attempted control, realizing that years of her father's training had made her words instinctive rather than thoughtful ones. Now, by saying what she had said, she was insulting her brother. His reflexes had been altered. The word *goyim* meant his wife. "I'm sorry Harry. I didn't mean to . . ."

"I realize that, El. I'm not angry. Being angry isn't the point. What's important is that you understand where the real difference exists. It's between me and . . . say Mama and the girls. I don't see things the way they do or Papa did. That way makes only trouble. And that's where the change has to take place. We're not living in Europe anymore. Don't you see that?"

"I do." His earnestness deserved that answer, but what he said she could not accept inside where his words sounded like a betrayal of their past, a past which she needed, even if he didn't, for nourishment, like someone needs to smoke.

"I agree that everyone's different, but it's not a question of being a Jew or gentile. It's more that they're just . . . well, they're different types of people. Like Martha's father for example. He painted his house a very strange color. He planted flowers in front of it. And Jews don't like flowers . . ." Suddenly, he laughed, realizing the circle he had talked himself into.

"Maybe you're right." Ellie brightened with his laughter, joined it without knowing why, but glad that he wasn't angry.

"Speaking of Martha, I better find a telephone and call her office. You can be alone for a few minutes, can't you El?"

"Don't be silly. Go ahead and call. Send my love." Waiting in the sunlight, Ellie watched a group of children advancing from the other end of the block. Lunch time from school. Gradually the group thinned as one or two at a time disappeared down alleyways. Finally, in front of Ellie there remained a boy and girl who looked up at her cautiously, uncertain of what they were to do or say, but obviously aware that Ellie represented the new tenant. "Hello. I'm Mrs. Howard."

"Hello." The little girl discarded the shyness that didn't match her fleshiness, her dark complexion. "My name is Carolyn. Do you have children?"

"Yes. Two boys and a girl."

Carolyn whirled gleefully. "My age? Is the girl my age?"

"I'm afraid not. She's older. But one of the boys is."

"Oh!" Her twisting stopped. Now the boy approached, slapped his sister's buttocks. "My name's Allan. Did you see my mother anywhere?"

"She's inside. Tell me, how much time do you have for lunch?"

"Half hour." Carolyn rang the entrance bell. Mrs. Silver appeared instantly, as if she had been listening nearby. "How many times have I told you to use the back door?" She pushed them inside. "Truck didn't come yet?" Ellie nodded. "You want me to call someone for you maybe?"

"No thanks. I'll just wait." The door closed hastily but Mrs. Silver's voice, yelling, continued to scold the children for their crime.

Ellie scanned the street, wiped perspiration from her forehead. It's going to be a scorcher. And still no truck. Something terrible's happened. The furniture's at the bottom of some river. "Irving? David?" They came running out of the alleyway.

"Ma, we met the kids," shouted Irving. "They came out of the side entrance."

David walked up the steps slowly. "What's the matter, Davie?" He placed his hand on Ellie's lap. "You feel all right? . . . Irving, stand at the corner and watch for Uncle Harry . . . David, what is it?"

"I'm hungry, Ma. I want to see Evelyn." Ellie brushed the hair from his eyes.

"We'll eat soon. Sit here with me."

"He's coming, Ma. He's carrying things."

"It's not necessary to scream, Irving. I can hear you."

Irving held his uncle's hand as they approached. "I got a few things, El."

Ellie smiled her gratefulness.

Upstairs, they sat on the floor and ate rolls and butter, and then Ellie managed to break open a cantaloupe. They munched it watermelon style.

"I'm going to have to go, El. I hate to leave you like this."

"We'll be fine."

"I do want to see Mama, and I've got to get back to the office. Martha's going to call the moving company."

"Don't worry, Harry. I'll call Morrie and he'll come home earlier."

He kissed Ellie, held her by the shoulders. "You'll like it here. You may never like your landlady, but the house's fine." He patted his munching nephews. "Be good boys now. Take care of your mother. I'll call you tomorrow."

Ellie kissed him again. "Don't tell Mama about this."

"I won't. Take care." He let his hand linger on her shoulder and Ellie accepted its pressure, silently thankful. It was like her father's touch, a remnant, changed, yes into a youthful hand but issuing from the same affection. Abruptly, he turned and raced down the stairs. In a few moments the Nash started up and then, gradually was lost in the sounds of traffic. The children gazed up at her. The empty house was frightening.

"The truck'll be here soon." She made them stand up, collect the gray speckled cantaloupe rind, wash their hands at the kitchen sink. "Come. We'll wait outside."

THE MOVING VAN ARRIVED AT 3:45. With it came the neighborhood children, home from school, and their mothers, standing on porches, inspecting the furniture as it was carried inside the house. Ellie stayed upstairs to direct the moving in. Twice the truck had broken down. They had tried to telephone her but the phone wasn't working yet. So what could they do? It's all in a day's work. Ellie nodded indulgently. From time to time she went to the front windows, frowned at the noisy, milling group that had collected. It was a show. A regular vaudeville performance. Mrs. Silver leaned against her tree, arms folded beneath her goiterish breasts, talking loudly, pointing to the pieces of furniture which were on display. The sidewalk was littered with cartons, and the children, unrestrained by the adults, were poking into them. Ellie shook with useless rage. These were *her* possessions being paraded before these women, some of whom would have to be her friends. For now she could only hate them. They had no right to do this. And there, in the middle of the melee, was David, trying unsuccessfully to hold his hands protectively over the cartons. Carolyn kept trying to help him, but each time she approached, he pushed her away. At first she couldn't find Irving, and then, further down the block, she saw him playing stoop ball with the boys, as if he had always lived here.

"Where does this mattress go, Mrs. Howard?"

"Put it anywhere. Anywhere at all." Then, redistributing her irritation, not wanting double work, she instructed the men to place it in the back bedroom. It was her mattress.

It took two hours to unload the truck. The house, by that time, was a confused jumble of half-opened cartons and crumpled pieces of paper. At first Ellie had tried to keep pace with the workmen. She had to give up that plan as she lingered over dishes, remembered wedding presents, pictures taken of the children and of herself. By the time Morrie arrived, the mountain of paper surrounding her, the chaos was beyond control. "Why couldn't you come earlier? Why?" She screamed. She cried hysterically.

"Don't start that."

"Twice the truck broke down. We were without everything all day long."

"I know. Martha called me. I . . ."

"You knew and you didn't come? Did you expect Harry to stay here all day?"

"I just couldn't, Ellie. Be reasonable. The president of the company wanted to see me. I couldn't say no to him, could I?"

"Of course not. But to me you can always say no." She brushed past him on her way to the kitchen. He followed, scanning the litter, stood behind her at the sink, not knowing what to do next.

"Did you at least see the boys outside?" She reached for a pile of dishes nearby. He quickly moved out of her way.

"Yes. They'll be up in a minute." He stopped her hand as it struggled with a load of dishes. "Ellie. Don't do this now. I'll take you all out to dinner and we'll just set the beds up tonight. How about it?"

"Set the beds up now," she ordered, "and then I'll go shopping for something and make supper here." She wrenched her hand free.

"For once do as I say. Don't be stubborn tonight?"

"No." She moved another load of dishes to a shelf above the sink. But she couldn't reach it. In confusion she turned to him for help. "Put these up on the top shelf."

He smiled. "You little shrimp." He placed the dishes where she directed him to. "Come on Ellie. Be a sport. You can't do everything in one night."

The boys, who had quietly entered during the exchange, stood alongside their father, hopefully waiting for her answer.

"Oh, all right. What's the difference. We'll go out to eat, but first we'll set up the beds. And we have to call Evelyn. When we go down, you'll call her, Morrie . . . Go wash yourselves, boys. I left towels out. And use hot water. Comb your hair." They raced down the corridor.

Morrie put his arms around her. Wearily she sagged against his chest. "You'll like the house? Won't you, El?"

"Yes. I'll like it." Her voice was muffled, flattened by the strain of the entire day.

"Come on. We'll set up our bed." He turned her, and they walked awkwardly down the corridor toward their room. The boys, looking out from the bathroom, giggled. It wasn't often they saw their mother and father so close together.

"I don't know where we'll eat around here, but we'll find a good place." Morrie kissed her before they entered the room. "You boys try to set up your beds. See if you can."

CHAPTER *Nine*

A WEEK WAS hardly enough time for Ellie to 'arrange' the new household and, at the same time, to prepare for her mother-in-law's staying with the children. Rushing to 'get done' had burned the edges of the hope that framed the prospect of a pleasurable trip. But the next morning they were to leave, finished or not. Finished she would be, and, as if to embroider the satisfaction of her accomplishment, Ellie had encouraged Mollie to come for dinner that evening and see the new house.

"It's a wonder," said Mrs. Howard at the dinner table, "how much is done. I don't know how." Reflexively, she started to clear the soup plates.

"No, Ma. I'll do that." Ellie forced her back into her seat. Mrs. Howard smiled benignly and shrugged her shoulders. She was not used to being served. "I'm like a queen, not doing a thing."

Mollie folded her arms across her chest, waited for the next course. "This house my mother's going to like."

"How is she feeling?" asked Mrs. Howard, rubbing her hand across the table cloth.

"Same as ever. Eats even less now."

"Still afraid to eat in her own house?" Morrie, pushing his soup plate in front of David's place, began his customary needling.

"That's right." Over the years, Mollie had fashioned her best protection against Morrie's little stabs: she reduced all communication with him to a minimum, never broadened the range of discussion. If she could have, she would have ignored him altogether.

"My mother's my mother." Ellie placed a platter of steaming pot roast on the table.

"Your mother's a religious fanatic." Morrie held up his plate for first service.

"Morrie!" Mrs. Howard shook her head, as if to apologize for her son.

"It's all right, Ma," said Ellie. "He just doesn't know any better."

Absorbed with eating, Morrie didn't react to the remark.

"Bubby?" David asked, "what's a fanatic?"

"Ask your father," Ellie interrupted. "You know how smart he is." But David said nothing, sensing that the word might be one of those his mother had cautioned him against using.

"I'm glad to see that at least one of my children has an inquiring mind." Morrie stopped eating. "He must take after me." David, unmoving, looked down at his plate. "A fanatic, Dave, is someone who doesn't know enough to give up stupid beliefs. Like your other grandmother."

"You certainly add to his intelligence by telling him that." Ellie glared at him. "Did you learn that from the *Saturday Evening Post?*"

"My brilliant one. What was the last thing you read?" Morrie's fork was poised midair. Everyone at the table, except Ellie, had stopped eating, waited. But she pierced her slab of meat calmly and said nothing. "What's wrong with that magazine, professor?" Morrie was going to insist on an answer.

"Nothing's wrong with it," suggested Mrs. Howard meekly. "Only eat, Morrie."

"Don't you interfere. My wife can talk plenty for herself." But Ellie's continued indifference roused his anger to new heights. "You've got nothing to say now?"

"Daddy," David began, fear softening his voice to a whisper, "after we eat would you show me on the atlas map how you're going to Canada tomorrow?"

Morrie's surprise made him, made all of them, smile. He nodded yes. The others sighed audibly. Even Mollie relaxed against the back of the chair. They proceeded with the rest of the meal in silence until Ellie, remembering, told Irving to place a call to Fanny. She turned to Mollie. "Evelyn's going on a hike tomorrow. We won't get her in the morning."

Ignored, Morrie reacted. "Don't tell me you're going to let your son telephone before *Shabbath* is over? Your mother wouldn't like that." He wagged his finger at her.

It was safe for Ellie to answer now. "With your training I don't have to worry that my children will grow up to be religious fanatics. That you can be sure of."

"Ellie," Mrs. Howard warned pleadingly. But Ellie knew all the danger signals by now. Morrie could control himself at this point and she couldn't resist picking at the corpse.

"Believe me, they'll be better off. They'll decide things for themselves. The orthodox Jew's a freak these days. He doesn't belong to this country or any country. You know that's true, Ma."

"I know only that people believe what they want." Mrs. Howard held up her hand. Don't fight with me, it said. "I think one way, another thinks another way. To me your mother-in-law is an exceptional woman."

"Who's arguing that? All I'm saying is you can't live in a modern world with old rules. You have to adapt. That's the way it goes."

"When you get older, maybe you'll understand that nothing's so different today." She picked at the table self-consciously.

"I understand right now. I know what's going on. In Germany. In Japan. I read, you know." He glanced quickly at Ellie; she didn't react.

"Mrs. Howard," Mollie began, "my mother's not bothering anybody. She's not forcing. She wants to be left alone. But now her fasting is too much. It's getting worse."

"She's stubborn," Morrie laughed, "like Ellie."

"Irving, go put in the call." Ellie started to clear the dishes and Irving dutifully left the table. From the kitchen the sound of the continued conversation was muted, otherworldly, like dreams that had suddenly become real as her mother-in-law told them of Jews banding together in Minsk, of the Cossacks beating and killing them, stories which Ellie had never heard from her own mother. But Budapest was different. Or perhaps her mother had decided never to tell them what it was like.

"Hello? Fanny? . . . Yes, it's Irving. How is everyone feeling?"

Ellie took the telephone from his hand, spoke to Fanny and Benny and finally Evelyn. Yes, they all missed her. Yes, they were ready for their trip. Morrie entered the kitchen and grabbed the phone from Ellie. Next it was Mrs. Howard's turn. ". . . when you come I'll make it for you . . . Aunt Lila is fine . . ."

"Can I speak to her, Ma?" David asked. Mrs. Howard was screaming into the mouthpiece.

"Yes, but only for a second." Ellie readied him next to her mother-in-law.

". . . Wait. Davie will speak to you."

"Hello. Evelyn? . . . I miss you." David extended the receiver to Morrie as if he were afraid to hold it any longer.

"Your brother's a man of few words . . . All right, now. Have a good time on the hike . . . Yes. We'll send you postcards . . . Aunt Mollie? . . . I'll tell her . . . Yes. Good night."

After the dinner dishes had been done, Ellie went to the master bedroom where, while the women watched, she packed. Morrie and his sons sat at the kitchen table while he explained the maps which had been given to him by the A.A.A.

"This is the line we'll take going out of New York. You see how it goes through this lake area? In blue here? I want to see that. They say it's beautiful."

"Who's they?" asked David. Irving, disinterested but afraid to break away, leaned back against his chair.

" 'They' are people who have been there before." Morrie waited for a further question, but David seemed content with the answer. "Probably we'll go to Niagara Falls and cross the border there. Your mother insists on seeing the Falls."

David left his seat and leaned against his father. "What's a border, Daddy?"

"It's the end of a country, stupid." Irving groaned with disgust.

"You don't have to sound like me, Irving." Morrie placed David on his lap. "He just wants to make sure. Anyway, I borrowed a camera from one of the drivers and I'll take a picture of each place we stop and you can see where we were . . . Hey, El," he called loudly, "how about some tea?"

"You just this minute finished eating." She appeared at the end of the corridor.

"So what. Let's have tea . . . Irving, put the kettle on and get the atlas from your bedroom." Irving moved quickly. This was his chance to escape into the living room where he could listen to the 'fights' on the radio.

"All right. Listen," Morrie warned him, "but keep it low." He began drawing a line on the map of the United States in the atlas. "We can keep a record of all the trips we take. Maybe next year we can go down here to Florida." His hand slid down the page. David watched. "And the year after that we'll go to Mexico and then California."

"Can we ever come?"

"No siree. When you get older, you can plan your own trips." Morrie twisted David's head and kissed him. "You'll get there. Don't worry."

By the time the kettle began to whistle, Mrs. Howard had joined them. Quickly, she readied the cups and saucers, rinsed the teapot. Morrie slammed the atlas shut. "I'm ready Ma."

Ellie and Mollie entered the kitchenette. "Your bath, David." Ellie beckoned with her finger. "Go start the water. I'll be in soon . . . Irving? Bath."

David kissed his father's cheek. "Yes, Ma." He ran down the corridor.

VERY EARLY the next morning, so early that only Mrs. Silver could watch the departure, Morrie carried the suitcases out to the car. Tensely, Mrs. Howard stood on the porch, hoping that no last minute fight would develop to cancel the trip. Irving and David leaned silently against the company car.

Ellie came out, shielding her eyes from the sunlight. Already it was too hot for what she wore. The black suit was not heavy, but it was black. And the red and white striped blouse with a flowing bow at her neck was itchy with perspiration. Yet, this was what she had planned to wear; this was the style for leave-taking. She couldn't convince Morrie to wear a suit and tie, but she was determined to look like a lady, hat included, a black pill box banded with the same fabric as her blouse. "It's easier for driving without all that garbage," Morrie had yelled that morning as he dressed. "I'm wearing this old sweater and a sport shirt, regardless, so don't bother me." And that was what he wore, a cardigan sweater his sister, Lila, had knitted for him when she was still in her giving years. "Who cares.

Do what you please." Silently now she descended the porch steps, walked awkwardly to the car, self-conscious of her outfit, placed, hurriedly, two bags of food and her white beaded pocketbook on the back seat.

"Just one more valise," Morrie said. "Everything'll go in the trunk."

"Have a good trip," Mrs. Silver called from the porch. Ellie waved her thank you. The boys stood next to the car door and Mrs. Howard joined them, waiting while Morrie settled the last valise in the trunk, slammed the lid, turned to his mother. "I don't think you'll need any more money, Ma, but if you do I left a check on the refrigerator and Mrs. Silver can tell you where to cash it."

"If anything should happen," Ellie stuck her head out of the car window, "to the boys or Evelyn, call my sisters. Their numbers are on a paper pinned to the wall over the telephone. Irving knows where." Ellie kissed each of the lowered heads. "Take care of Bubby. No fights and listen to what she says."

Mrs. Howard nodded continually. "They'll be good to Bubby. I'll take good care."

"Right, Ma." Morrie kissed them, moved them away from the car. "Let's go." He raced to the other side, got in, started the car. Ellie smiled nervously, waved to her sons. She was leaving them for the first time in her life. "Be good and listen to Bubby." The car began to move. "We'll write to you." She waved to Mrs. Silver, called Irving to the side of the slowly moving car. "Call Evelyn and see if her hike went all right."

Ellie could see them still waving as the car turned right at Utica Avenue.

MRS. HOWARD spent most of each day, while the boys were at school, preparing special dishes for them to eat. Toward the end of the week she got ready for Evelyn's arrival with *gefilte fish* and, her granddaughter's favorite, oatmeal and barley soup. The week had passed by uneventfully. Even Mrs. Silver couldn't dream up the slightest difficulty to report to the neighbors who waited eagerly to help, should there be any opportunity.

The boys played outside on the balmy June afternoons and worried the mailman until the first batch of post cards arrived.

For David, written in Morrie's rushed hand, was a card with the picture of a catwalk leading under Niagara Falls:

Irving read,

"*Dear David,*

Mother and I wrapped in raincoats walked here. Only your mother got wet. Be good. Love, Daddy."

Irving's card showed a view from the top of the Falls. Ellie had taken her time writing it:

"*Dear Irving,*

The weather is lovely. No rain at all. Tomorrow we shall cross into Canada. Take care of Bubby and David. Love, Mother.

Even Mrs. Howard received a card, written by Morrie, conveying the important fact that, so far, there had not been any arguments.

When Evelyn arrived late Friday afternoon, she read the cards sadly. None had come for her. "You absolutely certain, Bubby, that the boys didn't take my mail and hide it?"

"Maybe they mailed it to Fanny's?"

"Fanny didn't get one either." Evelyn walked into her new bedroom and fell onto the bed.

Mrs. Howard followed her. "One will come tomorrow. Maybe they thought you wouldn't be here until Saturday. No need to cry anyway." She loved Evelyn the way a grandmother must always love her first grandchild, especially a son's child. "Tomorrow for sure you'll get." Evelyn sat up, leaned against her grandmother. "I've got for supper all what you like. You set the table and we'll eat soon. Yes?"

Evelyn went to the kitchenette and between sighing and rubbing her swollen eyes began setting the table for four.

"Set for another two, darling. Aunt Lila and Max maybe'll be here in time."

"I hope so. I haven't seen them in such a long time." Evelyn got the extra plates. "Did you speak to any of my other aunts and uncles?"

"Everyone called. Even Mollie called for your grandmother. Toby and Leon may come later too."

"That'll be nice," said Evelyn without much enthusiasm.

"Darling, you'll go see if Irving's in front? I didn't have a time to get my *Forwards* this morning. I told Irving but he forgot." Mrs. Howard got her purse from the top of the refrigerator. "Give him money."

Evelyn walked through the house, enjoying, for the first time, the length of it. Looking out the window, she saw David on the porch playing 'War' with Carolyn Silver, but Irving was not around. She turned back, yelled, "I'm going down, Bub. I'll get the paper."

"All right, only come back soon. I'm warming the soup."

David and Carolyn were happy to join Evelyn on the search for Irving and the newspaper. "He's probably playing baseball on the Utica Avenue field," David informed his sister.

Carolyn took Evelyn's offered hand as they walked. "Are you older than my brother, Evelyn?"

"I don't know. I never saw your brother."

"Evelyn's older," David skipped in front, "she's going to graduate from high school."

Outside the candy store on the corner of Utica Avenue, a group of boys and girls lounged against the newsstand. Evelyn excused herself, tried unsuccessfully to unseat them.

"There aren't any papers here," one of the boys said, carefully patting the back of his hair as he spoke. "Yetta keeps the papers inside. The stand's for us to sit on." Each member of the group gazed at Evelyn. No one moved.

She stepped back with dignity, unruffled by their stares, started past them.

"You live in the neighborhood?" a tall, straight haired girl asked.

"We moved in last week." Evelyn spoke to the entire group.

"You live in the Silvers' house." The girl reached over and slapped Carolyn's behind. "I live down the block from you. My name's Harriet Goldstein."

"I'm Evelyn Howard." David yanked at her hand. "This is my brother David."

Harriet nodded. "Pleased to meet you." She waved her hand authoritatively. "I won't introduce all these kids. You'll meet them soon enough."

Nodding, smiling, she went into the dark coolness of the candy store.

Yetta, whose tawny hair was carefully arranged in tight ringlets and whose shortness was exaggerated by the long, white butcher's apron she wore, gave Evelyn the last *Forwards* she had. "You want I should save one for you every day?"

"Yes, please. Save one for the next week. My grandmother . . ."

"I know you don't read it," Yetta boomed with laughter, laughter which urged the same from everyone else sitting at the marble counter. "I'll save. Only remember to pick it up. There's no profit in this. It's a convenience."

Evelyn paid the money, collected David and Carolyn, who were rattling the gum machine, walked past the kids and started across Utica Avenue. They had to wait for a trolley car to rumble past, and before they could start again, a long line of cars turned into Lenox Road. "Don't ever cross this street yourself, David." She tried to sound like her mother.

Suddenly, David and Carolyn yanked hard at her hands. "Now." They raced safely across.

"This isn't Bayonne." Evelyn panted, enjoying everything about Brooklyn so far.

Irving was playing baseball, and only reluctantly did he leave the garbage strewn corner of left field to answer Evelyn's wave. The game was held up. Carolyn sprinted toward her brother at first base. Al slapped her affectionately with his mitt; she punched him, and then sprinted back.

"What the hell you want?" Irving remained a few steps from her.

"Why didn't you get the paper for Bubby?"

"Is that all? I just forgot." He began to dart away, but Evelyn managed to grab him. He tried to break her hold.

"I'll bet Bubby didn't forget what you wanted." He stopped struggling. "You better be home no later than fifteen minutes. Aunt Lila's coming." She let go; he dashed away, shouting, "Don't worry, I'll be there."

When they returned to the house, Max's car was parked in front. Evelyn forgot her dignity and raced down the alley with David.

Lila waited at the head of the stairs. Although a woman in her thirties, she always looked professionally older, as if she preferred it that way. Looking younger would come later, as a surprise. The hotel, or at least a part of it, which she had inherited from her father, and the headaches which had become hers as Morrie lost interest, had robbed her of the chance to be young. She was in business, and she might just as well look like a businesswoman. Without children, she and Max had devoted their affection, instead, to the proposition that the hotel could become a way of life that paid and also gave them plenty of free time in the winter. They maintained their dream even as bills mounted. And when they appeared willingly around the border of a family table, it usually meant one thing: they needed money.

"And where's the other?" asked Lila after kissing Evelyn and David.

"He'll be here soon." Evelyn extended the newspaper to Mrs. Howard.

"You'll put it please under my glasses?" indicating the top of the refrigerator where all odds and ends seemed to be ending up. She looked inside the oven, lowered the gas jet expertly. But being used to cooking for large quantities of people at the hotel, she worried over a small meal. "When Irving comes, we'll eat."

"What do you hear from your mother and father?" Max asked, already seated at the table. Evelyn knew this as politeness rather than interest. Mrs. Howard produced the post cards before Evelyn could answer.

"I've got to hand it to your brother, Lil." He glanced quickly at the cards and threw them down on the table. "He certainly must have some money stored away somewhere." Max's pudgy, but handsome face broke into an ironic, head shaking smile. "The whole country's starving and he goes on a trip."

"All the more credit to him," said Lila smugly, not so much defending her brother as baiting her husband.

"Credit? Why can't he invest some of it in the hotel?"

Mrs. Howard sighed. David went into the small bathroom, left the door open, let the water run as loudly as he could while he washed his hands.

"Not now, Max." Lila helped her mother carry fish to the table. "Evelyn, get the horseradish."

The bell rang and Irving appeared, dirty, but smiling.

"A man, Max. He's a regular man," said Lila, receiving Irving's kiss.

"Looks like Morrie. More like Morrie every time I see him." Max looked away, then down at the fish. "Let's eat."

During the meal, Lila and the children commended the food, but Max only nodded approval. His mother-in-law had learned to accept this grudging acceptance or rejection, the way a fly waits to be brushed from a plate of food.

"When are they coming home?" Max wiped his fingers fastidiously on a paper napkin.

"Another week." Mrs. Howard was stirring to clear the table.

"We'll have guests soon, you know." Max was now the boss, acting in his official capacity, as if he were the only one possessing foresight. "There'll be cooking to do."

"I'll do it until she gets back." Lila pushed her plate away. "Don't worry yourself too much."

"I understand my brother Leon will be here soon?" Max seldom addressed his mother-in-law directly, and she was never prepared for his attention. He waited impatiently. She nodded. "And is Toby coming too?"

"She's supposed to," David answered.

"We'll have to go to my mother's tonight, Lil. You and Toby don't have to." Max picked at his teeth with a match book cover, sucking loudly at his gums.

"Thank you." Lila shrugged her shoulders. "It's perfectly all right with me. Do as you please only don't make so much noise doing it." She helped with the dishes while Evelyn readied the tea cups. "Doesn't your mother ever want to see her daughter-in-laws?"

"My mother has more important things to worry about."

"Name one?" Even Irving had to laugh at his aunt's remark, but the others didn't. They expected battle.

"Nothing I would care to discuss with you at present."

"The only thing your mother has to worry about is what you tell her to worry about. Namely yourself." Now Lila laughed. She knew she was treading on touchy territory, but she also knew how to maintain a balance. When Max yelled, she yelled louder. Over the years, in that manner and because she had enormous reserves of strength, she had made her marriage prosper.

"I won't discuss it now."

"Yes, Doctor." Lila poured his tea. She had rubbed his sore spot.

"And with that now you can shut up? Yes?" Max did not so much question as command. Lila obeyed, but without the slightest trace of fear or anger. She had learned the method for silencing him, whenever she cared to use it. When Max, after three years of medical school had been forced to drop out because his father's money was whittled away by the depression, vanity became his only solace. He could have been something. It was his illusion and one which Lila usually nurtured. His years at college did, after all, represent an education. That had to stand for something. The hotel had become his prison, and, also, his only hope. If he loved his wife at all, it was because, unwittingly, she had given him another chance at self-respect. And she loved him because she knew he had been cheated by circumstances and not by lack of talent.

The unenthusiastic welcome given Toby, Mollie, and Leon set the mood for the remainder of the evening. Max displayed his characteristic melancholy moan, a trap which caused unsuspecting people to examine their gaiety, their contentment.

Mrs. Howard, now, acting in Ellie's place, honored Mollie's bitterness. She gave her tea and cake with ceremony and fuss. That was the only way of dealing with her properly.

Only Irving left the kitchen. Seated on Morrie's easy chair in the living room, he listened to the radio, removed from the bickering, turning up the radio's volume when they became too loud. Unlike his brother and sister, he remained neutral. He just wanted to be left alone.

Tea cups clattered, and the monotonous drone of conversation begun, in reality, months, years before, made this Friday evening only an extension of others. Max complained. Morrie was selfish. What did he care what happened to the hotel? Why the hell doesn't he sell out or turn over his control? He doesn't do anything to make it pay.

Leon's was the voice of justice. After all, Morrie had a family to be more concerned about. He had an important job. You can't do everything.

Since she had trained her husband well, Toby had little to say. Although they had tried and failed many times, no children served to deflect her energy. Instead, she had worked hard to put her words into Leon's mouth. And it was worth it. Her success was obvious. Her side of the entangled family was to be pitied. Ellie and Morrie had been used. All Max wanted from them was money. Toby always laughed when she reminded her brother-in-law that it was he who had introduced her to his brother. Did he regret the introduction? He never answered that question, but she knew how he felt. She had heard him say she was like a snake that didn't rattle a warning.

". . . but if you approached Morrie," Max was saying to Leon, "and told him you wanted to buy his share, I'll bet he'd do it."

"I don't need your kind of headaches. Besides, Ellie wouldn't let him. She's told you to your face already." Leon looked to his wife for approbation. Both she and Mollie were smiling.

"She'd do it for Toby." Max gave up easily.

"And who said Toby wants to be in the hotel business?" Toby remained smiling confidently.

"Please," warned Mrs. Howard, indicating her grandchildren. David and Evelyn were frowning, courageously angry, but forced to remain silent. Ellie had told them many times that they were never to interfere in these discussions.

"You stay out of this," Max pointed his well-manicured finger at Mrs. Howard.

"Stay out?" Color and control drained out of Mrs. Howard's expression of silent suffering. "It's not my hotel yet?"

"Not for long." Max's delight bloomed into a bright smile. He would dispose of her the way he did a smoked out cigarette, the way he had disposed of Lila's instinct to defend her mother. "I've got plans for the place," Max continued, "and if you're smart, Leon, you'll come along with me. You don't want to be a milkman all your life, do you?" Max leaned toward his brother as if to isolate him from any other influence. "You don't want Toby to go on working forever, do you?"

"Tonight you're trying a new approach." Toby placed her hand on Leon's arm. "But my advice to you is worry about your own welfare, not ours."

"I'm talking to my brother, so just butt out."

"In case you forgot, he's also my husband."

"How could I forget it."

"That's enough Max." Leon banged his teacup against the saucer. "And don't you say anything else, Toby."

"Max," Lila shook her head, "enough is enough."

"No," shouted Max, "it's not enough. That's the trouble. Nobody around here ever wants to stand up to Morrie."

"When have you ever?" And the anger with which Mollie asked the question, the truth which it told not only about Max but all of them, stopped him. Also, it roused Evelyn's adolescent indignation past control. She stood up suddenly, waved her arms in front of her uncle's face, screaming, "You don't have to sit in my father's house and talk that way about him." She grabbed David's hand and raced out of the room to her bedroom.

"See, Big Shot." Lila made a fist under her husband's chin. "I told you it was enough."

Mrs. Howard got up quietly, sighing with the accumulated stifled passion of her years, and went to comfort her grandchildren.

EVEN AT the Château Frontenac they came down to breakfast at an early hour. Nothing had awakened them. They just got up. It was their habit, and vacation was too short a period in which to change.

They stood nervously at the entrance to the huge dining room. Ellie pushed at the wisps of hair which had refused to stay underneath her white, wrap-around turban. Morrie shifted from foot to foot, impatiently waiting for the maître d'hôtel to recognize them.

Few people were eating and the stillness of the carpeted room was awesome. A coffee spoon clattered against the rim of a cup, or the rush of a waiter's foot on the carpet sent chills of discomfort down Ellie's spine.

Finally, under distant supervision, they advanced to a table for four near a window which looked down, far down, on the city of Quebec. This was to be their second day in the city and, after having climbed the steps of St. Anne de Beaupré the previous day, Ellie hoped it would be the last.

The glaring white of the table linen, the shine of the heavy, crested silverware did win grudging approval from Ellie. "At least it's clean enough to eat here. That I'm certain of."

"It's some hotel." Morrie stared excitedly out at the view. "A hell of a lot better than the place in Montreal."

The waiter came for their order, stood at attention, wrote quickly, and then asked, "And two coffees?"

"Only me. And one milk. You want milk, don't you, El?"

She nodded yes, embarrassed by the horrified look which the waiter directed toward her as he marched away. She inspected a teaspoon which had the escutcheon of the hotel stamped proudly on the handle. "Now here's something that would make a good souvenir for the kids."

"Take it," Morrie whispered, cautiously looking around to see if anyone had heard him. "They'll never miss it. They expect it."

"Don't be silly. I couldn't do that." She dropped the spoon as if it had suddenly burst into flames.

"Sure you can." Morrie picked it up. "Come on. Take it." But the more he urged her, the more reluctant she became.

When the food arrived, Ellie placed her beaded pocketbook on her lap and the huge napkin over it.

The dining room slowly began to fill up with people who reminded them very much of themselves. They would wait at the entrance, overwhelmed by the size of the room, advance shyly, only when directed to. Seldom were the sounds of comfortable conversation heard. The room commanded one to be still or to whisper. Only the waiters looked as if they had a right to be there.

"Remember, Morrie, when you write to the kids today make sure you send a card to Evelyn. Maybe of the hotel. We should have some memento." As she spoke she let the teaspoon fall onto her napkin and then, when she was sure no one was looking, slipped it into her purse.

"Will there be anything else, sir?" The waiter stood beside Morrie, materializing out of the air, and Ellie was certain he had seen her action. It would be just her kind of luck to be caught. Everybody is always doing this kind of thing, but she'd be caught. And she couldn't hurry Morrie with his coffee. He wanted to smoke a cigarette and look at the view. The waiter's gaze from nearby burned the back of her neck, or was it just perspiration; repeatedly she wiped her mouth with the napkin, shaking it so that anyone could see there was nothing inside it. "Let's go, Morrie."

"I'm not finished yet." He motioned for the waiter to bring more coffee, lit another cigarette.

Ellie imagined her mother saying, "Thou dasn't steal."

". . . and then we'll only be able to spend one night in Nova Scotia because . . . Ellie? Are you listening to me? . . . What's the matter?"

"Nothing. Only I wish you'd hurry."

"Relax. Enjoy the view. As I said, a night and day in Nova Scotia and then we'll head back for New England. Damn it, the time goes so fast."

"Not always."

"Oh come on. You're having a good time, aren't you?"

"Wonderful. Just wonderful." In spite of her anxiety she began to smile and then laugh, softly.

"What's so funny?" Morrie looked around to discover the reason for laughter.

"It's nothing, Morrie. Nothing at all."

Finally, they moved away from the table. The waiter's eyes followed them out of the dining room, of that Ellie was certain without turning around to check. They walked quickly into the elevator opposite the dining room.

When the door to their room was carefully closed behind them, Ellie sat down on the unmade bed and wordlessly removed the teaspoon from her pocketbook, holding it in front of Morrie's puzzled face. She laughed. "My mother should see me with this in my hand."

"Don't worry about *that*." Morrie produced another spoon from his jacket pocket.

The two of them tumbled onto the bed, laughing uncontollably. Ellie poked Morrie. She couldn't breathe. But each time he let her up, her laughter exploded with fresh strength.

"What's more," gasped Morrie, squeezing Ellie between his arms, "we're going to take some towels."

"No," she panted, struggling to sit up, "we can't."

"Yes we can." He pushed her back on the bed and roughly pulled at her turban.

"Morrie, no," she said, her laughter instantly subsiding.

"Oh yes we can."

Evelyn did finally receive a post card from her parents. It showed a huge, castle-like hotel, old, brown, and frightening. Her high school French allowed her to pronounce the name with appropriate ceremony, impressing even Irving. The card assured Evelyn that she was being missed, that she would have especially enjoyed the French type city of Quebec. She forgot about crying, and by the time that her Aunt Clara and Uncle Simon picked her up on Sunday afternoon in Brooklyn, she had decided that she was very glad that soon she would never have to go back to Bayonne. She had made further contact with the girls on the block and realized that she would care for them well enough. She might be younger than they were in years, but somehow, she felt miles older. After all, she was graduating from high school already and they weren't. And riding through the outskirts of Bayonne, she suddenly sensed why the days of the Girl Scouts had to come to an end. There just were too many other things to do. She was surprised that she felt no terrible sadness; instead, she was anxious to take on the future as part of a new regime. She loved that word. Regime. It fit perfectly. This was revolution and there was going to be a new regime. She wanted to organize her life like a master plan. Each year would be something new, leading her closer and closer to . . . goals. That's the problem. The goals. How was anyone sure what they would be. But, catching sight of Newark Bay sparkling in the last rays of the sunlight, she didn't doubt that they would present themselves in time. That's all you had to be patient about. There was plenty of time. Maybe she'd train for teaching; she loved children, most of them anyway; or a nurse. . . . The trouble was that her parents just never seemed to listen when she talked about the future; you'd think they were afraid of it, or something. "Only be what you want to be," her mother would say, "as long as you're happy. You'll know what to decide." And her father never wanted to believe that she was ready to plan. He always rambled on about Dale Carnegie's course about winning friends, and then lapsed into an explanation of how he had progressed because he knew how to influence people. Yes, he was right about himself; she couldn't deny that. But it's different for her. When her lipstick crusade had dwindled to nothing, Evelyn had accepted it as a fact of life that her parents should never be consulted about anything. Only she could decide whether what she wanted to do was right or wrong. Lipstick and dating—not smoking; that she never wanted to try—were her own problems and she could solve them. The first thing she would have to do as part of her new regime was to have her baby curls cut. They were finished. The money her father had left for her would pay for that . . .

She was ready to scream with excitement and expectation when she jumped out of Simon's car. She touched her dimples, suddenly aware that they had a power to help her get whatever she might want from the future.

Fanny waved from her upstairs window as Evelyn bounced up the steps, her curls bobbing an accompaniment.

DURING THE WEEK that followed, Mrs. Howard relaxed into a joyous routine. Just 'doing' made her feel younger, and she treated the boys as if they were her own children. She let them stay up later at night to hear the radio programs they never listened to when Ellie was home, and they repaid her with a simple, natural affection. Irving made sure he picked up the paper. David always cleared the table and even tried to do the dishes. She forgot about the hard summer that waited for her, the hours of standing on her feet in front of the enormous stoves, work that made it possible to have a place to live. The deaths she had lived through made it a necessity.

Now, sitting on the porch in the warm afternoon sun, the paper on her lap, eyeglasses slipping down her narrow nose, she experienced a sense of calm, watching the trees move in the wispy breeze. The grief that she had known for so long, the grief that she had wrapped in hard work at the bottom of all her other thoughts, felt remote, like a peacefully accepted reminder that, sure, she had lived and, of course, she would have to die. But, for right now, it was far away, on the circle, the outside rim of all that she had ever known, or experienced, or read about. The beginning, the end, but the same place, her hereafter. That she was sure of too. She picked up her paper quickly. Mrs. Silver had come to the front door.

"You need anything, Mrs. Howard? I'm going shopping."

"I was this morning around the corner." Mrs. Howard looked up from the paper, smiled politely. "Thanks just the same." As she feared, Mrs. Silver came to sit down on the chair next to hers.

"I noticed when the mailman came you had a card from your son. They're having a good time?"

"Wonderful."

"When they coming home?"

"On Saturday." Mrs. Howard did not immediately drop her paper. She hated *yentas* even though Mrs. Silver was the harmless kind. But she wanted her afternoon, before the boys came home from school, to be private, spent doing the nothing she planned.

"Time flies. It's just like they just went away and oops they're home again." Mrs. Silver settled more comfortably into her chair. "I don't know how you do your work so quickly. With me, before I turn around it's the afternoon."

Mrs. Howard nodded as if to say, '*Nu*, that's life. What can you do.'

"I understand you own a hotel in the Catskills?"

"My children and I, we do. A small hotel."

"Must be plenty hard work during the summer, I'll bet." Mrs. Silver was readying herself for further information. She smoothed the front of her cotton housedress, placed her purse on the ground.

"Sure it's hard work, but with good help it's not so bad." Mrs. Howard folded her paper. "My son-in-law Max, my daughter Lila's husband, he manages good. It's no money, but it's good to own something."

"You have two children, Mrs. Howard?"

"Now, two. Another son and daughter died years ago." She would not be left alone. That was certain. She removed her glasses, refolded her newspaper.

"They died when they were very young?"

"Not so young. First the boy drowned when he was nineteen. He just started night college, and the girl died a few months later from tuberculosis. She was sixteen." Mrs. Howard's expression remained placid, unmarked by the strain of these memories. Mrs. Silver's large breasts heaved in commiseration.

"Such troubles we have. It's terrible."

Now Mrs. Howard went on with her story, sensing that after Mrs. Silver regained her control the story would have to be told anyway so why prolong the waiting. "We bought the hotel for the girl. The doctor said fresh air and sunshine. Healthy food. So what could help in those years? He said mountains. We went to the Catskills. She died in my arms. She was resting on a cot under a tree—the tree is still on the hotel grounds. She called me. I was inside and I went to her and she said, 'Thank you, Mama,' and she died. Just like that." Mrs. Howard tried to snap her fingers, but there was no sound. "My granddaughter Evelyn is named after her." She paused, remembering, and without waiting for a show of pity from Mrs. Silver, went on with the next part of her story. "So we just stayed in the country anyway. It was better there. Like a farm in the old country. For my son, Morrie, it was hard. He stayed in Bayonne. The country was not good enough for him. But my husband and my youngest, Lila, were fine there."

"Your husband's still alive?"

"No. He died when Davie was born. We had the *brith* at the hotel, and a month later he died."

Mrs. Silver averted her gaze from the stolid mask of the old lady's face. "I'm sorry I brought it all up. I didn't think . . ."

"It's nothing to be sorry for. Don't worry. It happened. What can anyone do? Nothing. Thank God I have my grandchildren and the hotel."

"And such good children they are." Mrs. Silver was glad to change the topic. "You never hear them." She stood up. "You sure you don't need anything at the store?"

Mrs. Howard replaced her glasses. "No thanks."

"You got today's paper?"

"Irving will bring it home from school. This is still yesterday's."

"You certainly read all of it." Mrs. Silver started down the steps. "If you need anything be sure to let me know."

It would be minutes before she could start reading again. Memories, no matter how old, had to be put back where they belonged. Deep they had to be buried. That took time and the mood of pleasure which began the afternoon had already been disturbed. She removed her glasses once more, wiped them on the flap of her housedress, played with the tidy bun of hair that was slipping onto her neck. But no matter how she tried to prevent them, the hot tears did splash from her eyes. She folded her hands in her lap; the thin gold band on her finger glistened through the tears. Occasionally her shoulders would fall forward, yielding to the will of a sob. "*Liebe gutt*," she moaned.

From down the block she heard the noise of children. The tears stopped. She sat up straight, wiped her eyes with an old napkin she found stuffed into her apron pocket.

"Bubby? Bubby?" David called as he ran up the steps.

"Here, Darling. Here Davidel."

THEY KNEW THE DAY but not the exact time Ellie and Morrie would arrive home. David was on the porch at 8:30 A.M. and before long Evelyn joined him. No one else was outside yet. They could hear Mrs. Silver cleaning her Venetian blinds. She grabbed the bottom and shook them to unsettle the dust. Since it was Saturday, she was a little late getting started.

The sun was still comfortably warm; the haze had not yet settled into sticky heat. "They won't come this early, will they, Ev?" He knew the answer, but he was young enough to expect miracles.

Evelyn smiled, nervously pulling at her short hair. Her mother, like Fanny and her grandmother, would never approve. She dreaded the home-coming. No regime in the world was strong enough to prevent her from being afraid of what her mother might say. "I doubt that they'll be early, but you never can tell."

"It's not too far from New London, is it?"

"Far enough."

"I bet they get here earlier than you think." David was determined.

"Don't get your hopes up too high. Remember they're visiting Uncle Solomon, and you can't leave too early when you're visiting."

His head bowed under the force of that truth, then bobbed up defiantly. "Well, even so, it's not so far."

"Okay. Have it your way. Sit here and wait all day." She stood up, annoyed. "I'm going upstairs to help Bubby straighten up. Mama'll think the house's a mess."

"Fix it good."

David moved to the bottom of the stone steps for a better view of the street. From the alleyway the sounds of Mrs. Silver's banging blinds got louder and louder, the way a summer thunder storm does.

"Leah," called Mrs. Rosenberg who lived across the alley from the Silvers. "It's too early for that noise. Stop already." But Mrs. Silver continued. It was Mrs. Rosenberg whom she particularly wanted to bother. They had had a mah jongg fight. David knew it because all the women on the block were talking about the things they called each other. When the banging finally stopped, Mrs. Rosenberg got the radio treatment. Mrs. Silver turned it on full blast in front of an opened window.

Across the street, on the gentile side, shades were down. They would remain that way all day if the heat became unbearable. David wondered if the house did stay cooler that way. A woman came out and poked around in her little front garden. When she went inside she carried a bunch of pink roses. Then Mrs. O'Neil—everyone called her nuts—clanged her empty garbage can back from the curb and placed it underneath the entrance steps to her house. She turned to look at David before she slammed her door so loud it drowned out Mrs. Silver's radio. David hoped his ball never went into her garden.

A solitary sanitation man, pushing his squeaky wagon, appeared at the corner. He brushed bits of paper and piles of burned out punks down the sewer, and continued the motion of the steel bristled broom past it, along the curb in front of David. Then he stopped, went back for his portable garbage can and slowly made his way along the curb to the other end of the block, first brushing, then moving his wagon to collect the small pile of dirt; brushing again, moving so slowly that David, watching intently, thought an hour, maybe an hour and a half had passed before he disappeared around the other corner.

". . . sunny and humid in New York today." First the radio blared and then Carolyn screamed louder, "Why can't we go to Grandma's, Ma? He said it's going to be good. We could swim. Come on, Ma. Rockaway's not far. Please?"

"No, I said. Twice I said it already. Go get dressed." If Carolyn answered Mrs. Silver's shriek, David was not able to hear it.

Paul Kleinberg, from two houses away, passed on his way to work. "It's going to be a scorcher," he called to David. "Lucky you." David smiled and nodded as Paul speeded up his steps toward the trolley car at Utica Avenue. He was proud that Paul had said what he did, only he wished that he wasn't so afraid to answer. It was so different from Bayonne. No one spoke to him there. He was enjoying Brooklyn more every day. Even Mrs. Silver's noise was fun.

He jumped up suddenly, remembering the rubber ball in his pocket. That was something to do while he waited. Maybe for an hour he could throw the ball against the steps, and maybe by then they would be home. He aimed for the points of the steps so the ball wouldn't bounce before he caught it. It was harder that way. He wasn't very good at catching anyway. The ball kept missing the points and trickling away from his outstretched arm and he had to run for it. First hot, then bored, he stuffed the ball back into his pocket and sat down again on the bottom step.

When Irving suddenly came racing out of the alley, David was relieved to see him. "Where you going Irv?"

"Around the corner. Bubby wants farmer cheese." Even Irving was excited this morning, so excited that he stopped to ask David if he wanted to go with him.

"When you think they'll get here, Irv?" David walked as

quickly as he could to keep pace with his brother.

"How do I know." Irving's excitement translated itself into a lunging, jumping stride. David finally had to trot in order to keep up.

They passed the old apartment houses on the side street. From some of the open windows sheets and blankets were being aired, and down below janitors were rolling the empty garbage cans back from the curb.

In the market, on Clarkson Avenue, the smell of early morning freshness, the fragrance of cold water being spilled on scallions and radishes, greeted them as they moved down the narrow aisle to the white dairy counter. Mr. Millstein, the owner of this concession, didn't seem to be present, but then David spied his big behind sticking out of the little egg candling cubicle. "He's in there, Irv." David tried not to laugh. The black half-curtain began to wriggle open and suddenly Mr. Millstein appeared holding an egg. Surprised, he let the egg topple from his hand, caught it before it fell, and finally deposited it on a pile of loose eggs. "So *nu?* What you want without the laughing?"

"Quarter pound of farmer cheese." Irving held a dollar bill and only surrendered it when Mr. Millstein handed him the bag of cheese.

"Who's eating farmer cheese? You?" Now it was his turn to laugh.

"No. My grandmother." Irving started to move away.

"I figured it had to be someone older. Children, they don't like it. Who knows why. It's very good sonny." He handed Irving the change. "Thanks. Also thank your grandmother." Irving dashed away, and David, who had been examining the eggs, once more had to run to catch up with him.

"Why you in such a hurry, Irv?" David tried skipping.

"I got a ball game right away."

"Can I watch?"

"No. You can't cross Utica Avenue. Mama said so."

"But you could take me."

"I can't. I'm busy. Get Evelyn to."

As they came around the corner into Lenox Road, they both stopped suddenly. The car was there. Morrie was already removing suitcases from the trunk.

"Dad," David screamed. "You're home."

Morrie lifted David, swung him into the air. "Yes sir, we're home." Irving waited impatiently for Morrie to say hello to him.

"It's good to see you boys." Morrie placed his hand on Irving's shoulder. "Go see your mother upstairs . . . Here," he extended packages to each of them, "take these up." Irving raced into the alleyway but David remained stationary.

"Did you have a good time, Dad?"

"Wonderful. Marvelous trip . . . Don't you want to see your mother?" He looked down at David's sad face, bewildered by the fact that he didn't move. "Go upstairs and see her."

"Can't I help you, Dad?"

"The valises are too heavy."

David did finally move off down the alley. A half-hour ago he was so excited about the arrival and now he just wanted to cry. When he pressed the buzzer and opened the door on the ring of the bell, he pressed his eyes with the palm of his hand. Mrs. Silver opened her door when she heard him passing by. "They're home Davie. Hurry up."

He didn't stop to talk to Carolyn who had brushed past her mother into the hallway. "I'll see you later. Don't forget," she called coyly.

David opened the door slowly and there was Ellie, sitting at the kitchen table. Instantly his lost excitement returned. "Ma," he shouted, and, as if surprised by her presence, stopped in the doorway. "Ma," he repeated, leaping at her, kissing her even as he continued to yell. "You're home, Ma."

"Sure I'm home." She moved him back, examined him. "You look fine." David pushed back against her, crying, wanting to cry. So what if he wasn't the first one to see them.

Ellie returned each one of his kisses.

In the evening, after dinner, Max and Lila came for Mrs. Howard. They were to drive back to the hotel that night. Gathered around the kitchen table, Morrie and Ellie opened presents—little bottles of liqueur for Mrs. Howard—told the story of the spoons, thanked the boys for behaving so well.

"So good they were, I can't tell you how much." Mrs. Howard shook her head with pride. "And soon you'll all come to the hotel and stay."

Max frowned. Morrie laughed at his expression. "What's the matter, Maxie? You don't like that idea?"

"Sure he likes it," Lila said quickly not wanting an exchange now.

"You'll come, all of you," Mrs. Howard continued to smile defiantly at Max, "when school's finished and Evelyn's graduated. Everyone'll come."

After they left, Morrie and Ellie returned to the table but the previous mood had been changed. Their children seemed unusually quiet.

"That damn Max," Morrie grumbled.

"Ma," Irving whined, "do I have to go there this summer?"

"Of course. If I'm going how can you stay home?"

"I don't want to go either." Evelyn lowered her gaze.

"And I don't either." David echoed his sister's tone.

"It's unanimous then." Ellie laughed. "We'll all go."

"That bastard." Morrie's anger was drawing fuel from the children's comments. "All he wants from me is money."

"Not now, Morrie." She placed a hand on his chin but he brushed it away. "Not so soon."

"Everybody slaves for him all summer and he walks around getting fatter and fatter. What in hell does he want?"

"You know what he wants." Although she wanted to remain calm, it was difficult when the subject was Max or the hotel.

"I know all right and believe me I'd like to do it too. What do I need it for?"

"If you sell your share, so help me, I'm going to . . . to . . ." What could she promise to do? What act would be big enough to make him do what she wanted? But there was no need to complete the threat. Morrie was not listening to her. He went on talking, calmer now, reasoning out loud.

". . . but I can see his point. I don't do anything there. He's the one who has to get the money to pay bills. I told him long ago I wasn't interested."

"So what? So *you're* not!" She waved her hand in deprecation. "What about other people? How about your mother? Max would probably throw her out if he owned it completely."

"For Christ's sake Lila wouldn't let him do that. What the hell do you know about it?"

"Nothing. I know nothing as usual." Ellie pushed her chair back from the table. And that's how soon the vacation, the peace is over with. She wanted to remain calm. "But one thing I do know for sure is that Lila will do whatever Max tells her to."

"Dad?" Evelyn interrupted, unable to remain silent any longer.

"What are you going to add now that your mother's had her say?"

"Well . . . the other night . . ." she hesitated, unsure, but trapped now into speaking.

"What about the other night?"

Evelyn went on, told it all. ". . . and so they didn't try to hide it from us. Uncle Max is going to try and get you to sell your share to Uncle Leon."

"He said that?" Ellie's mouth twisted with an angry sneer.

"You're sure?" Morrie slammed the table, more surprised than angry.

"Yes," whispered David, wanting to help his sister. "It's true . . . I promise I heard him say it." He crossed his heart.

"And what did Aunt Toby say?" Ellie leaned closer to Evelyn.

"She said that you wouldn't like it."

"You see?" Morrie pointed his finger at Ellie, as if she were responsible for everything by insisting on staying at the hotel. "Max wants to get his brother into it. Okay! Well I'll just sit down with all of them and straighten things out a little bit. That bastard."

"Fine. Sit and talk to them. And make sure you say the right thing." Ellie could not have said what the right thing would be, but, in any case, Morrie would not ask for her opinion. If Toby wanted to be at the hotel, that would be a different case. Then Ellie would turn out to be the criminal if she made Morrie hold on to his share. But she wanted that place. She needed it, damn it. When the children were growing up, Morrie agreed that it was best for them to be there. Now, even they hated the idea of going there. They were too old for it. She looked at Evelyn, who squirmed with fear and shame, tried to remember the missing curls, curls that she had, so often, proudly arranged, realizing, like it or not, that time runs us down, makes changes behind our backs, without asking. Soon only David would go away for the summer. Soon Evelyn would want a real job, then Irving . . . That's the way it happens. Her head throbbed, confused. Vacation one minute; curls and hotels the next. "I'll call Toby tomorrow too, Morrie." And this was to be the unwilling product of her mind's movement forward; only to prepare for the next loss. Well, so that's life.

"Ma?" David tugged at her arm. Ellie did not respond. "Ma? You all right? You look funny."

Ellie heard the blood pumping out of her heart. She put her hand on the table, as if by touching something solid she could calm its beat. She opened her eyes wide, blinking them to catch her breath.

"El? What's the matter?"

"Nothing. Nothing at all." She breathed deeply. "I was picturing Evelyn's curls."

"Is that all! You had me scared for a second." Morrie went to the refrigerator, removed the seltzer bottle. Evelyn sat down in his chair, blushing. "My hair isn't too bad, is it Ma?"

"No. It's very nice. Beautiful." A tremor of fatigue made her want to yield up whatever remained of her private hopes. "Morrie, why don't you show them the other things we brought home."

"Sure. And maybe Irving will go down to the corner and get us some ice cream?" Morrie gave some money to Irving.

Ellie stood up, unsteadily walked down the corridor to the bathroom. She locked the door, slowly moved to stand before the medicine chest mirror. Her skin was so pale, repulsively pale. She frowned at the reflection, at the brown hair too soon streaked with dull strands of gray, at the protruding mouth, at the chin, which even as she looked at it, was losing its tightness. She opened the door of the chest; the image was gone. On the highest shelf, among Morrie's assorted home remedy tubes and tins, she found the package of Anacin tablets, removed two, closed the chest, avoiding the mirror, that picture of herself. From the kitchen came the sounds of David's laughter. Ellie rushed water in the palm of her hand from the faucet to her mouth.

The knocking at the door was soft. "Ma? You all right?" Evelyn called. "Ma?"

"Be right out."

NEITHER Ellie nor Morrie could fall asleep. The heat in the bedroom, with all the windows wide open, was suffocating. Ellie kept wiping her forehead with a washrag, but its relief was a delusion.

From outside, the noises of a hot city night were unabating. Only children, she thought, could sleep on such a night. And the loudness of Mrs. Rosenberg's radio didn't help matters. "I hope they don't play that radio so loud every night," she said into the darkness.

"If it wasn't Saturday night I'd get them to shut it off fast enough." Morrie got out of bed and removed his pajama bottom. He had long ago removed the top. "It's brutal tonight, El. I can't take this heat."

"Don't stand in front of the window that way. Someone will see."

"Let 'em." Nevertheless, his threat offered, he got back into bed. He tried to lie still, but the sheet beneath him was wet with perspiration. Turning, he looked at Ellie, her body stretched out, still, her eyes closed, hoping for sleep. "Head still hurt, El?"

"Yes."

"Why don't you take some more aspirin?"

"Two's enough."

"Suit yourself." For a moment there was silence. The radio had been turned off. "Thank God." But then the wail of an ambulance exploded the stillness. Morrie reached for his cigarettes.

"I hate when you smoke in the dark." Ellie did not have to open her eyes to know what he was doing.

"I'll be careful." He leaned back against the pillow, balancing an ashtray on his chest. "I don't hear anything from the kids."

"They don't have any cigarettes to smoke."

"Very funny."

"You can hear the people next door talking," Ellie whispered, trying to fan herself now with the washrag.

"What's their name?"

"I haven't met them yet, but they're quiet and that's a help in this alley."

"Next year," Morrie began, finding a way out of his present discomfort, "we're going to California or maybe even Mexico. I'll take a longer vacation."

"That's what you're thinking about already?"

"Why not?" He stamped out his cigarette, replaced the ashtray on his night table. "I feel a breeze somewhere."

"In California, probably."

"Are you funny. How is it you're not funny any place but in

bed?"

"There's nothing to laugh about anyplace else." She pulled herself up to lean on the headboard. She could see the outline of his naked body turned to face her, and then she heard him pass wind. How she hated that. He didn't even have the decency . . . Oh well, that he'll never learn.

"What are you thinking, El?"

"Nothing at all," but anger spiked her words, making her head ache with new pain.

"You want a cold drink, El?"

"No. It only makes you thirstier."

"I suppose so." He rolled onto his back. "What do you think I should do about the hotel?"

"You're asking me? How come?"

The bitterness of her words was so familiar, so far from sounding threatening that Morrie could choose his responses. If it were earlier, if it were cooler, if he were not so tired, he might have raised his voice to challenge her. But now he only wanted calm. "Yes. I'm asking you."

"Well, in that case, I can only say I don't know what to say yet. I'll have to speak to Toby."

"You don't really think they want to go into it, do you?" Morrie propped himself on an elbow.

"Who knows? Max could talk Leon into anything."

"But he couldn't talk Toby into it." Morrie almost sounded proud of his sister-in-law.

"That I'm sure of."

"Me too. But I'm also thinking about my mother. As crummy as that hotel is, it means a hell of a lot to her. She'd have no kind of security if I sold out." Morrie leaned over her. "Seriously, El. I know what you want from that place—you've told me often enough—but do you really think it's sensible?"

"As sensible as anything else is." Although her failure was certain, she just couldn't give up without saying what was expected of her. "Why shouldn't you own the place? Your mother wants you to. That's two shares. That only leaves Lila's."

"True, but remember that Max keeps it going. He deserves something. Just because he's a bastard . . ."

"All right. So why ask me?" Ellie turned on her side, but her head hurt too much that way and she rolled back again. "He'll take it over. So what's the difference what I want?"

"But he has worked hard to . . ."

"And your mother hasn't worked hard? And I haven't worked hard every summer in the kitchen? What do I get now?"

"Be realistic, El. You couldn't run that place, and I'm surely not giving up my job to help you run it. That's a certainty." He sat up to light another cigarette.

"Look, Morrie, I don't feel well tonight. Leave me alone. Do what you want. You always do anyway."

Trying to control himself, he breathed deeply, spoke, "I want to know what you expect. My father said—you know it as well as I do—before he died, keep the place. But what the hell do I need it for?"

"For me and the children. That's what your father meant."

"They hate it. You heard them tonight. They don't want to go there."

"Of course they don't, because Max treats them like poor relations. And you let him. He makes them eat with the help all summer and do this and do that . . ."

"All right. I know that's not the right way, but what . . ."

"But what? But you never did anything to stop him. How many times did I tell you to? And what happened? Nothing!"

"Oh shit," he muttered and rolled away from her.

"It's always the same." Now she was forced to maintain her advantage. "Everything that happens to you happens because you want it all to be easy and smooth. Your way. No troubles. I want a house? No. No house. Too much trouble. A car? No. No car. Too much trouble looking for a garage. I want you to own one thing. Just one thing that's yours. But no. Never. All you know is your job. Work for someone else all your life. Go ahead." Her outburst, controlled and low as it had to be in the darkness, made her head ache so that it seemed like the only part of her that was alive. She forced herself into a more comfortable position, but the whirling inside increased. A giddy panic rose in her throat.

"I'll speak to Max and Leon," Morrie murmured as if he were falling asleep while she spoke. "I'll decide what to do."

A new kind of fear pulsed through Ellie's body. Her fingers tingled as she pulled at them. Suddenly she felt as though she were about to die. She trembled, cold in the heat of this night. She sought solid bits of memory. Niagara Falls. Boston's narrow streets. She felt faint. She sat erect, looking wildly for an object that would crush her fear. Papa! If only she could scream for him, for some comfort. Little Ellie a woman, he used to say. A woman with children. Nausea grumbled in her stomach. Try. One step at a time, she told Irving. One step. Two steps. He learned. Davie learned. We all learn. "Morrie?" The softness of her voice shocked her. He didn't answer. "Morrie!" She thought she was screaming now.

He sat up, noisily alert to the low, crying sound of her call. "What is it, El?"

"Morrie," she repeated as if she hadn't heard him.

"What El? What's wrong?"

"I'm going to . . ."

"What hurts? Where?"

"My head. My chest." She tried to raise herself as if to show him where.

"What should I do? Should I call a doctor?" He switched on the bed lamp, saw her face pale, twitching, little. Gently he moved her against his chest, letting her head rest there, rocking slowly, moaning, "Ellie, Ellie. What's the matter?"

Gradually, this way, the throbbing diminished, the trembling subsided. She felt the warmth of the night flowing back into her body. But the nausea remained. It churned, rumbled in her stomach. She looked up at Morrie's head bent over hers, protecting, leaning on her, afraid. "Bring the pan. From the bathroom. Quickly."

Just as the retching started, he placed the pan beneath her bobbing head. Frantically, she pulled at his free hand, and then it came, in a rush, into the pan. Over and over again came the dribbled slime of her fear, of her death. The retching subsided, erupted, subsided until there was nothing left inside but a burning dryness. She wiped her mouth with the washrag and fell back against the pillow. She closed her eyes.

The pan banged in the bathroom; the toilet was flushed; water sloshed in the pan. It was far away, very far. But the washrag moved nervously across her forehead, cool, warming her back to the reality of her lighted bedroom. Morrie leaned over her, his bathrobe brushing against her arm. David stood beside her. She pulled him to her. "Don't be afraid, Davie. I'm all right. I just threw up." She squeezed his hands.

"Should I call the doctor, El?" Morrie continued to brush her face with the washrag.

"No. It's not necessary." She stopped his arm. "Enough. I'm fine now." Her head still ached, but it was comfortable, dull, real. A breeze had started somewhere.

Morrie reached for her hand and held it. "You're going to a doctor right away for a check up. Do you hear me?"

"Yes. I hear you . . . Davie, go back to bed now."

MORRIE ARRANGED to have Max and Leon visit him at the office. It was better that way. No one could interfere. Since Leon was one of the drivers at the plant, getting him was no problem, but Max had to make a special trip from the hotel. He would expect something decisive to take place. But on the telephone Morrie had only said, "I want to talk to you," and then inquired about his mother and how many guests they were expecting for the summer. Saying that was enough for Max to drop everything else. Morrie never approached him directly unless it was an important matter.

And it was going to be another busy day for Morrie. A pasteurizer had broken down and in order to get the milk ready for the next day's delivery there would have to be overtime. That they wouldn't like at the front office. Also, he had a meeting with the union shop steward. Another driver had been fired by Morrie. There was continual shortage in his collection money and Morrie didn't stand for that. The union was angry. Leon and Max were scheduled for four o'clock and that would leave enough time for him to get home and take Ellie to the doctor's. He lit a cigarette. Since that night, she was worse. Lots of dizzy spells. Something really had to be wrong if she complained. What a day. Everything always happens together. He got up from his desk, looked down into the yard where the morning delivery trucks were just now arriving. The drivers clustered together, checking their route books. There was some order there. Thank God. He turned from the window and looked down the line of glass-partitioned offices. Everyone was present, appeared to be working. The girls, out on the office floor, were uncovering their typewriters. The day was beginning. Morrie motioned for his secretary to come in with her steno pad. She smiled, stood up, ready. In his office he had all the respect he would ever need. He felt the strong glow of pride at work inside himself, reminding him, not that he ever really forgot it, how far he had come in so short a time.

"Good morning, Mr. Howard." Grace seated herself in front of Morrie's desk and began sorting the mail.

"Morning, Grace. Pasteurizing men get here yet?" He sat down, leaned back in his swivel chair.

"No, but they called to say they'll be here very soon. They promised." From the lightness of Grace's tone he knew that she was doing her best to make the day start correctly. She understood her boss well, so well that Morrie was able to convince her to make the move from the Jersey branch with him. Morrie had never yet lost his temper because of her. Grace handed him a personal letter.

"Well, well! My California uncle. It didn't take him long to answer my post card." He read the letter slowly, finally breaking out into a laugh. "He's ready to have us come out there. Now all we have to do is wait 'til next year."

"How's Mrs. Howard today?" Grace asked without stopping her work.

"So-so. I'm taking her to the doctor's tonight."

"I hope it goes well."

"Thanks Grace."

The dictation was rapid. Grace usually composed most of the letters anyway, but Morrie did insist upon lending to each his special Dale Carnegie touch of persuasive optimism. In the office Morrie, after such a short time, was already known as the boss who said everything could be done easily, as long as you worried long enough. "I'm going to be working on that plant report most of the morning so keep everyone away unless you think it's important. Right?"

"Right. I'll type these." She slapped her steno pad and quickly left the office.

Morrie glanced down at the folders he had left on his desk the night before. They were arranged neatly: a folder for each division of the plant. From these he would construct the over-all report for the main office in New York. Retail sales increase—he was happy to report that for the month. Wholesale deliveries holding its own. The new cottage cheese drive would help that in the next month's report. The idea for the 'Snow White' glasses filled with cheese, to be followed each week by other glasses showing each of the seven dwarfs, had been his. The president really liked that one. "No question of your future with us, Morris." Those had been his words, spoken before all the other plant managers at the general meeting in New York. He leaned back in his chair. My wife should appreciate me half as much as my boss.

By midmorning the report was ready for typing, just in time for his meeting with Joe Torantella, the union shop steward. There was a warm greeting. Joe had known Morrie since before the days at the personnel office, when Morrie was just beginning to rise in importance.

"Damn, it's good to see you, Morrie. How's the Mrs.?" Joe, open-faced, with a long, flaring nose and a receding forehead, pleased also with his own progress, settled into a leather easy chair at the corner of Morrie's desk. He had a nervous habit of constantly checking the buttons on his fly. Morrie could never remember them being open, but that was just Joe's quirk. Each person, Morrie always said, had one or two distinctive gestures. If you study those, you really get to know a person. His own, the mirror told him every morning, was that tremor of his head. And when he got angry, well, then he could feel it shaking.

"Joe, my boy—I mean, father . . ."

"Father, hell." Joe laughed, sneaking a hand down to his crotch. "So how's Ellie?"

"Not too hot."

"What's wrong?"

"I don't know. We're going to the doctor's tonight. How's yours?"

"Same old hag." Joe offered Morrie a cigarette.

"Joe," Morrie's tone became businesslike, direct, authoritative. "Kranski was fired for stealing again. His route book didn't balance. It's not the first time."

"He told me he only took fifteen dollars. Needed it for the house."

"What about all the other times, Joe?"

"Same thing, he says. It's not right, of course, but Christ, why'd you have to fire him for?" Joe sounded as if he were pleading with his own son, as if what he would have to do or say would be counter to the instincts of his heart. "All the boys are complaining. They say you're too tight with the books." Joe fingered his fly, lowered his gaze to make sure all was in order. "They call you the tight Jew boss."

"Is that all they call me?" Morrie felt his head begin to tremble, but he was determined to stay in control of it. "It's tough if they don't like it. And if they all want to quit me, it's still all right. Plenty of men around these days dying to get steady work."

"Don't get so het up, Morrie. Stay cool."

"I am cool. Just tell your boys I'm not working here to let them steal money, Joe. I'm damned if I am. There's enough of it going on as it is. That's one of the reasons they brought me here. And don't start crying about low salaries and the rough times."

"It's true, Morrie. You know it is. It's too low all over the country. Union's going to start moving. Mark my words."

"I'm marking them. And that's a different thing." Morrie now had the man just where he had been aiming to put him. "If the union gets money for the men, that's good. That's what the union's for. But the stealing has to stop. Everybody, including us, is in the same boat. A few years ago we had nothing too. Remember? Now it's better. Next year it'll be better still. It takes time. But stealing's stealing no matter what else you try to call it."

Joe sighed. "You know, Morrie, if I live to be a hundred, I'll never be able to get the jump on you." Joe stabbed his cigarette out and quietly put the ashtray back on Morrie's desk. "But I'm in a corner this time. The guys are bitching. You're new here. They think they can get to you. I got to tell them something."

"Tell them to push their sales. They get plenty of commission on the cottage cheese drive."

"Peanuts they get, Morrie. You know it."

"At least it's honest peanuts. If they want bigger money they'll have to give the bosses a harder time at contract time. Don't say I said that, but that's the real answer. Milk companies can't afford strikes. People don't like it. Babies need the stuff. So then you can get to them."

"Okay boy." Joe smiled, shook his head. "You playing both sides?"

"No. Just one. I'm no millionaire. You get a raise, I get a raise. Same thing."

"I got to hand it to you, yid. You got the brains."

"Yid, shit." Morrie waited for Joe's defensive smile, waited for the fingers to return from the crotch. "You guys got a president in the White House who backs labor and you don't even make your big move. Who's running your union? Herbert Hoover?"

Morrie won. Kranski would stay fired until he paid back the money he had stolen. Then he would be reinstated and keep his seniority. "The union can pay it back out of his dues," he told Joe and rushed him out of the office.

By the time Max and Leon arrived at his office, Morrie's energy had waned with the increasing heat of the day. The fan in the corner seemed to do nothing but ruffle the papers on his desk. He had removed his suit jacket, rolled up his sleeves, but still the sweat came, trickling down his back, forming pockets of discomfort whenever he shifted in his chair. The fat was doing it, breaking out all over. He thumped his growing potbelly. That's the way it happens. First the stomach, then the heart . . . He wished he could call off this meeting.

"It's a real scorcher," said Grace as she placed another chair in front of Morrie's desk and then led the men in. They sat down, nervously silent, Leon fidgeting himself into a position of sweating discomfort. "It sure is a hot one." He removed his driver's jacket, meekly waiting for Morrie's nod of approval. He was in awe of his brother-in-law's promotion, his unmistakable ability. He had no illusions anymore about his own ability. He didn't have what it took. Toby had said that often enough. Facts proved her to be correct.

Max stared at Morrie, waiting for him to begin. It was his show.

"All right, Maxie. We won't waste time. I've got to get home early to take Ellie to the doctor." Morrie thought that might shake him a bit. He did react, but dispassionately. "What's wrong?" He could have been asking about the rising price of milk.

"Anything serious?" Leon was genuinely concerned. "Toby didn't tell me about it."

"She doesn't know. And don't say anything to anyone yet. She had some kind of attack. We'll find out."

"Probably indigestion," suggested Max professionally.

Since that approach hadn't produced the desired effect, Morrie shifted to the real issue. "Max, I've got an offer for you and Leon. Listen to it and then tell me what you think." He cleared his throat, swiveled on his chair. "I want to sell out my share of the hotel." Max beamed, immediately attentive. He sure was a bastard all right. "I want to sell to Leon and Toby if they want to buy."

Leon sat up, surprised. He lit a cigarette to fill up the silence during which they waited.

"Of course," Morrie was impatient, "there are conditions."

"For example?" Max, like Morrie, was anxious to get to the obstacles. If he waited for his brother to talk, they would be there all afternoon.

"For example, number one, my mother stays at the place as long as she wants, for as long as she lives—without working." Max nodded yes, having expected that one. "Also, my family is welcome, free of charge, for as long as they go up there." Max lowered his head. "And lastly, Ellie does no work in the kitchen, and my kids get treated better than they've been treated." By raising his voice, Morrie showed that this condition was more of an attack on Max than it was a request.

"Why you yelling, Morrie?" Leon's surprise had become confusion. "You're only asking normal things?"

"So, Mr. Professor," Morrie ignored Leon, "what do you think?" Max was not disturbed by Morrie's hostility. That was familiar.

"In the first place," Max leaned forward, trying to look hurt, offended by the implications, "you forget that your mother is also Lila's mother. She's not going to be thrown out whatever happens here."

"Thank God for that," Morrie interjected, "even if you don't really mean it."

"In the second place, I wouldn't think of charging you or any member of your family. If your kids want to work as waiters, or anything else when they grow up, that's all right with me. It wouldn't hurt them. We did it. Remember? That's how I met your sister." Max, too, would have his moment for sarcasm. "But I can't promise that they'll get treated like guests. Let's be realistic, the guests come first. It's only right. That's business."

Morrie nodded, accepting the logic of the statement. "What about Ellie?"

"As far as Ellie is concerned, I never asked her to help out. She always wants to. Sure she's a tremendous worker, but I never directly asked her to do anything. She has her reasons, I'm sure, for wanting to. But that's her business."

"Okay. Never mind that. But she doesn't have to. Right?"

"Right with me. And you, Leon?" Max knew it was time for his brother to get involved. He wouldn't stand for total dismissal.

Leon did want to say something, but he wasn't sure what it should be. "What you're talking about is all right with me. But the other part, that's a different matter. You guys talk as if it's all decided already. What about my opinion?"

"Okay. What about it?" Max couldn't completely eliminate his patronizing tone. "What is your opinion? Now's your chance."

"Well, I don't really know . . . I didn't expect this. Toby didn't say anything about it and . . ."

"Don't you ever decide anything for yourself, without Toby's advice?" Max squirmed with frustration. "What kind of man are you?"

"Look, big-shot, my wife's been working ever since we were married. It's her money too we've saved. But you wouldn't understand that."

"What I understand is that for a man over thirty you act like a goddamn baby." Max was more than equal to his brother's raised voice. It was a novelty for Morrie to find himself in the position of asking for some quiet. ". . . this is an office, fellows. Leon's perfectly right. He's got to talk to Toby."

"Would you ask Ellie?" Max demanded.

"That's none of your damn business what I do or don't do. Just remember that." He pointed his finger ominously. "Besides, we haven't talked money yet, and I'm getting tired of all your talking. It's a long day for me." Morrie stood up, walked to the window. Downstairs, the platform was quiet, the way it should be in the late afternoon. When I control things, he thought, I make them run smoothly. Let 'em call me tight Jew boy. "I'll expect a few thousand down, and the rest you can pay off in notes."

"That'll take all my savings." Leon looked sad, reflective.

"But you'll have something in return for it," Max reminded him, calmed by his brother's expression. "You'll own part of something and you'll have an income."

"Income?" Leon frowned. "From that place? I don't see you rolling in money."

"Maybe not now, but there will be. I guarantee it."

Morrie began straightening his desk, motioned for Grace to come in. She waited at the doorway.

"Have they finished with the pasteurizer yet?"

"Just a little while ago, Mr. Howard. They're filling it with milk right now."

"Good. Okay, I'll be leaving in a little while." Grace moved away, nodding. He turned back to Leon and Max. "Let me know by Friday. Ellie and the kids will be up there the end of next week, and I want things settled before then." He rolled down his sleeves, wiped his face with a sweaty handkerchief, put on his jacket. "I'm not trying to high pressure you, Leon. You do whatever you want, but I think it's a good chance you'd be taking. You're not going anywhere here." Leon's gaze was lowered in embarrassment. "Not that you don't do a good job. Don't get me wrong. There just isn't so much advancement. Those days are going fast. I'm the Jew boy they gave a break to."

Max stood up, ready to leave, ready to start breaking down his brother's resistance. "I'll let you know by Friday."

"Listen," Leon was standing now, "if Toby says no . . ." He hesitated, smiled suddenly, "it won't be because of the place and all. It . . . We're trying to have a baby for a change and this time I think it took."

"Great." Morrie patted him on the back. "I hope it did too. Can I tell Ellie?" Morrie thought of the doctor again and tried to speed them up by moving toward the door.

"I guess so. She's in her fifth month, past the hardest part. She's going to have to take it easy, so I don't know if now's . . ."

Max grabbed his brother's hand, pumped it. "The best place for a kid is the country. Tell that to Toby."

THE DOCTOR'S TREATMENT ROOM didn't frighten Ellie. Her old job made her feel like she was seeing old friends again. But she hadn't visited a doctor since before David was born, and some of the friendly apparatus had been changed. Being a doctor's receptionist is one thing; being a patient is quite another. She was no longer on intimate terms with the blood pressure pad, and when Dr. Siefert squeezed the air bulb and she felt the tightness around her arm, panic made the pressure gauge on the wall suddenly shoot up.

"You're too nervous, Mrs. Howard." He undid the pad. "We'll try again later. Lie flat now."

Ellie, when directed, breathed deeply, exhaled, adjusted herself to the benign hands probing her stomach.

"Sit up." The doctor was absorbed by his probing stethoscope, moving it constantly over her back, her chest, her exposed breasts. "Keep breathing deeply. Breathe. Exhale. Fine."

The breathing made her too dizzy to relax.

He removed the stethoscope from his ears, let it dangle at his neck. "I'll try the blood pressure again."

It was no better this time. The same panic seized Ellie as the air was pumped into the pad.

"What's making you so nervous, Mrs. Howard? I'm not going to hurt you."

"I know doctor. I know." Ellie folded her arms across her breasts. Being naked didn't help her feel less nervous.

The doctor smiled reassuringly. "All right, you can get dressed now and then come into my office."

All at once she felt overwhelmed by weakness as she stepped into her cotton dress. There were too many buttons up the front. Her fingers felt cold, worked sluggishly with each button. She sat down on a stool next to the bubbling antiseptic tray, watched the syringes roll in the steaming water. Whatever is wrong is wrong. Eventually something has to go wrong. She poked at her hair, rose, resigned to whatever he might say, and walked into the office.

The doctor motioned her to a chair beside Morrie. "The dizzy spells you mentioned started a number of months back? Is that right?"

"Yes." Ellie's voice sounded flat, colorless.

The doctor wrote in a folder. "I won't have the results of your blood tests for a few days, but you haven't lost any weight, have you?"

"No. But I never weigh myself so I'm not sure."

"She hasn't." Morrie smiled. "She hasn't gained any either."

"That's good too. You're too small for a lot of weight."

"I've never weighed more than 120 pounds." Feeling proud of that fact made her relax.

"Well, Mrs. Howard, to get to the diagnosis . . ." He closed the folder as if he had just finished reading a book. "In every day language, you've got a pretty high blood pressure. The headaches, the dizziness, that's all a part of it."

"When you say high, doctor," Morrie interrupted, "You mean that . . ."

"I mean that your wife has to take it easier or she'll become a sicker woman." His firmness made Ellie sit up rigidly. "Your heart is in good shape but you must rest it more. Too much pressure won't help it any. You must relax. Take naps. You don't do you?"

"Never. I'm not able to nap."

"You've got to learn how. You're too young a woman to be sick this way. I'll give you some pills and a diet to follow which should help."

"How about housework?" Morrie asked.

"It's all right as long as she rests. She doesn't have to change her life, just alter it a little. If she doesn't listen to me . . ." he wagged his finger playfully, "she'll have another attack like the other night and it could be very bad." Ellie did not flinch at the words. She remained tensely attentive. "I'll let you know about the tests. You'll come back in about three weeks. Meantime you'll get the pills . . ."

"Doctor," she leaned closer, "I'm supposed to go away next week with my children, for the summer and I won't . . ."

"Fine. You'll be able to rest?"

"Yes." Morrie spoke emphatically, looked at Ellie.

"In that case come back at the end of July. Just to check. If you don't begin to feel better come back right away. And remember, Mrs. Howard, it's all up to you. You can live forever if you live wisely . . . And you'll have to take care of her, Mr. Howard."

"I will doctor. I assure you."

Ellie said little on the drive home, but she did feel relieved. The doctor had told her; the words made sense. The hard part was to follow the rules. The furniture will have to stay the way it is for awhile.

". . . and I'll get the prescription filled tonight and you can start the pills right away."

Ellie nodded yes, continued to look out at the darkening evening, at the heavily laden trees rocking, nudged by a strong breeze. There'll be good sleeping tonight, she thought.

"You feel better now?" Morrie patted her knee.

"As a matter of fact, I do."

"I thought you would. And as long as there's no monkey business, if you do what you have to . . ."

"I'll try." She didn't want to talk yet.

"No trying, just doing." They stopped for a red light. Morrie turned to look at her. He was ready to tell her how he would promise to help, how he wouldn't get angry. He felt so different at this moment, as if he sensed the loss of something, something which had no name and which he couldn't touch, something which was bigger than himself and Ellie in this car. He did want to help. But how could he promise to change, just like that, overnight? For years he'd been one way, and now, suddenly . . . The light changed to green, and the car moved, his feet shifting from clutch to accelerator automatically, picked up speed.

Ellie allowed her mood to blossom in the blueing darkness, indulged the sense of weary, flowing weakness. Her head didn't ache right now. Her heartbeat had slowed down. Blood coursed through each thought, each twist of her mind with ease. But that wouldn't last. She rolled down the window, wanting the rushing air, not the knowledge that her head would hurt again, that in an instant the movement inside her could be fired and overwhelm her. The doctor gave it a name and now it was her job to postpone—what?—its conclusion. For how long? She sighed and rolled up the window. The sigh was not a complaint. Everything had an end. So hers would be high blood pressure. Pressure from what? Morrie's voice intruded, asking for an answer.

". . . do you really?"

"What?" She could not retrieve what he had said.

"About the hotel?"

"Yes. Whatever it is. I don't care."

"Who knows, maybe Toby will get some pleasure from it."

The false note of his words struck the edges of her mood. He didn't care about Toby or anyone. "Why should Toby get pleasure from it? No one else has."

"That's my girl!" Morrie laughed.

"It's the truth, isn't it?"

"Truth schmuth. Who cares about the truth? All I'm trying to get across is that they'll be better off up there."

"And all I'm trying to get across is that I don't believe you. If they take it off your hands, you'll feel better. That's all."

"For Christ's sake, what the hell are you talking about!" He turned the car off Utica Avenue onto their block.

"Never mind now. Do as you please." Her body was once more tense, angry, just as it should not be.

When the car stopped across from their house, Ellie got out quickly, slammed the door, and crossed the street, not waiting for Morrie, who remained dumbly immobile behind the wheel.

A knot of silently staring children blocked her path up the steps. They shifted their shoulders to let her by. "Why don't you go home?" she shouted at them.

"I'm home," Al Silver said ingenuously. The rest of them remained silent, the light from the street lamp showing them shadowy, absorbed. As long as Irving isn't with them! Who knows what they're doing. Morrie was behind her now, entering the dimness of the vestibule with her. He stopped her from moving forward, when the door closed behind them. "I'm sorry, El." He tried to press her to him. "I didn't mean to . . ." he fumbled for her hand.

She managed, in this moment of his unfamiliar weakness, to push him away. "All right," she whispered, sounding as if she were telling him 'ssh, the neighbors.'

He tried to kiss her, but she slipped through the open doorway leading upstairs. And then David was calling, "Ma? You home?"

"Yes. It's me." Morrie was not behind her when she reached the top of the staircase. The door downstairs was slammed loudly.

Irving and David waited before her, both afraid to talk.

"Everything's all right. Don't worry." She extended her arms forward, held them. If Evelyn were here now, it would be a perfect time to die. It would teach them a lesson forever. It's better to learn early that we die before we know it. That's the first secret of life. And then, suddenly, she was laughing. She nudged the children away. "What are you crying for, David? I told you I was all right." David rubbed his eyes and looked up at her, smiling. "Did you eat what I left for you?" They nodded. She walked into the kitchen. "And you even washed the dishes."

By the time Morrie returned with the pills and some ice cream, Ellie's head no longer ached.

CHAPTER *Ten*

MRS. PERLIN was hearing it from Mollie, who had heard it from Toby: Ellie was not well. She would never receive that kind of news directly from Ellie. Her children protected her from bad news. True, she had never made it very easy for them to talk; that was the way she was. What they wanted to say, they said; anything else was their own business. But when it came to sickness, that she did want to know. Since her husband had died, that was the one instinct she nourished, that and her religion. ". . . so you don't know more than that?" She was preparing Mollie's breakfast.

"Toby doesn't know more than that." Mollie, seated at the table, was impatient for her coffee.

"She went to the doctor?" Mrs. Perlin shuffled to the table carrying a bowl of steaming milk and the coffee pot. Her bedroom slippers slapped on the old linoleum.

"I told you yes already, Ma. High blood pressure he said."

"Like me. I knew it." She sat down opposite Mollie, her hand supporting her swaying head, making a clucking sound of despair with her tongue.

"Why don't you call her later and find out everything?" Mollie dipped a piece of buttered bread into the coffee bowl.

"She called when she came from Canada. Why didn't she say then?"

"Maybe she was all right then. Who knows. Call her and find

out."

"You think she's going to rest with Morrie and the children? And rest she'll need."

"She'll rest in the country. They're going in a few days." Mollie stood up abruptly, and went to the bedroom to complete the combing of her hair.

"You're finished already? You had nothing to eat."

"That's all I want," Mollie called, exasperated.

"You should eat a bigger breakfast when you work all day so hard." Mrs. Perlin collected the few dishes and put them in the sink.

"Every morning you say the same thing, Ma. When you going to stop already?"

"Some day I'll stop. I'll stop everything." She sounded neither querulous nor expectant. She awaited death as she awaited the sabbath, joyfully, but quietly.

Mollie, holding a bobby pin, looked in at her mother. "You're talking foolish again, Ma. I didn't mean it that way."

"It's all right." Mrs. Perlin smiled. "When I'm not here I'm not here. The only thing I want to still live for is to see you married."

Mollie turned away wearily, letting her hands fall limply at her sides. "Not now, Ma. Please?"

"Of course not now. You'll be late for work. I know. Go ahead my darling daughter. Go." Mrs. Perlin pulled her housedress as if she wanted to stretch out the wrinkles. "You'll be here after work to eat?"

"Where else would I be?" Mollie was ready to leave.

"Maybe you should go to Ellie's?"

"I wasn't invited."

"You have to be invited? To your sister's? I'm sure there's enough food."

"And what'll you do?"

"Harry said he maybe would come tonight. He'll call later. And if not, Toby will be with Leon."

"Well, maybe then. I'll see what happens and let you know." Mollie kissed her mother's forehead. "Goodbye and don't fuss too much for Harry, Ma. You hear?"

"I hear. Goodbye. Have a nice day."

Mollie rushed out, slamming the door.

Mrs. Perlin remained seated at the table, even after she had finished her coffee. At that moment she felt too tired for cooking. Her toothless mouth trembled through a morning prayer, the sounds barely audible in the quiet apartment. At the end of the prayer she intoned the name of her dead husband, "Avrum, soon." She stood up slowly, leaning on the table for support. Her stomach growled for food it would not get until the evening. She always fasted the day on which the *Shabbath* began.

Sighing, she went to the telephone, peered nervously at it, then, lifting the receiver, cautiously dialed Ellie's number. "Hello? Ellie? . . . It's Mama," she shouted into the mouthpiece. "*I'm* fine, but you, Ellie? Mollie says you're not well . . . Tell the truth. What did he tell you, the doctor?"

Ellie repeated the doctor's words and then changed the topic to the news about Toby.

"It should only go all right this time." Mrs. Perlin's pessimism was invulnerable; Ellie could not talk her out of it. ". . . Ellie? Mollie will be by you for dinner tonight, I think. It's all right? . . . *Nu*, that's what I told her." Ellie inquired about her brother and sisters. ". . . Fine. Everyone is fine. On Sunday you're coming with the children? . . . Good. And remember, you dasn't do so much work . . . All right. If you won't do work, I'll eat. Don't worry . . . So Sunday . . . Give my love . . . Goodbye darling." She replaced the receiver on its cradle, shuffled into the bedroom. She needed to sleep for awhile. Just a half hour. Also, she needed to do up her braid. Harry would be angry if she didn't do that.

Leon stopped in at Morrie's office later that same day. Morrie was anxious for an answer. He wanted the thing settled once and for all. If the plan wasn't acceptable, he would just sell out to anybody, whether Max liked it or not. The whole place wasn't worth all that trouble.

It was never easy for Leon to confront Morrie and now, with what was on his mind, he found it necessary first to talk about Toby's pregnancy, then to light a cigarette and squash it out, then to inquire about Ellie's health.

Finally, it was Morrie who spoke up. "Well? What's it going to be? Yes or no?"

"Well, I want . . . to do it but . . ."

"But?"

"It's Toby. She's dead set against it. She doesn't want to be tied up with Max."

"That's understandable." Morrie pushed back in his swivel chair. "But it's not enough of an objection."

"That's exactly what I said. My brother wouldn't screw me so badly. At least I don't think so. And if we had legal papers stating that I'm his partner he couldn't do anything out of the way. I said that to Toby but she doesn't believe that either. I don't know what . . ."

"For Christ's sake, Leon, that's the easy part of it. The important thing is if you'll realize any income from the place. I think you will, eventually. One thing you can't take away from Max is that he knows how to run people and the hotel. He'll make something out of it and you'll benefit."

"I agree. That's my whole point."

"Let's face it. If you don't do this, what the hell you ever going to be? A milkman? All your life?"

Leon's gaze shifted toward the row of glass enclosed offices. "That's it, Morrie. That's it in a nutshell. If you thought I could get promoted here . . . get something better . . ."

"To tell you the truth, I doubt it. It'll never happen. Even with me where I am. You'll go on driving a truck, working lousy hours. I can't just give you a job. I don't own this goddamn place."

"I understand. I don't have Max's brains. That I know."

"Damn it, it's not brains. It's the way Max sucks up to people who don't know him. How he makes them think he's on the level. You're honest, for Christ's sake. And honesty isn't worth so much on the open market any more."

Leon looked up, relaxed for the first time since entering the office. "All right, then. I'm going to do it."

"Good." Morrie reached across the desk to shake his hand.

"And you won't have to worry about Ellie and the kids or your mother. I'll watch out for them. I promise it."

"I'm sure you will." Morrie slid closer to his desk. "Now about the payment of the money."

"Whatever you say, Morrie."

"If I was only dealing with you, I wouldn't bother to ask. But Max is a different case. I'll expect something from you first, and some money by the end of this season."

"We'll sign notes and then he'll have to pay."

"I suppose so, but Max knows I won't sue him."

"Well maybe this time you should if he doesn't honor the notes." Leon shook his head. "You know, I feel sorry for your sister, Morrie."

"Don't. Just watch out for your own interests up there. Your brother's got plans." Morrie gazed down at the work on his desk. "I'll tell you what. The first weekend I come up to the place we'll sit down and make the entire transaction official. For now, you can consider yourself a partner, acting in my place. And don't let your wife talk you out of it."

"She won't." He stood up. "When she has a kid to think about, she'll be all right. I'm sure of it."

Morrie nodded, already distracted by his work.

"So long, Morrie." Leon walked quietly out of the office, smiling broadly at Grace. As he passed, she stood up, went to the office entrance. "Need anything, Mr. Howard?"

Morrie looked up, grinning. "Yes. A new family. Can you do anything about that?"

"Afraid not."

Mrs. Perlin turned her head slightly, away from the stove, and looked at her family. All of them had come. That had surprised her most of all. For Harry and Toby to come twice in a few days was the greatest prize, like winning on the numbers after playing the same one for a whole week. She smiled, content even with her one vice, the family joke. "Mama prays and plays," they always said. So what did she do with the little money she made? It went to the synagogue and her grandchildren on holidays. That couldn't be a real sin, to use the money that way. She had to have something to give.

She removed the finished *blintzes* from the pan, heaped them onto a waiting plate, and refilled the skillet with uncooked ones. For once she was getting the opportunity to finish *blintzes* without having the children eating the 'pages.' Evelyn had them all in the other room, playing some game, but when she heard them laughing she wished they were standing around the stove, grabbing for her offering. "You'll finish playing soon, Harry?" she called out. "I'm almost ready."

"A few minutes, Ma." He studied his pinochle hand. "350."

"It's yours as far as I go," said Morrie, folding his cards into a pack and rapping the table.

"Pass too." Simon dropped his cards, yawned and cracked each of his knuckles.

Leon, who had dealt the hand, turned over the 'to loan' for Harry.

"Nothing." Harry threw his hand down. "I was looking. Can't make it now." He paid each of them a dime. "Let's stop. Mama's ready anyway." They agreed. The game had been a listless one what with the noise to contend with.

In the bedroom the girls lounged on Mollie's bed. Toby leaned against the headboard, her hands arched across her growing stomach. "If the whole summer were only like this, I'd be happy. These'll really be the hard months." She had been demanding recognition all afternoon.

Ellie and Clara, leaning against the bedposts, exchanged knowing glances. They were the mothers. "The best thing is to go on doing what you always do," said Clara.

"That's not going to be so easy this summer."

Martha, the last member of the family to receive news of any venture, asked, "What are your plans? Something special?"

"Didn't Harry tell you?" Mollie's sarcasm flared brightly. "They're buying Morrie's share of the hotel."

Martha glanced at Ellie who nodded in confirmation. "That's wonderful." She tried to sound enthusiastic rather than disinterested. "Leon must be excited."

Toby gestured back and forth with one hand. "He is and he isn't. To work with Max is not exactly a happpy event."

Harry appeared in the doorway. "Let's go girls. Mama's ready." No one stirred. "Come on." He clapped his hands together loudly. "The kids will eat them all if you don't get in there." He stepped into the room, leaned over Ellie, and, suddenly, picked her up. "You're the oldest and smallest, so you're coming first."

"Harry," Ellie screamed, laughed, embarrassed. "Put me down. I'm too heavy."

"You weigh nothing at all."

"Harry, stop it," Martha pulled at his arm, but he continued holding her, moved into the kitchen, set her down in the chair at the head of the table. "Your daughter, Mrs. Perlin, has arrived. The others are on the way." He turned, grabbed his mother, kissed her with silent-movie passion. "Everyone's ready."

There was hardly enough room at the table. David counted. "Thirteen," he screamed. They quieted down immediately.

Mrs. Perlin, standing behind Ellie's chair, took her own count, pointing at each of them. "Fifteen." She counted again to make sure. "Yes. Fifteen."

The laughter was spontaneous. Mrs. Perlin covered her face, but laughed with them. "You dasn't sit down with thirteen, David. It's unlucky. Remember that." She squeezed him against her side.

"There's no room to sit down together anyway, Ma." Mollie was passing dishes of *blintzes* around the table. Hands grabbed, the noise increased, the dimly lit room echoed with the unfamiliar sounds of joking. Tears welled up in Mrs. Perlin's eyes. She leaned wearily against Harry. "If only your papa . . ."

"None of that, Ma." Harry embraced her. "Just enjoy it."

She wiped her eyes with the palm of her hand. "Yes. You're right." She reached up, smoothed his hair. "So *kinder*, everyone, *ess gezunter hayt*."

Suddenly Morrie held up a piece of *blintze*. "A toast to the new venture. For Toby and Leon. Plenty of business and kids." Everyone applauded. Leon, standing behind her chair, leaned down and kissed Toby.

Mrs. Perlin screamed, slapped her cheek, "I forgot to get sour cream."

CHAPTER *Eleven*

IF IT RAINED during the day at the Hotel Washington, like most of the other hotels in the Catskill Mountains, there was nothing else to do but find some game to play. On the long, narrow screened-in porch that fronted the dining room, tables were set up by the management. The guests played poker, rummy, mah jongg, pishe-pesha while a foot away the rain dripped steadily from the roof of the porch onto the formal flower beds.

In the casino, the children set up their own tables. Monopoly boards dotted the smooth dance floor. There were never enough tables, and any sheltered, unused area was sacred territory. Paper money changed hands. Green houses were swiftly and carefully placed on the colored rectangles, only to disappear in favor of a red hotel. Dice were rolled on boards, squeals of "Go to jail. Go directly to jail," rang through the hall as if it were the prescribed choral accompaniment to the rain.

In one corner, the out-of-tune piano was constantly in use. Chopsticks, scales, "Blue Moon," and, occasionally, an ambitious Chopin Nocturne pierced, mingled with the general noise. Evelyn, whose job it was to govern all, had collected a group of children on the stage and was trying to organize her "Kiddy Show" for Friday night. She did have the curtain closed, but it was no protection. And she could barely hear Milton Birnbaum singing, a capella, "The Merry-Go-Round broke down." Only when he "oom-pah-pahed" did she recognize the song. But she applauded when she thought he was finished. "Fine. Excellent, Miltie." She called David next. "You're going to sing 'God Bless America.' It'll be the finale. I'll put an American flag behind you. A big one." David looked peevish, reluctant, but nodded yes. Evelyn smiled. "Daddy'll probably get here in time to see you." She gestured toward the wing of the stage. "Open the curtain, Mark, please."

The littered dance floor wrung a sigh of dismay from Evelyn's collapsing spirit. Bedlam was too much even for her rocklike determination to do a good job. She removed a whistle from her pocket, blew it repeatedly until there was a startled quiet. But just as quickly, the noise resumed its former volume. She continued to blow the whistle until the quiet was sustained. "Lunch will be served in a little while," she screamed from the stage. "I want you to clear up all your games, put them along the walls, and then form a big circle for a new game." She surveyed the waiting faces to determine what degree of response she could expect. It looked promising. With this kind of weather they would try almost anything. "It'll be a race to see who gets to the circle first. First one there gets to go into lunch first. Get on your mark"—some of the children rose half-way—"Get set"—Monopoly money was already disappearing—"Go." The whistle blew once more. First screaming, then running, pushing children moved in all directions. Even Irving stood around the dance floor anxious to start the circle. Evelyn breathed her relief, looked up toward the ceiling thankfully, even though she knew it was the rain that made them happy to obey.

Behind the dining room, in the kitchen, whether it rained or not, the activity was the same. Each cubicle had its master. The dishwasher worked incessantly, his hands white and crinkled from the water. The mesh silverware baskets stood ready on the galvanized sink boards. "Dairy Dishes—Dairy Silverware" read the sign above the entrance to his space. In the next cubicle the meat dishes were piled in big wooden bins. The waiters passed in and out, loaded their trays with dishes, went out to the dining room to set up for lunch.

Mrs. Howard, in a white apron over a sleeveless dress, stood in front of the enormous black steel stove, stirring a vat of corn soup. She had ended up being the chef whether she wanted it or not. The guests that came expected her food. That was the way Max presented it to her; she had no choice. Winter promises melted with the first heating of the stove.

Lila, Ellie, and Leon filled the salad plates that lined the long rectangular serving table. They placed a small white fish on each bed of lettuce, then tomato slices, black olives, long wedges of cucumber, and a slice of lemon. They worked without talking, conscious only of the fact that the salads had to be ready in time. Waiters snatched up finished salads, replaced them with empty plates.

At the end of the stove, in still another cubicle, the baker was cutting squares of nutty brownies from old battered cookie trays, and Bob, the head waiter, sliced bread, putting the slices into straw baskets. He piled the baskets, carried out a load to the dining room, then came back for more.

For those bustling in and out of the kitchen, the rain meant nothing. Before a meal there was no time to think about anything but the guests and their stomachs. And by now, the middle of July, the kitchen staff had been so well organized by Leon's surprisingly firm, but winning manner that not a motion was wasted. The children's lunch was at 12 sharp. The adults' at 1. That was the deadline. There was never a variation. The Catskill routine demanded efficiency that never wasted a minute. In 1937, there was not enough money to spend at a hotel that didn't satisfy the spirit. And in the office, located in the large, gabled main house, that's what Max worried about. He left kitchen duties to those who were uniquely qualified to handle them. His appearance in the dining room during a meal was the concession made in order to play the role of proprietor. He would go from table to table, put his hand on someone's back, joke benignly. When he left the room, his guests felt that they had been honored in a manner which was their right. They were glad that they had come to the Hotel Washington.

Filled to capacity, the hotel could accommodate 160 by squeezing people into the five bungalows and main house. It took a good deal of maneuvering and persuasion. Toby, since she was pregnant and naturally disinclined to kitchen work, became—at least that's what she thought it was going to be—Max's secretary. She made out charts listing available room space, charts which Max would never condescend to use. He had his own image of space. She tried to keep active files of bills to be paid, only to find that her brother-in-law paid bills which demanded payment or suspension of service; the others, he threw away. She soon realized that her chief functions were to answer telephone calls, guest complaints, and to make sure that the chambermaids didn't steal any linen. It didn't demand much skill, but it was time consuming and, in the rain, depressing. There was a window in front of and to the side of her desk. By stretching her neck, she could view the entire sweep of the hotel's grounds and buildings. As much as she wanted to, she couldn't deny the fact that the setting was beautiful. Out in front was an important and much traveled state highway that led from the encircling mountains. They weren't high mountains but, sitting on the large expanse of vivid green lawn, under the gnarled locust trees, they did inspire a sense of awe, of well-being. Very sensibly, this was where two weeks could be spent in profitable relaxation.

At the back fringe of the lawn were three bungalows, built alongside one another, painted an eternally fading yellow and a suitably contrasting green trim. The handball court, forming a right angle with the third bungalow, the farthest from the dining room, announced the legendary splendor: Hotel Washington on Willow Lake. Of course, from where Toby sat, Willow Lake was not visible. But she could look down the gravel path that led from the main house, past the dining room, in between another bungalow and the casino building, curved under a huge, annoyingly prolific mulberry tree, yielded, temporarily to still another yellow bungalow, scalloped out again, then seemed to rush straight past an apple orchard governed by quick-biting fruit flies, the children's playground, and, finally, about one quarter of a mile from where she sat, there was Willow Lake, without a single willow tree in evidence. Its name was Max's big joke and the guests accepted it as an example of imaginative management.

Today, the lobby was crowded and noisy. Across the wooden counter that separated Toby from the lobby proper, the guests sat on the mohair furniture, smoked, grumbled about the weather, waited for the next meal to be served. The chambermaid gave up hopes of ever being able to straighten up the room. She leaned against the counter. "I can't work in here Miz Levinson. It's only gonna get dirty in two minutes no matter what."

Toby smiled disinterestedly. "All right. Just finish the rooms." She checked her wrist watch. "The kids'll be eating soon. When you go over will you tell my husband to remember he's taking me to the doctor's this afternoon?"

"Yes, Ma'm, I will if I see him still long enough. This time of day he's so busy I can't get my words out in time, but . . ."

Toby turned back to her view from the window as Lucy began still another of her stories. Being a local woman, Lucy had the habit of turning every commonplace request into an excuse for lengthy conversation. Toby seemed to forget this each time they spoke. "You better go now, Lucy, if you want to eat. The rain's let up a little." Lucy nodded, used to being interrupted.

"Mrs. Levinson?" A short, plump, elderly woman with a bandana tied over her curling blond hair, approached the counter. She smoked rapidly without inhaling so that a circle of smoke moved above her head.

"Good morning, Mrs. Feinstein." Toby's smile froze in place properly.

"Mrs. Levinson, I'm informing you we're going to check out Sunday. I want to know when's the check out time?"

"After lunch."

"Such terrible weather, you know. We wished to stay longer. But the weather makes me blue." She smiled coyly. "All I do is eat too much and that I can't afford."

Toby had heard this and similar complaints so often during the week that, by now, she had lost her ability to smile at it. She nodded sympathetically.

"My daughter called last night and said it isn't raining in the city. Might as well be home, I told my husband, Abe. Must be bad for business all over. My son rented down on the Jersey shore—him, he loves the ocean, what can you do—with his family. Three girls he has. Anyway, down there it's raining too. They're going crazy he says. At least here I can . . ."

"That's a shame," Toby interrupted, hoping to stop the flow of words.

"I won't bother you no more." Mrs. Feinstein was hurt. "I can see how much work you have to do." After a few minutes of Toby's cautious silence, she cleared her throat and walked away, pouting.

Toby had to learn how to listen without listening. Max insisted that was the first necessity. Without that you have no clientele. Well, it was just going to take her more than a few weeks to learn. Maybe she never would. Looking up, roused suddenly by the sound of a different noise, she saw a line of children being marched by Evelyn up to the handball court.

Max rushed out of the first bungalow and followed the line, screaming, "Evelyn? What the hell are you doing?" Quickly, he raced up next to her on the wet, broken concrete of the court. His shouts rose louder, like the shrieks of a hurt dog. "Why'd you take them out of the casino. Can't you see it's still raining? You crazy or something?"

"It's stopped." Evelyn moved her hands to her hips. "They need to get some air before they eat."

"They'll ruin the lawn. They'll run all over and fall. Somebody'll break a leg." He moved away from her, shaking his head in disbelief, slapping his legs with disgust. "Nobody, nobody knows how to do anything right around here." He headed for the main house. Toby readied herself for attack.

David, standing next to Evelyn, yelled at the departing figure, "You stink. I hate you."

Evelyn took David's hand, pulled him back. "Now he'll go and yell at Aunt Toby. Aunt Toby'll run to mama and there'll be another argument. I wish we were home."

"So do I." David made a fist, waved it at the main house.

Irving, watching from a distance, shouted over, "So do I too."

Evelyn scanned the mass of screaming, now disorganized children. "All right children," she just had to scream louder, "let's try and form another circle."

When Max arrived in the office, Toby's spirit of belligerence was bubbling with anticipation. Just the right day for a fight.

"That niece of yours," he muttered angrily. "She doesn't know a goddamn thing about kids and she's a governess. What a place!" He reached for some open letters on Toby's desk. "Any reservations?"

"No."

"We better get some soon."

"It's the weather."

"Don't you start with the weather business too. Your niece has the weather all figured out already."

Toby took the letters from his hand. "She's also your niece, just in case you forgot it."

"I'm very much aware of that fact. Every time you try to economize it's always wrong. I should have gotten someone with experience. That's what I should have done." He leaned on the counter, cradled his head in his hands. "It's no use. You can't run a professional business with amateurs."

"And you're the only professional, I suppose?" Toby stood up, moved closer to the window, peering out for courage.

"I know, at least, what I'm doing."

"A lot of people can learn quickly."

"Not quick enough to suit me."

"You know, you're not exactly serving royalty. They're just people."

"Toby, for once you're right. I want a better clientele here. Younger, more active. It's certain my relatives aren't going to help me get it. I've got more family eating at every meal than guests."

"So? What does that prove?"

"It proves that I can't make any profit."

"I notice how you're always saying 'I' like you're the only one involved." Toby turned from the window. She was ready to face him now. "In case you don't remember, let me remind you that the situation's been changed a little. Not much. Just a little."

"You always remind me very fast about the change. There's no chance to forget."

"Good. So you know where we stand."

"I know, goddamn it. I know." Max spun around so fast he startled Toby into a backward step so that she was pressed up against the window. "Why the hell don't you just shut up for once?"

Max's rage was Toby's limit. She left the office, purposely pushing him out of her way, and then headed for the kitchen. The children were milling around the dining room entrance, anxious for lunch. David ran to catch up to her. "Aunt Toby, are you . . ."

"Not now, David." Impatiently, she waved him to a stop.

Inside the kitchen, preparations for lunch were still in progress. Lila was stacking monkey dishes in readiness for the inevitable sour cream orders. Ellie and Mrs. Howard stirred the vats of corn soup, anxious to serve it before it burned the bottom of the pan.

Toby entered, marched down the space between the cubicles. She stopped alongside Lila. In a voice that seemed louder because of the surrounding noise, she began, "I'm getting tired of your lousy husband insulting me and my family."

Lila smiled, unloaded a stack of dishes on the table. "So am I.

What's wrong now?"

Ellie approached them. "Not now Toby. After lunch. Wait 'til after lunch."

"No. I'm not waiting. Who does he think he is? No one's good enough for him."

Mrs. Howard was the next one to try quieting her.

Leon entered through the swinging dining room doors. One glance told him that this lunch was going to have an extra complication. "Max?" he questioned wearily.

"Yes. Your lousy brother."

"Toby, let's wait 'til after lunch, please? The kids are just going to eat. Please?"

"I'm not going to let this go by. I'm warning all of you. But I'll wait." She turned, walked back toward the exit and out.

Leon shrugged his shoulders. "Ralph?" he called, breaking away from the group of staring women, to a young waiter watching the scene, "let's serve the kids." Leon went to the switch located on the wall alongside the stove. When he turned it on, the sound of a siren was heard on every part of the hotel grounds. It was a short blast, announcing the children's meal. Ralph left the kitchen. Leon readied himself at the serving table.

WHEN THE ADULTS ATE, it was part of Evelyn's unsalaried job to keep the children amused so that they wouldn't run into the dining room and annoy their parents. Rain forced her back into the casino and, although the noise was deafening, at least it was all in one place. She could lock the one exit and let them do as they pleased without having to run after them.

Her free time came in the afternoon. The parents collected their children and tried to get them settled down to some activity before they themselves settled down again to afternoon card games. Talk had started about taking the children to the movie house in Ellenville. Evelyn hoped not because if Max agreed to the plan, he would agree for her too, and she had more important things to do.

There were only a few guests left in the dining room when she entered. Seated around the corner table, near the entrance to the kitchen, was the family. After the adults, it was their turn to eat. Today, there was silence at the table. Toby picked at her food. Leon tried to encourage her to eat more. Max was not present and Evelyn assumed that he had done just what she expected him to do.

Mrs. Howard smiled at Evelyn. "You ate already? No? I haven't seen you all day."

"I ate with the children, Bubby."

"Where's Irving and David?" asked Ellie who had given up the idea of food.

"They're playing monopoly in our room with two of the kids." Evelyn pulled a chair to the table and sat down next to her mother, but her gaze was directed at the waiters and busboys who were now engaged in clearing the tables as quickly as they could. The sooner they finished that, the more free time they had in the afternoon.

"Get the livestock in," Leon shouted to the boys. "Glasses and silver last, Ray, like I told you. Livestock first." Leon gulped his coffee, stood up to see if they were following his order.

"Can I help, Uncle Leon?" Evelyn asked, blushing with uncontrollable embarrassment.

"Sure, if your mother says so." He carried his cup and other dishes into the kitchen.

"Ma? Can I?"

"Don't you have anything else to do with your time?" Ellie didn't like her spending five minutes in the dining room.

"It's raining again, Ma. There's nothing else to do. Let me help?"

Ellie finished her glass of milk, placed it on the table, and then reluctantly nodded yes. Evelyn jumped up instantly.

"You better be careful, El," said Lila, wiping the bottom of her apron across her forehead until it glowed red and dry. "That's how I got Max."

Mr. Levinson, Max and Leon's father, a tall man with a pile of silky gray hair that kept falling onto his forehead and which he proudly pushed back from time to time, laughed as he stood up. There was seldom a time when he wasn't laughing. He leaned toward his wife. "I'm going into town, Annie." She smoked her cigarette sullenly. "Go. Go and drink, *shicke*." Her curly head shook with anger, an anger that surrounded her perpetually, especially when she spoke to her husband.

Ellie watched Evelyn working with Bob, the head waiter, at the other end of the dining room. She knew what was happening, but it seemed foolish to say anything to Evelyn. Bob, at nineteen, was too busy with the married women to be interested in a fifteen year old.

They called him a regular Gary Cooper. And Evelyn was no match for them. When the summer was over, the 'crush' would be over. Talking about it would only make it seem too serious. But Ellie could see that for her daughter, of course, it was serious. How she watched him move. How she talked to him almost in whispers.

Lila smiled at them as they passed with a load of butter dishes and bread baskets. "Don't drop anything, Evelyn." She lingered on the name. "Yes, El, you better be careful."

"You said that before." Toby needed to direct her anger at someone.

"Lila. Enough." Mrs. Howard, like Ellie, thought silence with this matter was the best way. "She's just a little girl."

"So was I, Ma. She's crazy about Bob."

"Let's not talk about it, please." Ellie brushed her hand across the tablecloth. "When the summer's over . . ."

"This is no summer romance," Lila interrupted. "I can tell. I know the symptoms."

"I wish my Fanny would come in here," said Mrs. Levinson to no one in particular. Fanny, her seventeen year old daughter, never came into the dining room. Max had ordered her to stay out, and whatever Max said, she did. Max had assumed control of her life. He knew what was best for his sister.

"That's Max's fault too," Toby said to her mother-in-law, glad to have something else to blame him for.

"He knows what he's doing." Lila couldn't let her husband go undefended indefinitely. "By the way, where is Max? He hasn't eaten yet."

"He's probably in the office," said Toby, "checking my room charts."

They all stood up, as if on cue, collecting their dishes for deposit with the dishwasher. Ellie called to Evelyn.

"What, Ma?" Evelyn made no move toward her mother.

"Come here."

"What do you want?" With Bob watching her, Evelyn was not going to yield to her mother's command.

"I'm not going to scream across to you. Come over here." Ellie pointed to the table and Evelyn trudged reluctantly to her side. "I don't want you in here more than a few more minutes. Understand?"

"Why?"

"Don't 'why' me. Just do as I tell you."

Evelyn wanted to plead her case, but Ellie quickly left for the kitchen. "It's unfair," she mumbled, on the point of tears.

Only Mrs. Howard remained at the table. "Do what your mother says, darling."

"But why, Bubby? What did I do wrong?"

"Nothing."

"So then why do I . . ."

"Because she wants that you should." Mrs. Howard placed her hand on Evelyn's shoulder, looked, smilingly, at her. "Your mother knows what she's doing. Just listen to her. Always listen and then everything's easier in the end. That way you have everything."

THE ROOM that Max assigned each year to Ellie and her family was one that no guest would pay money to stay in. It was large, but it was too hot. Below it was the hot water tank, and running through one of the walls was the chimney. On rainy days, however, it was the driest spot in the hotel. There were two doors to the room. One led to the dank hallway and into the lobby. The other led directly into the office. Whenever discussions were held that the guests were not invited to hear, Max would go into the room. Unfortunately, neither of the doors could be locked.

There were two double beds in the room. During the week there was no sleeping problem. Irving and David shared one bed; Ellie and Evelyn the other. When Morrie arrived, usually late Friday night, Evelyn moved in with Fanny who had another of those windowless, undesirable spots that could never be sold. Fanny's room was the smallest one in any of the buildings; just large enough for a bed, without sink or closet. Evelyn didn't really mind being moved there. She felt older on weekends, and because fat Fanny was also dumb, she could be bossed around, not cruelly, Evelyn always assured her mother, but just to help her.

The monopoly game, started during the adult lunch hour, had reached the hotel stage when Max entered the room followed by Lila, Toby, Leon, and Ellie. "You kids will have to move out," he ordered. The others were trapped behind him, but Ellie managed to squeeze past Max.

Irving and David looked to Ellie for instructions. "Just try to move the board to the lobby the way it is, Irving." Ellie bent down to help them, but there was so little space between the beds that pieces began to slide off the board. Irving refused to help. David gazed at his uncle with all the hate he could conjure up. Miltie Bernstein, a young cousin of Max's, said nothing, and tried to retrieve the falling pieces. He was a relative, but the other player, a guest, spoke up. "Couldn't you go somewhere else, Mr. Levinson?" Max controlled himself. "I'm afraid not, Allan. Why don't you go play in your room for awhile." Allan shrugged his shoulders, grabbed for the paper money.

Once more Ellie tried to lift the board without disturbing the placement of the pieces, but Irving brushed them all into the center. "We'll have to start all over again." Miltie and Allan nodded in agreement. David waited for Ellie's reaction.

"Why did you do that?" she asked quietly.

"Gee whiz, Ma. Can't we even play a game in peace?"

"Sure you can." Max was motioning them out of the room. "Just go into the lobby. You shouldn't stay in the room anyway."

"No more words, Irving. Go ahead," Ellie commanded.

They left, but David, lingered near the door. He watched his aunts and uncles take seats on the beds, then screamed at Max, "You stink. I hate you and I hate this stinkin' hotel."

Ellie was so startled by the outburst that she didn't move fast enough to catch him before he slammed the door.

"How can you blame him, El." Toby stood at the foot of the bed next to Leon. "He's right."

"Never mind that crap." Max paced the space between the two beds. "We've got other things to talk about." Ellie moved past him, took a seat next to Leon on her bed. Opposite was Lila, alone. She felt sorry for her, for the thankless task of standing by a husband who cared little about anything but himself. At least Morrie tried to care.

"Your wife has got complaints again," Max stopped in front of Leon, "and *I'm* getting tired of it. With all the things I've got to do I can't go around worrying about sensitive people all the time. This is a hotel, a business . . ."

"That's right, big shot," Toby interrupted, "and we're a part of it . . . Not that I wanted to be, but we are."

"As I was saying," his glance dismissed Toby's interruption as if she were an irritating child, "this is a business and the only one who has the burden of getting money for it is me." Still in control he paused to make sure that each of them accepted that fact. "We have to meet notes, pay grocery bills, the help, and hundreds of other things. Who worries about that? . . . Me!"

"You want it that way." Leon's calm was the calm of fatigue.

"Yes, because no one else can do it."

"How do you know?" Toby was still the only one shouting. "Maybe someone else could do a better job of it."

"I doubt it." Max stood in front of the office door. "If you don't think I can do the job, all you have to do is get out. I'll be glad to buy your shares."

Until this moment, Ellie had assumed that this discussion would follow a predictable pattern. She was determined to sit through it quietly. Let Leon take care of his brother. Let Toby yell. But now, with Max's plan laid open for them to see, her anger mounted instantly. She felt her heart pounding, and then the dizziness started. It happened, without wanting it, like an instinct. And when she spoke, she yelled, "So that's it. And my stupid husband couldn't see what you were planning. Max, you are absolutely no damn good."

"Don't get excited, El," Lila whispered. "Max hasn't planned anything."

"How do you know? Would he tell you?"

"Why don't you shut up and listen!" Max screamed. "No one asked for your opinion."

"Don't you talk to me that way." Ellie stood up, balancing herself against the edge of the bed. She breathed deeply as if to gather all the strength she had. "Talk to your wife that way, but don't you dare use those words to me."

Toby moved beside her. "Take it easy, El. He's not worth it."

Leon's anger took a different course. He wanted to control his urge to scream. There was a better way for him. "We're not getting out so fast. Nothing you can think of short of murder—which even that you might do—is going to get us out, so you might as well face it." He was able to smile now. "When Morrie comes, we're going to talk this over. You'll pay him the money you owe or I'll break every bone in your body. You'll stick to the bargain."

"What bargain?"

"The bargain we made in New York." Leon looked at the others as if to share his disbelief.

Ellie, still standing, trembling convulsively with rage that she wanted, needed to control, said, "You expect *him* to honor a bargain? I told Morrie to put everything down in black and white."

"There's nothing to put down." Max was calm again, challenging.

"Not for you. There never is." Ellie's arm moved in a gesture of powerless disgust. "But I'm telling you now that if you try to rob my sister, I'm personally going to see that you get put in jail. I promise you."

"Ellie! Please." Lila pleaded. "There's no need to scream. No one else is screaming."

"Of course there is. That's all your husband knows. And that habit I know from experience. He has to yell even at children. Which is another thing while we're at it. You get my children to do things for you. You give them nothing and then bully them. That's going to stop too, Mister."

"Your children?" Max laughed with disgust.

"Yes! My children! My children!" Ellie's voice seemed to raise to a thin thread of sound, become a shrill cry. And then she crumbled back on the bed. There was a banging at the hall door and Evelyn, Irving, and David ran in as the others crowded around her unconscious body. Evelyn screamed; David ran to Max and started punching him hysterically until Max pushed him away and moved toward Ellie. He lifted her up, moved the others away, except Leon who helped get her head down between her legs. A silence of tears stilled the room as they waited for Ellie to regain consciousness. "She'll be all right in a few minutes." Max was cool, professional.

"Thanks a lot doctor." Lila pushed him away from the bed.

"If I thought it would do any good, I'd say you were the biggest bastard I ever saw in my life." Leon's eyes were glazed with helpless disgust.

The children, frozen by fear, stood next to the bed. Toby, her hands draped protectively around them, stood behind. Ellie's eyes fluttered open. She looked into the faces of her children. Her gaze found each of the people in the room, saw Max leave, and then the lids closed as if the effort to take in all that had occurred were too great.

Toby fixed some pillows at the head of the bed. Leon helped

Ellie to sit up. All of them wanted to lean over her, to help in some way.

"Everyone move away from the bed," Lila directed. "Let her wake up."

Ellie opened her eyes again. "Don't worry," she whispered, "I'll be all right."

"Don't talk." Toby brushed her sister's forehead with a wet face cloth. "Just rest."

Evelyn took the cloth from her aunt's hand, continued to wipe the clammy perspiration from her brow until Ellie stopped her. "It's not necessary. I'm better already."

First Irving, then David leaned over and kissed her. She tried to hug them, but there was no strength in her arms. They remained next to her. And, at the foot of the bed, Lila and Toby cried softly, self-consciously. Leon stood by motionlessly, his arm on Toby's shoulder.

"Don't anyone worry," Ellie whispered. "I'm just getting started."

LATER THAT EVENING, when she was sure that her mother was sleeping comfortably, Evelyn left their room and headed for the casino where Bingo Night was in progress. The rain had stopped and the air was cooler, lighter. A breeze rushed the clouds away from over the valley toward the northeast. As she walked, she could see a crescent moon appear vividly white in the clearing sky, then disappear again behind another speeding cloud. It would clear completely by the next day. The dampness would dry. The heaviness she felt would lift.

The casino was filled with benches and people holding bingo cards. Mounds of lima beans dotted the benches. Lou Sobel, the social director, called the numbers from the stage. Hands would swoop down on the lima beans, grab one, cover a number on the cards. Lou reached into the glass jar, closed his eyes, picked out a wooden disc, then yelled through the microphone. "B-12." All over the casino a mumble of repeated "B-12" sounded from the lips of the players as they scanned their cards. "N-32," Lou called, and again the echoing whisper, like uncertain praying, hissed into the room.

Evelyn stood at the entrance. She spotted Bob: David was beside him, and Irving, seated, studied the card they all shared.

"O-72."

"Bingo," shouted Mrs. Tunick, slapping her face in disbelief. "Bingo, I got."

"Calm yourself, Mrs. Tunick." Lou laughed. His toothy smile munched like a monkey. "The jackpot is yours. Just read off your numbers slowly and I'll check it." Lou did a few steps from a soft-shoe dance.

"*Oy vay*." Mrs. Tunick clapped her hands, delighted. She pushed her glasses higher onto the bridge of her nose. Everyone turned toward her as she called her numbers. Lou nodded yes. "Correct," he shouted, jumped from the stage, shaking a bag of change, the prize. When he reached her, amid playful applause from the audience, he kissed the hysterical woman loudly on both cheeks, danced a mocking, mincing curtsey before her. The other players howled as Mrs. Tunick reached for Lou, held him by a lapel, kissed him. Max, watching from the back, laughed. The guests were happy and that was what he paid Lou to accomplish.

Bob, waving, moved away from David, through the laughing rows of guests, joined Evelyn. "Your mother any better?"

"She's sleeping."

"That's the best thing right now." He gestured toward the crowd. "You want to play?"

"No thanks." She blinked at his intense, appraising stare. "Did you finish setting up?"

"Just about. I'll finish in the morning. You want to walk?"

She nodded. "Let me see my brothers first."

Bob, standing at the entrance, was aware that now the eyes were turned toward him. Max came over, relieving the embarrassment.

"The boys finish?"

"Yes, but Leon's still in the kitchen if you're wondering why the lights are on."

Max left the casino. Bob listened to his slow step crunching the gravel.

Evelyn tugged at his sleeve. "Okay. Let's go."

Play was resuming and quiet once more descended on the casino as they walked off. "I-22." The filtered buzz of echoing sound oozed out into the darkness, followed them until, when they reached the main house, the whir of cicadas in the locust trees drowned out all other sounds, even the talk coming from the card games on the dining room porch.

They sat in front of the main house, away from any other people. Intermittently, headlights zoomed by on the highway, briefly lighting up their faces, making the darkness seem darker as they passed them. Evelyn pulled her sweater together, shivered, chilled by the clearing evening breeze.

"You want to go inside?" Bob whispered, unwilling to intrude, to disturb the dark silence.

"No. I'm fine here." She tried to fill in the silhouette of his face, which was turned toward the road. The black hair had fallen onto his forehead. That she could see. His eyes were blurred, obscured. Only when he started to speak again could she determine the shape of what, away from him, she was always able to imagine in her mind. "Is your mother going to stay in bed for a while?"

"She should, but she won't."

"Can't your father make her?"

"Never." Evelyn sighed. "My father can't make her do anything she doesn't want to do."

Bob laughed, quietly, cynically. "My mother was the same way. That's probably why my father left all of us."

"Is your mother divorced?"

"Jews don't get divorced. He just lives somewhere else. I never see him anymore."

"My mother isn't that bad." Evelyn spoke emphatically. "She means well. She just seems so unhappy about the way things go, like today, for example. It's such a mess." These thoughts were new for Evelyn. Before, they had only been vague feelings, buried beneath irritation when her mother refused her something. Now, suddenly, with someone she could talk to, someone to whom she wanted to tell everything she felt, she understood that there were truths of all kinds that needed to be sorted out.

"It's sad when it's like that. My mother's just gotten nastier. Hard to get along with. Selfish. You know." Bob, too, seemed anxious to explain himself. "She doesn't even want me to go back to school in September. Afraid she'll die while I'm away."

"But you've got older brothers, don't you? Why can't they take care of her? You should finish college."

"Sure. I wish it were so easy. They refuse. They're all married.

Moved away. When you grow up in the country, like we did, you can always find another place you think you have to go to, like New York City." A car passed on the road, lighting up Bob's face so that Evelyn saw there a softness, a sadness which, during the day, she had never seen. The expression confused her. As the darkness returned, the image lingered. How could he take her seriously when there was so much she didn't understand about him? Why did he bother to sit and talk with her? Sure she cared, wanted to find out. He must be able to see that.

"It doesn't matter where you move to, Bob, does it? I mean what you have to do is still the same, isn't it?"

"I suppose you're right." He shifted in his chair. "But . . ."

"What is it, Bob? What else? Please tell me."

"Oh nothing, really. I was just surprised."

"At what?"

"The way you said that." He leaned forward, away from her. "I guess I shouldn't talk like this to you. I admit I want to, but there's just no point saying things that . . ."

"That what?" She wanted to insist that he continue, that he treat her the way she knew she had become, that he recognize the changes inside her which, before this moment, had meant nothing. None of her dates ever spoke this way; none of the boys at school. "That what?" she repeated.

"Oh well, it's hard to say things to a young girl. I mean, you are young."

"So what. I'm not a baby. I know what you're thinking. I know what those women run after you for."

"That's not what I mean."

"Then what do you mean?"

"Hell! It's silly. I'm not even sure what's bothering me."

Evelyn stood up suddenly. "I better get my brothers since you don't really want to talk." She waited for an instant, then began moving away.

Bob stood up, grabbed her arm. "I don't want to hurt your feelings, Evelyn, but I feel strange. I like you, but it's so complicated." He turned her around slowly, so that she had to face him. When he leaned down and kissed her mouth, her trembling frightened him. He let go of her arm. "Remember, I do like you."

She raced off across the lawn, leaving him in the darkness.

THE THREE OF THEM tiptoed into the room, but Ellie was awake. "You can put the light on. I'm up."

The glare of the overhead light made her squint at the sight of her children, huddled together, trying to create their noiseless entrance. She laughed and the boys jumped onto the bed, kissing her.

"You feel better, don't you, Ma?" David urged her to say yes.

"Much better . . . To bed now." She pushed them away. "Come on."

They undressed quickly, the boys turning away as Evelyn got into her pajamas. Each of them waited at the sink to brush his teeth. Ellie followed each movement, content that they did what they were told, understood things, like what happened today, that she would not have understood at their age. But she never had to. Her life at their age seemed so much easier. Anger had never been responsible for her mother's illness. Perhaps too much love from her father, but not anger. Her children, she had to admit, didn't have too much of the love business. But, maybe that's better. Who knows.

"Ma," called David as he jumped into the other bed, "I played Bingo with Bob and Irving, but we didn't win anything."

"That's too bad." Ellie watched him shiver himself to comfort under the blanket.

"I don't care. It was fun anyway and Bob paid for all the cards."

"I don't like that. He doesn't have money to waste."

"He asked us," said Irving as he pushed his brother toward the wall to make room for himself in bed.

"That's no excuse—Irving, leave him alone. You'll hurt him—You should use your own allowance money."

"We don't have any left."

"If you wouldn't buy so many Milky Ways you would . . . Evelyn stop combing your hair so much and come to bed."

"We spent it on the movies, Ma." David leaned on his elbow so he could look over Irving. "You said we could."

"So I did. Well, you'll get more from your father tomorrow."

"I really need more, Ma." Irving sat up now.

"I do too." David waved to Evelyn before she shut the light.

"You're so quiet tonight." Ellie whispered her words to Evelyn as she crawled to her spot next to the wall. "You mad at me?"

"I'm not mad, Ma." Evelyn settled herself beneath the cover, stretched. "I'm just thinking."

"About what?"

"You wouldn't want to talk about it."

"How do you know?"

"I just know, Ma. I can tell. Anyway, you should sleep."

"Thank you, but don't worry about me so much. I'm fine. What's wrong with you is what I want to know."

Evelyn remained silent.

"What's the matter, Ev?" David called.

"Just you go to sleep . . . You too Irving." Ellie heard them turn noisily and feign the sounds of deep sleep. "Don't act, just sleep." She waited a long time before she spoke to Evelyn again. The boys were moaning themselves into a sleep that was real; guests were shuffling down the corridor and up the staircase: the signs of the day moving into another night. "Evelyn? You sleeping?"

"No."

"I thought not. Tell me what's bothering you. They're sleeping now."

"It's nothing, Ma. Just the kind of day it was. What happened to you, and everything."

"What's the everything? Not just me, I know."

"Myself too. I admit it. The way I feel."

"What way do you feel?"

"Oh Ma. It's so hard to say . . . you know . . . it's people . . . and love . . ."

"Love?" Ellie's sigh escaped before she could stifle it. Talking now would be harder than she wanted it to be. "That I can't help you with. When the time comes for you to know . . ."

"That's the point, Ma."

"Why? What is?" Ellie lifted herself higher on the pillow. "Are you getting married tomorrow?"

"Please, Ma. You asked me and I told you."

"Yes, but I didn't expect . . ."

"That's just it. I need to know now. I didn't expect it either." She stopped talking long enough to breathe deeply and then she blurted out what she realized her mother, or anyone else, would not take seriously. "I really do think I love someone, Ma."

"Not Bob. Don't tell me that. It's . . ."

"But I do. I can't help it." She seemed to stutter, trying to keep the words low, painless.

"It's ridiculous. You're only 15. What do you know?"

"Nothing. That's why I'm asking."

Ellie slipped down under the cover again. Her head was spinning. "I can't talk about it now. I can't. I'm tired."

Evelyn said nothing. She knew what her mother, what everyone would say. But her feelings, strong, joyous, sad, were there, inside, living apart from everything else.

They turned away from one another, but, for a long time, neither of them slept.

In the late afternoon, when most of the guests were either swimming at the lake, sleeping on the lawn or in their rooms, they gathered for the second conference of the day. Max had arranged it, had even instructed the handyman to set chairs on the front of the lawn, near the highway, underneath the tallest locust trees. Usually, this was the pleasantest time of day for all of them. The hours before the dinner meal were without chores. The guests could be forgotten. On good days it was the time when Leon and Toby went for a lazy drive into town or sat on the lawn listening for the sounds that only being in the country could offer. This seemed to be the only joy their new venture had delivered. It was the time when Mrs. Howard read her *Forwards*. None of them liked the idea of talking then. But Morrie refused to let another weekend go by without settling matters. Evelyn had told him about Ellie's fainting. And again, David and Irving had begged him to take them home.

When Mrs. Howard arrived, by habit carrying her *Forwards*, the conversation could begin. Their chairs faced the fence and the highway. They did not, at least, have to look at one another.

"I hope we won't have to raise our voices this time," Max began immediately. "Everybody's tired and I'd like Lila to get some rest before she goes back to the kitchen." Lila twisted to look at him, bitterly thankful for this day's first statement of consideration.

"All right. Let's talk." Morrie folded his arms across his chest.

"First of all, I'm going to be perfectly candid with all of you. We're in a bad way financially."

"That's news?" Leon interrupted.

Max was disinterested in the sarcasm. "I've been trying to get a loan from the bank since the beginning of the summer, but they're acting very slowly. Our credit is not the best." He lowered his head, leaned forward so that anyone who cared to would recognize and appreciate his earnest expression. Only Lila nodded compassionately. "I've been under a hell of a lot of pressure from my—our . . ." his correction sounded rehearsed, patronizing, "creditors."

"I thought you used the money we gave?" Leon reminded him.

Max waved his arm in deprecation. "A drop in the bucket. We need thousands more."

"Why didn't you give us the facts before?" Leon was no longer sarcastic, only earnestly concerned.

"It's my problem."

"It's mine too if I'm your partner. Damn it, I've got something to lose too."

"You're right," Max spoke quietly, and the quietness of his concession, the surprise of the admission, made each of them shift uncomfortably. "From now on, when I go to the bank, you'll come too, Leon. You'll see what it's like. I can tell you right now, it's not easy."

"So?" Leon was holding Toby's hand.

"So, you'll probably be sorry you ever left the kitchen. At least each meal is something finished. Over with. This stretches on forever. It'll never stop. Every year there's something else needs to be improved."

"For Christ's sake," Morrie interrupted, "how much do you owe?"

"Enough so Sakowitz groceries doesn't want to sell me anymore on credit—and they're friends."

"How the hell can you go on then?" Morrie, sensing that his question was a trap he set for himself, let himself be drawn into it. Ellie recognized the new twist to the plan. If she were still a shareholder, she could have spoken up. But now, her sister would have to learn how to handle Max. She tried to gain Morrie's attention, to prevent him from making it so easy for Max. But he wasn't looking at her. Of course not. He never looked at her when decisions had to be made.

"I'm really not sure we can go on." Max's head dropped lower. "If we have to pay off you and your mother," he slapped his thighs, "we're not going to have anything at the end of the season, unless, of course, we get the loan. Also, we have to have a full house for the rest of the summer. And the weather's been no help. Who knows what's going to be." Max did not raise his head. He waited. The silence deepened beneath the locust trees. As if in embarrassment, a chorus of sighs discharged the drama of Max's narration. Ellie watched a car speed by on the highway, her neck stretching to follow it around the bend, her ears lifted, then, for the sound of its grinding motor, disappearing.

"I get it Max." Morrie gazed toward the low mountains far behind the corn field on the other side of the road.

"Get what, Morrie?" Max seemed surprised, hurt.

"Simple. Elementary, Dr. Watson. You're smart. I've really got to hand it to you." Morrie pulled at his fingers nervously. "If I ask for the money, I end up the big bastard. I . . ."

"Who said anything about . . ."

But Morrie would not let him continue. "You said we could talk honestly for once, didn't you? All right. Let's. I don't give a damn about this hotel. I don't want anything to do with it. My wife here," he waved his hand, almost slapping Ellie in the face, "she's the one. She wanted me here."

Toby looked at Ellie, followed her gaze to a bird walking along the fence top. Ellie knew what was about to happen. Morrie's quivering voice stopped momentarily, then sputtered past a previous resolve. "With her it's always something. The same crap all the time. A house. A hotel. Always."

"That's so terrible?" Mrs. Howard fearfully interrupted.

"Stay out of this, Ma," Morrie shouted, but Mrs. Howard, who had been silently turning her paper back and forth in her lap, would not be stopped. "How should I stay out? Your father didn't buy this place? He should rest in peace."

"Why don't you stop?" Max yelled, but Lila's angry look silenced him.

And then, as if engrossed in the ritual of her remembrance, Mrs. Howard strung together the difficult words, sounds to speak for her alien existence. "For your sister he bought this farm. A farm it was then. Then you didn't care and now you don't care. All right. Let it be that way. You have your own family. You take care for them the way you want. You work hard your way. But your father, he bought something. When your sister died, I wanted you should help him build it into something else. No, you said." She rocked her chair in time to the music of events that had no sound for anyone else. "If Izzy were alive . . ." she wiped tears roughly away with the back of her hand, ". . . he would be here. That I know."

"Will you please, Ma!" Morrie reached across Ellie, trying to shake his mother alive to now. Ellie pushed him back.

"I know. What's gone is gone. *Ah zoy gayt dus.*" Mrs. Howard refolded her paper, loudly, alerting them for her next words. "Morrie, you sold my part to Leon. No askings. You sold. And your part too you sold. Let it be. But if Ellie wanted something, she's wrong?" She paused, but expected no answer. "No, my sonnele. She worked like I worked, and for nothing."

"What the hell has that got to do with it?" Max would no longer suppress his annoyance with the turn the conversation had taken.

"What it's got to do with is that n-ooww," she held the last sound until it became a rising cadence so that when she finally released it, what followed would be heard carefully and forever, "Morrie and Ellie will have nothing, and I'll have a bigger nothing because where can I go? This is not mine no more." She twisted to look behind her at the lawn, the buildings, the sky.

"Damn it. You'll stay right here. And of course I'll pay them." Max moved to the edge of his chair, as if to get up, to stand before them and teach them a lesson of life. "I said nothing about not paying them."

A wry smile closed the deeply webbed corners of Mrs. Howard's eyes into a clearer vision. "I know better."

"Never mind her, Max," Morrie roared. "You'll pay me and Mama when you can. My family stays here. Ellie does no more work in the kitchen. That's final."

"For who is it final?" Ellie roused herself from fatigue. "I'll do just as I've been doing. My share. I get what I deserve. You understand Max?" She stood up, moved behind her chair, looking past the fence, the fields, the mountains. "When the summer's over, we'll leave, but I won't be coming back next summer or the summer after that or . . . That I promise. What I do now, this summer, I do for my own reasons . . ." She paused, scanned the uplifted, twisted faces. "My children are a different story. Irving and David, maybe, will have some benefit. Evelyn maybe too. But I doubt it." Her final comments were directed toward Morrie. "If you let your mother work in that kitchen anymore, you'll be responsible for what happens. Nobody will ever blame Max. Let him hire a chef. My only regret is that I didn't die before I let you talk my sister into this mess." As she walked away, she could hear Max burst into words, but she had no desire to listen. It was too late. She quickened her pace, feeling lost, small, like she did at Toby's wedding, so long ago, or when her father died and she stood next to his grave and watched it fill up with earth. It was no use to fight at all. She managed to smile, her business reflex, at the guests who nodded, but her mind was already inside her room.

David was working a jig-saw puzzle, alone, on the floor between the two beds. "Go outside, Davie. Please. Mama wants to rest." He stood up, moved closer to her as she settled herself at the edge of the bed. "Go for a swim instead of staying in here."

"You okay, Ma?"

"Fine. Just fine." She rubbed his hair. He smiled bashfully, and fell against her. "Everything's hunky-dory." She moved him back. "Go. Find Evelyn and tell her to take you for a swim."

Quickly, David changed to his bathing suit and before he left the room kissed her. "You can sleep now, Ma."

She nodded. "Be careful swimming." She hugged him and he left, smiling, as if the hug, the kiss were treasures, more precious because only he had them.

Ellie fell back against the pillows, closed her eyes, thinking that there was time to relax before going back to the kitchen. Maybe even a nap. But with her eyes closed the spinning was worse than ever. And something else was bothering her now. Her eyes. They felt as if sand had been poured into them. She raised herself higher on the pillow, but rubbing them, they began to tear. Closed, the whirling was faster. One way or the other she couldn't lose the sensation of being bound to what was happening outside or in here.

She heard the sound of steps in the corridor. No one came to the door. The steps pushed up the stairs. To be left alone. Good. The shades were down. There was imagined coolness in the room. Concentrate on nothing. That was the way to sleep. Even the spinning was better that way, like a ride that is pleasurable because it doesn't have to end.

But, in what seemed like the next moment, the door was opened, slammed loudly. Morrie stood next to the bed, looking down at her, anger beating in his jaw. She sat up. So it would be just another afternoon without sleep.

THE WEEKENDS of the summer passed with surprising rapidity after that. The soothing effect of yielding to what was inevitable lingered whenever the family gathered. Even the complaints of the children entered, merged with the familiar gray routine of each day. Time didn't have a chance to hang heavily for any of them. If you like roast chicken and know that every Friday night you will have it, then Fridays loom large in the imagination, are longed for ferociously. The management anticipated *their* roast chicken, their Friday, the favorite of the summer: Labor Day weekend. For a Catskill hotel manager, the Labor Days of one's life were like musical preludes, the activity that precedes long winter vacations, vacations of idleness and indulgence, only broken by the creditors' demands and an opening for the Jewish holidays, maybe Christmas for the ambitious owner.

The mood of the Labor Day weekend was a unique blend of happiness and melancholy, the long desired goodbye. The staff could 'stick it out' now. Miraculously they mined from the depths of their collective fatigue a measure of brilliant, smiling energy. The waiters, mentally counting tips, became more solicitous of each guest's feeding whim. Max could forget that he was meant for other dreams, found time to joke and laugh. Ellie framed her thin-lipped, business smile with deeper pockets of displeasure at the corners, already arranging her Monday afternoon departure. Just three more days. This waiting does have its end. Toby and Leon stayed close to the reality of 'cash-in-the-box.' When the baby arrived they were going to need some money. Only Mrs. Howard remained apathetic. All her Labor Days now ended in the same share of left-over chaos, of moneyless dependence.

In the casino Lou Sobel and the band rehearsed all day Saturday for the extra demands of that night's show and Sunday night's Midnight Supper, the gala of the summer.

Only the children of the guests were glum. Their freedom was almost at an end. For David and Irving, joy overflowed. Their freedom was about to begin. Labor Day, for Evelyn, meant upheaval. She would leave; Bob would stay. Back in the city, having ruled out college—Morrie said a girl didn't need it; Ellie had argued for it and lost—she would have to start searching for some kind of job. And the long time between Monday and a letter from Bob would be how long? Breathless most of the summer with wonder and fear for what she felt, fear because she had told him what she felt and that had made him cautious, too conscious of a responsibility that made her wonder what he really did feel, she tried to create the best games for the children to play while the adults ate their last few meals at the hotel.

All day Sunday the kitchen staff remained on duty. Preparations for the Midnight Supper demanded that kind of loyalty. The baker baked small rolls which would be placed at each setting, and since the hotel was squeezed full, he started early. Next to the roll would be the fresh smelling fern which Max took his nephews, his niece, his sister to help him collect after the regular evening meal. He was back and forth to Ellenville all day securing cold cuts, flowers, candy, the liquor necessary to insure the success of this most special occasion. Tradition, too, required particular and new offerings. If last year he had given every woman guest a rose, then this year he had to do something better than that. Every hotel owner wanted to outdo the other, and when they met in town they stopped to compare purchases like women at a dress shop, adding more to their orders than they could afford. What difference did it make; they could spend all winter paying the final bill. This was the last splurge, the last taste in the customer's mouth.

Morrie, who on this day never entered the kitchen, did enjoy accompanying Max to town, forgetting, for the time being, all of their recent arguments. This Labor Day, he realized, was more important, for it would change the way in which all of his future summers would be spent. Ellie had assured him, each weekend, as July blurred into August heat, that this would definitely be the last summer she was going away. "Count on it Morrie. Arrange it so that you remember. We're finished here." She would not change her mind. He was prepared to accept what next June would bring, but not that day. You just couldn't help but laugh at Max's extravagance.

Lila, however, did not laugh. She screamed with useless desperation each time Max returned from town with another load of provisions. "What are we making these turkeys and brisket for if you get delicatessen? You're crazy. You're a child."

"Come on, Lil. What's the difference?"

She turned to Ellie and her mother. "And then you call us crazy. All right." Max grabbed her, playfully contrite. Lila pushed him away, trying to act disgusted. "You pay the bills when it's time. And don't come complaining." Max pinched her behind.

Leon, and even Toby, readied the pickles, the cole slaw, the plates of celery, olives, and carrots that would nestle, finally, among the fern later that night.

As soon as the evening meal, a conspicuously light one, had been served and the 'live-stock' returned to the huge refrigerator, Max eventually took over control of the dining room. The tables, which normally followed a pattern of formal disarray, were arranged so that they created a horseshoe around the perimeter of the room. Clean floral tablecloths came from seldom used cupboards in the kitchen. The dishwasher had no opportunity to stack the dishes from the evening meal. Still wet, they were taken back out to the dining room.

"I want this floor mopped and waxed. And Bob, make sure you have the boys put that resin on it. They'll be dancing here." Max yelled his commands to scurrying figures as he began to place the pieces of fern on the tables. "Let's get those dishes out here. We don't have all night." He walked toward the kitchen, held open one of the swinging doors, "Leon? You ready with the relish trays?"

"Don't worry. Just get out of here."

Max didn't move. "Ma? The turkeys done?"

Mrs. Howard, surprised by his direct address, could only mutter "yes."

Lila laughed. "What a change."

Ellie checked the briskets, anticipating Max's next request.

All evening the four waiters and busboys raced in and out of the kitchen, carrying, arranging trays, stopping occasionally for a gulped cup of steaming coffee.

By ten thirty while music from the casino filtered into the kitchen, accenting, sustaining the rhythm of movement there, Max adjusted a final fern. The staff gathered in the dining room to survey the finished product, Max assembling them in triumph. "I think it looks better than ever. Don't you?"

"Why did you have to use the *Rosh Hashanah* candlesticks?" Lila smiled even as she questioned. Max expected his wife to find fault publicly. Later, in their room, she would announce her admiration.

The flowers, the fern, the candlesticks, the shape of the tables all blended, creating the proper mood. If necessary, tonight they could force themselves to be festive.

"Beautiful, Max." Ellie undid her apron.

"Marvelous how *you've* done it all." Toby would never completely surrender.

Max ignored her. "Just before twelve, the band will lead them in. So you should all be back here no later than eleven forty-five . . . Bob, I want the boys in clean shirts. Everyone with a black bow tie . . . Make sure their pants are clean too."

The group dispersed silently. Leon remained. "I hope it turns out as good as it looks."

"It will. Just leave everything to me."

"Come on Max," Lila yelled from the kitchen. "You know how long it takes you to get dressed."

"Coming." Left alone, he tried the doors to the room. He didn't want anyone to break in and spoil the look.

THE BAND PLAYED "Darktown Strutters Ball" as they led the parade of guests from the casino to the dining room. The screaming mob was kept in some kind of order by the prospect of what they knew was before them. The line twisted, broadened, squeezed together at the entrance. Herbie, the trumpet player, blew the darkness back, warmed the September chill for them. They waited.

Max and Lila, Leon and Toby waited at the door to greet each guest. Lila and Toby wore corsages of camellias which Max had selected. They looked as if they were beginning the summer, not ending it.

The band entered first, quickly setting up their instruments at the open end of the horseshoe, never stopping the music. The guests marched in, followed the horseshoe around, remained standing on either side of the tables, hands readied on the backs of chairs, 'oowing' and 'aahing' over the decorations.

Max signalled to the band. They played "Hatikvah," followed immediately by "The Star Spangled Banner." The silence of the guests broke into cheers with the last note of the anthem. The band blared a fanfare. Max walked to the center of the floor. "Be seated." He waved his arms. The chairs slid on the slippery floor. "I'm glad you're glad to be here." Applause, shouts of approval greeted his opening words. "And it's my pleasure to extend my best wishes for your enjoyment this evening." Leon, listening near the kitchen doors, reddened with anger. Toby turned her back on the guests. ". . . Since I won't have a chance like this again, let me say that I'm pleased you are here and I hope to see you healthy and here next summer too." More applause. Toby entered the kitchen, refusing Leon's effort to keep her with him. Max turned slowly as he spoke, looking at all of the guests, making sure they watched him. "So have as good a time tonight as *you* wish. The staff is ready to honor any reasonable," he laughed devilishly, paused for their nervous titters, "request. So eat, drink, dance, and be sure to call on me for anything you need. Thank you for the opportunity to serve you." He lowered his head. Applause exploded. The band struck up a foxtrot; the waiters, as if on cue, emerged from the kitchen carrying platters of turkey and beef; the laughter, the shouted conversation rose toward the low ceiling: the guests had paid for the right to scream.

Max, followed by Lila and Leon, walked around the horseshoe, chatting amiably, drinking when it was offered.

In the kitchen, Toby muttered, "That bastard. Of all the nerve."

Only Ellie heard her. "What did you expect?"

"Well, at least he could have . . ."

"At least nothing. He's the big cheese. He'll always be." She moved Toby away from the edge of the work table. "But you won't change it by staying in the kitchen. That was my mistake. Don't let it be yours. You should be with Leon." Ellie led her toward the swinging doors, past the rushing waiters.

"And what are you going to do? Stay in here all night?"

"No. I'll be out as soon as my husband remembers I'm not out there with him."

"Just remember yourself you didn't get all dressed to stay in here."

"Don't worry." Ellie pushed her through the doors and jumped back, away from the noise.

Bob, passing, spoke. "You ought to get out there, El." He walked alongside her, slowing down.

Ellie tried to smile, tried to be congenial to Bob, whose progress with Evelyn was, by now, the topic of all lawn whispers, the talk of any card game that Ellie became a part of. She liked him as a coworker; he accepted all tasks; nothing was too much. But as a son-in-law? That was a different matter. "I'd like to speak to you before we go tomorrow," she heard herself saying involuntarily, without first having planned it.

Bob gazed down, unashamedly. "Sure, El. Whenever you say." He rushed off.

Mrs. Howard joined her. "Ellie, darling, go." She pointed to the door.

"Soon, Ma." She turned back to the work table. "Let's cut up this meat first."

"You'll get dirty. Let me do it. The dress is too pretty for meat cutting."

Ellie rubbed her hands down the front of her polka dot dress. It was the first time she had worn it that summer. It wasn't that she had saved it; she had had no occasion to wear it before. The dots were the color of her hair, a brown that wasn't dark enough or light enough. But the white background was pretty when the skirt twirled. The top fit tightly but not so tightly that her breasts stood out too much. She wasn't as comfortable in it as in her unfitted tops. But Evelyn and David had complimented her when she left the room earlier. Not Morrie. He had no time for that. He had to rush to the casino.

Mrs. Howard, watching Ellie smooth her dress, sensed her sadness, moved closer to her, kissed her forehead. "Go outside. Have a good time. Find Morrie. Go." As Ellie had done to Toby, Mrs. Howard tried to move Ellie to the doors, but Ellie resisted.

"No, Ma. I'll go later." She picked up a knife and began slicing the piece of brisket.

Mrs. Howard sighed with renewed despair. "At least let me put an apron on you."

As she worked silently, Ellie registered the progress in the dining room: the mounting roar of laughter that echoed incessantly; the shrieked shouts of drinking women; and then the opening notes of a conga and a new burst of roaring approval. The evening was proceeding successfully without her. I hope at least, she thought, that he's watching out for the children. The screaming I can do without. I don't need it. Just tomorrow I need.

Max, Lila, and Morrie were suddenly there, standing before her, watching.

"Why the hell don't you come out there, El?" Morrie started to undo her apron. Ellie squirmed away from him, dropping the knife, holding her greasy hands up so that he would leave her alone. "I'll be out soon."

"You can go now, El. Mama can cut the rest of the meat." Max stuffed a scrap of turkey into his mouth. Mrs. Howard did not look up, did not stop her work.

"Why don't you all get out of here. We started and we'll finish." Ellie tried to brush them away as if they were flies hovering around a cake. "The owners should be with the guests. The workers will work."

Morrie took the knife out of her hand, turned her around. "You're finished working." She could smell the liquor as he leaned toward her. "You'll enjoy your last night here." It was a command. He held her arm and pulled the apron so that it fell to the floor. "You look too good to be stuck in any kitchen." Ellie looked to her mother-in-law.

"Don't worry, Ellie." Mrs. Howard waved her away. "You too, Lila. Go."

"You come too." Max felt trapped into the words. "We have enough."

Lila took her mother's arm. "Bob will take care of things."

For those that drank, the evening was a success. For those who only ate, it was still a success. The sound of enjoyment was echoed in the music, the congas, the waltzes, the horas which even Mrs.. Howard and Mrs. Levinson joined. And the band played with a warmth engendered by the sure knowledge of the finale, and, because of this knowledge would have played all night. But at 2:30, when the flowers and ferns had wilted, and the waiters were no longer bothering to replenish the food, the 'good nights' began, mingled with other sounds. People, settled into languid positions of fatigue, drank long last drinks. Morrie, stumbling, eluding Ellie's stretching fingers, made his way, finally to the band and got them to play his favorite Labor Day song. It was, conspicuously, the wrong song for that moment, but the oldtimers, accustomed to, expecting even this part of the night's entertainment, turned to watch Morrie sway to attention. He sang, surprising even himself that he was actually singing:

"Oh April showers, they come in May;
They bring the flowers that come your way
So when it's raining . . ."

First year guests were shocked into listening. The voice was deep, serious. He was drunk; he mixed up the words, but the sound evoked the mood of another time, another singer. Ellie folded her arms in embarrassment and waited.

"Because it isn't raining rain, you know,
It's raining violets . . ."

He was free; his eyes were closed; his voice was forced higher until it caught a note balanced at the crest of his imagination's mountain. His head was thrown back. He screamed the tune of his optimism, believing for this moment that he was a singer.

". . . whenever April showers come along."

As he finished, his tall body, forced upright while singing, sagged forward dangerously. It was not a bow to accept the applause. It was a return to the knowledge of what he had done, what he had done at that moment for so many Labor Day Eves. He saw Ellie's hands beating, slapping with the others, and his mother's nod of approval, Evelyn's proud grin. In confusion he walked toward the kitchen doors, as if that were the way off the stage. When the noise of laughing conversation resumed, and the band played a slow, ending song, Ellie went to join him.

He leaned against the stove, one freckled hand covering his eyes. A shudder shook his body with a regularity that told her he was crying.

"Morrie," Ellie spoke softly, held his other, limp arm. "Do you feel sick? Do you think you'll throw up?" She forced him to stand straight. His hand uncovered swollen slits of eyes.

"Ellie . . ." His arms flopped over her shoulders and Ellie began to totter under the burden.

"You were marvelous, Caruso." She set her feet firmly, holding him up against the stove.

"I want to go to bed," he moaned.

"All right, but I can't carry you. Stand up." She was a mother again, commanding, sternly loving. She led him to the back door of the kitchen, past the smell of old garbage, around the laundry room, onto the fresh darkness of the side lawn with the sound of a breeze rustling the leaves of trees and the crunch of brittle twigs as they moved toward the main house.

He wanted to sit on the porch before they went in. The moon stopped him. They sat silently, Morrie trying to rub his face into order. The music had ceased in the dining room now and Ellie could hear the slow moving departure of others, the footfalls on the gravel telling the direction.

"Ellie?" Morrie's voice was an insistent whisper, a muffled call to affection, understanding.

"Yes?" She tried to echo his tone.

"So what if we don't come back here anymore."

"So what." Her voice was like a shrug.

"It's all right what I've done?"

"Yes. It's all right." But she could not hold back the sigh.

"Let's go to bed. The boys must be sleeping by now." He stood up, stretched, steadier now. She followed him inside, to the dark room and the low, sleeping moan of her two sons. She didn't want to think of where Evelyn was. She can take care of herself.

It was very late in the afternoon before they finished loading the car, and the sun was lowering behind a haze of wispy cloud. Morrie had borrowed Louis Kriegel's big Reo for the occasion. The company car couldn't hold the trunks and the five of them.

The dining room staff lounged lazily on their porch. All afternoon they had waited, making themselves available for the guests. Their presence shamed some into a bigger tip. Otherwise, if they couldn't be found, a dissatisfied guest, one who would never return, might drive off, his car loaded with family and obligations, without leaving anything. Max was nearby to warn them of that. The waiters' pockets bulged with crumpled money, money slavishly earned, but money which, for some, might mean another year at college, or, if it were a small amount, another year at a job. They were as available as diplomacy allowed. Max and Lila, sitting with them, demanded that. After all, offending a border-line guest was bad business. But they did enjoy watching the awkward, self-consciously ambling guest approach one of the boys, shake his hand, leaving some bills in the palm. Later, Lila would playfully urge each one to tell her the total 'take.' It was a pleasure, she said, to see her staff rewarded.

"How many you think there'll be for dinner?" Bob asked indifferently, his gaze fixed on the movement around the parked Reo.

"Five or six." Max rocked his chair, exaggerating this motion of relaxation.

"I'm leaving late tonight," Sonny, the other waiter, informed them.

"I'll be staying until tomorrow," Bob lit a cigarette. "My mother'll probably have the cows waiting to be milked already. If she thinks I'm going to . . ." he paused, watching Evelyn walk toward the car, ". . . to stay on the farm *this* year, she's sadly mistaken."

"You think you'll make it back to school?" Lila questioned, following Bob's gaze.

"That depends." Bob patted his pocket. "I hope so. They're expecting me."

Ellie stood next to the car, waiting. David, then Irving, joined her. Evelyn walked toward the porch. "We're ready to leave," she called, too loudly for it merely to be an invitation for her aunt and uncle to come say goodbye.

From different directions the relatives converged on the car. Toby, Leon, and Mrs. Howard descended the main house steps. Mr. and Mrs. Levinson, followed by Fanny walked from the lawn. Max, Lila, and Bob stopped their rocking and stood up.

Bob did not come very close to the car. Evelyn had to walk over to him. They looked at each other, embarrassed by the presence and stares of the others.

There were few words, only long embraces. Ellie held Toby closely and whispered. "No fighting. Just take care of yourself. I'll come up with Mama when it's time." Toby moved on to the children, kissing each of them as if she would never see them again.

Mrs. Howard was next. Ellie rested her cheek against the wrinkled, yielding skin of the older woman, "You'll come to us when you're ready and stay as long as you want."

"You should only live and be well." She rocked her daughter-in-law. That was the only evidence of the lament within her. "It's over," one hand moved across the view of lawn, "here."

Ellie kissed her again. "Don't worry, Ma." She continued down the line, and, at the end of it, with David, Irving, and Morrie trailing her, anxious to leave too, she remembered that she had never had that talk with Bob. Now there was no time. She approached him, and Evelyn moved to stand alongside him, facing her mother.

Extending her hand, forcing herself to smile, Ellie said, "I hope you have a good year." She sounded sincere and Bob sighed, relieved.

"Thanks, El. You too . . . Maybe I'll see you this winter. I'm thinking of staying with my sister in Brooklyn and going to night school there."

Ellie knew that there was little sign of encouragement on her face, nor could Evelyn refrain from criticizing it. "Ma!" she muttered. Bob's gaze shifted to the gravel. He kicked at it.

"You'll always be welcome to our house." She shook his hand.

Evelyn leaned toward Bob, kissed him lightly on the cheek, then moved quickly inside the car. The others watched the episode as if it were a scene enacted for their amusement. "Love!" Max exploded with mocking laughter. Ellie wheeled around, glaring, but Morrie pulled her back to the car, patting Bob's shoulder as he did so. "Let's go, already." He directed Ellie into the front, shoved the boys into the back with Evelyn.

Leon checked the rope that held the bulging baggage trunk together. "It'll hold, Morrie."

The car started up sluggishly, spurted into whirring action, then lurched ahead. Morrie leaned out of the window, waving toward the rear. "So long."

The group joined forces behind the slowly moving car. All except Evelyn twisted for a last look.

"I'm so happy," David shouted, clapping as they gathered speed down the curve, the hill, moving past the Post Office, across the erector set bridge that spanned a dried up creek.

The sun was ahead of them, moving lower on the horizon, its rays shining spokelike in the valley.

Toby's baby, a boy, was stillborn. For Ellie, who had traveled with her mother and David by bus through the November snowy grayness to the Ellenville Hospital, the event was marked by a head shaking sense of foreknowledge, as if part of her own summer feeling of defeat had prevented an ordinary birth. Mrs. Perlin, slowly losing her powerful hold on life, was stoical, but difficult. There was no complaint, only acceptance. But at the hotel, where they were to stay for a few days, she would eat nothing but—Lila couldn't help but laugh each time she told the woman how kosher they were in the kitchen—sour cream. If you could eat sour cream, you could eat anything. Lila's words had no effect, and her laughter produced a look of compassion. Lila gave up. Mrs. Perlin remained steadfast to a code for which only she could supply the rules. Mrs. Howard, at least understood and kept a supply of sour cream on hand.

David told Ellie that he would enjoy this vacation. Leaving school in the winter made going to the hotel different. He was only vaguely aware of what had prompted the leaving. When he overheard a whispered conversation between his mother and Leon in which the words 'blue baby' occurred, his mind stuck fast to the picture of those words and once more he was urging Ellie to take him home. But he was brought to the hospital, made to stand beneath his Aunt Toby's first floor window and smile up at her. He could tell that she was paler than the grayness that dusted the new snow. He could tell that she did not want to smile at him, even when Uncle Leon pointed excitedly toward his upturned face. And when they were back at the hotel, between visiting hours, sitting in the empty lobby while winter dusk settled in shadows around them, David saw his aunt's face, cold and white, staring at him from a patch of darkness on the wall. He wanted to but was afraid to light a lamp.

Mrs. Perlin's mouth worked constantly, shaping incoherent Hebrew prayers, the sounds of which were barely audible. Ellie tried to quiet her for the mumbling irritated Max, who expressed his anger with sharp words for Lila.

"We'll go home tomorrow, Ellie," said Mrs. Perlin during their second afternoon. "I don't want to stay." She looked at no one as she spoke, listening to the voice she heard inside herself, the voice that directed all her actions, all her words.

"But Ma, we should stay at least until Toby gets back here," Ellie whispered, not wanting the others to hear.

"We dasn't stay longer."

"Ma! Please."

Leon joined them on the leather sofa. "It's all right, El. My mother's coming and Lila's here," he gestured toward the rest of the room, "and your mother-in-law. We'll be fine. Mama's not happy." Leon leaned his head back against the rim of the sofa, closed his eyes.

"I can't understand you, Ma." Ellie motioned to David to stay away from the lamp and sit down near her.

"What is there to understand?" Mrs. Perlin watched David rest his head on Ellie's lap. "Mollie is home alone. I must cook for her. You have your family."

"They can all take care for a few days. It won't hurt." Ellie nudged David to an upright position.

"You're welcome to stay as long as you want, Mrs. Perlin." Lila spoke shrilly as if each word was a slap for her petulant husband rather than an invitation.

"Thank you, but I dasn't stay." Although decayed by the passage of pain through her life, Mrs. Perlin's aristocratic bearing required a respect that even Max found difficult to resist. She did not crumble. The words of those she disliked could not penetrate deeply or disturb the force that protected her. "You will have children, Leon. Don't worry." Like a Biblical prophet, her tired eyes pierced unknown quantitites of time. "You will again. Soon."

Leon turned his gaze toward her. The room was now almost totally dark. "I don't know. Toby's not convinced . . ."

"Don't worry." She interrupted majestically. "You are both still young. Now you can settle here and raise a family. God knows what He is doing. Remember."

David, who had moved to stand before his grandmother, put his arms around her forbidding, unbent neck. "God? Grandma!"

"Yes, God. He knows everything. And if you listen to Him you will know it too. She patted his back and then made him stand before her. "You'll learn in Hebrew School." She looked at Ellie as if in command.

"He's going, Ma. Don't worry."

Mrs. Perlin stood up, smoothed the front of her dress and walked into the darkness of the corridor that led to her room.

WHEN THEY RETURNED to Brooklyn, arriving in the evening, Morrie was requested to take his mother-in-law home. Ellie insisted. Mrs. Perlin refused to stay.

"Just give you a car, and you start arranging the world. I should have left it at work." Ellie stood above him as he folded his newspaper and threw it down on the carpet near his easy chair.

"All right." Ellie turned away. "I'll take her home on the subway. You listen to the radio and read your paper."

"Damn it," Morrie mumbled, striking the arm of his chair. He got up, followed her into the kitchenette where Mrs. Perlin, in hat and coat, sat waiting. She watched Irving struggle with his homework. Evelyn was finishing the dishes from the evening meal which she had hurriedly but enthusiastically prepared after returning from work. David, seated on the radiator in front of the kitchen windows, watched his sister.

"You ready Ma?" Morrie snapped. "It's late."

"I'm ready." She stood up.

"In a few minutes," said Ellie, content with her little victory. "I just want to change my dress." She started down the corridor. "I'll bring your coat, Morrie. You just stay there."

Mrs. Perlin stood behind Irving's chair. "Soon you'll be *bar-mitzvahed?*" She smiled down at his now upturned face. "You're studying already. No?"

"Yes Grandma. The rabbi says I'm good. You want me to read for you? I got my book home."

"Not now," Morrie threaded his fingers, bent them until the knuckles cracked. "Come on, El."

"I'm coming. Another minute," Ellie called from the bedroom. "A little patience."

"Can I drive with you?" Evelyn asked. She was replacing the dishes in the cupboard above the sink.

"No!" Morrie leaned against the refrigerator.

"Why not? After all I did tonight the least . . ."

"I said no and that's final. You're staying with the boys."

Ellie was ready. She stood next to Evelyn. "Put them to bed in an hour."

Evelyn nodded but would not look up.

"Don't be angry with your father. He's not . . . serious now." Ellie looked at David. "And you get off the radiator. You'll burn your behind. . . . Go kiss Grandma goodbye."

When Irving heard the outside door slam, he yelled, "What a lousy father," and slapped the table the way Morrie did when he was angry.

David and Evelyn laughed until finally both of them rolled on the floor.

CHAPTER *Twelve*

Mrs. Perlin was willing to stay at her daughter's house only once during the year, for the Passover holiday. She was certain then that the house was sanctified. But the yearly game was started a month prior to the holiday. Ellie would telephone as usual and the reminder, the request, would become part of the daily conversation. And Mollie would reinforce the plan at home, in the evenings, after work. In the end, her acquiescence became a prize which, like most prizes Ellie realized, was not always worth all the effort to obtain.

She arrived with Mollie in the very early afternoon, when the house was completely *Pesadiche,* devoid of the familiar dishes, pots, silverware used the rest of the year. The packages of *matzos* and *farfel,* the crate of country fresh eggs brought to the house earlier by Leon were lined up behind the kitchen table, and on top of the stove, as well as inside, the items prepared for the *seder* dinner waited to be heated.

Mrs. Perlin did not help Ellie. She watched. She said a prayer over the first piece of *matzo* snatched by Irving as Ellie scolded him for having opened the box too early. Mrs. Howard, who had come down from the hotel the day before, spread thick chicken fat all over the blessed piece, then sprinkled it with the coarse koshering salt. But the necessary vigil, the one for which she allowed them to convince her to come, began in the dining room. There, seated in a straight, armless chair moved back from the table to the wall, Mrs.

Perlin held her *Haggadah* in readiness for the *seder* ceremony which would not begin until she determined that sufficient darkness outside made the turning on of the electric lights essential. Occasionally the boys would sit with her while Evelyn set the table, but they were too excited by the kitchen smells and the exotic activity of their mother to remain stationary for long. And their grandmother's unblinking reverie, her trance, made her too remote, too cut off from the reality of their excited expectation. Mollie, who never entered kitchens, finally, out of desperation and not knowing what else to do, became the ally of her mother's vigil. She sat closer to the table, untalking, rubbing first one hand, then the other, aimlessly across a patch of unused white tablecloth, listening to the sounds of the house that brought them all closer to nightfall.

Each year, since Mr. Perlin had died, the day of the first *seder* proceeded this way. And now, in April, 1941, it was established as law that in the afternoon Grandma and Aunt Mollie sat in the dining room and that the *seder* was always held at Ellie's house.

"Ellie?" Mollie called into the kitchen. "When do you expect Toby? It's getting late."

"She said by five. She's walking over with the baby from her mother-in-law's."

"Alone?"

"Leon's somewhere with Max." Ellie entered the room, holding one hand beneath a dripping soup ladle. "They're hiring for the summer."

"Today they had to?" questioned Mrs. Perlin, waving her head so vigorously that her unkempt bun threatened to come undone.

"What's the difference?" Mollie snapped. "Today? Tomorrow? It's all the same."

"They'll be here before sundown." Ellie returned to the kitchen. Mrs. Howard was already preparing the matzo meal for her special chicken soup *knadles*. "Isn't it too early, Ma?" Ellie put down the ladle and leaned against the sink.

"Maybe." Deferentially, Mrs. Howard ceased her motion with the box of meal.

"I think everything else is ready." Mentally nodding with each item, Ellie checked the familiar list: fish, hot *borscht*, chicken soup, chicken, pot roast, sponge cakes. . . "Only the *knadles*. We'll do them when we do the eggs and potatoes." She rested her hand behind her on the sink, watched Evelyn counting out the necessary silverware and dishes. "Why don't you go rest for awhile, Ma. You haven't stopped all day."

Reluctantly, Mrs. Howard backed out of the kitchen, undoing her apron. "And you? No resting?"

"I am. I'll shower now. The boys are outside. Evelyn can take care."

"I'll sit with your mother." It was duty rather than desire and Ellie appreciated her mother-in-law's generosity.

"You could read your paper if you . . ."

"Paper?" She shrugged her shoulders at the suggestion as if it were the last thing in the world she cared to do.

Ellie lingered with her shower, sapping up energy for the evening ordeal. She washed her hair, carefully rinsed it twice, hoping that the wetness would magically hide the plenitude of grayness which was gradually overtaking the brown, turned on the four needle sprays, indulging an almost lost sense of playfulness. The spray tickled her into a smiling, rejuvenated wakefulness. The water splashed against the glass shower door, blurring her reflection, seeped onto the tile floor outside the door. And that reminded her that she must stop. The water was turned off immediately.

She draped the huge towel, bigger than she was, over her hair, let it dangle down her body. She stood on the bath mat before the glass door, her dripping form now once more mutely reflected. At 41 she was no longer what you could call lean, but neither was she fat. Patting her mid-section proudly told her that. It was the face which revealed the sagging sickness, the blood pressure attacks which made her seek help from too many doctors. She pulled at her eyes, lifting the lids to relieve them of the feeling that something was inside. But there was no helping them. The newest doctor had said that was where her pressure had settled and would stay. Her glasses didn't help. Some days it was impossible to see. Just rest, they told her. Rest and you'll be fine. And come for your injections. Ellie smiled in derision at her reflection, at the doctors. Rest! These days the only rest she offered herself, apart from the movies with Morrie, were the gin rummy games with her lady-friends. As her mother said, "Believe it or not Ripley, Ellie's a card player. Her mother plays the numbers and she plays cards." Well, if Morrie could play pinochle every Friday night, then she had a right to her games. These days you needed to have something. And that was her rest.

She moved before the medicine chest mirror, powdered with 'April Showers,' enjoying the sweet cheap scent mixing with the steam in the room. Next she brushed her hair, skillfully avoiding the picture of her face, looking everywhere but at the mirror. She knew too well what she looked like. And what difference did it make now? Vanity was for when you had time, and time she had very little of.

She put her brush back on the shelf, suddenly not caring how she looked. Her hair was still too wet to worry about anyway. It would curl as it dried and she was beginning to perspire all over again. Quickly, she put on her underthings, listening to sounds of activity in the other rooms. The boys were upstairs. Evelyn was telling them to start getting dressed.

In a bathrobe, which she held together because there were no longer any buttons on it, she dashed into her bedroom only to find Mollie stretched out on the bed. "You feel all right, Mollie?" She closed the door. Hanging behind it was the black crepe with the short lace-capped sleeve, waiting where she had put it earlier that day.

"Fine. Just fine." Mollie sat up, rested against the headboard, watched Ellie step into her dress then move toward the bed so that she could have Mollie zip up the back. "But tired. The store was busy with Easter shopping."

Ellie sat at her dressing table, applied a dull lipstick artlessly. "I hope there's no fight tonight."

"It wouldn't be *seder* unless there was one." There was no humor in Mollie's tone. She only represented the facts.

"I suppose so." Ellie pushed her hair into the suggestion of a wave.

"And if Martha doesn't come with Harry we'll have the same old trouble." Mollie closed her eyes momentarily and sighed. "Mama won't say anything but rest assured someone else will."

"He told me she was definitely coming." Ellie went to her bureau and extracted a fresh apron, a white gauzy one, embroidered with pale roses. "So if we're careful there won't be trouble."

"What's going on at the hotel these days, El?"

"To tell you the truth, I don't ask and nobody tells. Toby never talks unless you ask her a question."

"Just like you." Mollie sat up to emphasize her remark.

"Like all of us." Ellie smoothed the front of her apron self-consciously, as if her sister had uncovered her secret of survival. "Lila told me that Leon and Max hardly talk to each other anymore. That was never meant to be a partnership."

"And they never mention the money they owe Morrie?"

"Never. And they won't either. Instead they'll get more. My husband . . ." she waved her arm instead of completing the sentence.

"Well, El, he should do something if he's going to keep his mother up there. She can't live on charity."

"Max gets his money's worth." Ellie wondered how her own sister could view the situation in those terms. But to explain how wrong she was would not help. "I've got to go to work. You coming?"

"No. I'll rest a while longer."

Ellie walked down the corridor toward the kitchen, the pleasant effects of the shower lost in the whirling dizziness of annoyance.

"MA NISHT HA NAW . . ." David trembled as he asked the 'four questions,' conscious of all eyes riveted on him. He faltered with the Hebrew pronunciation, but the sweetness of the soprano sound diminished the flaws. The rising and falling melody, the family melody, learned by instinct, by vague recollection made all of them move their heads in time to memories of other *seders*. For a moment, as David chanted, they were together, quiet, smiling wistfully, listening. Even Mrs. Perlin had closed her *Haggadah*.

"Pa-ah-pa," David trilled the middle syllable, "give me an answer for my four questions." He sat down and the smiles and his mother's kiss assured him that it had gone well. He reached up to make sure that his skull cap was in place before he made the expected journey around the table. First Evelyn, seated next to Ellie, kissed him loudly. Mrs. Howard suffocated him with a tearful hug, moaning. Clara's two children giggled. Mrs. Perlin patted his face and smiled. David was glad she was satisfied. His aunts kissed; his uncles shook his hand except Harry who squeezed his shoulder; his brother punched him lightly in the stomach. He came full circle, back to Morrie, seated at the head of the table, who grabbed David and pulled him to his lap. His kisses were loud and wet. David wiped his cheek, felt annoyed by the laughter, but as he regained his seat and glanced at the red wine that rocked against the brim of the etched silver goblet set for the prophet Elijah, he had the sense of a duty accomplished for another year. He was the youngest; he had to do it anyway. He felt happy.

Morrie was ready to continue. Each wine glass was filled; the platter on which the *seder* symbols—a chicken neck, a circle of horseradish, an egg, a sprig of parsley, a sliver of potato—rested, was ready to be raised in benediction. He felt the folded napkins underneath the dish to make sure the *matzo* was there for its special use later on. He picked up the *Haggadah* from his plate, cleared his throat. "All right. I'll skip a little so if you try to follow, be careful." Morrie saw Ellie's angry twitch. "I'm hungry," was his response.

Ellie fought back words forming behind her closed lips, words which were as familiar to the others who waited for them as the ritual of the *seder*. Only the twisted, almost toothless mouth of Mrs. Perlin continued to hiss the sound of prayer. Then Harry solemnly joined his mother's chant. His baritone drowned out the tension of the moment. Morrie read, skimmed incoherently over the Hebrew words. And Simon's voice, flat, out of tune, his pronunciation perfect, rose higher in proud combination.

As usual, this beginning was the signal for conversation to start. Clara, sitting between Simon and Toby, whispered. Evelyn and Mrs. Howard mumbled. Ellie looked over, trying to silence them, but it did no good. Max, bored by the familiarity of the process, closed his eyes for sleep. Lila prodded him, but he pushed her hand away.

Ellie stood up as quietly as possible.

"Where the hell are you going?" Morrie's voice rang out, louder than the chanting.

"I've got to check the eggs."

". . . same damn thing every year." Morrie slammed the table. The private conversations ended. Harry looked sympathetically at his sister. Mrs. Perlin's eyes steadfastly scanned her prayer book although tears were visible.

"Please Morrie," Ellie pleaded, her hands stretched toward him.

"Don't please me."

"Morrie, ssh," begged Mrs. Howard, leaning toward her son,

aware that if she lived to be a hundred she would always feel responsible for any of his outbursts.

"Don't you enter the picture." He glanced angrily at his mother and then back to Ellie who was frozen in indecision like a rabbit caught in the headlight glare of an automobile. If she returned to her seat, she would only have to get up again later. If she continued on her way to the kitchen, Morrie might follow. Mrs. Perlin reached out for her daughter's hand, indicating that she should return to her seat, but Ellie shook it off.

"I start the damn *seder* and right away everyone's talking. No one pays any attention." He removed his skull cap, threw it to the floor. David, conditioned by a religious reflex, retrieved it, kissing it before he handed it back to his enraged father. When he realized what he had done, how he had interfered, David sheepishly lowered his gaze. But that was enough. The trembling of Morrie's head abated; the white ridge that was his lips reddened. Sighs of relief rose from the table. Ellie went into the kitchen.

Somewhat contrite, but having to maintain at least the semblance of irritation, Morrie said, "Now will you all shut up and let *me* do this *seder!*" He looked at Harry who, until this moment, had not recognized the real source of anger. Harry, pressing a nerveless finger on his bushy mustache, would be silent now.

The story of the "Exodus," continued in the *Haggadah*, unfolded in sketchy outline, quickly. Morrie lingered only over the narration of the plagues faced by the Israelites, making sure that each person, including the children, dipped a finger into the wine glass, let the wine dribble onto the saucer, each dribble a new plague. The Hebrew words blurred into one sound as Morrie read on, sliding into suggestions of melody, pushing rapidly toward the dinner which would come at the midway point.

David tried to follow the story in English, but each time he glanced at his father's book, he found himself too far behind. And when his father came to the part with the 'little sandwiches' of horseradish and the special *matzo*, he gave up entirely. It was time to find out whether or not the horseradish was strong enough. Each person would make a comment; Ellie would wait nervously for the verdict.

Morrie placed a large glob of the grainy redness between two small pieces of *matzo*. The others copied his action. The reaction was delayed, but then, suddenly, his hand darted up to the top of his head. "That's strong," he gasped, tears streaming down his cheeks. "Marvelous El. If they had stuff like that when they crossed the desert, their lives must have been bitter all right."

Tears of tingling, self-induced pain flooded the eyes of the others. David felt a burning, breathtaking spray of red explosion in his nose and head. He pushed at his temples to make it stop. Ellie offered his wine glass and the sweetness of the wine mixed with the bitterness made his stomach heave and rumble. Morrie slapped his son's back; the others laughed.

"Can't take it, can you?" Irving taunted, but Morrie silenced him with an angry glare.

When Mrs. Perlin, reading each word in her book, arrived at the bitter herbs, the others were ready to proceed. She placed a huge amount of horseradish on the piece of *matzo* resting on her plate.

"Ma," Ellie squealed. "Be careful. It's very strong."

The old lady deftly stuffed the sandwich to the back of her mouth and crunched complacently. If she responded to the strength of the radish, no one was able to discover any sign of it. Her wrinkled mouth formed a smile of pleasure.

Morrie was already skipping on to the next break: eggs dipped in salt water; after that, dinner.

Only Mrs. Howard and Evelyn were allowed to help Ellie in the kitchen. Lila offered, but was refused. "Sit where you are, all of you. Evelyn will clear the wine glasses."

And so the ceremony, the ritual of this family's *seder* endured. The fish was praised; the *knadles* were devoured. Morrie had a bowl of chicken soup and then a bowl of his mother's hot *borscht*. He made no comment concerning taste, but the rushed slurping sound was proof that he was content. Mrs. Perlin ate only a bowl of chicken soup. She resisted the continued offering of other food and finally Ellie did not insist. "Why I try to make you eat, I'll never know. But have it your way."

"Another one of your great meals," Harry shouted.

Ellie nodded, pleased, but confident now, after all the years during which she had perfected her methods. It was almost unnecessary to think when she cooked.

Morrie pushed his plate away so that it landed on the edge of David's who looked up, squinting with annoyance.

"Must you always do that when you're finished? He's still eating." Ellie adjusted the offending plate.

"Do what?" Morrie rubbed his stomach. He was too full to be angry.

"Why can't you leave your plate in front of you like civilized people do?"

But Harry quickly interrupted before Morrie could respond. ". . . Uh . . . How's business these days?"

"Not bad." Morrie continued to glare at Ellie.

"The holidays help, don't they?" Max, at the other end of the table, joined the game of deflection, too weary for arguments.

Morrie nodded, lit a cigarette and motioned Irving, who was still eating, to get an ashtray from the living room.

"There's not supposed to be smoking *during* the *seder*, at least," Ellie mumbled, nibbling at her food.

"Don't start with that crap now." Morrie rolled the cigarette back and forth between his fingers. "Where did it ever say you couldn't smoke?"

"Nowhere!" Ellie's hand waved at him, her gesture of disgust.

"Jews'll never learn." Morrie shook his head. "How many times you have to be told the same thing? You've got to keep up with the age you live in." He struck at each word as if he were a teacher laboring with a backward student.

"I agree." Max smiled facetiously. Lila grunted. "What's that animal sound for?"

"For you." Lila laughed. "You know about the Jews like I know about Easter Sunday—nothing."

"What I know is," and Max's tone immediately revealed his oratorical intention, "that in Europe, in the year 1941, April, Jews are being butchered, gassed, tortured because they wouldn't wake up to the reality around them. I know of hundreds of cases where . . ."

"What do you mean wouldn't wake up?" Simon, whose parents were rigidly orthodox and who had insisted that Clara keep a similarly kosher home, rose to a defense.

"Just what I said. The Jews were sleeping and Hitler knew it."

"You speak," Harry felt obliged to join in, "as if the Jews were the only ones asleep."

"They're the only ones being persecuted." Morrie found himself in the unusual position of defending Max's point of view.

"Of course," Harry, the lawyer, found it difficult not to be patronizing, "but why are they? Certainly not because they were asleep, as you both seem to think, but just because they are Jews. They are always persecuted. History proves that much." Martha, sitting opposite, smiled her support. "The very story we're reading tonight is a story of persecution. And how old is that?" Everyone listened now. Even Mrs. Perlin had raised her eyes to gaze proudly at her son.

"All I say is that," Morrie, anxious to talk, began, "the Jews have to learn how to fit in better, not keep themselves separated. Look at my case. I've done well enough because I'm not a *yidel*."

"Why are you so proud of that?" Harry knew, but didn't care now, that he was stepping onto slippery land. "You think the Jews dying in Europe would be happy to hear you say that?"

"Look, Harry," Morrie's voice quivered with a familiar sound of anger, "I know all about Europe. Don't forget I saw some *pogroms*. Don't forget that my mother and father came here because of them . . . All I'm saying is if the Jews want to be liked and accepted, they've got to give up some of their outdated ways. They've got to move with the times."

"Why should they? Why do they have to?" Simon, in order to be heard, was screaming, but Clara encouraged him by nodding confidently at him and her children who crowded against her chair.

"For Christ's sake! What the hell do you know about it?" Morrie tried to silence him with a wave. "They have to change to stay alive. Look what's happened already. Look what Hitler's doing."

"Is he doing that because they're Jews or because they're backward?" Harry leaned toward Morrie, his hand cutting through the air.

"Of course because they're Jews. I know that much." Morrie squeezed a piece of sponge cake, looking at it abstractedly. "But if they'd been alert they would have left Europe when they had a chance."

"Do you know there is such a thing as immigration laws?"

"I know all about it, Harry. Don't worry. But I read this article in the *Saturday Evening Post* . . .".

"Oh Dad, the *Saturday Evening Post!*" All of them, but Evelyn most of all, were surprised, startled by her interruption. She had expected that phrase, had heard it too often when the course of a discussion turned against her father. Her reaction, readied in silence, had merely slipped out.

"And what the hell's wrong with it, Miss? It's the best magazine in this country, maybe in the world."

"I know, Dad, but you're always quoting from it as if it's the only authority." Evelyn, placatingly, wanted to withdraw, but she was caught now. Ellie looked at her as if to say, 'How could you.'

"Well, I'm not so informed as you. After all, you go to night school, to Brooklyn College. And you're a big lawyer's secretary so you know all about everything . . ." Morrie's sarcasm, his subdued anger, caused his head to tremble violently. ". . . I just went up to the eighth grade. I'm just a plant manager for one of the biggest milk companies in the country. I'm only self . . ."

"I wasn't trying to be insulting." Evelyn returned his stare with a sense of her own anxiety and because she felt that, she also felt confident. "All I meant was that the *Post* has been called an isolationist magazine, so its point of view is prejudiced."

"Isolationist?" He savored the word. "Well, that is something. You are growing up. But what the hell has that got to do with it?"

"It's got a lot to do with it." Max roused himself from a listening torpor. "What Evelyn means, simply, is that we, here, in this country, could do more to help the Jews before they're all wiped out. We should be in this war already."

"Don't worry, Max," Harry spoke quietly, "we will be soon. All of us."

For a moment there was silence, a silence in which each of them, the children in expressions of open fear, heard the echo of Harry's words.

Evelyn was the first to respond. "I agree with Uncle Max. After all . . ."

"After all," Morrie mimicked, but he had, during the silence, shifted his mood to gentle resignation, "Bob shouldn't be the only one in the army, should he?"

Evelyn smiled, caught off guard, blushed, lowered her gaze.

Lila laughed. "Trapped you, didn't he? . . . By the way what do you hear from him, anyway?"

"He's fine. Still in Panama. Probably at a *seder* too right now." She glanced across the table toward the darkened living room.

"Well, if he is, I hope he's not talking so seriously as us." Leon's words produced uncomfortable, forced laughter.

Ellie stood up. "Well, I'll clear the dishes and we'll continue with the next half."

ELLIE HAD DESCENDED the front stairs to open the door. Upstairs they stood as Morrie read from the *Haggadah*. David's gaze was fixed on the large silver goblet. Elijah would pass into the house, the room, hover above the wine glass, drink, and depart. The rabbi at Hebrew School told him so. And each year he waited for it to happen. The wine at the rim of the goblet trembled. David was sure it moved. "I did see it. I swear I did," he shouted excitedly as Ellie returned.

"Ssh!" she whispered.

The others sat down once more.

The wine glasses were filled for the fourth and last time. The drugged silence of overeating and the solemnity of the fleeting moment remained with the company until the end of the *seder*. No one—Mrs. Perlin followed her own tempo—cared that Morrie was turning pages of his book, barely inspecting them for importance. He mumbled incoherently, his little finger settled into the final page, ready. Mrs. Perlin's lips moved slowly. Simon studied his book, gradually yielding to his drowsiness. Harry slouched back against his chair, an expression of sad reverie obvious to anyone who cared to look. Only Martha's eyes registered any apprehension. The other women waited in various positions of inattentiveness. The candles, burning lower in their holders, flickered into a dying white brightness. Ellie cupped her chin, brushing aimlessly at the wine-splattered tablecloth.

Morrie closed his book loudly. "We're finished. Drink the last glass. *Boruch ataw adonoy* . . ." He swallowed before the prayer was concluded. "All right. You can sing now."

The men stood up, on cue from Morrie, removed their jackets, drifted languidly toward the living room, to the soft sofa, the easy chairs, the darkness that wine-fuzzed minds seek. The ladies and children remained seated. The candles had burned down to the wick which floated in the liquid wax. Ellie switched on the overhead light.

"Come on, Dave. We'll sing." Evelyn pulled her brother to her.

Mrs. Perlin, just finishing her reading, looked up, gazed, smiling at her grandchildren.

"*El bene*," Evelyn lingered on the phrase, waiting for her brothers and cousins to find the song in their books, continued, "*bene vayso be-kaw-aw-rov* . . ." For Mrs. Howard the *seder* was now official. She moved her head in time to the tune, hummed. The others talked, listened, laughed as the children sang.

"What a *seder*," said Mollie. "It's over before it starts. Papa's probably continuing it in his grave right now."

"What's the difference?" Toby pushed back from the table.

"You dasn't say that." Mrs. Perlin frowned at Toby.

". . . *be-kaw-rov*." Finishing, the children burst into embarrassed laughter.

"Bravo," Harry called from the living room. "Sing another and drown out the conversation entirely."

Mollie glared at Martha.

"*Ha-gad-yaw-aw-aw-aw, ha-gad-yaw* . . ." Evelyn quickly started the song of the goat.

"My brother!" Mollie turned to Ellie. "He probably doesn't remember how it used to be. Remember, El, how we didn't finish 'til two or three in the morning? Everyone in white robes, reclining on pillows?"

"I remember that," Clara nodded as she spoke, "and how Harry asked the four questions. And papa used to kiss him until he cried."

Mrs. Howard gazed at Lila. "My husband too with Izzy. He too had a voice. You remember Lila?"

"I remember, Ma."

The song ended; the children waited in the silence of the dreaming adults.

"Well?" Evelyn questioned. "No appreciation?"

"Very good," said Mrs. Howard.

"Thank *you*, Bubby." Evelyn stood up, walked to the kitchen where the dishes waited. Irving led the other children to the bedroom he shared with David.

And in the living room Morrie was organizing the inevitable pinochle game.

"That's what's wrong with the Jews." Ellie pointed to the living room. "All my husband can do is play pinochle."

"Ssh," Mrs. Perlin whispered.

"Ellie," pleaded Mrs. Howard.

"It's all right . . . There's not going to be any game tonight, Morrie." Ellie's voice was raised so that he would be certain to hear.

"That's what you say." Morrie was standing next to her now. "If you clear this junk, I'll show you."

Ellie did not move, but Clara, Toby, and Lila began reaching for the wine glasses and cake platters.

"Nobody takes anything off this table. Just sit still." Ellie motioned them back.

"If this table isn't cleared in five minutes, I'll clear it myself. And you know what that means." He leaned toward her menacingly. "What's the matter? Aren't you the queen of the Lenox Road card tables? You play often enough to be."

Nothing revealed Ellie's anxiety, only the tremulous spluttering of her voice as she spoke, finally determined, "Go ahead and clear it, and then go to hell. We're staying here." She moved her head, looked up, saw the cold whiteness of his skin. "I decided that this *seder* was going to be a little different."

Morrie fidgeted awkwardly, searching for an action other than attack, held back by his mother, who pulled at his arm.

Mrs. Perlin stood up, reached for Elijah's goblet and her own wine glass. "Come Ellie," she said, her voice tired, resigned to losing.

"We're not going to play, El," Harry spoke emphatically, gazing at the other men standing nearby.

"*You're* not going to play, you mean." Morrie pointed at him. "Max and Leon'll play, and you too Simon."

Simon shook his head. Clara smiled at Toby triumphantly.

Morrie slammed the table next to Ellie. The glasses tingled; wine sloshed onto the cloth. "This is the last *seder* in this house." He walked quickly back into the living room, fell heavily into his chair.

Ellie remained rigid, only her fingers moved, pulled at the embroidered tufts of roses on her apron. "Good. Perfect with me."

"You better see if the baby's up," Leon said to Toby.

"Get the children." Clara motioned to Simon.

"Amen," whispered Harry, reaching for his wife's hand.

Ellie stared blankly at the preparations for departure. She did not try to stop anyone. The goodbyes were solemn, brief.

From the top of the staircase, Ellie waved each group into the night. Mrs. Howard, Mrs. Perlin, and Mollie remained seated at the table, gazing down at the spotted cloth.

"I'll help Evelyn," Ellie said on her way through to the kitchen. Her mother-in-law stood up. "No, Ma. You stay here and rest."

There was a great deal to be done in the kitchen, especially the greasy pots and pans. "I'll do the rest, Evelyn." She began to nudge her daughter away, but Evelyn resisted without turning to face her mother. "Didn't you hear me, Ev?"

"Yes, Ma."

"Well? Go ahead then. You did enough." Ellie turned her around, saw her eyes, swollen with crying. "What are you crying for? It's not the first time you've seen your father like a madman, is it?"

"No."

"Well?"

"I was just wondering," Evelyn's gaze now rested unashamedly on her mother's face, "if when I get married it's going to be this way." Evelyn waited; Ellie was unable to say what she thought was the truth. Morrie passed through the kitchen, and in a moment the bathroom door was slammed. Irving and David appeared, in pajamas, and still Ellie held her daughter's arms, not speaking.

"Ma?" David questioned, "can we have milk and sponge cake?" Ellie moved her head to see them, to gaze at the three of them, and then smiled.

"Sure you can." Ellie did not turn back to her work; how odd it was that tonight she wanted so much to resist the familiar impulse to give in, to fight the way things were. Before, when she dared Morrie, she had won. Now the dishes could just wait. Everything could just wait. She poured milk for her sons, cut an entire cake for them, made them sit at the kitchen table with Evelyn and herself.

In the dining room the women talked quietly. Down the corridor Morrie made sure they all heard the slamming doors, the coughing as he lit a cigarette, the squeaking of the spring as he got into bed. The sounds were all around her, but, for now, Ellie wouldn't honor them, wouldn't allow them to trap her. Her children. Let them ask for anything. If they wanted to sit here all night long, she didn't care. "Take more cake."

"You all right, Ma?" Irving, now taller than his mother, touched her forehead to see if she had fever.

"I'm fine. No fever. You like the cake?"

"Great." David munched contentedly.

They were all smiling at once. It was so rare and it took so little to make it happen. Perhaps, Ellie thought, feeling bands of tension loosening in her head, her stomach, they can keep this moment, instead of the one before it. Still, it's got to be a crooked scale. I'll have to keep my hand on one side when they measure it all out. For too long she had forgotten what her father had said, so long ago, about getting older. But there was still time, and there were still occasions. Evelyn would get married, have children of her own. She'll learn from my mistakes. The boys will be *bar-mitzvahed*, be married. Everything in time. In time. And that's the problem. Would she last to see it all? To enjoy it after she saw it? Who has such a bargain? So you say to yourself that you deserve the time for all you didn't get. Who hears that? Everybody has the same listener, whoever it is, and inside is where the talking goes on—no one else hears it—and anyway you can always make up your own answers. All right. Then make yourself happy. Like now. If Morrie were sitting here, it wouldn't be the same. The answers would be different because inside my listener would hear the question differently. And they would not be smiling. And Morrie too. "So," she said out loud, "that's the way it is."

"What is, Ma?" Evelyn was puzzled by the silence, by the smiles, by the words. The boys looked at their mother, waiting.

"You heard me?" Surprised, Ellie pulled at her hair.

"You spoke, Ma." David reached for her hand. "What did you mean?"

"Nothing." She stood up, remained motionless, as if she couldn't remember what she had to do next. "I was daydreaming."

"About what, though?" Evelyn persisted.

"Oh," she waved her hand over them, "about you . . . about how good you all are."

"Even me?" Irving looked up seriously.

"Even you."

"Even if I won't take the garbage out?" He smiled again.

"Even then." She leaned down, kissed him; then, moving, kissed David; and Evelyn, standing up, hugged her mother.

"Do you think we'll never have another *seder*, Ma? Like Daddy said?" David leaned against Ellie. Even he reached her shoulders.

"We will. Don't worry. And we'll have plenty of other things too. Weddings. *Bar-mitzvahs.* Whatever we can have, we'll have. You should all just live and be well."

"You too, Ma." Evelyn squeezed her mother's hand.

Ellie tried to shake the tears out of her eyes. "To bed boys . . . Evelyn, now you'll help me finish what I started to do there?" She pointed to the sink and the dishes.

THE FIRST RING of the telephone awakened her, but only her eyelids fluttered open. By the second ring she was out of bed, reaching for her buttonless robe, watching Morrie stir himself to a mutter of complaint. Alarmed,—it was too early for the call to be anything but trouble—she raced down the corridor of the sleeping house. Who could it be? 'Who' was all she had time to think about.

And then Martha's voice told her. The words, the facts, sobbed, garbled. It's a joke. He was just . . . Ellie refused, absolutely refused to hear the fact. She leaned against the wall, suddenly aware that she was screaming, that Morrie had taken the telephone from her hand, that he was holding her, preventing her from slipping to the floor. She had no sense of her body, of the filmy nightgown, of her arms struggling to reach her mother and Mollie who stood, mutely staring, bewildered, before her.

"Slowly Martha. Tell me. What is it?" Morrie screamed into the mouthpiece.

Evelyn, holding her arms around David and Irving, waited, watched.

And then Mrs. Perlin turned away from Ellie's sobs and Mollie's screams. Resignation stilled her gaunt, sunken face. "God's will," she muttered. "My son." She covered her face, fingers trembling, the rest of her body rigid until Mrs. Howard embraced her, rocked her.

"Your Uncle Harry's dead." Morrie looked toward his children. "Just like that." He snapped his fingers. "A heart attack and it's over."

There was no movement in the room, only sound, the sound of wailing, of rage. And outside, the grayness of early morning lightened, started to become day.

PART *III*

CHAPTER *Thirteen*

EVER SINCE THE DOCTORS had warned her of the possibility, Ellie expected that each of her attacks would end in death which, when she felt her worst, she insisted would be the best thing anyway.

"Why do you still have to talk like a goddamn kid at your age? I can't stand it." And Morrie would sigh, angry out of habit rather than passion, nervous about when it would happen to himself. "I'll be dead long before you will and then what'll you do?"

"Do? I'll wait like everyone else. What else is there to do?" It did seem to her, after all, that waiting was what she was most used to, that it was part of the big plan. True, now she had grandchildren who made the waiting less frightening, but what they looked forward to, their opportunities were too unlike hers or Morrie's to really understand them. She loved them. She was relieved to know that they were there. But it was exhausting to keep up with them. She had so little memory of youth's shiny possibilities. Only the vivid picture of her father's funeral remained untarnished. Then, last year, at her mother's funeral, fleeting, compressed into the moment it took her to turn from the sight of still another coffin being lowered into a grave, she remembered seeing inside, while reaching for her crying sisters, the rapid unreeling film of her mind, seeing herself as a young girl, greeting her father in the snow, watching her mother cook. And then there was the stilled slide of Harry's death, reaching unexpectedly, without concern for the correct order, past her, shaking her sense of proportion. From that day on, it seemed that whatever else the film contained was being buried under the weight of each day's details. There was no way to shake free from the fact of her age. As old as the century. That was her constant reminder. Forty-nine now. No longer forever sixteen as David, when he first registered at the Brooklyn library, decided she would be. The century recorded two wars, so far; an influenza epidemic—that she could still remember because it had taken cousins, aunts, uncles and tossed them aside like so many old toys; and the depression which had made hope, for some, a joke; and the special shuddering pain of Hitler and the Jews, the ceaseless distant howl that ended serenity forever and created a bomb. Those facts told time on a different clock, ticking louder than all the weddings, the births, *bar-mitzvahs* of her recorded history, depleting her often-praised stockpile of energy and endurance. The drab pile of years she carried around as she shifted in bed, pinched Morrie to stop him from snoring, or worked around the house, or played canasta and gin rummy with her lady-friends, or went to visit at Evelyn's and Irving's was like a growing mountain that blocked her view, prevented her from seeing what she had been like, once. So, perhaps, one day, when her head whirled her into bed, sick, the dizziness would fill her vision completely and, just like that, she would be finished.

After Harry's death, she had gone to visit the doctor dutifully again. It made everyone else feel better. She even had her teeth fixed, kept a weekly beauty parlor appointment. It felt good to do that, like revenge. And it eased Morrie's conscience, she knew, to pay for these things, to buy her new clothes even though she said she didn't want them. There was no longer any need for a house now with just David left. Neither of them spoke of the hotel. They went on trips instead. To California, to Florida. Just the two of them. And Morrie could give these things with ease, so she just stopped going to the doctor. Not out of spite, she told him. Absolutely not. She didn't want to be bothered, she would say, or the doctors didn't know what to do for her anyway. She could be her own doctor. Morrie would shrug his shoulders, continue reading his magazine. It was her own grave she dug, not his. If she wanted to be obstinate . . .

But whenever he found her stretched out in bed, trembling,

clutching the sheet, he did, frightened both for himself and her, whatever he could to comfort her until the doctor arrived.

"Mrs. Howard, you haven't been to me in a long time." The doctor unwrapped the blood pressure strap. "It's much too high. Didn't you care for the injections?" He looked down at her, shaking his head. "I'm no magician, you know."

Ellie shifted her gaze to the open slats of the venetian blinds.

"All right, doctor." Morrie nodded impatiently. "What should she do now? Old history doesn't help."

"She should stay in bed for as long as possible, say two or three weeks, even longer. She should do nothing at all." The doctor prepared a syringe, Ellie followed his movements.

"That's what she'll do then." Morrie sat down on the bed, reached for her hand, which she refused to let him hold. "I'll get my mother to come."

"No." Ellie glared at him, her eyes unchanging as the needle punctured her skin.

"What do you mean, no?" Now, as always, Morrie found contradiction unbearable. "She'll come and that's all there is to it."

"Well, if . . ." the doctor hesitated, looked from the husband to the wife, began to pack his bag, "if your mother-in-law irritates you . . ."

"She doesn't. But she's not getting called here again. My daughter can come. And my son will be home."

"Look, El, you can't expect Evelyn to come here every day. She's got a husband and kids to take care of."

"She'll do it."

"I know she'll do it, but . . ."

"But nothing." She rolled further away from his hand.

The doctor sighed. "You'll have to settle it somehow. In any case I'll leave a prescription and a new diet. Follow it and please stay in bed. That's the most important thing." He leaned closer to Ellie. "And your flushes? Are they any better?"

"No," she answered softly, embarrassed, glanced quickly at Morrie.

"I'll give you something for that too." He stood up. "The pressure complicates it all. But we'll take care of each thing. Don't worry." Rapidly his hand moved across the prescription pad, ripped off a piece of it, officiously, solemnly handed it to Morrie, nodded, grabbed up his case. "I'll stop in at the end of the week. Call if you need me."

"Dave?" Morrie stood in the entrance to the room, calling. "Show the doctor out." He extended his hand. The doctor buttoned his overcoat. "Thank you for coming so late, but I thought she was almost done for."

"It's quite all right." He moved briskly down the corridor.

Morrie listened for the descending steps, for the slam of the door, feeling with each sound of the doctor's departure, the return of his own helplessness. But he sat down again at the edge of the bed. "Okay. You heard him. You just have to stay in bed."

She nodded, huddled on her side.

"You're no spring chicken any more, kiddo." He forced himself to laugh.

"That I know, thank you."

David entered the room, stopped, waited for Ellie to look up at him, moved to the other side of the bed, leaned down and kissed her.

"We're going to have to keep her in bed. The doctor said for at least three weeks." Morrie slapped his leg in resignation, looked over Ellie, past his son, toward the window.

"I'll stay home from school." David held his mother's hand.

"Just like that?" Fiercely, Ellie looked toward Morrie for support, but he only shrugged apathetically. "You can't do that."

"All right, then. I'll quit school." David watched his father.

"It's all right with me." Morrie waved his arm. "You're old enough to know what you're doing. You're nineteen. And you do a lousy job in school anyway, so what difference . . ."

"How would you know what I'm doing?"

Morrie pointed a finger menacingly at David. "Don't get smart alecky."

Ellie tried to sit up against the pillows and David, puffing them up with his free hand as she leaned forward, helped her. "You're not leaving school. That's final." With her eyes she denied his decision.

"Let him." Morrie moved closer to Ellie. "Let him go out and work. Let him see what the world's like."

"You talk like I never worked . . ."

"A bookshop? On weekends? You call that work?" Morrie's limp, twisting hand dismissed his son. "When I was your age I really had a job. I did . . ."

"Please," muttered Ellie. "Not now." She saw her son's full lips thin angrily, heard his answer, nasty, goading Morrie to expand the familiar facts, begin once again the endless exchange. "Please let me sleep." She closed her eyes.

But Morrie was trapped in his own story, in the words, the memories, oblivious to his wife's request, or even to the fact that David had moved to the window to poke through the slats of the venetian blinds. ". . . so you'll never have to know what that was like, lugging those crates. You're lucky."

"That's what progress is for." David's back faced Morrie.

"Look Mister, . . . turn around when I'm talking to you."

"Morrie! Will you please." Ellie put her hands to her head, shutting them out. "I'm tired."

"So am I. I'm tired of having my son treat me like a piece of dirt."

"Do we have to do this now?" David did turn then, his voice trembling as an echo of his father's anger.

"What's the difference? Now or later!"

Ellie stared at David, demanding silently that he be still, but his words erupted, uncontrolled. "If you don't know, there's no point in telling you." He waited, not looking at Morrie, for a still louder outburst from his father.

But Morrie remained silent, staring at the wall behind the bed, his face opening and closing on the whiteness of stifled rage, his fleshy cheeks sagging into the sadness of fatigue. When he spoke, it was to both of them. "You think I have no feelings? You think I'm a dumb bastard? Well, just go on thinking so, but meanwhile I've got something to show for my work. I started with nothing. Now I've got men working for me. For me! Do you understand that?" His eyes, scanning an inner landscape of accomplishment, dared them, contritely, to deny his truth. "You remember that, Ellie. Don't you?"

Wearily, she answered. "Yes. I know it. I remember." But what she remembered would always be different from what he remembered. And she cried for that, pitying herself and him because he didn't know it, and because he never would be able to. So she lied; it was so much easier to lie that way, for that reason. It was not so easy for her children. And when she died, what would they do to him? "I remember everything."

He reached for and held her hand. "As long as you're all right."

"I will be." She looked at David, at his pout of annoyance because she did not face what he liked to call 'the truth.' "We'll all be fine."

David did resign from school. Ellie continued to protest, but protests from a sick bed produce the opposite result, and, finally, she had to submit to Morrie's certainty that it would be the best thing for him. During the three week period allotted for Ellie's convalescence, Evelyn did come to the house every day with her children and prepared food for the family. Betty Pulaski, Ellie's closest friend, visited every afternoon. Irving and his wife, Beth, came two Sundays in a row with their two children; for the second visit Ellie got out of bed and made 'something special' for them. From there it was only a matter of days before she was back in control of the household. And Morrie told Evelyn it wasn't necessary for her to come. David's decision had proved a useless sacrifice. All he did during that period was wash dishes, 'straighten' the house, and empty ash-trays.

And when Ellie cleaned now, she had to confront him reading in his bedroom or listening to his phonograph. "I told you not to do this, but you wouldn't listen. Of course not. You're just like your father."

"That I deny."

"Don't deny it so much. Look and you'll see it's true." Ellie sat on the bed she had just made up, watched David fidget on his desk chair, smoke from his cigarette, letting the smoke sift from his mouth to form a protective cover around his face. "And why must you smoke when you don't even inhale?"

"I'll learn."

"It's not essential that you learn *that*. Other things I hoped you would learn."

"You don't have to worry about me, Ma."

She saw the honest plea in his eyes, the lean, bony look of her brother glowing there beneath the silky brown hair which had always fallen across his forehead. And she recognized his sadness, like an inheritance from her. He wanted too much from her, just as she had wanted too much from her father, "I'm not worrying, Davie.

Only I don't want you to look so old when you're so young. It's now that you should have good things happen to you, things that you'll remember when you're older." David looked up, surprised, and Ellie, speaking the words of another voice that had suddenly found sound in her throat and that only she could hear, a distant voice that had told her the same thing so many years ago, smiled, warmed by the recognition of its source, twisted her wedding ring so that it pinched her skin.

"What is it, Ma? Are you laughing at me?"

"Laughing?" She stood up. "No, not laughing. Thinking. About something that wouldn't interest you."

"How do you know it wouldn't? Why don't you tell me and see?"

"Not now. I've got too much to do." She started out of the room. "Anyhow, I want you to talk to your father and straighten things out with him."

David nodded.

"You will won't you?"

"I'll try, Ma. That's all I can say."

But it was Morrie who tried. He waited for an evening when Ellie had fallen asleep early, an evening when David was quietly reading in his own bedroom.

"Your mother wants us to talk." Morrie cleared his throat, waited for David to close his book. "I don't like this kind of thing. It shouldn't be necessary." He lit a cigarette, nervously dragged on it in quick successive puffs. "And I'm not going to spend more time than I have to . . . I know what you think of me . . ." his voice was low, controlled in a way it seldom ever was, ". . . but that's beside the point . . . I'm still your father and . . ."

"I don't forget that."

"And never mind being sarcastic. It won't work." He paused, getting a firm grip on the cigarette he was dangling over an ashtray on David's desk. "Sometimes you forget your mother and I have been married a long time. Maybe you think I yell too much, but there's lots of things you don't know about, lots of good things that . . ."

"When did they take place?" David's interruption was neglected.

". . . Anyhow, we're getting older and changes take place. People get afraid. I . . . I don't want anything to happen to your mother and . . ."

"I don't either."

"That's just what I was going to say. I'm sure you don't. But you have a hell of a way of showing it." Morrie stamped out his cigarette, delicately extinguishing each spark. "First of all, you're irresponsible. You sulk around here like an old man. All I want to find out from you is what you intend doing."

"That's all?"

"All right. I asked you not to get smart with me. When it comes to yelling, you know my power." Morrie laughed but David would not join him. "You are nineteen. Your mother's worried about you. I'm worried . . ."

"About me?" David's eyes rounded into mocking pockets of disbelief. "You really are?" He threw his book behind him onto the bed.

"Why you so shocked?" Morrie watched for a sign that would make it easier for him to talk. "You're so surprised that I'm concerned?"

"Frankly, yes." Slowly, David lit a cigarette, blew the smoke in his father's direction. Morrie raised his hand; David leaned away from it, but then the hand only stirred the smoke, pushed it away.

"Well it's not the truth." Morrie's head began to tremble with the effort to control his words. "I wouldn't be in here now if it were the truth. Would I?"

"All right. So now you're interested." David stood up, leaned against the high maple bureau which he had always shared with Irving and which was now completely his. "What about all the other times? What about the times *I* came to talk to you and you were too busy with the *Post* or with your radio broadcasts. What about my going to a free college so you wouldn't have to spend any of that money you've been saving—for what I don't know. Or how about the fact that I've been working summers and weekends since I'm fifteen? You interested in those facts or would you rather read the newspaper?"

Morrie stared at his son. He was no longer trying to hold his trembling chin, and whatever words he chose would be good enough. "That crap I've heard from you before, only you never ask how hard it was to get what we've got in this house. Not once did you ever offer to help out with your salary . . ."

"Did I have to?" David stopped pacing the floor next to his bed. "You always had money to do what you wanted. I needed mine. To go to school with. To buy clothes. For a movie. A date. For everything you never would think about giving . . ."

"I never heard Irving complaining. He got his money the same way you did."

"I'm not Irving. I wasn't sent to school. No sir. To me you said do as you damn please. Why was that? Did you suddenly lose interest in me? Your favorite child?" David turned away, leaned heavily against the bureau again. "What's the difference," he mumbled. "You don't know anything about me. You never will. So let's forget it."

"What's to know? You're a snotnose kid growing up who's afraid to work. Who had advantages I never had, who . . ."

Whirling around, David screamed into the confines of the small room, "Just don't come to me now to be a big time father. Don't lecture. Read your *Saturday Evening Post* and go on believing you know everything." There was no surprise in the slap when it came. They both nodded at its naturalness. Morrie paused to touch the redness on his son's cheek before he left the room; David sat back down on his bed.

WHEN HE RETURNED to his own room, Ellie was not sleeping. She had listened, heard the raised voices, David's final words, the sound of the slap.

Morrie sat down on the edge of their bed, looked over at her, rubbed his eyes to push back the tears he did not want. "It's no good. He doesn't want to talk."

Ellie sat up, put her hand on his back. "All right. You tried. That's all you can do."

"You'd think he hates me the way he acts."

"He doesn't *hate* you. What a way to talk."

Morrie twisted, pulled her against his chest. "Do you *hate* me?"

"Why should I?"

"You shouldn't." He squeezed her until she pushed him away.

"I don't." Her mind went on talking to herself. And if I do I wouldn't say it now.

"You'll have to talk to him. I can't. Only Evelyn ever listened to me anyway. She's the only one with sense enough." He helped Ellie back onto her pillow, undid his bathrobe and got into bed. "Now that I hit him, that's the end . . . But he had it coming to him . . . He's so damn stubborn. Just like you . . . He'll never forgive me for that."

"He will. Don't worry." She held the hand he extended across her breast. "Just go to sleep now. I'll talk to him." She laced her fingers in his, felt his arm sag. Flicking her eyes closed, she imagined tugging at that arm to make him hear the truth, telling him, yes, your son hates you, I hate you. You're selfish. Money you give. Trips . . . She could even picture that look of his. How his head would start to shake and then the yelling, 'What do you know? Look at how hard I worked. You never went without anything . . .' And finally, she knew, they would be back at the same point they had always been at. It's better this way. Hating, if you could stand it, was as much a way to live as loving. Maybe they even meant the same thing in the end. Neither feeling had any clear reason for existing and so every reason made sense. No one was free to choose how he lived or even if he lived at all. It happened to you and because you wanted to stay alive you accepted everything. The trap was everyone's, like a mass grave in a concentration camp. The whole world was in it with you, trying to pick its way out, knowing that was the only way to stay alive. Why should she or Morrie be exceptions? . . . She removed her hand from his, turned on her side away from him . . . The older you get, the better it is to lie anyway . . . after all, what else is there to do? He tried and I tried and the rest of it . . . She blinked that thought down into the deepness of sleep and with it the 'ifs' of her father, her mother, Mollie, and herself. The next years were for her children to manage. Whatever she had given them, whatever Morrie had or had not done for them was part of them. Good, bad, or indifferent they'll have to manage . . .

Morrie was snoring. That was the last thing she heard before she fell asleep.

CHAPTER *Fourteen*

NEVER AS EXCITED an eater as a preparer of food, Ellie did not realize immediately that over a period of a few months, ever since she and Morrie had returned from visiting David at the army camp in Georgia, she seemed to be eating less than the small amount she usually ate. It was having to cook for two people that was responsible. By the time she finished fussing, by the time Morrie returned from work, the food had no appeal. And then, too, it depressed her to find that her proportions were all wrong. She bought too much meat and then had to split it into several meals; she was not used to leftovers. Or she made too much cake on a Friday, out of habit, and had to make sure that Bob stopped by so that he could take some to Evelyn and the boys. So much effort, and for what? Just mistakes.

But, finally, it was a fact. She was losing her appetite. Even Morrie remarked about it. "If you did more, anything, during the day, you'd eat more. Playing cards isn't activity, remember." She agreed, but he had no further suggestions, only, "You've got to find something. Cooking and cleaning, the *Hadassah*—you don't even go there anymore—and cards. It's not enough." So she read his magazines, the newspapers, tried to get through some of David's books but by now, that was a hard occupation. She did enjoy listening to his records. And twice a week she called Clara and Mollie. Once a week Mollie came for dinner. Twice a week she wrote letters to Toby at the hotel. Every other day she took a long piece of the afternoon to write David. Every day Evelyn phoned. And Irving, " . . . well he's a different story," she told Morrie when they watched television in the evening. Morrie would grunt and nod, absorbed with watching.

"When David comes home, I'll feel better. It's been all the worrying about him going to Korea that does it," she would say to herself with anticipation, carrying the fear of that through each day, knowing that when he did come home he would surely be changed. Maybe then he would decide, on his own, to go back and finish school. So, to use up time, she would plan to send him another package of brownies and pinwheel cookies. Tomorrow she would feel up to it.

Tomorrow arrived and she cleaned the house in the morning, dragging herself in a desultory fashion from one spotless room to another, imagining that there really was some dirt. But it was the kind of game that served to fatigue rather than amuse her. This apartment was too big for Morrie and herself. If they had a smaller one, a few rooms . . . that would be nothing to clean. And when David comes he won't stay with us for long.

She prepared her baking ingredients, got the dough from the refrigerator. That will take awhile and it'll be done in time to go to Betty's for the canasta game.

It was while she showered that day that she felt it for the first time. She was rubbing the soap down from her armpit to her breast, and the soap seemed to slip out of her hand as it went over something hard and bobbing. The water splashed onto her hair—again she forgot to use the shower cap—spilled blurringly over her face, but she couldn't remember to shut it off while she explored. Unwillingly her fingers played with this thing, each time hoping that they would tell her it was gone, that it was just her imagination. But even that game wouldn't work. Her fingers stopped exploring. She froze under the tepid flow of water. It *was* there. And she did know what it was.

As she dried herself, she tried to ignore it, to think it out of existence. But, involuntarily, her fingers, acting with a will of their own, slyly, beyond her mind's panic to control them, sought it again and again. She didn't want to touch the spot. Yet, now, it had suddenly become the only part of her body that really existed. She would not be able to avoid it. She finished drying, powdered herself heavily, although this morning the sweetness of 'April Showers' made her nauseous, left the bathroom and dressed quickly.

Once in the living room, going there because it was the closest to the outside, she sat down on the chair she kept in front of the window, stared out at the glaring winter sun, at the dirty snow, melting rapidly, sending a rush of water along the curb to the sewer. She didn't want to call Morrie. Not yet. Not Evelyn. There would be time for that later. Maybe Betty? But Betty had her own sister dying of it, and Ellie had accompanied her to the hospital too often to add another trouble to Betty's day.

Cancer. That's what it is. She repeated the word over and over in her mind. When, finally, she said it out loud, just once, she felt her heart squeeze tightly, like a fist, as if it were stopping, and then, when it started to pump again, it seemed different, as if, in that way it told her that it would never feel familiar for the rest of her life. She tried to stand up, to fix her gaze on Morrie's chair across the room, to walk. And she was in motion without knowing it, dizzy, trembling with anger as she stumbled against the sofa, banged into the dining room table.

She clutched the telephone in the kitchenette and carefully dialed Betty's number, steadying herself that way. "I can't come to the game this afternoon . . . No. Nothing's wrong . . . I'm positive . . . I . . . I just want to send a package off to David. I promised him . . . Send my regards to the ladies . . ."

Next, what?

She found her coat, hat, and handbag. When she was half-way down the stairs, she remembered her gloves, debated going back up for them, recalled her mother's words that you 'dasn't return to the house once you leave . . . It's always bad luck.' She continued down the stairs. Mrs. Silver was waiting in the vestibule, scanning the mail. Ellie forced herself to smile.

"You all right, Mrs. Howard?" It suddenly seemed ridiculous to Ellie that after so many years of living in the same house, they never addressed each other by first names. "You look so pale."

"I'm tired is all." Ellie started to open the heavy front door and today it seemed beyond her strength. She pulled, wedged her foot in the opening she had managed, steadied herself for the final pull, aware that Mrs. Silver was watching her curiously.

"You're sure you're all right?" She helped Ellie with the door. "You're not having one of your attacks, are you?"

"No. Really Mrs. Silver, I'm fine. Just tired, but you know," smiling, settling into the weight of the door on her back, "the shopping still has to be done." Mrs. Silver held the door open, followed Ellie's cautious movement down the slippery stone steps. Ellie felt as if she were running away from those eyes on her back. She walked rapidly—realizing she had also forgotten her galoshes—toward Utica Avenue and hailed a cab.

"St. John's Clinic," she told the driver and sank back, noisily, against the hard leather seat. Only then did she give way to the throbbing spot of fear near her breast. Covering her eyes, blocking out the glare of the sun, she cried quietly, hearing the crunch of the tires on the melting snow. She felt dwarfed by the cold indifference of the taxi, as if everything, the resolve of years, had been reduced to this one ride in a car she didn't own. Soundlessly she screamed, muttered "Papa," once more a child, wanting to be soothed out of still another nightmare . . . She sat up straight, leaned forward. "Could you hurry, driver?"

"I am, lady. It's the snow." He motioned to the outside. "It's there, you know."

SHE WENT TO St. John's because Betty's sister had gone there first. It had a special cancer clinic. But it was too crowded, and the line she waited on never seemed to move. She unbuttoned her heavy coat, swinging the front fold to circulate some air onto her sweating body. She followed the movements of the nurses and doctors as they sped down the corridors. She heard the announcements, the calls. She watched the frightened people around her on line, shared their fear. But it didn't help to know that there were others. Only her trembling mattered to her. Repeatedly she stepped out of line, checked on the movement. It was so slow. One desk was all there was. One nurse behind the desk.

She stopped a nurse who was racing down the corridor, held onto her arm, was dragged a few paces that way. "Isn't there any other place to go? Must we all wait here?"

The nurse shook her arm free. "That's right, lady. Right here." She smiled cruelly and sped away.

Ellie left the clinic. If she waited any longer, she knew she would faint.

She went home, climbed the stairs, removed her coat, returned to the window seat in the sunlight, dazed by her decision, and waited.

When Morrie arrived home that evening, he was annoyed that the bell was unanswered. He had to use his keys to get in for the first time since they had moved to Brooklyn. The house was dark.

"Ellie?" he called, switching on the kitchen light. "Ellie?" he called again, walking, as if by instinct, to the living room, his hat and coat still on. In the darkness, he saw her seated by the window. "Ellie?" His call was quieter, tentative. He moved toward her, stumbled on his hassock. "What's wrong?" He made her stand up. "Ellie, what's wrong?" He didn't realize he was screaming.

"Don't yell, Morrie. Please don't yell."

He led her slowly out of the room toward the kitchen light.

SINCE SHE WOULDN'T LET HIM CALL anyone, he took care of her that night. They went to bed very early. Morrie insisted upon feeling the lump, and when he did he became frozen by the same panic that Ellie had lived with all day. "It doesn't have to be what you think it is." He held her close to him, patting, rubbing her back. "We'll go to this doctor in the morning. The one Louis Kriegel had before he . . ." He sucked back the word 'died' and squeezed her tightly, afraid.

"I can't breathe, Morrie." Ellie tried to move him, but his arms tightened with each of her movements. She stretched her head free, gulping for air.

"I'll call Evelyn and . . ."

"No. You won't call anyone," she whispered. "We'll find out first and then we'll see who we'll call. No one now, remember."

"Why not, El? Why shouldn't I?" He struggled with his fear, his irritation, whined, and each time he spoke, Ellie gained more control of herself.

"I don't want anyone to know. That's all."

"But El, I can't take this thing alone."

"You will. You'll have to for once."

"Just Evelyn. After all, she's . . ."

"Not Evelyn. Not anyone. They've got their own things . . . I mean it, Morrie . . . No one, until we know what's what."

"All right," he yielded, finally, "if that's the way you want it. But it's wrong. I swear it." He loosened his grip, rolled onto his back, stared into the darkness. Next door the television set was on loudly, in spite. And the Silvers were arguing. "There they go again for a change." Morrie was surprised that he was able to laugh.

"Yes. There they go." Ellie tried to close her eyes, but she kept shuddering and automatically they opened, searched the darkness for some familiar object. The only light was the glowing dial of the electric clock . . . If she died before David got home . . . If she died before her grandsons' *bar-mitzvahs* . . . If she died . . . If she died . . . "Morrie," she cried out, "you've got to help me. I can't help myself."

He held her again, patting her back. "Don't worry. I'll do everything. All the money I have. Everything."

That way, both crying softly, eventually they fell asleep.

THE DOCTOR Morrie took her to the next day had come to America from Germany just before the war had started. His office was part of his apartment in one of the old, rococo residential buildings that line Eastern Parkway. The waiting room was shabby but cheerful, as if you were stepping into a friend's house. That relaxed Ellie, made her more willing to submit to the examination which followed, that and the fact that the doctor's manner matched the surroundings. He was casual, calm, compassionate as he listened to Ellie's fears come spilling out.

"Now, Mrs. Howard. You must not jump to conclusions. I have handled many such cases in Europe, and many times," he removed his pince-nez, rubbed them on his white coat, smiling as he reached out to touch Ellie's arm reassuringly, "it is not nearly so serious as one should expect." He stood up, replaced his pince-nez. "We'll have a look. Come." He motioned Ellie into an adjoining room. Morrie remained in the outer office.

The doctor's treatment room was unusual. Ellie noticed that there was no steaming sterilizer, no fluoroscope screen, no scale, nothing that she recognized as medical except the blood pressure gauge on the dark walls, and the black leather treatment table covered with the white barbershop paper. She remembered then, not having seen any diplomas hanging in the other room. She said nothing; the doctor, himself was comforting.

"Please to undress yourself, Mrs. Howard." The doctor opened his bag which rested on an ordinary end table and produced his stethoscope. Ellie undid her blouse and brassière, the customary embarrassment of being naked curiously absent today. She lifted herself onto the treatment table, conscious of her sweat staining the paper. He listened to her heart, nodded, then checked her pressure. "It's very high. But you are nervous, no doubt?"

"I do have a blood pressure condition."

"Ah! Everyone does these days. You have children, Mrs. Howard?"

"Yes."

He returned to his stethoscope. He urged her into conversation about her grandchildren.

When he finally found the lump and tried to move it around, she stopped talking; she heard only the thumping of her heart.

"Ah!" He exhaled. "This is it. So." He felt in various spots around her breast, touching gently, always smiling. And then, suddenly, he was finished. He made a movement that was like a bow. "Please dress yourself."

"Is that all, doctor?" The examination seemed too short, incomplete.

"You think there should be more?"

"Well, no . . . if you say no. But I've been to so many doctors and they usually . . ."

"A good doctor can hear and sense. There is no need to do more unless he wishes to impress his patients and is interested more in a large fee." His smile was frank, encouraging her to believe in his insight.

Returning to the other room, he motioned Morrie to remain seated. "I am convinced," he began immediately, "that what your wife has is not a malignant tumor." He paused, looked comfortingly from one to the other. Smiles of hope, astonishment instantly appeared on each face. "I believe, am, as I said, convinced that your wife has a calcium deposit which, through treatment, I should like to dissolve."

"Are you sure?" Morrie was afraid to believe the verdict too quickly.

"Who can be sure of anything one hundred per cent?" Once more, very slowly, he removed his pince-nez. "It is my professional belief. If you want me to be your doctor, you shall have to accept my belief as the truth."

Ellie, the strain of doubt, then relief skimming across her face, alternately firming, then easing the corners of her mouth, blurted out. "But how can you be so sure so quickly?"

"So much have I dealt with these cases in Europe." He hesitated, seemed to wait for the return of their trust. "Today everyone talks nothing but cancer. Not everyone has cancer." When he used the word, he seemed to grind the force out of it, but Ellie recoiled; her mouth opened and shut involuntarily. "There are other illnesses as well. You, fortunately, have another illness."

Morrie nodded. "It's true everyone panics, but still and all . . ."

"If you follow my treatment," the doctor interrupted with renewed warmth, "I shall help you. Of that I am sure."

"We will," Morrie said, looking at Ellie, annoyed by her doubtful expression.

"I just can't believe . . ." Ellie did not want to complete the statement. What didn't she believe? That she didn't have cancer? That she would live? Morrie was speaking for her.

"What does she have to do?" It was settled.

"I will write out prescriptions and a diet and I shall see your wife twice a week for the next few months."

When they left the office and walked in the cold sunlight to the company car, Morrie labored to convince her and himself. "He must know what he's doing. Can't you tell?" Ellie held on to his arm, unwilling to answer. "He sounds honest, El. You have to admit that. No pretense."

Ellie opened the door to the car and as she slid in she seemed to burrow herself deeply into the folds of her coat. She was cold, doubtful and cold. She heard the car start, listened to Morrie's continuing praise of the doctor, but she felt no relief. It's too easy, her mind repeated. Much too easy. She knew better than to rely on the easy way. Yet, she could not rouse herself to contend with him. It demanded energy and her supply had, overnight it seemed, disappeared.

Silently, they drove the rest of the way home. Morrie had to return to the office, but he took her upstairs. Before he was ready to leave, he held her against him, her head resting on his chest. "Don't worry, El. We'll see what he can do. If you don't start feeling better soon we'll go to another doctor."

She lifted her head. "You really believe him?"

"Yes. I do." He held his hand beneath her chin.

"All right then." She let her head fall back onto the roughness of his tweed coat. "I'll do whatever he tells me to do. But you're not to tell anyone. Not the children. No one." She drew away from him. "Remember. It's between us . . . the way it should be."

He nodded yes, kissed her awkwardly, and left the house.

Ellie forced herself back into a routine. She played cards, as usual, twice a week, once on Friday night when Morrie had his regular pinochle game. Even Betty was unable to tell that anything was wrong. Ellie even forced herself to continue visiting Betty's sister. Those days were the hardest and so she made sure to follow them with trips to Evelyn's or a dinner out with Morrie, telling herself over and over again, I do not have cancer. She wrote to David, sent him packages, and looked forward to his discharge as if his return would resolve the pinpoint of doubt that burned buried within her acquiescence.

Yet, with each visit to the doctor, she did feel closer to acceptance. He became more confident. And her energy did pick up. Her appetite returned to normal. Cleaning the house was fun again. That was proof. It was only when she stopped to relax during the day, or waited for a friend to play a card at a game, or tried to fall asleep at night that the fear returned. "Suppose he's wrong?" she would question Morrie.

"How can he be wrong? You look a hundred percent better. You feel better, don't you?"

"I think so." Sighing, she would eventually fall asleep, her arm curled around Morrie's shoulder, and if she dreamed, she was not aware of it.

Ellie was unsure of exactly when David would arrive home. She knew the week, but not the day. Each time the bell rang, she would race to answer it, and once, certain that the ring was his special one, she slipped running down the corridor, hurt her shoulder and arm. It was Betty wanting shopping company.

Later that same afternoon, however, the bell rang again. This time, forced to by the pain in her shoulder, Ellie carefully walked to the buzzer, waited for the slam of the door, listened at the side door. And David appeared before her, a duffel bag poised on his shoulder. She backed into the kitchenette, her tears spontaneously present, blurring her sight of him. He hugged her tightly, kissed her, held her at arm's length.

She looked up at him, wanting to sob her relief. She had lasted this long, reached one goal, and, at that moment when her doubt seemed to diminish into nothingness, she sensed the power of another truth that told her she would not reach another. There was no clear reason, exactly, for feeling it, but seeing her 'baby' a grown man, she was sure. She cried, her arms hanging limply at her sides, unwilling and unable to stop the tears. David, smiling, gazed at her, waited, then became embarrassed by her sobbing. "What is it, Ma?"

"Nothing. Nothing at all." She tried to hold her sore shoulder straighter. "This morning when I answered the bell—I thought it was you so I was running to answer it—and I fell." She showed him the swelling arm, glad that she had that to call his attention to.

He laughed. "Maybe you'll have to go to the doctor for a change."

She laughed. "Never mind it now. You hungry, Davie?"

"Starved."

"I've got something special. I just have to heat it up."

"What is it, Ma?" He followed her into the kitchen.

"You'll see . . . Go wash first." She turned, suddenly, but he was not irritated by the familiar request. Instead, they both began laughing.

THE LONG STRETCHES of silence when they ate dinner, the furtive glances between Ellie and Morrie, their apparent disinterest concerning his future plans for a job and then, in September, his return to school aroused David's open irritation and, finally, the ultimatum that " . . . if you don't tell me what's wrong—obviously something is bothering both of you—I'll leave this house for good. I'm not going to fool around anymore . . ."

And so Morrie, encouraged by Ellie, her fear flowering with the presence of someone else in the house, told him.

David's response put an end to Morrie's sworn silence. For that he was grateful, but not for what he said. "You call that man a doctor? Are you kidding? In this day and age?"

"What do you know about it?" Morrie's voice rose in self-defense. "She's been better every day . . . until you came home."

David rejected the invitation to that battle. He gazed at Ellie who, listening from the kitchen, leaned back against the sink. "Look, Ma. If this man is right about what he said, it can't hurt to have it checked by another doctor, can it?"

"I know what we're doing," Morrie slammed his open palm against the table.

"Maybe you do, but either Mama goes to another doctor or I'll bring one here."

"Just stay out of this." Morrie pointed his finger at David, but the face that challenged his son was contorted in a grimace of hurt and confusion.

"I can't stay out of it. Don't be crazy." He leaned toward his father, urging him to listen, not to fight.

"Don't yell," Ellie muttered, by instinct playing her role of the failing peacemaker. "I'll go to another doctor." She came to the table, sat down between them, rubbed her sore arm which had not healed satisfactorily and which her doctor had told her to ignore. "What's the difference. It's probably too late now anyway." She stared dumbly at David, her face set in its expression of resignation, to cancer now, as it had been to her husband's yelling, to his unwillingness to honor any of her old requests.

"There's no reason to say that, Ma." Unconvincingly, David stared at them with unfelt optimism.

Morrie looked down at the white tablecloth. His trembling face on which the handsome features had long since been cancelled by fleshiness, sagged in defeat. But this time he was glad to lose. It wasn't only his secret now. David would call Evelyn. Evelyn would tell Clara and Mollie. Mollie would tell Toby and everyone would share it then—and help. "It's right," he said softly. "I'm the fool." He cupped his head in his hands.

"Don't start crying now," Ellie said as she stood up. "Save it for later." She moved toward the sink and the dinner dishes.

THE NEW DOCTOR, a cancer specialist with modern offices, confirmed in words what each of them had suspected in silence. He ordered an immediate operation. The machinery of preparation went into effect and they were carried along with it, hoping. The hospital was selected; the date for the operation set. The hour and minute specified. Ellie, with all the determination she could achieve after so many months of private dread, allowed the rapid swirl of events to suck her to its center. She was floated along the current to that specified moment when she and the others would know.

The day before the operation—it was early May and the warm spring day soothed her sufficiently to let her hope that perhaps she would not die—she had her hair done up in a loose, soft row of waves, and even let the beautician give her a manicure. She told them at the hospital that night as she lay in bed that the girl asked if she were going on a trip because, " 'It's special when *you* have your nails done.' No, I said, I'm only going to the hospital. She dropped her whole tray of bobby pins and bottles."

The windows of her private room at the Polyclinic Hospital in Midtown Manhattan looked out to a red-mauve sunset on the Hudson River. Thin wisps of cloud drifted in front of the declining sun and the rays of color, the warm glow in the sky softened the yellow harshness of the room. No one switched on the overhead light. Morrie sat on the bed, holding Ellie's hand, gazing toward the river and the sun. Evelyn and Bob leaned on the iron railing at the foot of the bed. David was on the other side of Ellie, sitting against the headboard. The conversation was constant, nervous, evasive. When one of them stopped abruptly, lost in a thought they could not give voice to, another began. Evelyn, at least, could talk about the children, what they told her to tell Grandma. The darkness deepened in the room; the sun was lost behind the Palisades; the lights of Palisades Park glittered. A sad, appreciative smile lingered on the edges of Ellie's half-opened mouth.

"It'll be all right," she said, interrupting Evelyn's flow of words. "I'm ready and I'm glad that it's going to be done." Each of them gazed at her. "If it's not good, it's not good, and no one's to blame . . . remember that." Morrie winced, embarrassed by the guilty lowering of his head. "I repeat. No one's to blame for anything." She put her hand under Morrie's chin and lifted it so that he had to look into her eyes. "I mean it. Whatever happens, happens. Just promise me that you'll take care of . . ." her lips quivered, parted, and then resumed their firmness, ". . . that you'll take care of me until . . ."

The light was switched on and an apologetically smiling intern wheeled a square cart of capsules and tiny tubes into the room. "I'm sorry to disturb you, but I've got some work to do. All right Mrs. Howard?"

"Yes, doctor. They're just going anyway." They stood up, hovered near the bed while the intern waited, shifting from foot to foot. No one made a movement toward the door.

"Go ahead," Ellie commanded. "I'm fine." Her smile was frozen in place.

Each of them kissed her silently, Morrie, lingering near the bed had to be edged away by the intern.

"Go ahead, Morrie. Go." Ellie waved him away.

They huddled in the doorway, unwilling to leave. David threw her a kiss. "We'll see you tomorrow."

Ellie leaned forward in bed, suddenly. "Just one more thing." The intern was wrapping a blood pressure strap around her arm. Morrie made a movement toward the bed, but Bob held him back. "Call Irving. Maybe something is wrong. He didn't call."

The last expression they saw on her face that night was disappointment.

CLARA WAS IN THE WAITING ROOM with Morrie and David. Evelyn had gone to the desk to check once again.

"Nothing yet," she whispered, sat down next to Morrie.

It was now one o'clock. Ellie, they knew, had entered the operating room at nine that morning. "It's no good. No good," Morrie muttered, shaking his head, his eyes glazed, focusing on nothing but what he saw inside himself.

"You can't tell from that." Clara put her hand on his arm. "Sometimes the longer you wait the better it . . ." She smiled, nervously shaking his arm to gain his attention, looking into his unlistening face, biting her lip for control. She turned to David for help.

Slowly, he stood up. "Anyone want some coffee? Dad?" Morrie did not respond. "Dad?"

"What?" Morrie stared blankly.

"Some coffee?"

"No. I'll stay here. The doctor'll be looking for me right away." He looked up at the clock on the opposite wall.

"Go ahead, Dad," Evelyn tried to get him to stand up. "You didn't eat anything this morning. You should . . ."

Morrie moved away from her hand. "What's the difference." He slapped his thighs with a new finality, looked around at the other people in the room. Their silence seemed to rouse him. "You absolutely forget that there's anyone else here."

"It's true," Clara agreed quickly, hoping to get him talking. "I always say that. When people come into our shoe store, you can always sell them another pair of shoes if you remember they're human and talk to them that way. But Simon's different. He does it by . . ."

"Clara," Evelyn interrupted, pointing toward the entrance of the waiting room.

Clara followed her niece's finger. The doctor was waiting.

Still wearing the gown from the operating room and letting his mask dangle from a finger, he approached Morrie, the only one he knew. It was a careful smile he had fixed on his tired face. Morrie stared up at him, still seated, his breath caught, waiting.

"She's in the recovery room." The doctor moved his head slowly so that his information reached all of them. "As you know, it was a rather long operation. You won't be able to see her for a number of hours . . . Would you please join me for some coffee, Mr. Howard."

As Morrie walked off down the corridor with the doctor, his mind alert now, he tried to formulate the honest questions he knew he had to ask. He didn't want any lies. Just the honest truth. Yet, each time the words formed in his mouth, they seemed to slip back into his throat, forced there by a will of their own. Once asked, they couldn't be taken back. Once answered, they hardened into fact, escaping into the air, to live with the answers. And throughout his life with Ellie and even before that he had been determined to eliminate facts that he had no use for. That way truth was what he wanted it to be.

When the coffee was set before them, the doctor spoke without hesitation. His words were careful, scientifically honest, so honest that Morrie had to avert his eyes. ". . . because it is better for me and for you to say exactly what the situation is than to hide what may be inevitable. As a doctor I have tried many approaches and the direct one, although very hard to take at first, is, in the long run, the best . . ." He lit a cigarette, offered one to Morrie, and continued. ". . . Your wife does have cancer. The biopsy was done right there. There is no doubt. We were forced to remove her left breast and to cut deeply into the tissue of her chest and arm. I cleaned away whatever I could see, and more, in the hope that we may arrest it. But I feel that it has already spread into the lymph system and we . . ." he stopped abruptly. Morrie struggled to control his tears, wiping them with the heel of his palm. ". . . we don't think it's absolutely hopeless. There are X-Ray treatments. Sometimes they work miracles." He drank from his coffee cup, his eyes peering over the rim at Morrie. And Morrie now stared back. Everything he was forced to know had been spoken except for one item.

"How long . . . will she . . ." Morrie stammered, stopped completely.

"How long, I cannot say." The doctor shifted his gaze to the clock on the wall. "It depends on so many things. And then, the treatments may . . ."

"I'll tell you one thing, doctor. I'm not giving up." Morrie's hand flailed the air above them in a sudden burst of anger. He had never faced futility before, and his instinct told him that nothing was impossible. He had no use for miracles. That wasn't the way you won something. It's work, hard work . . .

"That is the only attitude to assume. It is best for your wife, for you, and for your family." The doctor's sustained, pretended apathy began, suddenly, to dissolve. "I have watched my own wife die of cancer, Mr. Howard. I have been helpless. But I tried everything. One must. There is no other way."

"I will. And there's one other thing I'm going to do. I'm going to get that other bastard doctor if it's the last thing I do." His voice had risen and people nearby turned to look at him. "How could he do that? How did I let him do that?" And, admitting his part, he admitted his helplessness. His anger was ended in the crumbling body movement of guilt. "It's more my fault."

"That is really not the issue now, Mr. Howard. It is more important to think about what we can try to do for your wife now." He touched Morrie's arm. "I must go. I have still another operation. I will let you know as soon as you can see your wife." He paid for the coffee, directing Morrie back out into the corridor, walking slowly alongside him. "You will have to demonstrate to your wife that there is still a chance. She will feel otherwise, but you must not let her refuse to resume the form of her past life. That is very important. I shall arrange to do everything in my power to help. Count on that." He patted Morrie's back, "Until later." He walked quickly away.

The others, watching from the edge of the waiting room, moved cautiously toward Morrie. Seeing them, he felt defenseless, as if he would have to say that *he*, not cancer, had killed Ellie. It was true, he told himself, and there would never be a way, now, to make up for it.

"Well, Dad?" David put his hand on Morrie's shoulder.

"We'll be able to see her in a while . . . The doctor . . . he thinks they got it in time." This first lie was not hard. In the months to come the other lies he told would separate his grief from the others, would allow him to feel the full weight of a responsibility which was, and should be, after all, his alone.

WHEN ELLIE RETURNED to Lenox Road two weeks later, she walked up the steps of the porch under her own power, although Morrie and Bob were on either side of her, and David, his hands ready, stood behind, in case she should fall backwards.

Mrs. Silver was on the porch, her frightened smile of welcome, the only expression she could safely permit herself. She and the other neighbors had visited Ellie in the hospital, had seen her always small presence shrunken even smaller, and had guessed, without naming it, what was wrong. "It's good to have you home," Mrs. Silver spoke, then looked away quickly.

Upstairs, the rest of the family had assembled, waiting since early that morning. At the foot of the flight of stairs to her house, Ellie finally hesitated. She heard the muffled requests for quiet, Evelyn's attempts to silence her sons, and then Andy, the older of her two grandsons, appeared at the top, shouting "Grandma, Grandma," and raced down toward her. He kissed Ellie with the unrestrained passion of the very young, and she, recoiling with fatigue, nevertheless accepted his embraces until Bob could free her from his son. "Okay Andy . . . Enough. Upstairs." He lifted Ellie. "Let me get grandma upstairs." He carried her up the steps, through the kitchen, down the corridor, and, finally, placed her on her bed. A line of relatives had followed him down the corridor, but when he left the room he motioned them all back. "Wait a minute," he whispered. "Let her catch her breath." They retreated slowly, like unwilling children, except Mollie who tried to push Bob out of the way. "I've got to see her. You've got no right to keep me out."

"You'll see her, Mollie." Bob hugged her playfully, but she moved his arms down, glaring at him for daring to stop her.

The scuffling aroused Ellie, and she called from the bedroom, "Be a good girl, Mollie. Just wait 'til Evelyn gets me into bed." Morrie pulled at his sister-in-law's arm, scowling for compliance. Pacified, she turned toward the kitchen with the others. Toby sat glumly in the corner near the pantry entrance. She had never been able to face sickness and now she was willing to wait as long as necessary before seeing her sister. Clara and Mollie came to her, leaned against the wall, ready to help if signaled to. Mrs. Howard and Lila waited in front of the kitchen sink, their arms folded, realizing that probably they would be the last ones to see Ellie. Irving, seated on the cold radiator next to the stove, averted his gaze, looked with exaggerated interest through the window behind him, at the narrowness of the alley, at the shaft of sunlight which managed to insert itself between the two houses. The sight of his mother being carried through the house had made him willing to wait.

When Evelyn appeared in the dinette, immediately flanked by her sons, she blinked back her tears and gazed at each of them, the women tense, the men, Leon, Max, Simon and Bob, expectantly crowding the entrance to the dining room, she wanted to push through them, to walk away from what she had just seen as she undressed her mother. She spoke quickly, before panic made her unable to speak at all. "Mama wants to see you, Irving." She leaned against Bob and cried, ignoring her sons who tugged at her dress.

For the others, watching Evelyn, and then Irving, his eyes cast down on the linoleum floor as he walked past them and down the corridor, there were no further attempts to hold back tears.

Irving closed the door of the bedroom as he entered, then stopped. David and Morrie stood along the far side of the bed. Ellie, the pallor of her skin emphasizing a bitter smile, turned toward Irving. "Come here," Ellie spoke as if Irving were once more a little boy. "Don't be afraid. I won't bite you." Her fingers pulled at the edge of the cover.

"Ma!" Irving moaned as if he expected to be hit, moved to kneel alongside the bed, rested his head on top of her hands. "I'm sorry, Ma." His eyes were closed.

"For what are you sorry?" Ellie's hand played with his wiry brown hair; all traces of the silky blond strands had disappeared years before, but she touched his head as if she remembered the feel of it. "Nothing to be sorry about. So you didn't visit. You called every day. That's enough."

"No! it wasn't." He lifted his head, waiting for something else to happen. "I know it wasn't."

"It's all right." She nodded. "You're here now, aren't you?"

Then he smiled, looked toward his father and brother, but they did not return his smile.

"Whatever you do or don't do," Ellie raised her hand in front of his face, "is my fault, not yours. That I know." Her eyes closed. Her head fell back against the pillow.

ALL THROUGH THE SUMMER Morrie drove home from the office three afternoons a week and took Ellie for her X-Ray treatments. He would allow no one else to do it. No matter how busy he was, no matter who was with him, he left at 1:30. Grace tried to schedule appointments accordingly, but if the president of the company wanted to see him, she couldn't prevent it. Morrie told her it made no difference to him. They would have to understand. If they didn't like it, they could fire him. After he left Ellie at home, in bed, or on the porch, he would return to work. If he had to remain at the office to catch up, at least he knew that David would be home from work.

Slowly Ellie did seem to regain her strength. She did little things around the house. But the furniture was no longer moved, the pantry was never the storehouse of cookies and cake for her grandchildren. And a maid, for the first time in her married life, attended to the major housekeeping. Although Ellie brooded over this development, complained about the items carelessly cleaned or left undone, she was wearily content to sit on the porch in the afternoon, talk with the neighbors, play cards or scrabble, keep contact with each day. And there was always someone to be with. As soon as she made an appearance on the porch, a neighbor would join her. It was as if the entire neighborhood had conspired to be with her, or shop for her, or sit quietly with her. Betty Pulaski had arranged that much. But even Mrs. Silver learned how to allow the slowness of a summer afternoon to soothe as they sat together.

Ellie's pain was invisible to them. Her arm would not work properly, and she tried to hide it by keeping shawls over it no matter how hot it got. The X-Rays made her skin peel and itch. And inside her dress was the other shame, the false breast. She could not avoid seeing it, pointing youthfully, mockingly upward. But when she sat with her friends, she played the game of convalescence solicitously. "Every day you look better. You're gaining weight," one would say, and Ellie, nodding yes, smiling, tried to forget how hard it was to eat. Or her hands would fumble with a scrabble tile and Betty, quickly retrieving it, would call attention to her own ancient backache. So Ellie buried her fear. If they can do these things for me, she thought, I'll do what I can do. If they think they're curing me, let them think.

The summer moved into its sweltering, lazy August heat. The air pressed down, waving, visible in the sunlight. Car tires slapped monotonously against the melting asphalt. Ellie watched the movement of time turning in the trees before the house, in the children who no longer played when it got hot in the afternoon, in the sweat marked packages the ladies carried to the porch when they sat with her after having shopped. "The corn's getting good now . . . the melons are finished, but the tomatoes . . ." To all of this Ellie was alert as she never had been before. To David's sunburn when he returned from a day at Brighton Beach. To Morrie's sweat smell at night as she lay beside him wanting so much to join the sound of his sleep. To the way David set the table for dinner, making sure that it was exactly as she would have done it. To her growing grandchildren when Morrie drove her to Evelyn's or Irving's for a weekend trip. To the frightened smiles of David and Morrie, silently united for the first time, as they helped her into a complicated dress, helped her to walk the steps upstairs. Whatever she saw that summer, she coveted. Whatever she experienced that was pleasurable, she wanted to extend it, especially in the evenings when the three of them sat on the porch wishing a breeze into existence. Morrie smoked, his paper folded on his lap. David sat on the stone partition that separated them from the connecting house. She knew their fatigue, their interrupted sleep, and loved them both with a new passion that demanded quiet for them, now, as they sat together. The street in front of the house hummed with the whir of slow traffic. Lights, dimmed behind drawn shades, glowed peacefully. The only hush Brooklyn ever knows, a subdued fusion of separate noise, surrounded them and they were stilled in it.

"It is beautiful tonight. Good breeze," Morrie said, trying to rock his porch chair.

"It is, isn't it." David strained his head upward as if to see beyond the layer of light that always hangs above the city and blocks out the imagined stars.

"Yes," said Ellie. "I don't want to go upstairs yet."

"We'll stay as long as you want, Ma."

She smiled, unseen in the darkness. For a while then her nausea vanished, the pain in her arm felt only like a tickling sensation. She believed she was getting better, that she was healthy, forever healthy, and that there would be other evenings like this one, other summers.

IN SEPTEMBER, very early one morning, she sat up suddenly in bed. The alarm clock on Morrie's night stand said five o'clock. The ring of pain in her chest choked her scream. Her mouth opened and shut. She gulped for air. And that moment she knew was the beginning of her death.

Her flailing arms awakened Morrie. He jumped out of bed, walked around it to her, held her, rubbed her back. And finally the scream came, whistling gradually out of her gaping mouth.

David appeared immediately, stood beside the bed, immobilized by disbelief.

When she could breathe again, the trembling started. She insisted upon walking to the living room, to the front window. David hastily put her bathrobe around her shoulders.

"Should I call the doctor, El?"

No, she nodded vigorously. She sat on the chair before the open, screened window, forcing herself to inhale deeply. "Better. That's better."

David rubbed his eyes so that she would think he were merely getting them opened for the day. And Morrie sought help from his son, looked into his reddened eyes, saw there, instead, a question, a request, 'Why was this happening?'

Morrie was still the only one who knew that this moment would arrive. He had waited for it to begin, never allowing himself to believe that it would not. He continued to rub Ellie's back. She leaned against him.

"It's better. Much better." But her words were swallowed in the next spasm of pain.

MRS. HOWARD was called to the house. Evelyn came every other day and Clara in between. David, who had returned to school, and Morrie took over in the evenings.

Ellie remained in bed now. She refused to get out of it.

"But Mrs. Howard," the doctor would plead with each daily visit, "you *can* get out of bed. You should continue to do all the things you were doing."

"I can't doctor. I don't have the strength."

Sometimes, playing the game, he would shrug his shoulders in disappointment. But each day he would give her an injection of morphine and after it she would revive, sit up, ask for a dish of jello or soup, anything that she could eat with ease. Mrs. Howard would rush the dish to the room while Evelyn or Clara hovered hopefully nearby.

But, although at these times she wanted to, Ellie could not eat.

"Maybe it's not hot enough," Mrs. Howard suggested. "I'll heat it again."

"It's all right, Ma. I just can't eat." Ellie's head moved back and forth on the pillow.

"It's not good soup. I'll throw it out and make new." Mrs. Howard struggled to find any other reason but the right one. Always she left the room in tears, feeling that if she could only succeed with the soup everything would be all right.

In the evenings, after dinner, David took his school books to the bedroom. He used Ellie's dressing table as a desk. Morrie read his paper seated alongside the bed. He had moved his easy chair in there. They would not leave her alone. Only that way was she able to sleep, was she willing to accept the two sleeping pills, sinking into a twisting, moaning torpor.

During the night, Ellie's screams, determinedly stifled, nevertheless ended the scraps of their rest. David and Morrie, on either side of her, held her hands. Her nails dug into flesh, but even as the spasm of pain subsided, she would not let go. They smiled down at her decaying, wax-pale face, and for as long a time as it took her to be dragged wearily back to the nightmare of her tossing sleep, they sat that way. Some nights, they never left her. But each morning, after Evelyn or Clara had arrived, David went to school and Morrie went to work.

Ellie allowed no one to visit her. When the neighbors stopped in, she persistently refused to see them. "I can't stand them to see me this way. This is not the way I am." She buried her head under the pillow.

The anger which Ellie aroused in those who stayed near her was a source of constant shame. If she didn't want to eat, they tried to force her to do so. If she didn't want her hair brushed or her face washed, they made her submit. David, on the day he finally yielded to the truth, went so far as to urge her out of bed. She collapsed in his arms. Mrs. Howard stood alongside them, covering her eyes, crying.

Toward the middle of October, Ellie was brought back to the hospital. Bob carried her from her bed. She was wrapped in blankets that hid what was left of her. The car waited in the alleyway next to the side exit. Ellie was stretched across the back seat of the car. Morrie and David sat in the front. Bob eased the car slowly out of the alley, backed onto Lenox Road, and sped Ellie away from her house. Those women who watched from porches or from behind closed curtains, turned from the departing car to sigh themselves back into the performance of their day, to wait for their children to return from school, their husbands to return from work.

CHAPTER *Fifteen*

No ONE STOPPED THEM as they emerged from the elevator. The nurse at the desk knew where they were going, and there were no visiting rules for cases on the critical list. Morrie and David halted, glanced over at the cubicle across from the nurse that served as a waiting room. The sun streamed through the shadeless windows and the grimy beige of the walls showed streaks of dirt. The trees outside waved energetically in the autumn wind, a match for the brisk, scurrying efficiency of the nurses. No other members of their family had arrived yet to sit in the wicker chairs and wait.

They started up once more. David walked behind his father, past the nurses' room, down the corridor, both of them tiptoeing instinctively. Their pace quickened, then stopped altogether. They stood in the doorway of her room.

She looked exactly as she had the night before. The sound of hissing oxygen filled the silence. There was a film of moisture collected along the edges of the tent's plastic window. She was breathing laboriously, her eyes closed. Morrie moved around the bed so that Ellie would see him if she opened her eyes. Evelyn, who had just arrived, stood at the foot of the bed.

David came up close to the tent. Ellie's head turned toward him, her eyelids fluttered open. She raised her thin arm in recognition, then wiggled her fingers toward him under the flap of the tent.

David moved his hand to meet hers. Their fingers touched briefly. Ellie relaxed the stretching of her fingers. Her eyes closed again.

A nurse entered and motioned them out of the room.

They walked down the corridor to the waiting area opposite the nurse's desk.

Morrie slumped into one of the wicker chairs, resuming his post, determined to remain there for as long as necessary. He stared blankly at the moving figures. The wheel chairs. The bathrobes. The sliding slippers on the cold marble floor. The nurses carrying bed pans, syringes—the routine setting of disease and death. Words, if he cared to find out what they were, coldly medical, unfamiliar could explain what he stared at. ". . . I told her I'd stay with her 'til the end," Morrie muttered, the words trancelike, fixed on a single sight in his mind, ". . . I won't leave . . . as long as she's alive . . ."

"No one will move you, Dad." Evelyn leaned to kiss his forehead. He put his arms around her body and wept. She rocked him as if he were one of her own children.

"Only I'll be there at the end . . . that's the way it was at the beginning and that's how it'll be at the end." He moved Evelyn away. His voice rose, not in anger, but in an agony of desire. "No one else . . . No one."

Throughout the morning other members of the family arrived, took turns walking down to the room. They stayed briefly, long enough for Ellie to recognize them, and when they returned, their tears were quiet, controlled, resigned. Max and Lila arrived, assured everyone that Mrs. Howard was better off at home. The neighbors are with her. "She's just crying anyway," Lila informed the group. "She wants to come but I told her no."

The group of relatives stood, sat, leaned, waited. The doctor appeared, told Morrie that he was going to tap her lungs once more. "She won't feel a thing, Mr. Howard. I can promise that much." The doctor kept his hand on Morrie's shoulder as he led him back to the group. He smiled sympathetically, but the smile only elicited stifled sobs from Mollie. As he moved off he motioned to the head nurse.

They settled into their waiting. Some gazed out the windows. The sun's intensity had burned the breeze into fitful spurts that whirled the pile of leaves down below. It became hotter inside. Some of them drifted off to the coffee shop, reappearing shortly, afraid to be away too long.

By the time the nurse finally told them that some of them could return to the room, it was late afternoon. "She's out of the oxygen tent, but please don't tire her."

Morrie went first. Then Irving and his wife joined him. They had not seen Ellie earlier. No one objected, but instinctively they arranged themselves for the order of the visit, certain that this would be their last.

Mollie, Clara, Toby, and Leon went next. David, although it was not part of the tacit plan, joined them.

The corridor was quiet. Other patients were resting, waiting for the evening meal. There were no other visitors present.

Ellie's head jerked alertly toward the door as they entered. Morrie stood at the far side of the bed, holding Ellie's hand. The bed had been cranked high, and her back seemed to be pushing against the support, enmeshing her in a swirl of white sheets and coverlets. Only her graying-brown hair suggested color. She smiled at each one as they leaned to kiss her forehead. There were no tears. Her smile forbade them. She held on to Morrie's hand with a fierceness that showed in the brilliant whiteness of her straining knuckles. Occasionally her mouth twisted in a grimace of pain and her chest heaved uncontrollably. But when the spasm was over, her eyes would open, the smile would reappear.

She freed her hand from Morrie's grasp, then meshed her fingers across her stomach. She moved her narrow gold wedding band, first one way, then the other, back and forth until all that looked at the movement became mesmerized. The band was worn flat on one side. Her engagement ring had rested alongside it for so many years and now it had been placed in front of a glass of water in which floated a gold dental plate on the night table next to the bed. Only her wedding band she had refused to remove.

No words were exchanged. The sisters looked at each other. Ellie bit at her lips. Her eyelids blinked open, shut, open, rapidly, but she did not cry. Finally, with an effort that creased her forehead, that raised the loose skin of her cheeks, embarrassed because of her missing teeth, she spoke. The sound hissed from deep within her chest. "I'm hungry for something."

They were stunned into smiles. Clara moved first. "What, Ellie? What would you like. Tell me."

The others moved closer to the bed, for the moment less afraid.

"Jello. Some jello." Ellie repeated the word as if more for its soft sound than for the food it represented. "Jello again this . . ." The effort overtook her memories. She looked at them, urging them with her eyes to remember for her.

Clara rushed out of the room, her heels tapping, staccato down the length of the corridor. "We'll let the others come down, El," said Toby.

"Tell Evelyn and Irving to come," said Ellie. Mollie nodded yes and they left the room. David remained.

When Evelyn appeared with Irving, she carried a dish of Jello and a paper cup filled with ginger ale. Ellie tried to raise herself but as she did a redness seeped onto her white bed dress. She covered it with her blanket and remained still. "Feed me, Evelyn."

The family watched as Evelyn spooned the jello into Ellie's waiting, opened mouth. With each spoon she took, the heaviness of the room seemed to lift. The nurse, standing at the door, observing expectantly, not intruding, switched on the lights.

Evelyn held the cup to Ellie's lips and she sipped slowly, rolling the liquid around in her mouth, savoring the sharp sweetness. She raised her hand to signal no more, and relaxed against the pillows. The tension seemed fled from her sagging shoulders. She tested them into a position of straightness. Her smile brightened.

The children ranged themselves around the bed. David next to Morrie, Evelyn facing them, and Irving at the foot.

Ellie's gaze lingered on each face in turn. And gradually her smile faded. Once more she pulled at, twisted her wedding band, averted her eyes. "Kiss the children for me." Her words were a scratchy whisper to Evelyn. David took her hand and held it tightly. She returned the pressure, looked up at him, nodding as if in approval, continued to speak to Evelyn. "Bob has finished painting the house?"

"Yes, Ma . . . It's turned out beautiful. The colors you picked."

"You can look at me, Irving. Don't be afraid."

Irving did try to look at his mother, but only fleetingly. His eyes sought the anonymous darkness at the window.

"You'll take care, Evelyn . . . of all . . . of them." Ellie waved her hand and, as it dropped back to the blanket, it clutched the edge, then let go.

David did not loosen his hold on Ellie's hand. He followed his mother's gaze to Evelyn, his mind filling with a blur of moments, tastes he thought were lost but which had always been there, ready. His mother seemed to walk across the floor of his brain, to wave, to turn away toward darkness and then return. He leaned over and kissed Ellie's cold lips. Each of them followed. Irving leaned and lingered. Ellie whispered to him, "It's all right . . . All right." The three of them stood near the doorway, looking, Ellie and Morrie returning the gaze, exchanging this moment for all that had come before, the five of them frozen in each other's mind. And then Ellie, suddenly, lurched upward, choking.

The nurse who, all this time had waited in the corridor, rushed in, immediately spreading the oxygen tent over Ellie's twisting figure. The hissing sound filled the room once more. The nurse pried the wedding band from Ellie's finger. Ellie struggled, but could not resist. The attending doctor, as if he had known that at precisely this moment death would begin, rushed past the stunned children into the room. He injected something into Ellie's uncovered leg. Evelyn and Irving, sobbing, walked away down the corridor. David, numbly watching, saw the furious activity of the nurse and doctor, heard the low, choked moans of his mother. The oxygen tent was flung back; the flow was turned off. They moved to the side of the room away from the bed.

Ellie's arms flailed the air like the wings of a butterfly caught in a strong wind. Morrie tried to hold her hand, but it continued to elude his stretching fingers. And just as suddenly as they had begun their reaching, searching spasm, her arms now dropped onto the twisted white cover. Her chest stopped heaving. Her eyes rolled up, up, beneath the wavering eyelids. And she was still.

Morrie bent over her, lifted her half out of the bed, sobbing, squeezing, rocking her gently, kissing her finally.

When morrie and the others returned from the hospital, all of the people present in the house responded as if they had been taken by surprise. Mrs. Howard, the least informed on the progress of Ellie's cancer, was the most affected. She sat on the hassock, Morrie's hassock, in the corner of the living room—she had sat there all day waiting for news—began to sway and wail when she saw the faces of her son and grandchildren. Each came up to her, kneeled as they embraced her. "Everyone. Everyone," she sobbed. "And now my Ellie."

In the kitchen, Betty, Ellie's closest friend and therefore, by tradition, the one to prepare food for anyone who entered the house, steadfastly tried to set the table. The other friends, members of the canasta group, stood around, blank faced and frightened, determined, as custom prescribed, to fill up every corner of the house. Cigar and cigarette smoke filled the air. Mr. Silbersweig, who played pinochle with Morrie, led him into the kitchen and got him seated at the table.

David entered from the living room and, as if prompted by a long forgotten instinct, seated himself on the radiator next to the stove. He watched Betty frying potato pancakes. They were too thick, too green. They didn't look like his mother's. Every so often Betty reached out a free hand and touched David's face. "Cry. Cry," she told him.

People walked into the kitchenette. They looked at Morrie, listened to his sobbing, wailing grief, and walked away, unable to say what they had forced themselves to be ready to say. Morrie's voice was raised in rage. " . . . I did what I could . . . Money was no object," he screamed. ". . . What could I do? . . . What's the use now! . . . What's the use."

David walked past his father and down the corridor, into his parents' bedroom. He went to the window, pulled up the venetian blind. The night was clear and the sky's cloudlessness invited his eyes to look out, to see upward. The clothesline pulley banged gently, regularly against the wooden window frame; the canvas clothespin sack rocked in the wind. Across the narrow yard lights blazed in another house. He heard the sound of a radio announcer. Someone came to a window, lifted a shade, seemed to look toward the empty clothesline, then quickly disappeared. Below, he heard a window in the Silvers' bedroom slam shut.

He left the room, agonized by its emptiness, by its lingering smells of alcohol and morphine. He returned to the kitchen.

"David," Morrie shouted. "She's dead, David. Your mother."

"Ssh, Morrie." Mrs. Howard leaned over her son, smoothing his hair, stretching out her other arm toward David.

THE SUNDAY LINEUP of cars wanting to leave Brooklyn for the country green of Staten Island on perhaps this last day of summer warmth yielded to the funeral entourage. The attendants ushered them on to the waiting ferry. Soon the grinding departure subsided, followed by the monotonously pumping engines. The water of the bay splashed, thudding against the sides of the boat. Car doors slammed, loudly hollow in the dark passageways, and on the narrow catwalks people squeezed past the hearse on their way to the open air at the front of the ferry.

In the limousine behind the hearse sat the immediate family. They remained in the car. The collective gaze was forward, each of them now allowed his private, silent scrutiny of the hearse and its content. The burial was all that remained. Morrie turned his head, watched his mother grind her teeth, her head bobbing 'yes, yes.' "You okay, Ma?" He leaned toward her.

"Fine. I'm fine." The rhythm of her shaking head was altered. 'No', it said now. 'No. No.'

"Don't worry about Mama." Lila touched her mother's hand. "She knows all about dying. She wrote the book."

David, on the jump seat between Evelyn and Irving, squirmed to attention. He tried to smile at his grandmother, but failed as he saw Morrie's pallid face twitching back the flow of fresh tears. "Dad?" Morrie did not answer. "Dad?"

"She's dead." He looked up at David. "Do you know that? . . . We're carrying her away forever." He cupped his face and sobbed loudly. And then, just as suddenly as he had started to sob, he became quiet once more. He slapped his knee. "Well, that's it. It's over."

"Morrie . . . don't." Lila shifted away from him, sighed.

"Don't Morrie me." He looked up at the hearse and smiled, remembering. "Don't ssh me, Ellie," he muttered.

The rocking of the ferry became more pronounced. Bob, who had stood next to the open window of the limousine, holding Evelyn's hand, moved back toward the car he was driving, located further down the line. The driver of the limousine, who had sat silent and tranquil said, "We'll be docking soon."

Passengers slowly, reluctantly returned to their cars, walking rapidly only when they passed the hearse. Doors slammed, the sound reverberating as if from a great distance. The buildings of the dock complex loomed larger and larger, as they approached. The ferry thudded once more against the wooden pilings. The motor of the hearse was started; it idled, humming, merging with the noise of the mooring. Next, the limousine motor was turned on. Down the line of cars motors thundered into readiness, waiting; headlights blinked on. The criss-cross iron railing was opened and the cars slipped onto the land. The hearse led them.

THE SUN'S WARMTH gleamed on the glassy smoothness of the nearby headstones. The rabbi, the same rabbi who had married Evelyn and Bob, stood at the foot of Ellie's grave. The coffin rested above the opening, suspended on three green bands drawn tautly at either side. Morrie, Irving, and David, the men of the family, stood next to the opening, looking down at the polished brownness of the coffin, shifting from foot to foot. The rabbi craned his head, requesting silence, waiting for the shuffling to subside. Behind him were Evelyn and Bob. Mrs. Howard, a shawl framing her face leaned against Lila. Ellie's sisters and their husbands pressed close to each other. A semicircle of friends and relatives fanned out between the other graves of the plot. Beyond the group, beyond the fenced confines of the United Hebrew Cemetery was the natural fence of tall, sparsely leafed trees, stilled, on this windless October day.

The rabbi began, first in Hebrew, then in English. He spoke the prayer which asked God, in His infinite wisdom, to accept into eternal protection, one of His children. His voice trilled high, soaring, broke loudly upon the hushed stillness of the frightened viewers. Then the sound of weeping, of stifled sobs and coughs became a melancholy, choking harmony for the rabbi's words. It grew louder, sweeping through the strands of the watching semicircle, drawing them together. Men and women, alive, thought of death and of Ellie. And as they swayed, mesmerized by the grief laden Hebrew sounds, living through another death, the rabbi led each of them closer to his own end. Death was not just for other people, the words said.

From the front row David's gaze lifted, followed, as the sound of crying rose behind him, the line of trees, and above the trees to the blue, cloudless sky; shifted down once more to his mother's coffin, to his father, beside him, sinking closer and closer to the ground.

"If I forget thee, O Jerusalem, let my right hand forget her cunning. If I do not remember thee, let my tongue cleave to the roof of my mouth . . ." The rabbi's words pierced the groans, the wails.

"Ellie, Ellie," Mollie shrieked. Morrie turned to that sound and nodded.

The Psalm was finished. The rabbi motioned to the sons. "Repeat after me," he commanded. "*Vyisgadahl, vyis* . . ."

The death prayer issued through the unwilling lips of Irving and David. The rabbi pointed to the coffin. The attendants began to lower the coffin. The bands of green slipped from beneath the polished wood. Slowly, stopping for the next verse of the prayer, moving again, lower it went, guided by the slipping bands, the mumbled Hebrew words, traveling the shortest distance to the longest silence. The rabbi continued his chant. The crowd pressed forward. Morrie slipped to his knees, bent above the opening, rocking back and forth, grief making him defenseless once more, a child again. Mrs. Howard stood behind him now, her hand holding him back, moaning softly.

David and Irving struggled through to the end of the prayer. Men, friends, relatives pushed cautiously to the grave, gathered fists of dirt to throw as tribute on the descending coffin. The sun was blocked out by their pushing, advancing, retreating movements.

The coffin settled down, at rest in the earth.

"Amen," said the rabbi.

"Amen," the crowd repeated, already turning, shuffling up the path, away from the hollow sound of earth being shoveled rapidly into the grave by the attendants. Morrie stretched his arms forward as if to stop them. He bent low, peering into the space that separated him from the coffin. "Soon, Ellie. Soon." His whispered words mingled with the striking sound of falling earth below. Turning then, grunting with the effort to stand up, he scanned the waiting faces, tottered forward, leaned heavily against Evelyn. "Help me." His hands darted out to hold David and Irving. "Help me."

"Come Morrie." Mrs. Howard called, urging them to her. "Come children. Away from here."

They started off obediently, down the gravel path that led between the other graves, behind Toby and Clara whose arms supported Mollie's struggling body, all of them, now, moving reluctantly away from this moment and into the next moment that waited, this one like a seed taking root, even as they entered cars, slammed doors, drove off, already budding in the nourishing darkness of each mind, sending out powerful threading shoots of growth, forward, binding it to other lives that have no other power over death but memory.

THE AUTHOR

GENE HOROWITZ was born in 1930 in Bayonne, New Jersey, and later moved with his family to Brooklyn. After a stint in the Army as a radio repairman, he received his B.A. in English from City College. He has been a teacher of English, first at Marlboro, New York, and then at Horace Greeley High School in Chappaqua, New York. While teaching, he also attended New York University Graduate School. In 1964 he decided to devote full time to writing.

Mr. Horowitz now lives in Manhattan. *Home Is Where You Start From,* his first novel, was written over a period of years during the summer vacation months. Of his book, Mr. Horowitz says, "Circumstantially, the availability of a cabin located on a lake on Long Island made the writing possible. But, of course, in a deeper sense, the events of my life led to the writing of my book."